BOOK ONE OF
THE DARKWOLF SAGA

WIZARD'S KEY

MITCH REINHARDT

WIZARD'S KEY

ACKNOWLEDGEMENTS

First and foremost, I want to thank my mom for everything. She's always been the rock of our family and she's the sweetest lady you could ever hope to meet. I would like to thank my childhood best friend, David H. Seibert. He's an army veteran, firefighter, family man, and still the best man I know.

I have to thank my writing team as well. Without these gifted professionals, this book would never have been completed. Charlotte Rains-Dixon, my mentor, sounding board, haranguer extraordinaire, and good friend throughout this writing project. Valerie Williamson, another wonderful haranguer who helped shape this book with her keen edits and advice. Glendon Haddix and the team at Streetlight Graphics for using their considerable talents to create the cover of this book.

I want to thank the mother-daughter team of Sue and Stacey Call for taking the time to be fantastic beta readers and offer wonderful comments as well as constructive criticism. I'd also like to thank Criss Hanson, who bravely battled through an illness to beta read this manuscript and provide excellent feedback. Special thanks to my friend Danny Hay for his help in proofreading this book. He noticed several details I missed along the way. I can't forget to mention Svetlana Tretiakova, whose indomitable spirit and determination were an inspiration while writing this book.

But most of all, I want to thank you, the reader. This book was written for you and I sincerely hope you find something within these pages that resonates with you and entertains you.

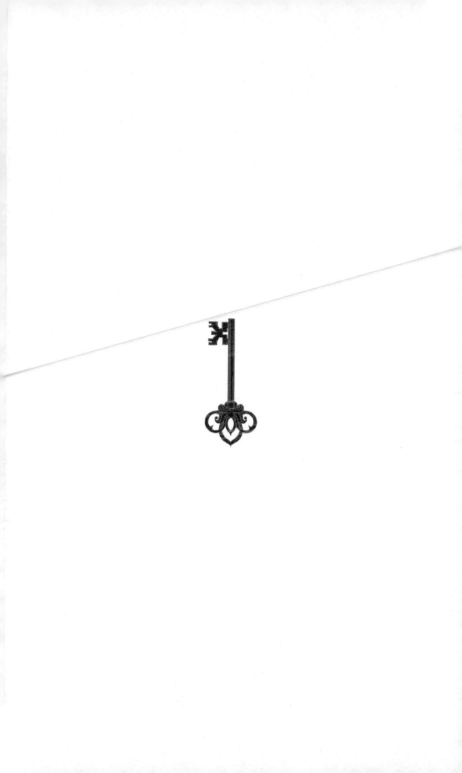

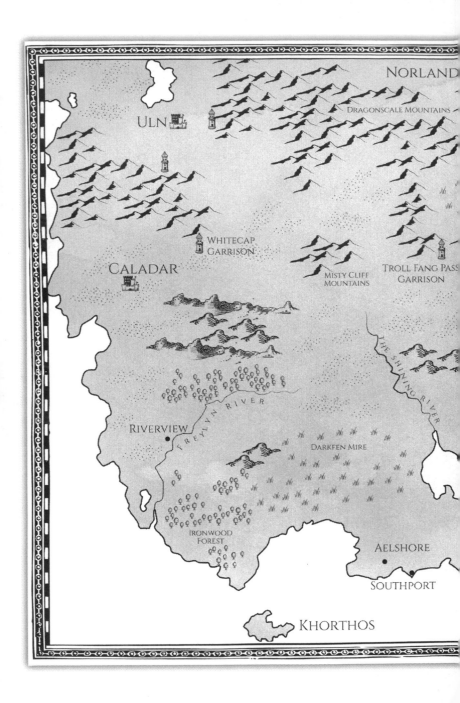

CHAPTER ONE
THE ARCHWAY AND THE KEY

Tiptoeing came naturally to Geoff. In fact, the slight, blond teen was very adept at the "toe-heel" method when he found it necessary to sneak. He was sneaking now. His curiosity concerning the contents of a package that had been delivered to his father the previous night had been gnawing at him all day. He crept down the hall to the small den where Rosa, the housekeeper, usually sat and watched television during her break. Geoff inched his head around the corner just enough to peek in. The den was empty. He quietly continued down the hall to the kitchen, which was also empty.

"Hello! Anyone here?" called Geoff. He waited but there was no answer. The mansion was quiet. Satisfied he had the house to himself, Geoff grinned and turned to go back down the hall. As he did, he saw a note taped on the refrigerator door. It was beside an envelope simply labelled 'For Jane'. The note was from Rosa:

Hola Geoff! Your mother said to let you know she is out shopping and will return by 3:00pm.

Rosa

Geoff crumpled the note in his hand.

"She isn't my mother, Rosa," he said as he tossed it into a nearby waste basket. "She's my stepmother." He glanced up at the antique clock on the wall.

"2:30," said Geoff. "Not much time."

He made his way back down the hall. It ran past the living room and stopped at the foyer with a large, showy chandelier hanging from the ceiling. Beyond the foyer, leading out of the mansion, were two handmade French doors. There was also a wide staircase leading to the second floor and Geoff's destination; his father's study. It was his favorite room in the whole house and inside was the box filled with mysterious contents.

What intrigued Geoff the most about the box was the perplexed look on his father's face as he had read the label.

"How odd," said his father as he studied the writing. "Sending materials directly from a dig site like this just isn't done. It's highly illegal to smuggle artifacts out of a country. I'm surprised it arrived."

Now, a day later, Geoff had his chance. He was determined to see what was in the box. His heart beat fast as he grabbed the mahogany banister and hiked up the stairs. As he neared the top, a loud creak came from a step. Geoff grimaced. It was the third step from the top; he had forgotten it always made a racket. He held his breath and looked over his shoulder, once again listening for sounds of anyone in the house. Silence. If he were caught trying to sneak into his dad's study again, he would probably be grounded for the rest of his life. After a few seconds, he allowed himself to exhale.

Geoff climbed to the top of the stairs, then turned and listened one more time. The house was quiet.

"Alright," he said to himself, and he hurried to the oak door at the end of the hall. Beside the door was a small table on which stood a large, leafy tropical plant. He had seen where his father hid the key to his study over six months ago, so Geoff knew where to search. He groped around the base of the plant. The dust that had settled on it wafted upward, making him sneeze. Again he stopped and listened, but there were no sounds of approaching footsteps.

Geoff had approximately thirty minutes before his stepmother returned. So, he resumed his search and soon felt something small and solid tucked into the moist soil. He freed the small object, a door key, from its earthy prison then quickly turned and unlocked the door to his father's study. Geoff stepped inside and closed the door behind him, making a tiny *click*. He looked about the large, sunlit room until his gaze settled on an opened box that rested on his father's desk, along with a box of surgical gloves, a large lamp, some magnifying glasses, and some delicate brushes, as well as tools for examining artifacts.

"There it is," said Geoff. He walked to the box and read the label.

From: Central Carpathian Mountains Dig Site, Romania
To: Dr. Richard Vincent, Ph.D., Archaeology Treemont University
Contents: Lithic tools and materials
Origin: Undetermined

Geoff's eyes lingered on the last word. *Undetermined*? That's new, he thought. What *was* in the box?

He removed a pair of surgical gloves from the nearby box and put them on so as not to damage any relics or leave oily fingerprints behind. As he had learned last year, fingerprints could result in his father discovering Geoff's intrusion. Peering inside, Geoff saw several small boxes and what looked like fancy sandwich bags containing stone chips and rocks. Each item was neatly packed in the box. He picked up a bag and held it up in the light so he could see. The earthen and stone chips were brownish-gray, and some were black. Geoff shrugged, put them back in the box, and moved on, this time picking up a small square box. A printed label said: *Sedimentary Fragments.* Geoff popped open the box top, revealing small bits of various rocks. Some contained tiny shining flakes of other minerals, but most looked like the dark brownish-gray chips in the plastic bag.

Geoff replaced the cover and picked out another box. This one was narrow and rectangular. The label said: *Unknown key— characteristics do not match other artifacts found in the surrounding sediment and area.* Geoff's heart beat faster.

He opened it. Inside, wrapped in a plastic bag, was a key. It resembled a plain old skeleton key, and was encrusted in reddish-gray dirt and stone. It was nearly five inches long and slender. Geoff frowned. That's it? It's just an old key. He sighed and set it on the desk. As he did, he received a small shock. A tingling sensation shot from his hand up to his elbow.

"Ouch! What was that?"

Geoff shook his hand and looked at the nondescript key in the plastic bag. That's weird. Static electricity, maybe, he thought. He dismissed the key and reached for another box. Hopefully a more promising one that was full of mystery. Suddenly the doorbell rang.

Geoff looked up in horror. "Oh no," he whispered as he quickly stuffed the small boxes back into the larger box. He yanked off his surgical gloves and raced out the door.

"Coming!" he called out as he closed the door to his father's study. He bounded down the steps as the doorbell rang again. When he reached the front door, Geoff looked over his shoulder. Definitely no one else here, he thought. Relieved and secure in his surroundings, he reached for the door knob.

Geoff's hand trembled slightly as he opened the door. If for some reason it was his father—if he had forgotten his keys or something—then it would be all over. At a minimum, his punishment would include being grounded for a couple of weeks, not getting any allowance, and doing more chores around the house. The chores were the worst part. They usually included cleaning the bathrooms and the attic, and straightening the greenhouse out back, which was always a particularly long and nasty task that included stacking pots, spreading soil, and sweeping the floor.

He opened the door. A tall, muscular teenager with thick, dark hair was standing there. It was Sawyer Collins.

"Hey," he said. "Here's your book back."

"Huh?" Geoff blinked and looked at the book Sawyer was holding out to him. It was his copy of T. H. White's *The Once and Future King* that Sawyer had taken earlier at school. Geoff was eating lunch in the cafeteria when Sawyer and his pals, Andy Nifong and Stewart Jones, surrounded him. They were all sixteen, two years older than Geoff-and much bigger. Andy had poured his juice all over Geoff's sandwich while Stewart tried to force a spoonful of mashed potatoes into Geoff's mouth. Sawyer slapped the back of Geoff's head, which brought laughter and giggles from other kids sitting nearby.

"Huh?" said Sawyer, tilting his head and mocking him. "Seems someone ratted me out. The principal and my coach said if I didn't return it to you pronto I'd be suspended and miss the next game. Did you rat on me?"

Geoff took a step back. "No."

"Right. Whatever," said Sawyer with disdain. "Here's your stupid book. Take it."

Sawyer tossed it at Geoff, who caught it with both hands.

Having Sawyer suddenly show up at his home upset Geoff. He felt safe when he was home. He had no idea Sawyer knew where he lived.

"Thanks," said Geoff. He kept his eyes on the book in his hand as he started to shut the front door.

"Hey!" said Sawyer as he jammed his foot in the door and forced it open.

"Is that a real suit of armor?" he asked, pointing at a shiny, bronze inlaid suit. Geoff turned and looked at the suit that had caught Sawyer's attention.

"Yeah. Dad won that one and the others in an auction last year. Got a good deal on them, too," Geoff answered.

Sawyer pushed past Geoff and entered the house. Geoff blinked at Sawyer's nerve. He opened his mouth, but didn't say anything. He was afraid to confront Sawyer, even in his own house. Instead he continued, "They just needed to be cleaned up some, but they're in great condition. Dad says they're from England."

Geoff felt his face become warm, and he knew he was blushing. Oh great, he thought. He was talking too much, wasn't he? And acting like a geek. Again.

Sawyer walked to the first suit of dark gray armor and ran his hand along the smooth, cold surface of the helmet.

"They're way cool. They must weigh a ton."

"Not really. You'd be surprised," Geoff said as he glanced at Sawyer. "That suit is from the fourteenth century and weighs around forty-five or fifty-five pounds."

"That's all?"

"Yeah," said Geoff. "That's less than what modern soldiers carry and it's less than the gear a firefighter carries into a fire."

Geoff watched as Sawyer moved to the next suit of armor in the entry, a black, decorative suit with intricate engravings covering it entirely.

"I bet it took a long time to make a full suit of armor," mused Sawyer as he ran his fingertips over the engravings.

"Probably," said Geoff. "There weren't many deadlines recorded by armorers in the Middle Ages, so we can't say for sure."

"You really know all about this kind of stuff, huh?"

"I guess," said Geoff.

Sawyer looked around the living room and foyer. "Your house looks like a museum," he said. Geoff followed Sawyer's gaze. "Yeah," he said. "Dad always brings cool old stuff home to study." Geoff saw Sawyer notice a sword hanging over a round shield on the wall and walk over to it. Without asking he took it down and swung it back and forth a few times. Geoff held up his hand and opened his mouth. Geez, he's rude! Wish he wouldn't handle stuff. What if he breaks something?

Sawyer's size intimidated Geoff, so he thought the best policy for the moment was to let Sawyer handle the sword with a simple plea. "Just please be careful," he said.

"I thought it'd be heavier," Sawyer said as he looked at the blade.

"Most one-handed swords weighed around ten or fifteen pounds."

Sawyer slid the sword back in its resting place on the wall and walked into the living room. Geoff tried to think of something to say that Sawyer would think was cool, but he swallowed and remained silent.

"Now this is a helmet," said Sawyer as he picked up a shining conical helm and placed it on his head. The helm had a metal bar that extended over his nose and down to his chin. It was several sizes too large and wobbled around as Sawyer tried to steady it. He looked like a bobblehead doll with the helm wriggling back and forth on his head.

"It's a Viking helmet from Scandinavia," said Geoff with a chuckle. Sawyer took it off and looked at it again.

"No way," he said. "Where are the horns?"

"They didn't usually have horns on their helmets."

"Geez, who wore this, Bigfoot?" asked Sawyer.

He set the helmet down. "This is so awesome. Your house rocks."

Geoff looked around the room. It occurred to him that most homes didn't have suits of armor in the foyer or authentic swords and shields hanging on the walls.

When people see this stuff for the first time they may be impressed, he thought.

"Dad's been bringing stuff home for as long as I can remember."

Sawyer nodded and sighed. "You must have the coolest dad ever."

"He's all right, I guess," said Geoff, gaining confidence. "Mom doesn't like him bringing all this stuff home. She says it's junk."

Sawyer ran his finger along the crest of the cone-shaped helmet. "Yeah? Does your mom get mad at him a lot?"

"Actually," said Geoff, "she's my stepmom. My real mom died a couple years ago. My stepmom isn't around much. Neither is dad." Geoff's eyes wandered to the floor and his face again became flushed. He had never shared that with anyone before and he wished he could take his last remark back.

"You're lucky. My parents can't be in the same room with each other because they fight all the time."

Geoff swallowed again. This was awkward. He wanted to change the subject. An idea suddenly occurred to him. He turned to Sawyer.

"Wanna see some other cool stuff my dad has? Some of it he even found himself while he was digging in Europe."

"Yeah, okay," said Sawyer. "Why not?"

Geoff led Sawyer up the wide staircase, then they turned right and continued down a hall. At the end of the hall was the door Geoff had closed minutes earlier. Geoff stopped at the door. Should he really do this? If Sawyer broke anything then he would be in so much trouble. But maybe Sawyer will like him better if he sees what's in here. Geoff pushed the door open and they entered.

He smiled and watched as Sawyer's jaw dropped as he looked around the room. Sunlight filtered through the windows and revealed stacks of boxes and crates all around the room.

Geoff watched Sawyer's eyes wander to several partially reconstructed suits of armor, along with a wide array of utensils, statues, weapons, and wooden carvings displayed throughout the room. The entire wall opposite the windows was one giant bookshelf full of books. Geoff stood on the plush carpeting and watched Sawyer wander back and forth, unable to focus on any one object.

"Oh wow…," said Sawyer.

Geoff again smiled at Sawyer's amazed reaction to his father's study. "This is incredible," said Sawyer as he walked into the jungle of crates and relics.

"How much is all this stuff worth?"

"Don't know. Dad says some of it is priceless," said Geoff.

"Oh, man! I believe it! This really is a museum!"

Geoff beamed as he looked around. Sawyer's enthusiasm and excitement thrilled him. Sawyer picked up a large, heavy tome.

"Sawyer, please be careful," said Geoff with a hint of alarm in his voice. "Here, put these gloves on. We have oils in our fingers that can damage some of this stuff."

Sawyer gently set the tome back in its resting place and took the surgical gloves Geoff offered.

"Yeah, okay. So is your dad going to study all this stuff? That'll take forever."

Geoff looked around at the stacks of crates, each containing artifacts and relics of an age long gone.

"Yeah, I guess. He just got this box of stuff yesterday. Some other archaeologists need help identifying what's in it," he said as he motioned to the box on the desk. "Maybe someday I'll get to finish what he's started. When I get out of college he might let me help him with his research."

"Where's your dad now?" asked Sawyer.

"Teaching," said Geoff. "He works at the university and won't be home for another couple hours or so."

"Then we better not get caught," said Sawyer with a slight smile. He weaved his way among the crates and boxes, pausing to admire a partial suit of blue and black samurai armor that was hanging loosely from a mannequin.

"Are you piecing this armor together?"

Geoff looked at the ancient suit of Japanese armor. "Dad kind of is," he said, "when he has extra time." Sawyer kept his eyes on the samurai armor as he walked around a stack of large crates. He was completely out of sight when Geoff heard a loud *thump* followed by Sawyer's "Ouch! Damn, that's heavy."

Geoff's heart nearly stopped.

"What happened? Are you okay?" he called with a higher pitch to his voice.

"Yeah, yeah," grunted Sawyer. "What the hell is this?"

Sawyer held his hand out from behind a large stack of crates and beckoned Geoff to come over. Geoff hurried around the crates and saw Sawyer standing in front of a large object covered with a single white sheet.

"It's huge. It must weigh a ton. I almost broke my toe on it." Sawyer lifted the sheet from the tall object to expose a gray stone archway. It stood over seven feet tall and was cracked and chipped, and from the black, sooty residue that covered one side, it looked as if it had been in a fire. Even in such a damaged state, Geoff could see remnants of once beautiful carvings all around it. There were small figures that reminded him of gargoyles, and he was sure he could make out part of a dragon's head at the top.

"What is it?" asked Sawyer.

Geoff ran a gloved finger along the cold, gray surface and shook his head. "I don't know. I've never seen it before. It looks like either a doorway or perhaps it was once a window or mirror, maybe from a cathedral or something."

"It was hidden behind all these crates. It must have taken a lot of big guys to bring it up the steps and put it here."

Geoff looked at Sawyer. He was right. It would have taken a small army to heft this heavy stone archway and drag it up the steps, something Geoff would certainly have known about.

"How did they get it in here?" asked Geoff. "Look. You see this archway is much bigger than the door."

Sawyer looked back at the door that led into the study and then back at the archway. "Yeah, you're right. Maybe they used a crane and brought it in through a window."

"No." Geoff shook his head. "I would have noticed that. And besides, they would have had to take out most of the wall in order to get this thing in here."

Sawyer shrugged with his arms out wide. "You got me. I have no idea how it got here, unless the Great Pumpkin left it last Halloween." Geoff smiled and chuckled a little. He had never spoken to Sawyer this long and he liked Sawyer's sense of humor. Geoff stepped closer for a better look at the carvings, "I've never seen this kind of sculpture before. I wonder who carved it. It's very detailed."

Apparently already bored with the archway, Sawyer walked back to the desk and peered into the box Geoff had been rummaging through earlier. "Looks like a bunch of rocks and dirt," he said as he gently sifted through the bags and small boxes. He picked up the rectangular box and read aloud, "Characteristics do not match other artifacts found in the surrounding sediment and area. What characteristics would that be? Geoff, can I open this?" Geoff pulled his attention away from the archway and looked at Sawyer. He recognized the box Sawyer was holding. "Yeah, sure. Go ahead. It's just some old rusty key inside, but be careful with it."

"Key to a treasure chest, maybe?" asked Sawyer with exaggerated excitement. Geoff chuckled again and watched Sawyer open the box and pick up the clear bag containing the earth-encrusted key. He turned it over and looked at the other side.

"Yep," said Sawyer. "Just an old key." He was about to place it back in the box when Geoff noticed he stopped and examined the key more closely.

"Hey, Geoff, this reminds me of some of the carvings on that archway," he said as he walked over to Geoff and held the key up for him to see. Geoff took the key from Sawyer and looked at it.

"No. There, on the other side. Doesn't that look like a dragon or snake to you?" asked Sawyer as he pointed to the small shape that caught his attention.

Geoff looked closer. The shape did indeed look similar

to the carvings on the archway. He slowly opened the bag and removed the key. It weighed next to nothing in Geoff's hand and it was as cold as the stone archway. He held the key up to what appeared to be the partial carving of a dragon's head on the archway.

"Yep," said Sawyer. "I thought so. I bet whoever carved that archway also made the key."

"I think you're right," said Geoff. Now this was more like it, he thought. Geoff loved a good mystery and Sawyer had discovered an extraordinary one. Sawyer's keen eye had revealed a connection between the key and the archway, but what exactly was their connection?

Geoff felt his heart pound and the hair on the back of his neck seemed to be standing up. A tingling sensation enveloped him, giving him a warm, energized feeling.

"Uh, Geoff," said Sawyer, "what's going on?" Geoff looked at Sawyer, who was backing away with an alarmed expression on his face.

"What's happening? I feel strange. Sawyer, what's happening to me?" asked Geoff

Sawyer pointed. "Whoa! Your hair...it's standing up! And what's that sound?"

Geoff raised his hand and felt his head. His hair was indeed rising from his head. He heard a slight rushing sound, like wind whistling through a keyhole. Suddenly Geoff felt a movement in his hand and he quickly looked down at the key he was holding. Bits of dirt and stone were starting to crumble and flake away right before his eyes, but there was something else—something beneath the fragments of stone and earth. It was smooth and white.

The doorbell rang.

CHAPTER TWO

JANE

JANE WAITED AT THE FRONT doors of the large Tudor mansion, admiring the thick walnut wood surrounded by beautiful oval stained glass windows. The vivid blues, reds, and yellows reminded her of windows in a cathedral in Italy her family had visited three years earlier. She turned her back to the doors and looked out over the well-manicured front lawn. She loved this house. What a wonderful place to call home.

Each year Geoff's parents had hosted a party on Christmas Eve and invited the entire neighborhood. Jane always enjoyed those gatherings; they made her feel warm inside. Near the end of the evening Geoff's mother would play the piano while everyone gathered and sang Christmas carols before leaving.

When Geoff's mother suddenly passed away, however, those wonderful parties stopped. Jane realized she really missed those holiday celebrations at the Vincents'.

Recently Geoff's father remarried after a surprisingly fast courtship. Geoff's stepmother was cold and mean. Jane remembered the time when she went to the door to ask for a donation of canned goods and his stepmother just glared at her before slamming the door.

Still, this house was amazing to Jane, almost magical, even. Like the lawn, the hedges were meticulously maintained. She especially loved the large greenhouse behind the mansion. When Geoff's mom was alive every imaginable flower and plant grew there. Jane thought it was a slice of paradise when she strolled through the greenhouse. Now it was in a state of neglect and in need of a good cleaning.

She felt a breeze lift her shoulder-length hair and for the thousandth time she wished it was a color other than brown. She was desperate to dye it blond, but her mom wouldn't let her. She tilted her head back and closed her blue eyes. She took a deep breath, surrendering herself to the refreshing gust as it swept over her.

Opening her eyes, she saw that no one had answered the door yet.

That's strange, she thought. Geoff should be home right now. Maybe he didn't hear the doorbell. She rang it again.

A few moments later Geoff opened the door. His normally well-combed blond hair was standing nearly straight up, making him look like he had stuck his fingers in a socket. Jane giggled. She couldn't help herself.

"Hi, Geoff!" she said.

She watched as Geoff blinked for a moment before letting out a sigh of relief.

"Oh…hi, Jane." Geoff stood at the door, his eyes darting back and forth while he apparently searched for something to say.

Jane giggled again. "Geoff? Hello? Geoff, are you okay?" She waved her slender hand in front of his eyes. "What's up with your hair?" She reached forward and smoothed Geoff's hair.

Geoff snapped out of his mental torpor. "Oh, hey, Jane. How're you doing?"

"I'm fine. You look a little rough, though." Jane smiled.

"I'm okay," said Geoff. "I was just…kinda—"

Jane laughed as Geoff stammered.

"Relax, Geoff," said Jane, holding up her hand. "I don't want to know what trouble you're about to get into. I'm just here because your dad signed my pledge sheet for the muscular dystrophy walkathon last week, and I've come to collect."

Geoff snapped his fingers. "Oh, oh yeah. I think he left an envelope for you in the kitchen. It's on the fridge." He held the door open for Jane to enter. She wiped her shoes on the welcome mat and walked into the house.

"Hey, your dad has added a few things since the last time I was here," said Jane, pointing at the suits of armor. "I don't remember these."

"Yeah, he got them in an auction. Pretty cool, huh?"

Jane nodded. "Mmhmm."

"Hey, Jane." Sawyer was perched on a plush brown leather couch in the living room, flipping through a magazine. Jane stopped. She was surprised to see Sawyer. In fact, she didn't think Sawyer knew Geoff, much less visited him.

"Sawyer? What're you doing here?" she asked.

Sawyer smiled. "I just returned a book Geoff let me borrow and now we're hanging out."

"Oh really?" asked Jane. "You *borrowed* a book from Geoff?"

Sawyer raised his eyebrows. "Yup."

"So I didn't see you and your friends bully Geoff in the cafeteria? I didn't see you *take* his book? And now you two are hanging out?"

"Yup," said Sawyer again.

Jane glanced at Geoff, who was standing quietly nearby.

"And how often do you two hang out with each other? You never seem to know each other at school." Jane's eyes narrowed and she smiled. "Sawyer, are you trying to get Geoff into trouble?"

"Me? No. No way. We were just talking about those suits of armor. Did you know they weigh less than a fireman's gear does?"

"Mmhmm." Jane became more suspicious. "Sawyer, you don't care about suits of armor or medieval stuff. Why are you here?"

"No, really. I just returned Geoff's book," said Sawyer as he motioned to the novel Geoff had laid on the coffee-table.

Jane looked at Geoff, who shrugged and nodded.

"Okay, whatever. It's just that I've never known you to be interested in anything besides sports or girls."

Jane looked at Sawyer, who was the epitome of a hot, hunky guy. Then she looked at Geoff, who was the skinny nerd type. Something is going on, she thought, and she didn't want to know what it was.

"Alright," she said. She didn't have time to indulge the boys in whatever foolishness they were currently involved in. Jane turned back to Geoff. "I'll just get the envelope and let you guys get back to hanging out, okay? Thanks." She walked toward the kitchen, glancing over her shoulder at them as she left the living room.

"Okay," said Geoff. Jane's mind was now on other things. She had to collect pledges from two more neighbors, feed the dogs and cats at the animal shelter, and get home to help with dinner.

Her pace quickened. She went to the kitchen, found and removed the envelope with her name from the refrigerator, and turned to leave when she suddenly came face to face with Sawyer.

She started and gasped. "Oh! Sawyer! You scared me!"

Sawyer held his hands up. "Sorry. I didn't mean to. How's it going?" Jane blinked and looked at him. He now looked like a guy who wanted something.

"Good. How about you? Shouldn't you be talking with Geoff about knights and the Middle Ages and stuff?"

Sawyer flashed that gorgeous smile with the irresistible small dimples in his cheeks as his eyes caught hers. Wait a minute, thought Jane. Is he flirting with me? Oh my! This is so cool! Oh wait, Kylie is my friend. No, this isn't a good idea. Didn't they just break up again? They seem to break up every other week. She tried to squeeze past Sawyer and the doorway to leave the kitchen, but he stepped in front of her.

"Whoa there. Wassup, girl? Hold on. Why the rush? I just want to talk for a sec."

Jane looked at Sawyer, whose eyes were now roaming over her body. She bit her lower lip to keep from laughing.

"Do some girls actually fall for that?"

"Hmmm? Fall for what? It's all good," said Sawyer. "You look good."

"Okay, Sawyer. Wassup?"

Jane's slight mockery of Sawyer went unnoticed, as she half expected.

"Hey, did you see the game? I threw for two touchdowns and ran for two more. We won 35-17. That puts us in the state semifinals."

Sawyer's arrogance was the one thing about him Jane didn't like. For all his good looks and athletic ability, he was still a bit of a dumb jock who thought he was "it".

"Semifinals? Great. That's great," said Jane, feigning interest. "I'm sure you're going to do awesome. Really. Congratulations. I mean it."

"Yeah, I think we can take the state title this year. We have a great team. All I need is 252 more yards passing and I will have the state record for most passing yards in a season."

Jane nodded. "Really? That's awesome!"

She raised an eyebrow. She couldn't resist playing the part of devil's advocate, "Do you think you'll get the record?"

"Oh yeah," said Sawyer. "I guaran—."

"Okay," she said. "Great. I gotta go. See ya."

"Are you coming to the game tonight?"

"No. I doubt it," she said. "I have too much going on. I'm supposed to be at the animal shelter. They're really short-staffed." She hoped she didn't sound like she was stuck-up just then.

"Oh yeah," said Sawyer. "You like animals, huh? It's cool that you volunteer and all that. Still, maybe you can leave early and make the game? Maybe see some real animals play?"

Jane watched through narrowed eyes as Sawyer slightly scratched a bicep and flexed. He is so arrogant, she thought, hitting on me in Geoff's house. He thinks he can do anything. He probably just wants to use me to upset Kylie.

Jane was Sawyer's age and while she was considered by many to be cute, she was a bit of a bookworm herself. She studied hard; she planned to attend veterinarian school and spend her life helping animals.

"I have to go now," said Jane as she stuffed the envelope containing the pledge money from Geoff's father into her purse. "See ya."

"C'mon. You don't have to go now, do you? Maybe I'll save a spot for you on the bench. You can see things up close. Whadda ya say? Then we can grab some pizza after the game."

"Oh, that is tempting," said Jane, "but I really can't. Sorry."

She walked back down the hall and stepped into the living room to say good-bye to Geoff, but he wasn't there.

Jane shrugged and walked to the front door, stopping to call out to Geoff. "Geoff! I'm going now! Thanks!"

There was no answer.

Jane placed her hand on a doorknob and waited for Geoff to appear, but he didn't. She wondered where he was. He usually comes running to show a guest out.

"Geoff?" she called again.

Jane noticed Sawyer had followed her to the foyer and was looking around.

"Where's Geoff? He's not here?" he asked.

"No. Where did he go? I don't know if he heard me yell," Jane said. "Anyway, tell him I said 'bye." She turned back to the front door and twisted the knob. Suddenly, Jane heard what she thought was a high-pitched ringing sound as she opened the door.

"Oh!" Jane gasped and looked around, thinking that perhaps she had triggered an alarm. She quickly closed the door and held her hands up in a show of no wrongdoing.

"What is that?" she asked. "Did I set off the burglar alarm or something?"

The ringing sound grew louder and more frantic, with small pauses.

"Oh no," said Sawyer as his face turned white and his jaw tightened. "That's Geoff! I bet he messed with that key we found!"

"What? What key? What are you talking about?" Jane was sure Sawyer didn't hear her as he rushed past her and bounded up the steps two or three at a time.

"Geoff's in trouble, Jane! C'mon!"

"Wait! What? Sawyer, what's going on?"

She watched from the bottom of the stairs as he charged through the door to the study, trying to process what Sawyer had just yelled to her. Once the door was fully opened, Jane could hear the high-pitched sound more clearly. Someone was screaming. It was Geoff. He was screaming at the top of his lungs. She also heard the rushing sound of a strong wind and there were several bangs and crashes, followed by a loud *thud*.

"Geoff!" called Jane.

She had never heard anyone scream so loud. Jane followed Sawyer up the steps as fast as she was able. When she rushed into the study she was nearly knocked off her feet by a strong gust of wind. A whirlwind was whipping around, sending loose pieces of paper, boxes, and other objects flying about the room. She could barely hear Geoff and Sawyer shouting over the wind.

"Hang on, Geoff! Hang on!"

"Help! Sawyer! Help me!"

Jane's hair whipped around her head and stung her eyes. She pushed her hair back and looked about the room, but she didn't see Geoff or Sawyer.

"Sawyer! Geoff!" she called. She noticed what appeared to be a pale green glow coming from behind some large crates near the back of the room.

"Jane! Over here! Help me!"

The call came from behind the crates, from where the green glow emanated. It was Sawyer, and he sounded like he was under terrible strain. Dodging a box and a couple of books as they flew by, Jane moved toward the glow. When she rounded the last stack of crates she suddenly stopped and stared. She couldn't believe the scene that lay before her.

"Oh my god!" she cried.

Sawyer had one foot propped against an old stone archway and was straining for all he was worth, pulling on something. The muscles in his arms were taut. He grimaced and shook from the exertion. Jane gasped as she noticed that what Sawyer was so desperately trying to hang on to—it was Geoff's arm, and only his arm, protruding from the archway. Jane screamed. She couldn't see where the rest of Geoff's body should be on the other side of the arch.

A small wooden box struck the side of Jane's head and disappeared into the archway. She clutched the side of her head, wincing with pain. The intensity of the wind was

 31

much stronger here, creating a vortex in which Sawyer struggled to keep Geoff from being sucked into the archway. Jane staggered as she fought to keep her balance against the constant rush of air. She grabbed the edge of a large crate to steady herself as the gust pushed her forward. She moved her hair out of her eyes again and looked at Sawyer, who met her gaze.

"Hurry, Jane! He's slipping!"

Jane saw Sawyer was indeed losing his grip. Geoff's arm was steadily disappearing into the archway. Sawyer grunted and strained. "Jane! Help me!" At that moment, Sawyer lurched forward uncontrollably, nearly losing his balance and falling into the archway. He managed to grab it with one hand to prevent himself from being pulled in as he held onto Geoff with his other hand.

"Jane!" called Sawyer again. "I can't hold him much longer!"

Jane ran to Sawyer, and grabbed him around the waist. She pulled, but felt him slipping from her grasp, so she also placed a foot against the archway to gain more leverage. She thought all three of them were going to be lifted into the air and swept into the archway. She glanced over Sawyer's shoulder and saw Geoff inside the archway, his body twisting and turning like a leaf in the wind. Behind Geoff, she could see green and gray billowing mists churning and swirling about.

Geoff's eyes were wide and darted back and forth as the ebb and flow of the swirling mists threatened to swallow him. Jane saw the fear and panic in his face. He screamed as he gripped Sawyer's arm.

"We're slipping, Jane! Pull!" shouted Sawyer, his body

shaking from the strain. With her arms still around Sawyer, she pushed off the archway with her foot and leaned back, pulling as hard as she could. She could feel Sawyer slowly pulling away from the archway and she saw Geoff's head and shoulder begin to emerge.

"That's it. Keep pulling! We got him!"

Jane's hamstrings began to ache from the exertion, and she felt her foot slip a little against the stone arch.

"Sawyer! I'm slipping!"

"Hold on, Jane! C'mon! Pull!"

Jane arched her back again, pulling with every bit of strength she could summon. It felt as if they were trying to pull a heavy object out of quicksand.

"Jane, grab his hand! Hurry!" shouted Sawyer. Jane blinked, trying to think how she could get hold of Geoff without being sucked in herself.

"I can't! I can't reach him!"

"Hurry! Pull!"

With one arm anchored around Sawyer' waist, she stretched for Geoff's hand. As she strained to reach him, another strong gust caused her to lose her balance and her foot to slip off the archway. She grabbed Sawyer's waist with both hands, clawing at his shirt to keep from being swept into the archway, but she was unable to maintain her grip. She screamed as the strong wind lifted her off her feet and she was pulled into the archway with Geoff. The gale force winds that were pulling Geoff now enveloped Jane. Her foot slammed into Geoff's head as she just managed to seize Sawyer's leg.

Sawyer grimaced and yelled in pain. The added weight was too much. He also fell into the archway, only barely keeping his grip on both Geoff and the arch. Jane wrapped her arms around Sawyer's leg and squeezed it. She and Geoff were tossed about like sheets in a breeze, crashing into each other while trying to hold onto Sawyer.

"Sawyer!" called Jane, "Don't let go! Hold on! Pull!"

"I can't! I can't hang on!" Sawyer called.

"I'm slipping! Sawyer!" screamed Geoff.

Jane watched Sawyer take a deep breath and muster whatever strength he had left. He strained against the swirling winds with the added weight of Geoff and Jane clinging to him, but his attempt was futile.

"It's no good! I can't pull us out!"

Jane looked at Sawyer. It was all he could do to hold onto the arch. She thought she saw him shake his head. The look on his pain-stricken face was clear.

"Oh no," sobbed Jane.

She looked into the swirling mists churning all about them. She could see no forms or shapes, only a writhing tempest that had no end. She tried to swallow, but couldn't. Tears rolled across her cheeks. There was nothing any of them could do now. Jane looked at Geoff. He was sobbing, but she could do nothing to help him.

Jane heard a loud *crack* followed by another *crack*.

"Sawyer!" she screamed.

She saw Sawyer's lips move as he shouted something, but the rushing wind was too loud for her to hear. His eyes met hers as they were suddenly swept away by the powerful winds, screaming and tumbling into the billowing vortex.

 34

Chapter Three

Enchanted Forest

Geoff's eyes ached. A bright light shined in his face. He winced and closed his eyes while he turned away. His head was spinning, or perhaps he was spinning. Geoff thought he was lying on his back. A loud yet muffled sound drummed in his ears. He groaned and tried to swallow but couldn't. His mouth was dry. His right shoulder throbbed and felt as if needles were sticking in it.

He lay still a while longer, taking deep breaths. A faint, sweet scent of wildflowers and grass drifted over him. Soon the drumming sound dissipated and he thought he heard something else. It was faint, but it sounded like cheerful music.

Is someone whistling or are there birds singing nearby? As he focused, the melody helped him regain his senses. It was calming and somehow lively at the same time. Geoff opened his eyes. He saw lots of flowers. He tried to raise his right arm to shield his eyes from the bright light, but a terrible pain raced from his shoulder down the length of his arm. Sawyer had pulled Geoff's arm so hard he must have injured some muscles or perhaps even dislocated his shoulder as he tried to keep Geoff from falling.

Wait, thought Geoff. Didn't he fall? What happened? Since he felt pain, Geoff reasoned that he was indeed alive. He could definitely make out the sounds of birds singing. The birdsongs were harmonious and the golden patch of light on his skin warmed and reassured him.

With some effort, Geoff raised his left hand to shield his eyes as he looked about. The grass he'd smelled was tall and the flowers were an incandescent hodgepodge of yellow, blue, red, purple, and white. He lifted his head and scanned the area around him. Jane and Sawyer lay a few feet away. Beyond them, on all sides, were trees and shrubs with another explosive array of colorful flowers.

Geoff gently rolled onto his left side and propped himself up with his elbow for a better look. He held his right arm close to his body, slightly bent, since it didn't hurt so much that way. The left shoulder didn't hurt, but he felt something hard in the grass next to his left hand. He blinked again to focus and looked at the object. It was the white alabaster key from his dad's study, but it wasn't glowing now. It wasn't doing anything. Geoff frowned as his memory started to return.

He remembered Sawyer and then Jane arriving at his house. They had been talking in the kitchen and he went upstairs to clean up the study, beginning with the key. It was lying on the floor where he had dropped it earlier. What harm could there be in picking it up and quickly placing it back in the small bag? If he were quick about it, then there wouldn't be any strange lights, or wind, or anything.

He was about to shove the key into the bag when he

noticed the swirling mists immediately returned to the archway. He thought he saw something in the mists—not just a shape the mists formed, but trees in a forest.

Yes, he had seen a lush, green forest full of colorful, flowering plants. He remembered reaching out to touch a tall purple hyacinth, and before he knew it, he was being pulled or wrenched into the archway. He managed to grab the side, but he began to slip away almost immediately. He remembered Sawyer and Jane rushing to try to pull him to safety.

Thinking of Sawyer and Jane made him look at them again. Jane was lying on her side, her back to him. Her body slowly rose and fell as she breathed. Then he looked at Sawyer, who was sprawled on the ground just a few feet away from her. He was also breathing. Geoff sighed in relief. They were alive.

Where are we? Geoff wondered as he painfully forced himself to sit up. He sighed heavily and looked about. They appeared to be lying in the forest he had seen in the archway. Yes, he thought, this is the forest. He rubbed his eyes and looked around again. It really was beautiful. Many of the trees towered overhead to fantastic heights. Their branches formed a thick canopy through which beams of sunlight filtered to the ground below. In the distance rose an awesome and majestic snow-capped mountain range.

Geoff slowly got to his knees, still holding his right arm close to his body. He crawled to Jane and gently shook her shoulder.

"Jane, wake up," he said. She didn't stir. He shook her again. "Jane. Hey, Jane." Jane suddenly took a long, deep breath.

"Huh?" she groaned.

"Wake up, Jane. Are you okay?"

"Geoff? What…what happened?" She grunted and rubbed her temples with her fingertips and she grimaced as if in pain.

"I don't know, but I think we died," said Geoff.

"Hmmm? Wha—?"

"Looks like we're dead and now we're in heaven or maybe the Elysian Fields," said Geoff.

"What? The what—? Geoff, what are you talking about?"

Jane sat up but kept her eyes closed, and she clutched her head with both hands.

"Are you okay?" asked Geoff again.

"Yeah. Yeah, I think so. Just a bad migraine. I get them from time to time." Jane slowly lifted her head and opened her eyes. She blinked several times and scanned the area. "Where are we?"

"I don't know. The Garden of Eden?" asked Geoff.

"Oh hush, Geoff. Wow, it's beautiful," said Jane.

A young doe peered at them curiously from behind a tree as it slowly chewed a mouthful of leaves. On the other side of the clearing, two plump robins flapped about a large shrub and chattered noisily at each other. Jane tilted her head back and rubbed her neck and shoulder. Sawyer was still lying on the ground nearby.

"Is Sawyer okay?" she asked.

"I think so. I'll check," said Geoff. He turned and crawled to Sawyer and shook him.

With a snort and a cough, Sawyer opened his eyes. He

blinked several times, trying to regain his vision. He also had to put a hand up to shield his eyes from the sunlight.

"Wha...Geoff?" He coughed again and mumbled something that was incoherent.

"Sawyer, are you okay?" asked Geoff as he shook him again.

"Yeah...yeah, okay. I'm up. I'm up." He raised himself a little, propping himself up on one elbow and looking first at Geoff and then at Jane.

"What happened? Where are we?"

"Good question," said Jane. "We were just talking about that." Jane looked about, still rubbing her neck.

"I think we're dead and this is heaven or something," offered Geoff.

"Geoff," said Jane sternly, "stop it. We're not dead. We can't be; my head hurts too much."

"In that case," said Geoff, "I bet we got sucked through an interdimensional wormhole in the space-time continuum. That could have caused your headache."

"Aww hell," grunted Sawyer as he pulled himself to his feet. "You watch too much TV."

Sawyer wobbled a little and then steadied himself and regarded their surroundings, taking in the beautiful and flourishing forest.

"What's going on? We were in Geoff's house and now we're...here. Wherever 'here' is. Hey, wait a minute." He turned, pointed, and took a couple steps toward Geoff.

"You touched that damn key again, didn't you? Why did you do that? I know what you did, you went back upstairs and played with that strange key again and got us all sucked into the archway."

The angry look on Sawyer's face frightened Geoff.

"I…I didn't mean to," he stammered. "I just wanted to start cleaning dad's study. I thought if I picked it up really fast…then…it would be okay."

Sawyer took a step toward him, and Geoff scooted backward on the grass.

"You little dweeb," said Sawyer, still advancing on Geoff. "It wasn't okay, was it? Take a look around. Where the hell are we?"

"That's enough," said Jane. "Leave him alone, Sawyer." Her voice was louder than usual. "Arguing and fighting isn't going to help."

Sawyer stopped and glanced at Jane, who was still sitting on the ground holding her head.

"Are you serious? Look around, Jane. We were in Geoff's house and now we're here…lost in the woods. We're up the creek without a paddle."

"And how is bullying Geoff going to help?" said Jane in an exasperated tone.

"I'll tell you how it's going to help," said Sawyer. "It'll make me feel better after I kick his ass."

"No it won't," said Jane. "Leave him alone. I mean it, Sawyer."

Geoff knew from the tone in Jane's voice that she meant business. He noticed Sawyer had realized the same thing as he turned and looked at Jane.

"Alright," Sawyer said. "Are you going to be okay?"

"Yeah. I'll be fine," she said. "I just need my headache medicine and to lay down for a while."

She went through the pockets in her jeans a second time.

"Great," she said. "I am always losing my medicine. I thought it was in my pocket, but I guess I left it in my purse. Wonderful."

She let out a long sigh as she eased back and lay on the grass again with an arm across her eyes. Geoff tried to stand up, but lost his balance and fell with a grunt. He grabbed his injured shoulder, which still throbbed painfully.

Geoff glanced at Sawyer. He was looking at Geoff's sore shoulder, but made no attempt to help.

"My shoulder and arm hurt," said Geoff. "I think it happened when you and Jane tried to save me."

After a few moments, Geoff's dizziness faded until all he felt was a dull throbbing in his head. He rubbed his forehead for a moment.

A pair of brown and white rabbits raced by their feet and stopped at the edge of the clearing. They rose up on their hind legs and sniffed at Sawyer and Geoff, their noses twitching, then they turned and hopped back into the shadows of the forest.

"At least there's wildlife we can kill and eat if we get hungry," said Sawyer.

A soft breeze blew, carrying with it the earthy smells of the forest and the aromatic scents of various flowers. Their fragrances were almost intoxicating for Geoff. He found himself standing still staring at the sea of wildflowers all around. There was something relaxing and peaceful here. He had been a boy scout briefly and had been on a few camping trips with his troop. While he had seen some beautiful places in the forest, nothing compared with his current majestic surroundings.

"Crap," said Sawyer as he tapped the screen of his phone. "I don't have any bars. Jane, do you get anything?"

"It's in my purse," said Jane dryly.

Sawyer looked at Geoff.

"Stay here with Jane. I'm going to look around a little," he said. "Maybe I can find a phone or a road or some help."

Geoff nodded and watched as Sawyer disappeared into the trees in the direction of the mountain range. Soon the sounds of twigs snapping and leaves rustling faded as Sawyer moved through the underbrush of the forest. Geoff walked to Jane, who hadn't moved.

"Sawyer is scouting around," said Geoff. "He won't be gone long."

Jane only grunted. Her arm still covered her eyes and she was breathing deeply. Geoff noticed she was tightly clutching the grass beside her.

"Jane—" began Geoff, but Jane immediately cut him off.

"Geoff, please be quiet and be still," she said. "This migraine really hurts."

"Okay," whispered Geoff. He lowered himself onto the tall grass beside her as quietly as he could, which was difficult to do with only one good arm. He watched Jane lie there for a few minutes, wondering if she really was going to be okay. He glanced back in the direction Sawyer had taken but didn't see any sign of him. Instead he caught sight of a familiar-looking piece of stone lying nearby.

It was scorched and had intricate carvings on its surface. It was a piece of the archway, the piece Sawyer was holding onto. Their combined weight must have caused it to break off in Sawyer's hand.

 42

Geoff picked up the charred piece of stone and examined it. He held the key next to the stone, hoping to reactivate it and send them back home. Nothing happened.

"The key doesn't glow anymore," said Geoff quietly. Jane did not respond immediately. She just lay there beside him shielding her eyes.

"Geoff? What key?" she asked finally.

Geoff looked at Jane and realized she wasn't there when he and Sawyer found the key. Nor had she witnessed the interaction between the key and the archway. Uh-oh, he thought. She's going to be really upset with him when she finds out.

"Geoff," repeated Jane, "what key? What key was Sawyer talking about?"

Geoff fidgeted in the grass, "I found...well...Sawyer and I found this strange key." Geoff held it up so the sunlight reflected off its sparkling surface. Jane uncovered her eyes and looked at the white key in Geoff's hand.

"Then I placed it in the keyhole of the archway and this big whirlwind started blowing and I got sucked in. That's when you and Sawyer tried to save me and then...we ended up here."

Jane was silent.

"I didn't mean for anything to happen, Jane. I'm sorry."

"Oh, Geoff," moaned Jane as she turned her head away from him. "What did you do?"

Geoff looked down and repeated, "Sorry." Jane sighed. "No way this is real. This can't be happening. It's like a bad dream."

Geoff couldn't look at her. He felt like crying. They

were lost in an unknown forest and it was his fault. He stood up and surveyed the glade in which they rested.

A large butterfly with wings of bright blue and green trimmed in black darted past his eyes and fluttered about Jane's head, but Jane was oblivious to her visitor's presence. It dipped and hovered just above her head. Another butterfly, slightly smaller and sporting red, orange, and white on its wings, soon joined the first one.

The butterflies appeared to be attracted to Jane, maybe because of the perfume she wore. Geoff didn't know what caused their behavior. Then two more butterflies joined the others and formed a collage of colors dancing about Jane. Every now and then one would land on Jane's arm or head only for a moment before leaping back into the air again.

Geoff blinked and watched. He had never seen such a performance from butterflies. He opened his mouth to say something, but decided not to disturb Jane. If she wasn't feeling well because of a headache then the quickest remedy for her was to continue to lie down with her eyes shut.

Geoff glanced up and frowned. The sun is starting to go down, he thought. Sawyer was right. They were lost in a strange, wild place. Who knew what dangerous animals roamed about in the forest after sundown? Geoff looked about for some shelter, but he didn't see any possibilities from the clearing. He opened his hand and looked at the white stone key again. Still no tingling or electrical flashes; it felt like any other key now.

There was a loud thrashing sound from the underbrush behind Geoff. He turned in time to see Sawyer emerge from the greenery carrying a thick tree limb over his shoulder like a club. "Hey, guys," Sawyer said, "I found a stream just over the next hill. The water looks crystal clear and clean. You can see all the way to the bottom and there are fish everywhere."

"You didn't drink any of the water, did you?" asked Geoff.

"Yeah, a little."

"Sawyer," said Jane from under her arm, "you're supposed to boil water from a stream before you drink it. There could be parasites and all sorts of bacteria in it."

"I don't think so," he said. "Not in this water. It tastes good. Anyway, how the hell are we going to boil water?"

"Um," began Geoff, trying hard not to sound like a know-it-all geek. "In the scouts we boiled water using large green leaves as bowls."

"Yeah?" said Sawyer. "Green leaves? How do you make a bowl with leaves? And how are we gonna start a fire?"

"I think I can try using the bow and drill method for maximum friction. We need to find some dry wood and a flat rock and I'll try to use my shoestring to make a bow."

"Are you serious? Are you some kind of Eagle Scout or something? You can do all that?"

Geoff looked at Sawyer and realized how he must have sounded. A wave of self-doubt washed over him. He was talking so fast he did actually sound like a know-it-all.

"Maybe. I think so."

Sawyer cocked his head to one side with a smirk while he regarded Geoff's plan.

"Okay," he said finally. "We can look for leaves and dry wood on our way to the stream. It's not far; maybe fifty yards. I didn't see any trails or roads or any other people. Looks like we're all alone."

"It's starting to get dark. Maybe we should also look for shelter," said Geoff.

"Okay. Then in the morning we can continue looking for a way home. How're you holding up, Jane?"

For a few seconds Jane didn't respond to Sawyer. Then she simply nodded twice and said, "Good."

"Do you feel up to walking?"

Jane didn't reply. She slowly raised her head and groaned. Sawyer walked over to her and helped her stand. Jane took a step and stumbled, but Sawyer caught her.

"Watch out. Easy there. I got you. Take it nice and slow. Hey, Geoff, get on the other side of her."

Geoff hurried to help Jane as Sawyer led them into the trees. Jane placed her arm around Sawyer's shoulder and clutched her forehead while Geoff wrapped his uninjured arm around her waist. He glanced up at her and saw she was grimacing with each step. As they left the glade a shadowy new world opened up to them. Rays of sunlight filtered through the canopies overhead like spotlights, with an occasional bird darting through them.

After a minute or so, Geoff's eyes had adjusted to the dimly lit forest. His vibrant surroundings reminded him of pictures he had seen of tropical rainforests. The trunks of the tallest trees were gigantic, something he hadn't realized until he was closer. He marveled at their magnificence.

Strange, these trees must be ancient, thought Geoff, but there aren't many dead trees or even leaves on the ground.

He could hear the sound of rushing water now. They were nearing Sawyer's stream. Geoff realized his mouth was still dry and the thought of a nice cold drink of water appealed to him. The going was relatively easy, only a few dips and hills along the way.

"How are we going to get back home?" asked Jane.

"No idea," said Sawyer. "Wouldn't it be nice to bump into a park ranger right about now and get a ride to civilization?"

"Tell me about it," said Jane.

Geoff didn't say a word, but he also wished they would find a way back home. The sooner the better, too, because he didn't like the thought of sleeping overnight in the forest unprepared. They had nothing. No food, no gear, no medical supplies. They didn't even have an aspirin for Jane's headache. Geoff couldn't help it; he was miserable. They were lost and it was his fault. If he could go back, he would never have touched that key.

The sound of rushing water grew louder as they reached the top of the next hill. Below, not more than twenty yards away, was a stream with the clearest water Geoff had ever seen. It was just as Sawyer described. Even from this distance, Geoff could see the bottom of the streambed. Small flashes of silver zipped along the bottom. As Geoff watched, the fish seemed to be playing a game of tag, or maybe they were dancing in the current.

"There ya go," said Sawyer proudly. "Boil the water if you want, but it tastes great." Lush green grass grew everywhere. Here and there more patches of wildflowers grew, providing colorful landing pads for bees and butterflies. Geoff looked downstream then upstream. His eyes widened.

"Hey, guys, what's that?" asked Geoff as he pointed upstream. Sawyer and Jane looked in the direction he was pointing.

"Wow," said Sawyer. "How did I miss *that*?"

Chapter Four

An Eventful Night

Jane's mouth dropped open as she stared in wonderment and disbelief.

"Yeah, wow," said Geoff, trying to decide if what he was seeing was real.

"Oh man," said Sawyer. "It's just like the Vikings from the Middle Ages, right Geoff?"

Geoff slowly shook his head. "I don't think the Vikings had anything like this."

The shattered remnants of a once great walled keep lay before them. Its dark gray moss-covered stones had provided ample protection from intruders and the elements alike. Most of the walls had long ago fallen away, revealing a small courtyard overrun with trees and thick with ivy.

The keep itself was nearly three stories high. The aged roof had collapsed, leaving only a few rotting beams jutting toward the sky. Over time, the stream had invaded the courtyard, winding through it and under what remained of the walls before cascading into a clear blue pool below.

Jane looked at Geoff, who was grinning as his eyes

roamed over the courtyard and then the keep, then back to the outer wall.

"I've never seen anything like this," said Geoff. "It's like an old keep from the Middle Ages. Like in dad's books. He would love to be here right now."

As Jane looked at the ruins, her heart sank.

"Geoff," she asked, "where are we?"

She pointed at the ruined keep. "There's nothing like this back home. I've seen ruins of old castles in Italy. This looks like one of those."

"I really don't know. This doesn't look like Italy or anywhere in Europe," said Geoff quietly.

Jane shivered and spun around.

"What is it?" Geoff asked.

"I...I just had a feeling we were being watched." Neither Sawyer nor Geoff said a word. They scanned the forest for a minute, then their attention returned to the remains of the keep.

"Guys!" Jane stamped her foot. Her head pounded from the activity, which angered her. "I mean it. I think someone is watching us."

"Hello!" called Sawyer suddenly, cupping his hands around his mouth. Jane winced. She put her hand up for quiet and stepped back.

"Oh," said Sawyer, realizing what he had done. "Sorry."

Jane's breathing became heavier and her eyes welled up with tears. Between Sawyer's shout and her stamping her foot, her head began pounding again. She sank into the thick grass by the stream and lowered her head as tears slid down her cheeks.

"Are you going to be okay?" Sawyer's voice was quiet. Jane sniffled and nodded.

"I'll go look around. Geoff, you stay here with Jane."

"Okay," whispered Geoff.

Sawyer turned and walked back into the forest, scanning for other people. Jane's head was throbbing so much it felt like it was going to explode. She had closed her eyes tightly, but she could hear the sound of cloth tearing and then she heard Geoff lightly splashing in the stream.

"Here, Jane," she heard him say as he placed a cold, wet cloth over her forehead. She opened her eyes a little and looked at Geoff. He had torn a strip of cloth from the bottom of his shirt and wetted it in the stream. The cool water soothed Jane's aching head and dulled, or least somewhat numbed, the throbbing.

"Thanks," she said as she took a deep breath. Geoff, careful not to further injure his right shoulder, lowered himself onto the ground next to Jane. She could tell he was trying to be still, but he was restless and fidgeting.

"Nervous?" asked Jane.

"A little," said Geoff as he glanced about. "I'm not sure I like this place. It's beautiful, but a little spooky."

"Yes, it is."

They lay in the tall grass for the next several minutes listening to the sounds of the forest. Occasionally she could hear Sawyer call out, but he was far enough away that his shouts no longer bothered her. The cool, wet rag on her forehead was working better than any medication. This is amazing, she thought. My head feels better. Much better. The pain isn't so bad now.

After nearly twenty minutes, Sawyer returned.

"I didn't see anyone," he said. "Not a soul. I guess if someone was out there they must've left."

"Someone was definitely out there," insisted Jane.

Sawyer regarded Jane for a moment, then shrugged. His eyes moved to the ruined keep. He scratched his head as he studied the debris around the structure.

"Looks kinda like a haunted castle from here," he said. "Think I'll go check it out."

Jane carefully sat up, still keeping the cool rag on her forehead.

"No, Sawyer. I don't think we should separate again. We should stick together."

Jane's voice was quiet yet firm.

"Relax, said Sawyer. "I'm just going to have a closer look. I'll be right back. Don't worry."

With that, Sawyer climbed a small, steep hill and clambered over a broken section of the outer wall. Jane and Geoff struggled to their feet and followed Sawyer, stopping at the wall. Jane looked at the ruined structure that lay crumbling within, and then the courtyard. She wasn't convinced they would be safe inside. Sawyer walked to the remnants of the inner keep and disappeared into a large fissure in the wall. Jane glanced at Geoff, who was looking over the courtyard.

"Geoff," she said quietly, "what are we going to do? What's happened to us?

"I wish I knew," said Geoff. "I don't see any landmarks I recognize. Look at this forest. The trees are huge. Everything is green and growing. It's like a fairy tale setting."

A few minutes later, Sawyer emerged from the keep,

brushing his pants off as he approached them. "At least we have a place to sleep tonight."

Jane let out a small incredulous chuckle. "In there? Are you serious?" Her voice quivered.

"At least it's shelter," said Sawyer. "Where else are we gonna sleep tonight? Out in the woods?"

He walked to a waist-high section of the outer wall, stood across from Jane, and placed a hand on the cool, rough surface.

"I don't wanna stay here either. But it'll be dark pretty soon, so if you got a better idea let's hear it."

Jane looked out at the forest again, hoping to see a sign of civilization or anything familiar. Finding nothing of the sort, her gaze returned to Sawyer. He had leaned against the wall and was looking at her, waiting for an answer. Jane sighed. Sawyer was right; they had nowhere else to go and it was getting late in the day.

"Look at this," said Geoff. "The stones in the wall are pitted and worn with age, but they're nearly two feet thick."

He ran his hand over the large stones.

"I wonder what happened here. The people who lived here… where did they go?"

"Dunno," said Sawyer as he jumped over the crumbled section of the wall, landing beside Geoff.

"The place is a mess," he said, motioning with a thumb over his shoulder. "We're gonna have to clean up a bit. It's all overgrown, but it should do for the night."

He pointed at Geoff. "Leaves for a bowl and firewood, right? Let's go find some. I wanna see if you can do all that stuff you said earlier."

"I better go too," said Jane. "Geoff's shoulder is hurt and I can help carry wood."

They set off to look for the materials needed to build a fire and boil water. The sun was setting by the time they returned with armloads of tree limbs, twigs, and leaves. Finding large green leaves was easy, but they had to search much longer to find dry limbs from dead trees because there simply weren't many dead trees.

Inside the keep, they found themselves standing in what had once been a beautifully landscaped courtyard. At least a dozen trees had grown and overrun the area, and a tangle of shrubs made it difficult to navigate through it.

Jane watched the rippling stream that had cut a swath through the middle of the courtyard, washing some sections of the wall away. The light from the setting sun made the surface of the rushing water sparkle and glint. Tall, thin reeds tipped with yellow and white flowers sprouted along the edges of the stream. The overgrown, mossy remnants of a carved stone fountain and two benches lay strewn about the courtyard.

"This must have been a beautiful place," she said, giving her temples a rub.

"Yeah, I agree," said Sawyer. "It's getting dark. Think we better get inside?"

Jane nodded and they followed Sawyer into the keep. The first room they entered was long and had narrow slits for windows. Large broken beams leaned against the walls and littered the floor, along with bits of wood and stone. The left wall contained a large fireplace. The far end of the room opened into a small twenty by twenty room with a smaller fireplace. In the other corner of the room was a rubble-strewn, circular staircase leading up and down.

Ivy snaked up the walls and covered much of the rough stone floor.

Jane sniffed the air. There was a dank, musty odor mingled with an earthy smell. The amount of debris, along with the ivy and even some saplings, made the space look cramped.

"That looks like a good place to set up camp, whadda ya think?" asked Sawyer, pointing to a corner of the room that was less cluttered with debris.

"I want to go home," said Jane.

"Me too," said Geoff. He walked about until he found a suitable place for a small fire.

"Maybe we can clear away those vines and junk and sleep here," said Geoff. "Hopefully there aren't any poisonous snakes hiding in all this mess."

"Ugh," said Jane with a shiver.

Sawyer smiled and grasped a handful of the thick leafy vines and began to pull them away from the floor. His activity disturbed a pair of brown and white sparrows that had nests wedged into cracks in the wall. Squawking, they flew away.

"Sparrows," said Geoff. "Hey, it's a good sign that we see trees, deer, rabbits, and other familiar animals. Isn't it?"

"I guess that means we can expect to find poisonous snakes and spiders and, like, bears, too," said Jane.

"Oh. I didn't think of that."

Jane watched Sawyer, his arms bulging as he strained to pull the vines up. Not only had the vines grown into nearly every crack and crevice, they had started to branch out, making them difficult to dislodge. Jane tied the rag around her head and grabbed a handful, too. Eventually, the vines grudgingly surrendered their long conquered homes to Sawyer and Jane.

Soon they had cleared enough space on the stone floor for Geoff to make a fire.

"Sawyer, can I borrow a shoelace? I need it to help me start a fire."

Sawyer looked suspiciously at Geoff. "You're not going to burn it, are you?"

"No, no," said Geoff. "You have the best shoelaces for using the bow and drill method. I'll give it back."

"You better," said Sawyer as he untied his shoe and gave the string to Geoff. "I seriously doubt you can do it. But go ahead, mountain man."

Using the shoelace from Sawyer, Geoff fabricated the rough tools needed to start a fire. Once he had everything assembled he began the task of quickly moving the bow backward and forward.

"Ow," said Geoff. He dropped the makeshift bow and clutched his shoulder. His injury prevented him from being able to work the bow back and forth to apply pressure to the drill.

"Geoff, you're hurt. Let me help," said Jane, dropping a handful of vines. She walked over to Geoff and knelt beside him.

"Okay," she said. "Tell me what to do."

"Here, hold this rock in place with your foot and push down on the drill here," said Geoff as he pointed to the thin, dry branch positioned perpendicular to a somewhat flat piece of wood with crumpled dry leaves at its base.

Jane held the flat rock as Geoff instructed and feverishly worked the bow back and forth as Geoff gently blew on the kindling.

Sawyer watched from a comfortable position against the wall with a disbelieving look on his face. "Ha! Like this is really going to work," he said.

It was dark by the time Jane saw a red glow under the leaves and smelled smoke. Geoff blew again and small flames burst forth. Geoff quickly placed more leaves and broken twigs on the fire. Soon they had a good-sized campfire that illuminated the area.

"Holy crap!" said Sawyer. "You did it! I didn't think it would work! Way to go, you two."

Jane smiled at Geoff and gave him a reassuring pat on his shoulder. Geoff flinched in pain.

"Oh, Geoff, I'm sorry. I'm so sorry. I forgot about your shoulder."

"It's okay," he said.

"No, it isn't okay, Geoff. Here, let me take a look."

Jane moved behind him and carefully lifted his shirt over his head. In the firelight, she saw his right shoulder was red and purple and swollen to twice its normal size.

"Oh, Geoff," she cried. "Why didn't you say anything? You must be in a lot of pain." She lightly ran a finger along the discoloration surrounding his shoulder.

"I think it's dislocated," she said. "I hope there isn't any muscle damage."

Sawyer, who had been adding kindling to the fire, stopped and walked over to Jane and Geoff.

"Ouch," he said. "Yeah, looks dislocated to me."

Jane thought for a moment, and then she saw the pile

of vines and undergrowth Sawyer had pulled up from the floor and walls.

"I think we can make a sling from these vines," she said as she gathered a large pile of the greenery.

"But we need to pop that shoulder back in place," said Sawyer. "I had the same injury last year in the state quarterfinals. Coach popped my shoulder back in, but I wasn't able to continue. It hurt like hell...," Sawyer's words trailed off. Jane remembered hearing about how upset Sawyer's dad was and how he had to be restrained by security. He had attempted to go down to the sideline and berate Sawyer for being too soft.

"I've never done that," said Jane. "Do you remember how they reset your shoulder? Do you think you could try with Geoff?"

"Yeah, maybe. I think I could do it," said Sawyer as he examined Geoff's shoulder more closely, "but it's gonna hurt, Geoff."

"Sawyer, if there is any doubt we better leave it alone. We could end up doing more damage to his shoulder."

"No," said Sawyer. "If we leave his shoulder all messed up there is a chance it will be permanently damaged. He's been walking around like this for hours now."

"Geoff," said Jane, "it's up to you. Do you think you can wait until we get home or do you want us to try and reset your shoulder?"

Geoff looked at Jane, then Sawyer. He was trying to decide what to do when Sawyer gave him a reassuring nod.

"C'mon," he said. "I got this. You'll be okay."

Jane noticed the confident tone in Sawyer's voice seemed to chase away any fears Geoff may have had. Geoff smiled.

"Okay, let's do it," he said.

"All right. Now we need some room to work. Here," Sawyer said as he turned and kicked a few stones away. "Jane, let's clear a place for Geoff to lie down."

Sawyer tugged at a few pesky vines that lingered in the way. Jane joined Sawyer and several minutes later they had cleared a place large enough for all three of them.

"Okay," said Sawyer. "Geoff, come lay over here by the fire so we can see."

Geoff's eyes were wide, and Jane could see he even shook a little. He took a step forward and then stopped. Jane went to Geoff and gently placed an arm around him.

"Don't worry, Geoff."

She helped Geoff get into place on the stone floor. Sawyer told her to position herself on the opposite side of Geoff.

"Geoff," began Sawyer, "like I said, this is gonna hurt like hell until we get your shoulder back in place. I need for you to relax, take a deep breath, and let your arm go limp."

Geoff inhaled and closed his eyes.

"Don't forget to exhale," said Sawyer. Geoff exhaled.

"Okay. I'm ready," said Geoff. Jane noticed he was gritting his teeth.

"Don't be nervous, Geoff. It's okay," said Jane in a soothing tone. "We're going to fix your shoulder. Just do what Sawyer said and relax. Let the tension leave your body. Relax."

As Jane spoke she felt Geoff's body unwind, and his breathing slowed and became deeper.

"Good. That's good, Geoff," said Sawyer. "Now, Jane, you're on the other side of Geoff. I need for you to put your arm around his waist and pull him toward you when I pull on his arm, okay?"

"Sawyer, are you sure about this?" Jane didn't want to insult Sawyer, but she didn't want to make Geoff's shoulder worse.

"Of course," he said with a wide grin. "I've had this done to me and I've seen it done to a couple teammates. No problem. It's the same thing. Now get ready to pull, nice and slow. Don't jerk." Jane reached over Geoff, placed her hand firmly around his waist, and waited for Sawyer to start.

Sawyer carefully straightened out Geoff's elbow so his arm stretched outward from his body. Then he grasped Geoff's wrist with both hands. Geoff took another deep breath.

"You're doing great, Geoff," said Jane. "It'll be over soon." She glanced up at Sawyer. He met her gaze and gave her a quick nod. As soon as he started to pull Geoff's arm, Jane felt him tense up.

"Ow! Ow! Ow!

"Relax, Geoff," she said. "We're almost done. You're doing great. Just relax." She pulled Geoff's body toward her, trying to match Sawyer's steady, slow tug. Geoff grimaced and as Sawyer kept pulling.

"That's it, Geoff," she said. "You're doing it. Hang in there. Almost done…"

The growing look of agony on Geoff's face was not a good sign, and Jane worried that Sawyer was doing more harm than good. Geoff's mouth was open now and it looked to Jane as if he were about to scream. She heard a faint pop and crack. Geoff's eyes flew open and he cried out.

"Ahhh! Stop! Stop!"

Sawyer released Geoff's arm.

"Good job," he said with a quick nod. "How does it feel now?"

"It…really hurts," he said. "But it's better, I think. I can move my arm a little more."

With Jane's help, Geoff laid his arm across his stomach and let out a big sigh. Then she leaned forward and had a closer look at Geoff's shoulder. She noticed the discoloration was still there, of course, but now it looked like everything was in the right place.

"Looks good," said Sawyer cheerfully. "You're gonna be okay. You'll be sore for a while, so just try and get some rest."

"You're going to be fine, Geoff," said Jane, echoing Sawyer's reassurance. She looked at Sawyer.

"Nicely done," she said.

He smiled and nodded.

"Here," she said to Sawyer as she handed him the rag Geoff had placed on her head. "Would you go dip this back in the water? I'll get to work on a sling for his arm." Without a word, Sawyer took the rag and scrambled over the ruined wall, disappearing into the growing darkness. Jane reached for the pile of vines she had set aside and began crudely weaving a handful together. Sawyer returned a few moments later with the dripping wet rag and handed it back to Jane.

"Here ya go," he said. Jane placed it over Geoff's shoulder, trying to cover as much area as she could.

"You know," said Sawyer, "I think you may be right.

I think someone is out there watching us." Jane looked at him. The serious look in his eyes gave her pause.

"What happened?"

"Nothing happened," said Sawyer. "I felt like you did earlier, but when I turned and looked back at the forest... well, I don't know."

"What did you see, Sawyer?"

"I don't know," answered Sawyer. "Just for a split second, out of the corner of my eye, I thought I saw some movement. Something in the darkness moved. It was big. I mean, really big. But when I looked I didn't see anything. Just a tree. It was probably a moose or something." He shrugged. "Maybe we should be careful. What if someone is out there and they aren't friendly? Or what if a wild animal is stalking us?"

Jane looked out into the darkness, considering what Sawyer said. They had no way of defending themselves and would be at the mercy of whomever or whatever happened upon them in the forest. She shivered a little, but tried to keep a stoic face. Sawyer handed her his makeshift club.

"Here," he said. "Just in case."

Jane took the club and laid it next to her. Sawyer stood up and walked back to the wall to look around.

"I'll be back. I'm going to get some more firewood."

"Sawyer," said Geoff, "it's not a good idea to get separated. You better stay here now that it's dark."

"It's okay," said Sawyer with the same confident tone he used earlier. "I'll be right back." And with that he hopped over the wall and was gone again.

Jane looked at Geoff and smiled. Geoff showed what

looked like a forced smile and said, "He likes taking risks, doesn't he?"

"All jocks do, I guess," said Jane.

She lifted the wet rag and looked at his shoulder. Geoff was right. Sawyer was always a reckless kid growing up, doing all sorts of dangerous feats like jumping a parked car on his bicycle and holding a firecracker until the last moment before he threw it.

Jane closed her eyes. A nagging throb in her head had returned and now she realized she was tired. She picked up Sawyer's club and positioned herself cross-legged beside Geoff, facing the wall and waiting for Sawyer to return.

The soothing breeze they felt earlier grew stronger. Jane could hear the limbs far above in the treetops scrape and scratch each other in the wind. Almost twenty minutes later, a smiling Sawyer dropped an armful of tree limbs over the wall and climbed back into their camp.

"Everything okay?" he asked.

"Yes," said Jane quietly as she put a finger to her lips and pointed at a sleeping Geoff.

"All right," said Sawyer in a hushed tone. "Sorry. I think we have enough wood to burn now."

"Good. That should keep the night chill away. Did you see or hear anything out there?" asked Jane. Sawyer shook his head, "Nope. Just crickets and fireflies. I must have been imagining earlier." Then he reached back over the wall and proudly produced a relatively straight six-foot-long tree branch.

"However, this is my new weapon." He looked at Jane. "Just in case."

"Just in case?" asked Jane.

"Yeah. Just in case," repeated Sawyer. "I'll pull off the smaller limbs and sharpen the tip. It should make a nice spear." He looked at Jane.

"Hey, maybe you better get some rest, too. I'll be up for a while working on this," he said as he held his soon-to-be spear up high. "Don't worry. I'll keep the fire burning."

"We should try to have a plan for tomorrow," said Jane. "We need food and we need to decide on a course of action. I wonder if we should follow the stream or perhaps build a bigger fire and hope someone will see it."

"Dunno," said Sawyer. "You and Geoff are the boy scouts. I'm just the shoelace guy."

Jane looked at Sawyer, who was smiling.

"No, really. What do we do tomorrow?"

Sawyer stopped working on his makeshift spear and thought.

"I'm not sure," he said. "I would like to follow the stream. I mean, sooner or later it has to come out somewhere, right?"

"I suppose so," said Jane. "Tomorrow morning Geoff and I will look for something to eat—berries or some fruit, maybe."

"Cool. That's a good idea," said Sawyer.

"Can you keep an eye on me while I go down to the river and wet my rag again?" asked Jane.

Sawyer chuckled.

"Not afraid of the dark, are you?"

"No," said Jane. "Just stay where you can see me, that's all."

"Yeah. No problem." Sawyer stepped to the wall and continued working on his spear.

Jane went to the courtyard and knelt beside the stream.

She glanced up at Sawyer, who could easily see her—if he was looking. His attention was focused on his spear, however. Jane dipped the rag that Geoff had given her into the cool, flowing water. How refreshing it was! She gave it a quick squeeze and then placed it on the back of her neck. Some excess water rolled down her back and relaxed her a bit. Jane took a long, deep breath. She was so tired. All she could think about now was going to sleep.

She stood up, and as she did a white flash or shimmer moved in the forest by the stream below her. She gasped and blinked. She was overwhelmed by the brief glimpse of something intriguing.

Without a word to Sawyer, she ran down to the stream to where she had seen the exquisite shape dash off into the darkness.

Her heart pounded in her chest. Did she really see it? Was she too tired and simply imagined that beautiful form in the dark?

Jane ran back and forth along the stream, peering into the forest for another white shimmer. She slipped on some large stones and fell on her rear. The stones were wet. She lifted her hands and in the moonlight saw they were covered with a dark, purple-red liquid. She smelled her hands and detected a faint trace of iron.

Jane began to tremble.

She glimpsed the white shimmer again. Her heart leapt.

She struggled to her feet and looked back at the keep.

"Sawyer!" she called. "There's something out here! Hurry!"

And then Jane ran into the forest.

Chapter Five
The Unicorn

Jane ran deeper into the dimly lit forest, small branches whipping at her as she ran. Jane glanced back at the keep. Two figures emerged, Sawyer carrying his spear and Geoff holding a burning stick from the fire as a torch.

"Sawyer! This way!" called Jane.

She turned and ran a few more steps before she saw something that stopped her in her tracks. Her eyes widened and her mouth dropped open. Standing not twenty yards away from her was the source of the white shimmering. Could it be? But how? She shook her head to clear it, then closed her eyes and opened them again. And still, there it was.

Its majestic head was adorned with a large, spiraled horn nearly two feet in length, and from its chin hung a tuft of white hair. It was drinking from the stream. The moonlight shone and danced against the unicorn's body and flowing mane, giving it an illuminating radiance. Jane stood motionless, not even breathing.

She had never seen anything so beautiful in her life, and was unable to take her eyes off the wondrous figure before her. She trembled and her heart raced. The unicorn looked directly at her, and she held a hand out toward the amazing animal. The unicorn backed away.

"Oh," pleaded Jane, "please don't go. Please."

She was about to get on her knees and beg the unicorn to stay. Before she could do so, however, it regarded Jane with a quizzical look and nodded. Jane was sure that somehow the unicorn understood her. It walked to Jane, its head bobbing up and down. As soon as it was within arm's reach Jane rubbed its nose. The unicorn stepped closer. She wrapped her arms around its neck and squeezed. She could feel its powerful muscles as she hugged it.

The unicorn curled its head around Jane's back and she knew she was also being hugged. As she embraced the unicorn, Jane finally remembered to breathe. She inhaled deeply and thought she smelled fresh gingerbread and roses, her two favorite aromas. She rubbed the long white mane and closed her eyes. Tears streamed down her face. She felt love, pure love, and nothing else.

Jane buried her face against the unicorn's neck and cried. All of Jane's fears and anxieties as well as her headache were washed away by the benevolent feelings she shared with this glorious creature.

"The fairy tales are true," said Jane. "Unicorns are real." She maintained her grip around the unicorn's neck.

"Sometimes unicorns come to maidens in the forest, don't they?" Jane sniffled and wiped her face. She lifted her head and looked into the large lavender eyes of the unicorn.

"Well," she said, "this maiden won't try to tame or trap you." Jane pressed her hands to each side of the unicorn's head and kissed its nose.

"Never," she said as she hugged its neck again. The unicorn pawed at the ground with a hoof and rested its head on her back. Their intimate embrace was all that mattered to Jane. She could stay with the unicorn forever. She stroked its neck and shoulder, feeling the powerful muscles beneath its soft coat.

Jane knew that she was in the presence of something great; something eternal and good. The unicorn's grace and beauty were intoxicating.

"Most little girls hear fairy tales of unicorns," she whispered, "but I must be the luckiest girl in the world to be here with you."

She felt the powerful, steady thumping of the unicorn's heartbeat as she pressed herself closer. Her fingers found a moist spot on the unicorn's shoulder. It flinched at her touch; something was protruding from its shoulder. Jane looked at her fingers and saw they were red again. She gasped and looked at the unicorn's shoulder. A broken, roughly cut arrow shaft was sticking out from the muscular shoulder. Blood ran from the wound, down its leg, and onto the ground.

"Oh, you're hurt! Who would do this to you?" Jane caressed the unicorn's slim neck while she gently grasped the broken wooden shaft.

"Easy, now. Easy. I need to take this out and stop the bleeding. Be still."

Jane pulled on the protruding arrow shaft, which caused the unicorn to flinch. "Whoa there. Easy. It's almost out." Jane stroked the unicorn's soft mane with long, calming strokes. Then she heard Sawyer and Geoff calling her. Apparently, she had lost them in the forest. She didn't want to answer just yet, though, because they might frighten the wounded unicorn.

"Okay. One more time," said Jane as she exhaled loudly and grasped the shaft again.

From somewhere in the dark forest came a terrifying shriek. The unicorn's muscles immediately tensed and it broke its loving embrace with Jane to look in that direction. Jane also looked, but she wasn't sure what she had heard. Perhaps it's just an animal squealing for food and nothing to worry about. A lower, more distant shout answered the first. Jane couldn't hear any words or language in the shouts; the sounds were too guttural.

Soon came a series of excited yelps and hoots from several other sources and Jane could see the glow of torches deep in the forest coming closer. The unicorn stamped its hoof repeatedly, tossed its head, and neighed. Jane reached out to calm it, but it reared on its hind legs, then turned and bolted away.

"No! Please, no!" Jane ran after it, but the unicorn disappeared into the darkness, its brilliant luminescent coat sparkling against the light of the rising moon one last time.

"Come back! Please!"

She heard another series of yells, this time much closer. There was grunting and snarling as well. Whatever was making the noises was not friendly; Jane determined that much. The hair stood up on the back of her neck and suddenly she felt alone and cold in the dark. She crouched behind a large tree. She saw the firelight from at least five torches pass by her, and she heard the unknown figures make snorting and sniffing sounds. As they raced by, Jane saw their silhouettes in the moonlight. They were roughly five feet in height, slim, and had a slight slouch. Suddenly Jane realized what they were doing. They were hunting the unicorn!

Her heart began to race again and her breathing became ragged. Oh no! What are those things? And why are they hunting the unicorn? We have to do something. Sawyer and Geoff need to be warned! Jane ran back toward the keep, hoping Sawyer and Geoff had heard the hunter's cries. She navigated through the trees as best she could in the dark and arrived at the stream, not far from the old ruined keep.

"Jane? Is that you?"

It was Geoff's voice. He and Sawyer emerged from behind a large tree on the other side of the stream. Geoff was still carrying a torch.

"Sawyer! Geoff! Come on! We need to help! Hurry!"

Jane motioned for them to follow her.

"Hurry! Come on, guys!"

"What's going on, Jane?" Sawyer asked as he and Geoff splashed across the stream.

"I think some people are out looking for us," said Sawyer. "I saw torches."

"Yeah, and we heard wild animals, too," added Geoff.

"No, no! Come on, guys! We have to help it! Hurry!" said Jane as she turned and dashed back into the forest.

"Jane! Where the hell are we going?" Sawyer's tone was insistent as he chased after her with Geoff close behind.

"We have to help the unicorn! Now come on!"

"The…the…what?" Sawyer blinked and stopped. Geoff stood beside Sawyer and looked at him. "I think she said unicorn," he said. Then he ran after Jane.

"Huh?" said Sawyer under his breath as he charged after Jane and Geoff.

Jane dashed headlong into the dark woods, the moonlight guiding her way. Her heart pounded with every step. Please, please get away, she thought. Please escape. Ahead, perhaps a hundred yards away, she saw the glow of several torches. Oh no. No, no, no. They're still after the unicorn.

Jane plunged further into the dark forest, paying no heed to the limbs that raked her arms and face and pulled at her hair. She felt a stinging pain on her right cheek. She touched it. Something warm and moist trickled down her cheek. Her pursuit in the dark left her with a scratch, but she didn't stop.

Soon she heard an awful commotion coming from the far side of a clearing just a little further ahead. She ran until she reached the edge of the trees before stopping to catch her breath. She blinked several times to clear her eyes to make out the flurry of activity before her. She moved a little closer for a better look while staying hidden in the trees. The unicorn was fighting five small humanlike figures.

As best she could tell in the moonlight, they were Geoff's size or maybe a little larger, but there was something not quite right about them. Their bodies were thicker than a boy's and their skin was darker, a dark brown hue with a green tint with patches of matted hair. She noticed they had jagged teeth and their eyes bulged and darted around excitedly. They were armed with swords and spears and wore dark hide armor which didn't fit them very well. They were yelling and shouting in some guttural language. They were trying to pull the unicorn to the ground with ropes.

No! Oh no! It can't be! The horrible sight made her heart sink. The unicorn fought valiantly for its life, having dispatched four of the little creatures, but five more remained and they had it surrounded. The unicorn's beautiful white hair was soaked red in a few places. Tears rolled down Jane's cheeks, and she watched in terror as the largest of the humanoids jabbed a wicked-looking spear into the unicorn's side. The unicorn reared on its hind legs and neighed in pain as it flailed at its attackers with its front legs. They're torturing it! No! Jane gritted her teeth.

Jane frantically looked around for anything she could use as a weapon. Sawyer and Geoff arrived a few seconds later as Jane grabbed a handful of nearby stones.

"Come on! Hurry! We have to save it!" she said, pointing at the chaotic scene not thirty yards away. Sawyer and Geoff stood transfixed, unable to believe their eyes. Geoff was the first to speak, "It really is a…a—"

"Unicorn," said Sawyer, finishing Geoff's sentence. "What are those guys doing?"

"Sawyer, they're killing it! We have to save the unicorn," said Jane, giving Sawyer a shove to get his attention. "Come on!"

"Wait, Jane," said Sawyer. "They have weapons."

"No! We can't let them kill it!"

Jane turned and ran toward the melee, her heart pounding with every step she took. The unicorn fell and lay on its side, breathing heavily and bleeding from a half dozen wounds. The largest of the humanoids was now jumping up and down, roaring in triumph and waving his spear. The other four humanoids also appeared jubilant, shouting and barking as they danced about victoriously.

Sawyer and Jane ran toward the unicorn. Sawyer was faster than Jane and overtook her. Geoff was a few yards behind.

"Stop them, Sawyer. Hurry!" Jane threw a few stones at the unicorn's attackers as he raced by. "Don't let them kill it!"

Sawyer saw the leader raise his blood-soaked spear into the air for the final killing blow. The unicorn wasn't moving; it was weakened from battle and loss of blood.

"Hurry, Sawyer!" pleaded Jane again. Sawyer rushed straight at the larger humanoid with his spear raised. He was a dozen yards away when the two closest humanoids noticed him charging. They yelped in surprise and moved to intercept him, but he was too fast. The bigger humanoid was still gloating over its kill when Sawyer swung his makeshift spear. His strike to the back of its head sent its body flying in one direction and its newly dented helmet in another.

The blow, however, also shattered Sawyer's spear and Jane saw him wince in pain and shake his hand. Next he turned his attention to the two charging, snarling humanoids. One was armed with a rusty sword and the other had a crude stone axe.

The first humanoid swung its sword at Sawyer's midsection, but Sawyer's quick reflexes enabled him to leap backward just in time to avoid the strike. The creature followed up with a thrust aimed at Sawyer's heart. Sawyer quickly sidestepped the thrust, but slipped and fell backward in the tall grass. Frantically, he reached about trying to find something he could use to defend himself.

The humanoid now stood over him glaring and

drooling. It raised its sword over its head and then *whack.* Something struck it square in the face, stunning it. Jane had thrown a bulls-eye with a rock and nailed the little creature.

"Get up, Sawyer," she called as she pelted the humanoid with a couple of more rocks. Sawyer scrambled to his feet and found a tree limb nearby. The humanoid with the stone axe rushed at Sawyer with its weapon raised. The look on its face was malevolent and filled with hate. Sawyer grasped his tree limb with both hands and swung it like a baseball bat. He struck his attacker squarely on the jaw, sending splinters and teeth flying and dropping the creature in its tracks.

The first humanoid had recovered, and in spite of being peppered with stones from Jane and Geoff, advanced on Sawyer. It was still a little unsteady and missed badly with another sword thrust. Sawyer brought what remained of his tree limb down directly on the creature's warty head, knocking it unconscious.

The remaining two humanoids were unsure what to do next. Their leader and two others had fallen so easily. Screaming, Jane rushed past Sawyer hurling rocks at them. Sawyer looked at the remaining nub of a handle in his hand and threw it at them as well. Faced with a screaming, rock-hurling maniac, the remaining two humanoids turned and fled. They yelped wildly as they disappeared into the forest. Jane ran to check on the unicorn.

"Oh nooo. No, no," she sobbed as she reached the unicorn and saw its wounds. She dropped to her knees beside it and as she did so, it raised its head and looked at her with sad eyes. Its breathing was labored and shallow.

 73

Jane tore a piece of cloth from the bottom of her blouse and placed it over a nasty wound in the unicorn's side. She gently stroked its neck as she looked into the unicorn's lavender eyes and started to cry again.

"Please don't die," she sobbed. "You can't die. Please don't."

Sawyer collected the weapons from their unconscious foes in case they awakened while they were tending to the unicorn.

"Why would anyone want to harm such a wonderful animal? So beautiful…please don't die…please," said Jane.

Sawyer knelt beside Jane. She was crying so much she could barely see as she tried to stop the bleeding from several wounds.

"Jane, I'm sorry. I'm really sorry," said Sawyer. He then placed his hand on the unicorn's neck and gently rubbed back and forth.

"It isn't your fault," said Jane between sobs. "You did everything you could. We were just too late."

The unicorn appeared to understand they were trying to help it and give it some comfort. It shifted its head and rested it neatly in her lap. Tears were streaming down her face; she couldn't bear to watch such a beautiful animal die.

"I wish we could do something," said Sawyer.

Jane nodded. She was sobbing too much to say anything. She didn't even look up when she heard Geoff approaching.

"Are you guys okay? I thought we were…," Geoff's words trailed off at the sight of the dying unicorn. "Oh…"

"Geoff, you're a scout," said Jane. "Don't you know of some kind of technique to stop the bleeding?"

Not able to take his eyes off the unicorn, Geoff slowly

shook his head. He removed the moist rag Jane had placed on his shoulder and covered one of the unicorn's wounds. As Jane watched, Geoff began to stroke the unicorn's chest and front legs.

"I'm sorry," whispered Jane. "So sorry."

Jane felt helpless; she wished she could do something, anything, to save this magnificent animal. She thought about how majestic the unicorn was when she first saw it in the forest, how affectionate it was to her. Geoff sniffled and wiped his face. Sawyer sighed and walked to the nearest prone humanoid.

"Jane, I'm sorry about the unicorn. I really am. But what do we do with these guys?" he said, nudging one with his foot.

"What are they, anyway?" asked Geoff, looking up from the unicorn.

"No idea," said Sawyer. "But we have a problem—other than not saving the unicorn. They'll eventually wake up and more than likely come after us next."

Jane didn't answer, nor did Geoff. Yes, thought Jane. They will regroup and hunt us just like the unicorn.

"I don't know and I don't care," she said solemnly. "Maybe we can tie them up."

"No," said Sawyer. "They'll break free no matter how we tie them up. And don't forget they have friends still out in the forest somewhere."

Jane scanned the dark forest, but saw no movement. Her eyes were blurred from her tears.

Finally she spoke, her voice breaking. "I don't care what you do with those horrible, ugly things. Do whatever you want. They deserve it." She heard Sawyer let out a grunt.

"Maybe we can just run as fast as we can, get far away, maybe even find people and some help," said Geoff.

Sawyer shook his head again. "I don't know. It doesn't seem right killing them like this. I mean, they're helpless."

"Yeah, right now they are," said Jane. "But what if they do exactly what you say? What if they come after us? Hunt us down? Will they show us mercy? I doubt it." She motioned to the unicorn. "They'll kill us, too."

"But is it, you know…," said Geoff, not wanting to say the word. "Is it murder?"

"More like self-preservation and justice," said Jane coldly.

"Yeah," agreed Sawyer, "and I don't think these things pass for human, either. They have to be human for it to be murder, right?"

"Then…who's going to do it?" Geoff's voice was almost a whisper.

Jane looked at Geoff, his expression clearly indicated he wanted no part of the grisly task.

"Well," said Sawyer, "we probably need to decide sooner rather than later. We're wasting time just sitting here waiting for…" His voice tapered off as he noticed Jane staring stoically at him with tear-filled, red-rimmed eyes. The unicorn shuddered and coughed, then tried to raise its head but fell back into Jane's lap. She saw blood trickling from its nose and gently wiped it away.

"Jane," said Sawyer somberly. "It's suffering. If it were a horse we would put it out of its misery."

"No," snapped Jane. "Don't you dare. Don't even think about it."

"I agree," said Geoff. "It's too beautiful to kill."

"It's already dying," said Sawyer. "Hey, I agree. It *is* beautiful. It's awesome. But look at it. It's in pain and the only thing we can do is make it quick. Then we get rid of these guys and find our way back home."

Jane shook her head. "You aren't going to kill it."

Sawyer threw his hands up in the air. "Okay, okay. Someone decide what we are going to do and let's do it." Jane was silent for a few moments, then she looked up at Sawyer.

"You have the weapons, Sawyer. You just said we can't tie them up and leave them here, so that means one thing."

"Yeah, it does," said Sawyer. "You two probably shouldn't watch."

He picked up the rusty sword and turned to finish the fallen humanoids. Jane leaned forward and kissed the unicorn on the side of its head, tears dropping from her face as she did so. She caressed its cheek and the unicorn slowly closed its eyes. Its breathing became shallower and more uneven with every minute that passed. Jane looked at Geoff, who also caressed the dying unicorn. His lower lip quivered and she saw his face was moist too.

"It won't be long now," she said quietly. "At least we got to see a unicorn, Geoff. How many people can honestly say that?" Jane tried to force a smile but only managed to make herself cry more.

"I thought they were just imaginary," said Geoff between sobs, "but they *are* real, Jane. All the books I read about unicorns—I never thought for a minute I would ever see one in real life."

Jane shook her head.

"Me either," she said. "I doubt we ever will again."

Jane wiped her face and looked at Sawyer. He was standing over the largest of the humanoids preparing himself. She saw that he hesitated. Jane wasn't sure he would be able to finish them. The hair on the back of her neck stood up again. The uneasy feeling of someone spying on them crept over her again. She quickly looked around, fearing the two enemies who ran into the forest had returned. She caught a glimpse of something overhead moving among the branches, but it was too fast for her to see what it was.

"Sawyer!" she called.

He looked over his shoulder at Jane.

"Yeah, what?" There was a slight rush of air and something landed in the grass beside him. A figure crouched near the ground, a figure with eyes like emeralds.

CHAPTER SIX

ARIEL

GEOFF COULDN'T TAKE HIS EYES off her. The green-eyed figure was lean, yet muscular and athletic. She wore a green cloak and was clad in a brown leather jerkin with a matching short skirt. Her skin was the color of a golden sunrise and her facial features were angular. Two white feathers with vivid blue-green markings dangled from minibraids in her long, dark blond locks. She rose slowly, observing Sawyer, June, and Geoff as she did. Her sculpted figure tapered at the waist, and she wore a curved sword on each side. The leather jerkin stopped at her midriff, revealing a firm stomach. Several small pouches dangled from a dark brown leather belt.

She stopped suddenly and stared at Sawyer, who still held the rusty short sword he had taken from one of the humanoids.

"Sawyer," whispered Geoff, "your sword."

Sawyer was so transfixed with the image of the Amazonian beauty in front of him that his mouth had fallen open.

"Sawyer," Geoff said again.

"Hmmm? What?" Sawyer looked confused. Geoff motioned at the sword he was holding.

"Oh! Oh, yeah. Sorry," said Sawyer as he dropped it in the grass.

Geoff's gaze returned to the newcomer. She had relaxed a little after Sawyer dropped the sword. Her deep green eyes continuously darted between the teenagers. They reminded Geoff of the eyes of a bird of prey, never missing even the slightest movement.

"Um…hi," said Sawyer, trying to sound confident.

The leather-clad figure walked toward them, maintaining eye contact with Sawyer. Her movements were catlike and graceful. She didn't make a sound. She stood over Jane and the unicorn, watching Jane try to stop the bleeding from multiple wounds.

Now that she was closer, Geoff thought she smelled like wildflowers and honeysuckle. Protruding from beneath her dark blond hair were pointed ears. Jane looked up.

"Please," she said, tears rolling down her cheeks, "can you help? I can't stop the bleeding. It's dying."

Geoff saw the green-eyed stranger tilt her head and regard Jane for a moment, but she said nothing. Then she knelt beside the dying unicorn and examined its wounds. With a single, quick motion, she removed the broken arrow shaft from its shoulder.

"I think she's a Vulcan, or maybe an elf," Geoff whispered to Sawyer. "Look at her ears."

The stranger's green eyes darted to Geoff, and he felt so uneasy he was unable to maintain eye contact with her. Geoff stepped behind Sawyer, who was still gawping at her.

"Ye...yeah," mumbled Sawyer as the stranger's green eyes fell upon him. Geoff heard Sawyer clear his throat.

"I'm Sawyer, that's Jane, and the little guy is Geoff," he said. "Who...are you?"

The stranger only raised an eyebrow and returned her attention to the unicorn.

"I told you," said Geoff. "Vulcan. Hold your hand up like this and say *live long and prosper.*" Geoff held his hand up to demonstrate the split-fingered gesture.

The woman brushed Jane's hand aside and examined the most grievous of the wounds, the one inflicted by the attacker's spear. As Geoff and the others watched, she reached into one of the small dark pouches on her belt and withdrew what looked like small dried leaves. She gently crushed them in her fingers as she spoke, "*Ilinara tae ullnara taethos.*"

Then she sprinkled the bits of dried leaves over the wound and placed her hand over it. She closed her eyes and took a deep breath. Geoff was the first to notice that the unicorn's wounds stopped bleeding and began to close. A moment later the unicorn's breathing became less labored, deeper and more regular.

"Wow! It's like...like—" stammered Geoff.

"Magic," answered the green-eyed beauty as she opened her eyes and looked up at Geoff.

"It is druid magic. Healing magic of the forest."

She gently patted the unicorn on the neck and scratched its ears before standing. She was every bit as tall as Sawyer, if not a little taller. She looked at Sawyer.

"In your human tongue my name is Ariel."

 81

Her voice reminded Geoff of a beautiful, harmonious tune. It was both soft and comforting.

"How did you do that?" asked Jane as she looked up from the unicorn while wiping away her tears.

Geoff saw Ariel raise an eyebrow again. She regarded Jane for a moment and then said, "I already told you. Magic."

Geoff watched as the unicorn slowly moved its front legs and then opened its big lavender eyes. It looked at Jane and blinked, then shifted its position and snorted. Its head still rested on Jane's lap. Jane smiled and happily sobbed at its playful behavior as she stroked its nose and scratched its ears. The unicorn responded to Jane's pleasurable touch by slightly stretching its neck, thereby giving her full access to rub under its chin.

"What an incorrigible flirt you are," Ariel said.

The unicorn responded with another snort and a flick of its thick, bushy tail.

"That was awesome," said Geoff.

"Thank you," said Jane, smiling at Ariel.

Geoff watched Ariel. While she didn't attack them, she didn't smile or otherwise appear to be friendly. He noticed her hands remained close to her weapons and she continued to observe their movements.

"You're an…elf," said Geoff without thinking as he stepped from behind Sawyer. Ariel looked at Geoff and nodded once.

"That's impossible. There's no such thing as elves," Sawyer managed to say.

"Or unicorns," added Geoff.

"Indeed," Ariel said. Then she turned and pointed at

one of the prone humanoids that had attacked the unicorn. "Or goblins."

"Goblins?" asked Sawyer.

"This is so weird," said Jane, shaking her head. "Where are we?"

"You are in my forest, the Spirewood Forest," answered the elf. "I am the custodian of this woodland."

"Spirewood Forest? We've never heard of that," Jane said.

"How did you come to be here?" asked Ariel, ignoring Jane's comment.

Sawyer turned and pointed at Geoff, who felt accused by the action. "He found a key and we got sucked through… an archway…in his dad's study…and…"

Geoff stepped back a few steps as Sawyer's words trailed off.

"Key? What key?" she asked.

Geoff noticed Ariel had narrowed her eyes at him and seemed content to wait for an answer.

"Go on, Geoff. Show her the key," said Sawyer. Geoff swallowed hard and then reached into his pocket, but didn't find the white alabaster key. Then he remembered he left the key back in the old ruined keep. His heart sank.

"Oh, no. I…I left it back at our camp when Jane called for help. I better go get it." Geoff looked around nervously and turned to go back to the keep.

"Wait," said Jane. "Sawyer, you better go with him. Remember two more of those…those goblin things are still in the forest somewhere."

"Okay. But what about these?" He motioned to the unconscious humanoids nearby.

"And why were they hunting the unicorn?" asked Jane in an accusing tone.

"They are a goblin raiding party and like you, they should not be here," said Ariel.

"Can you help us? We need to get home," said Jane. "Our parents will be looking for us by now."

"And I have an algebra exam tomorrow," Geoff said.

Ariel's demeanor became icy as she first stared at Jane, then him, then Sawyer. Geoff looked at Sawyer, who was looking at Jane with a questioning expression. The awkward silence made Geoff fidget. *Is she going to help us?* He didn't think they did anything to offend her.

"I will take you to the nearest humans. Perhaps they can help you find your way home."

"Humans? Woodland? Whatever. No one talks like that," said Jane. "But yes! Take us there, please!"

Another moment of awkward silence followed, and then the unicorn snorted and stood up. *It looked majestic,* thought Geoff. And it was, in fact, regal in its bearing. Its muscular flanks glistened in the moonlight. Jane rose with the unicorn and continued to rub its mane.

Ariel playfully rubbed its nose and then grabbed each side of the unicorn's head, "And you should go, my friend. These woods are not safe this night. Go."

Geoff noticed Jane frowned when she heard Ariel's words.

"Wait," she said. "Does it have to go? Can't it stay with us a little longer?"

"He will be fine," said Ariel. "Unicorns have homes as well."

The unicorn bobbed its head and nuzzled Jane one more time before it disappeared into the darkness.

"You have made a friend," said Ariel with a slight smile.

"I guess I'll go get the key now," said Geoff, fearing he had loitered too long.

"You say this key opened a portal to this world and you were drawn here?"

Before Geoff could answer her, Sawyer cleared his throat and spoke.

"Yeah, that's right. When Geoff there touched the key he lit up and so did the archway. Pulled us all through."

Now Geoff felt Ariel's green eyes looking at him again, as if they were probing him.

"And how does a human child come to find such an item, much less use it?" Ariel asked as she continued to observe Geoff.

Geoff's eyes widened. He opened his mouth to speak, but no words came out. He didn't know what to say, and he trembled slightly.

"We…we…didn't know it was a magical key," he said finally. Ariel studied him for a moment.

"A magical key? Are you a wizard?" asked Ariel.

Geoff shook his head, and answered with a simple "No."

Ariel walked over to Geoff, keeping her gaze on him. She stopped a few steps away.

"And you are not a wizard's apprentice?"

Again Geoff shook his head.

"This is silly," said Jane. "He's just a kid. We all are. We aren't wizards or goblins or whatever. We just want to go home."

Ariel ignored Jane, remaining focused on Geoff.

"Do not be afraid," said Ariel. "Curiosity at your age is a healthy thing. Get your key. I doubt it is the sort of thing to leave lying about."

Geoff picked up a torch that was dropped by a goblin and looked at Jane, then Sawyer, expecting them to join him as he made his way through the darkness back to the keep.

"Go," said Ariel. "I will not be far behind."

Geoff turned and ran to the keep. Sawyer and Jane followed several yards behind. Geoff thought he heard Ariel unsheathe one of her scimitars and begin the grim task of dispatching the unconscious goblins.

"Do you think those ears are real?" asked Sawyer. "I think she's hot."

Geoff glanced over his shoulder and saw Jane cast a disapproving glare at Sawyer. Geoff thought about what Ariel had said, that the key they found in his father's study was not to be left lying around, so he ran faster.

He didn't realize how far ahead of the others he was until Jane called to him.

"Hey, Geoff, wait up!"

"I gotta get the key! I'll see you at camp," said Geoff without slowing down.

Soon Geoff arrived at the stream and the first thing he noticed was no glow coming from the fire they had built earlier. He assumed the unattended fire must have died out on its own. He crossed the stream, easily hopping from one rock to another, and went into the keep. He began searching for the key in the faint light his torch provided, but suddenly an uncomfortable feeling came over him. Something was wrong.

A huge tree trunk now stood where the fire had been and he saw no sign of the key. Wait a second, thought Geoff. That tree wasn't here befo—. His thought was cut short when he saw a large hoof at the bottom of the trunk. It was a leg! He heard a low, deep growling coming from overhead.

Geoff looked up as a gigantic clawed hand grasped him and lifted him ten feet off the ground. The movement was so sudden that he dropped his torch. The hand was almost as large as he was, and it felt like a vice. Geoff was trapped. A pair of malevolent black eyes peered at him in the torchlight.

He screamed and tried to wriggle free of the giant's grasp. In the giant's other hand, Geoff saw the white glint of his key. He felt his chest becoming tighter as he gasped for air and flailed about helplessly.

He heard voices as he struggled. Sawyer and Jane were calling his name. The giant stopped squeezing the life from Geoff and sniffed the air.

"Ariel," muttered the giant. It frowned and dropped him. Geoff landed on the stonework floor with a thud. As he lay there gasping for breath the giant changed its shape.

Long black wings sprouted from its back and the thick body of the hulk became slender. In a matter of seconds, a dark, winged dragonlike creature with a fanged maw and barbed tail loomed over Geoff.

Sawyer and Jane emerged from the darkness along with Ariel. As Geoff watched, the winged intruder launched itself upward. It flew straight through the rafters, exiting through the roof of the keep and disappeared into the night sky.

 87

Geoff coughed as he began to catch his breath, attracting Jane's attention.

"Geoff! Geoff! Are you okay?" asked Jane, kneeling down beside him. "Oh my god! What did it do to you?"

Ariel also knelt beside Geoff. "Are you unharmed?"

Geoff managed to nod. "Yeah. Yeah, I think so."

Jane looked at Ariel. "What was that thing?"

"Not now," she said, turning her head toward the forest to listen. "We must go."

"Go where?" asked Sawyer as he leaned on the spear he captured from the goblin leader.

"We don't even know where we are," said Jane, "much less where to go. I feel like we're in a video game or something and we can't get out."

"Quiet," said Ariel. "Geoff, can you stand? We must leave."

"Yeah, I think so," Geoff said. "I just needed to catch my breath."

Geoff got to his feet with assistance from Jane and Ariel. Other than some bruising, he felt fine.

"That thing," he said between breaths. "It took the key."

Sawyer and Jane looked at each other and then at Ariel, who was already leaving.

She turned and looked at them. "Come. We are in danger."

They looked at each other, trying to decide if they should trust her. Geoff shrugged, then went after Ariel, with Jane and Sawyer close behind.

The four of them made their way through the dark forest. Ariel made no sound as she moved among the trees and underbrush. Geoff, Sawyer, and Jane did make noise, however. A lot. The moon had disappeared behind thick clouds, so they stumbled over moss-covered rocks and tree roots. Geoff wished he hadn't forgotten his torch in the ruined keep.

As silent as she was, Ariel was also much faster than they were. She had to stop on several occasions and wait for them to catch up. Geoff noticed she continuously scanned the forest around them for any unseen enemies.

It wasn't long before the sounds of the stream had faded and they came upon a clearing.

Ariel suddenly stopped and grabbed Geoff's arm.

"Get down," she whispered as she crouched in the darkness, pulling Geoff down with her. Sawyer and Jane did as she said; their breathing was the only sound. Then Geoff realized what had concerned Ariel. The forest was quiet. Too quiet.

"What is it?" asked Jane.

Ariel held a slender finger up to her lips "Shh. We are not alone."

She pointed to a glade just ahead. Emerging from the trees on the other side of the clearing were larger, dark, apelike shapes....

"More goblins?" asked Sawyer.

"Orcs," whispered Ariel as she narrowed her eyes. "What are they doing here? They have never dared to venture so deeply into these woods before."

"What the hell is an orc?" asked Sawyer.

As they watched, the dark, brutish figures spread out and started to search the tall grass of the moonlit glade.

Their arms were thick and muscular and their faces looked more

humanlike than the goblins.

"What are they doing?" whispered Jane.

"They are hunting us," Ariel answered as she turned and looked at Geoff.

Geoff trembled. His skin tingled with goose bumps and his heart thumped in his chest.

"Us?" asked Jane. "Why are they hunting us?"

Sawyer tightened his grip his spear and asked, "Can we take them?"

Ariel shook her head. "No. There are too many. Orcs are much stronger than goblins. We must leave before they catch our scent."

Ariel slowly backed up while remaining crouched. The others did likewise. When they were far enough away from the glade they changed direction, giving the orcs a wide berth. As best as Geoff could tell by looking at the moon, they were making their way north along the tree line between clearings. Ariel was in front, followed by Geoff and Jane, then Sawyer. Once they had traveled for nearly a mile they came to another clearing.

It was a large clearing and in the moonlight they could see tall grass and a thousand tiny flashes of light that flitted about in the meadow.

"Look at all the fireflies," said Geoff.

The insects flying about flashing their tiny lights created a surreal appearance.

Ariel stopped again and crouched. Geoff and the others did so as well, not knowing what unseen dangers lurked ahead.

"What is it? What do you see?" asked Jane.

Ariel shook her head. "Nothing, but we must hurry across this meadow. We will lose too much time if we try to go around it. Be careful; we are vulnerable in the open."

"Vulnerable to what? Orcs? Goblins?" asked Jane.

"Everything," answered Ariel as she stood up, hands on her weapons.

"We are vulnerable to everything tonight."

"Where are we going?" asked Jane.

"The nearest human village is over the next ridge," Ariel said as she pointed across the clearing.

"Cool," said Sawyer. "This place would be alright if it wasn't so spooky and full of bad guys."

"Yeah," said Geoff.

"Shh. Orcs are relentless and have a keen sense of smell. They can easily track us in the dark. We must hurry."

They set out across the meadow as fast as they dared run, following Ariel. The moon illuminated their way, making it easier for Geoff, Sawyer, and Jane to cover more ground. The grass and wildflowers grew as high as their knees and slowed everyone but Ariel.

Geoff, being the smallest, had a more difficult time keeping up with the others. More than once he stumbled as he ran through the tall grass. They were nearly halfway across the meadow when Ariel stopped and held out her arm for them to stop. Geoff kept his eyes on Ariel, who slowly and silently drew her scimitars and crouched down. Geoff crouched beside her.

"What now?" he whispered. He noticed the muscles in her forearms were taut and she was coiled like a spring. Then he smelled a disgusting, fetid odor and he thought he heard footsteps approaching. He turned and looked at Jane and Sawyer. Jane was holding her nose from the stench.

As he turned back to Ariel, a large, brutish figure suddenly sprang up just in front of them with a massive two-handed battle-axe. The orc was taller and more powerfully built than a man, with skin that was dark green-gray. It had large teeth, which looked more like tusks to Geoff. A helmet adorned with ram's horns and a thick mane of long black hair covered most of its head. It wore pieces of different types of armor, which added to its grotesque appearance. The armbands and chest and breeches were made of stitched leather, and the shoulders, helmet, and gloves were constructed of plate.

It raised its axe high overhead and let out an awful roar.

Ariel leapt forward and whirled, slashing its midsection with her scimitars. The orc was stunned. It gasped and dropped its axe. Then it covered its wounds with its hands and crumpled to the ground. As it fell, Geoff saw the shapes of two more similarly armed orcs bearing down on them. Ariel crossed her scimitars in front of her and uttered, "*Tae'nalara!*" and the closest oncoming attacker was violently thrown backward, sailing through the night air and landing with a loud crash almost thirty feet away.

The second orc rushed at Ariel and swung his axe at her right side. Ariel ducked the blow. As she did so she slashed at the legs of her opponent. It howled in pain and dropped to its knees. Ariel's next blow was across its neck, silencing any further sounds except the gurgling sound it made before it fell to the ground.

Geoff had not moved; he was shocked by what he had just seen.

"Hurry. The others will be here soon," said Ariel.

"Oh, no," said Geoff as he pointed to at least a dozen or more orcs coming toward them from the forest.

Chapter Seven
Journey to Silverthorne Manor

Each of the approaching orcs looked to be almost seven feet tall and carried wicked-looking serrated axes and swords. Like the first orc, they were clad in mismatched armor. The moonlight that illuminated the flowers in the glade ignored them. The orcs appeared to be wild black shapes amid the blue, white, and purple hues of the wildflowers.

"Guys, we've got to get out of here!" said Jane from her crouching position. She grabbed Sawyer's sleeve and gave it a sharp tug.

"Now," she said. "Let's go!"

"Holy crap," said Sawyer. "They're huge."

Jane looked at Sawyer, who didn't move. Why isn't he moving? Thought Jane. He seemed to be in awe at the oncoming shapes. She punched him in the arm. Sawyer grabbed his arm and looked at her.

"Now!" said Jane.

Sawyer sprang to his feet.

"Run back the way we came," said Ariel. "Hurry!"

Jane jumped up and started running back to the forest.

Sawyer and Geoff were right behind her. As they ran, Jane looked over her shoulder at Ariel. She had knelt on one knee and was chanting *Bar'athel envora* repeatedly as she watched the grass and trees sway in the night breeze.

The orcs spotted the teenagers almost immediately and charged across the meadow, but as they gained on Sawyer, Jane, and Geoff their sprint slowed and then halted when they reached the middle of the clearing. The attackers' legs had become wrapped and entangled by an overgrowth of grass, weeds, and flowers.

The orcs roared in anger as they strained and struggled to free themselves. They tried to cut and hack their way out of their grassy trap, but whenever they chopped away the entangling greenery more arose and wrapped around them. Ariel stopped chanting. She grabbed her weapons and ran after the others. She caught up with them as they reached the tree line.

"The entangling growth won't hold them for long. We must hurry," she urged.

Jane turned and looked behind at the struggling orcs.

"Oh wow! What did you do?" she asked.

Ariel shook her head. "We have some time, but the spell will eventually wane and the orcs will be freed."

"How did you do that?" asked Jane.

"Forest magic," said Ariel. "Hurry."

As Ariel led them deeper into the forest, Jane could still hear the orcs trying to free themselves, but their grunts and screams subsided with every step they took.

"Where are we going?" asked Jane.

"I know of a safe place. A grove. Evil pursues you, and I do not know why." Ariel looked at Geoff for a moment.

Jane noticed her glance and frowned. Why is she looking at Geoff?

"Oh, and what was that thing in the keep that attacked Geoff?" asked Jane.

Ariel did not answer. She continued rushing them through the forest. All three suffered scrapes and small cuts as they pushed through the undergrowth.

"Well?" said Jane, who was determined to have her question answered.

"Look," said Sawyer, "we just wanna get home. We don't know what's happening. This is all weird as hell."

"Yes," said Ariel. "It is strange because orcs and goblins would never dare to venture so deep into this forest. Something compels them. As for you returning home? If what you have told me is true, if a wizard's key brought you here, then only a wizard's key can send you back."

"What he's trying to say," said Jane as she brushed past a sapling, "is we don't have unicorns or goblins or magic where we come from. We shouldn't be here at all. It was an accident. We don't belong here. So if you can help us we would really appreciate it. I bet our parents have the police looking for us by now."

"Home. The sooner the better," Sawyer said.

"I cannot return you to your home," said Ariel. "As I already told you, the best I can do is take you to the nearest human village. Once there, the lord or magistrate can decide what to do with you."

"Magistrate? Lord? Medieval villages and towns had those," said Geoff. "Did we go back in time?"

They waited for an answer from Ariel, but again no answer was forthcoming; she simply continued to lead them into the dark forest. Something in Ariel's voice and manner struck Jane as aloof, perhaps even self-centered. She opened her mouth to say this to Ariel but stopped. Whether she liked this strange elf-girl or not, Ariel was leading them to where other people were located. And more important, she was leading them away from danger. Jane shivered a little as she walked.

In addition to her fears, Jane was beginning to feel overwhelmed by the events she had witnessed. Who would ever believe her? What would they say to their parents?

Somewhere far behind them came a bloodcurdling howl that pierced the night. Ariel whirled around, her green eyes searching the trees.

"What the hell was that?" asked Sawyer as he tightened his grip on the spear he carried.

"A wolf," Ariel said. "A very dangerous wolf."

"A wolf? Are you sure? We have wolves back home, but I don't think they sound like that," said Geoff.

"I doubt you have wolves like this," said Ariel as she knelt down on one knee, placing a palm on the ground. Jane opened her mouth to ask her what she was doing when Ariel spoke.

"Stand back. I am trying to conceal our trail."

"*Udair'lalnaron ethel tonari*," chanted Ariel. As they watched in the moonlight, their footprints disappeared, broken limbs and twigs repaired themselves, and plants that were trampled underfoot straightened themselves.

"Cool!" said Geoff.

"We must hurry," said Ariel. "Our trail is masked, but not our scent."

"How much farther?" asked Geoff.

 96

"Not far. You will be able to rest and eat," said Ariel.

Jane realized they hadn't eaten for most of the day. She felt a hunger pang as she ran.

"I wish you hadn't mentioned eating," Jane said. "My stomach is starting to growl."

"Same here," agreed Sawyer.

"Me too," said Geoff.

"This way," said Ariel as she led them further into the forest and into a thick copse of trees.

Jane saw a faint glow ahead through the trees. It wasn't an eerie glow; it was more like a warm, welcoming light. The sweet scent of wildflowers wafted over her. It reminded her of the colorful flower-laden meadow they found themselves in when they had awakened. She heard a babbling brook as they trotted toward the friendly glow.

A few minutes later they emerged into a tranquil grove. Jane, Sawyer, and Geoff all stood awestruck. The grove was almost fifty feet in diameter and ringed with apple, pear, peach, plum, and cherry trees. There were also raspberries, blackberries, and strawberries scattered here and there.

The grove had an upward slope with what looked like a round dais supporting a large stone bowl. A small waterfall trickled from the base of the hill and filled a crystal clear, rock lined pool. Everywhere the grass was thick and littered with flowers.

"This must be what paradise looks like," said Geoff.

"Yeah," said Sawyer. "Paradise."

"You are safe here," said Ariel. "Eat your fill and drink from the pool. You will find the water refreshing." Ariel walked up the hill to the dais and bowl. Jane thought she heard her mutter something that sounded like an incantation, but Sawyer was making too much noise picking apples for Jane to fully hear.

"So we don't need to boil the water before we drink it?" asked Sawyer.

"No," said Ariel.

"Mmhmm. That's what I thought," said Sawyer, glancing sideways at Geoff and Jane.

"What is this place?" Jane asked.

Ariel turned her attention to Jane, "This is a druid grove. Every druid is the caretaker of a forest and within each forest druids have groves like this one. This is a sacred place. Only the purest of souls may enter."

Sawyer chomped down on a large juicy apple. "So does that mean we're all pure? I mean, we're here, right?"

"In your case, I have made an exception," said Ariel.

Jane smiled and giggled under her breath. Then she saw from the look on Ariel's face that she was serious.

"Here, Jane. Try these," said Geoff as he held out a handful of the most succulent raspberries Jane had ever seen. She popped one in her mouth. The sweet, juicy taste was simply delightful. Jane rolled her eyes in approval. "Mmm. That is the best raspberry ever!"

"I know, right?" Geoff said while he handed the rest to Jane. Jane eagerly ate a few more delicious raspberries. Sawyer and Geoff went to every tree, bush, and vine collecting what amounted to a feast. Jane picked a few blackberries herself, then she stopped and looked around. The moonlight shone directly on the grove. It's almost like daylight here, she thought. The stars overhead shone brightly and there wasn't a cloud in the sky.

"Everything here is perfect," said Jane, addressing Ariel. "How's that possible?"

"As I just said, I am the caretaker of *this* forest, Spirewood Forest. This is my grove. My magic sustains this forest and everything in it. I protect it."

"Well," said Sawyer, who was finishing off the last bit of his apple, "looks like you haven't been doing a good job. I mean, your forest is full of goblins, wolves, and those big orc dudes."

Jane looked at Ariel. She was sure Sawyer's comment would draw her ire, but she only nodded.

"And what's to stop the orcs and wolves from walking right in here and attacking us?" Sawyer helped himself to a pear, tossing it in the air and catching it.

"Forest magic. Evil cannot set foot in a sacred grove," explained Ariel. "There are powerful incantations and blessings in place to prevent that."

"Okaaay," said Sawyer. "Forest magic for the win!" He took a bite from the pear.

"Alluria is on the verge of tearing itself apart. War is coming. I fear a dark age is nearly upon us. If what you have said is true, then you have come to this world at the wrong time."

"Tell me about it," Sawyer said.

"Alluria? What is Alluria?" asked Jane.

The elf tilted her head slightly and raised an eyebrow. "Alluria is this world, the world in which we live."

Jane, Sawyer, and Geoff fell silent and sat in the grass around Ariel, nibbling on their harvest.

"I was tracking the goblin raiding party when I

happened upon you. The three of you had already defeated the goblins when I arrived."

"It's a good thing you did," said Jane. "Otherwise, the unicorn would have died."

"What was the giant that grabbed me and stole our key?" asked Geoff. "You never did answer Jane."

Jane nodded and looked at Ariel. Ariel sighed and thought for a moment. "You should know that most druids are peaceful, compassionate, and strive to maintain a balance with nature," she said. "I suspect what we saw tonight was a druid who has been corrupted. A dark druid."

Jane watched Ariel as her gaze drifted downward and the look on her face was no longer stoic. She looked sad, she thought. She isn't telling us everything.

"Well now, hang on a minute," said Sawyer as he pointed at Ariel. "You said we can't get home without the key, right? And this dark druid guy took it. So we gotta get it back."

"How? He flew away," said Geoff as he munched on some strawberries.

"That's a good question," said Jane. "Will the people you're taking us to help us get Geoff's key back?"

"Eben Silverthorne is a good man. He will help you," Ariel said.

"Who is he?" asked Jane.

"He is the lord of Silverthorne Village. He commands a garrison there."

"When I get home dad is going to be angry and ground me forever," said Geoff. "It's bad enough I was in his study, but staying out this late too?" Geoff shook his head. "No way he'll believe this."

"I think we're all pretty much grounded when we get home," said Jane. "I just don't like making my parents worry about me."

Sawyer lay on his side in the grass, eating another apple while Geoff picked at the strawberries in his hand.

"I said it before," said Jane. "We don't belong here. This world is full of monsters and magic and stuff we don't understand. We have to get home."

"I'm scared," said Geoff. "If we are being chased by orcs, will we be safe at Silverthorne Village?"

"Yes," Ariel said. She had regained her stoic demeanor. She looked to Jane as if she had steeled herself for something yet to come.

"I have a question," said Sawyer. "If those orcs are in your forest, why don't you use your forest magic and get rid of them?"

"I have. This forest can protect itself," said Ariel. "I will see to them after I take you to Silverthorne Village."

"Shouldn't we have dealt with them while you had them tied up in that meadow?" asked Jane. "I mean, what if they're still out there tomorrow?"

"Have you ever killed before?" asked Ariel, raising an eyebrow.

"No," said Jane. "None of us have. And I hope we don't ever have to, either."

"You should rest," said Ariel. "Sleep while you can. We have a long way to travel tomorrow."

"I am tired," said Geoff, "and my shoulder still hurts a little."

Another howl came from the nearby forest.

"Man, that was close!" said Sawyer, jumping to his feet.

Jane scanned the darkness beyond the trees surrounding the grove. She didn't see anything, but Sawyer was right; that howl was much closer than the first one. Ariel stood up and walked along the trees lining the grove. While she was away, Jane whispered to Sawyer and Geoff.

"Guys, what're we going to do? You don't trust her, do you? And how are we going to get that key back?"

"No idea," said Geoff. "But I trust her. If she wanted to kill us I think she would've done it by now"

"But what if this Silverthorne guy doesn't want to help us?" asked Sawyer. "What if we bump into more orcs and Ariel isn't around?"

"I'm not sure we have a choice," said Jane. "At least we'll be in a village with people and not out here in the wilds."

"That's true. But what about this war stuff?" asked Sawyer.

Jane shook her head. "Who cares? It's not my fight. It doesn't concern us. Let's get the key and get out of here. Agreed?"

Sawyer and Geoff nodded. Jane felt better now that they had something of a plan, but she had no idea how they were going to accomplish it. How were they going to take it away from the giant? They would just have to figure out the details later.

Ariel returned to the group, "Sleep. There is no danger."

"Are you sure?" asked Jane.

"Yes," replied Ariel.

"Sleep sounds good to me," said Sawyer with a yawn.

Ariel nodded and walked back to her stone bowl. Jane stretched and then lay down in the grass. It's like lying on a plush bed, she thought. She looked over at Geoff, who was already curled up beside her. She closed her eyes.

The next thing she knew, it was morning and the sun was shining. She sat up and yawned. Sawyer and Geoff were still asleep, and Sawyer was snoring. Beside each of them sat a napkin-sized cloth with a piece of flat bread, cheese, apples, and berries on it. She picked up the bread and took a bite.

"We should be on our way as soon as you finish your breakfast," said Ariel. "If we hasten our pace we can reach Silverthorne Village by nightfall."

Geoff and Sawyer required a nudge or two from Jane, but they awakened and ate their breakfasts. They were on their way in no time, but they had a difficult time keeping up with Ariel, who was running.

"Wait," said Jane after a fast-paced hour. "We need to rest a little."

She and Geoff sat under a nearby tree. Sawyer, who was also breathing heavily, plopped down beside Jane.

"What's the rush?" asked Sawyer.

"As I mentioned last night," said Ariel, "we must arrive in Silverthorne before nightfall."

"I thought we didn't have to worry about orcs during the day," stated Geoff.

"The orcs are dead," said Ariel. "They never left the meadow."

Jane looked at Sawyer and then Geoff.

"Did you go back and kill them?" asked Jane.

Ariel shook her head. "No. Before you awakened I went back to the meadow hoping I could find their tracks and determine which direction they had gone." Ariel squatted beside them. "I found what was left of them still in the meadow. Something had attacked them."

"You mean to say that all those big orcs are dead? What could do that to them? The wolves? Those orcs were massive!" Geoff said.

"I know you are tired," said Ariel, "but you can rest at Silverthorne Manor. We cannot delay for much longer."

"Hey," said Sawyer, "maybe whatever killed those orcs is after us now."

"Come on, guys," said Jane. "We better get going. I want to get back to civilization."

They continued for most of the day, taking quick, regular rest breaks with Ariel's approval. The forest seemed to be serene and pleasant. At one point a small herd of deer darted by. Looks like they're going to Silverthorne Manor too, thought Jane. She also noticed the trees were much smaller now. She started to see some dead trees the farther they traveled from Ariel's grove. The trees thinned out and the terrain became rockier.

Geoff slipped on a rock and took a small tumble downhill. The others stopped.

"Geoff, are you okay?" asked Jane.

"Yeah. I'm fine. Just slipped."

He got up and brushed himself off. Jane and Sawyer walked down to Geoff as Ariel scanned the horizon.

"I thought I was the only clumsy one here," said Jane with a smile.

"You sure you're okay?" asked Sawyer.

"Yeah, yeah. I'm fine. No problem," said Geoff.

They started back up the hill but something caught Jane's attention.

"Hey, guys," she said, pointing at the ground. "Look at this!"

Sawyer and Geoff went to see what Jane had found.

"Wow! That is huge!" said Geoff.

"Hey, Ariel, we found something," said Sawyer, motioning for her to come have a look. She joined them and crouched to study it.

"What do you think made that track?" asked Jane. "A bear?"

Ariel shook her head. "Wolf," she said.

Chapter Eight
The Tattered Man

"No way!" said Jane as she looked at large clawed footprint.

"There aren't any wolves that big!" Jane looked at Sawyer and Geoff for agreement. They only shrugged. Jane put her foot next to the deep impression Ariel was examining.

"I can get three of my feet in that footprint," said Jane.

"That's a big wolf," said Geoff. "It must be as big as a horse. Are you sure it's a wolf track?"

Ariel nodded and continued to study it.

"Look at the size of those claws," said Sawyer. "I hope we don't run into the wolf that made that track."

"Yeah. Me too," agreed Geoff.

Ariel stood and took a few steps in the direction they were headed. Jane thought she heard Ariel say "What are you doing? Why are you here?" under her breath.

Jane walked over to Ariel and stood behind her. A shiver ran down her back. She swallowed before asking, "Ariel, are we in danger?"

A few seconds passed, then Ariel looked at Jane and

smiled. "No. The wolf that made this track is far away by now."

"Good," said Sawyer. "One less thing to worry about trying to kill us in the middle of the night."

Jane, however, was not convinced by Ariel's answer. Ariel had smiled for the first time, but the tone in her voice indicated the elven druid was worried.

Jane looked into Ariel's green eyes for a few seconds. The emotionless expression had returned. Now she doubted whether she could trust Ariel. What reason did she have to help them? She had saved them the night before, but why? Ariel looked worried but had composed herself quickly after seeing the large wolf track.

"Come," said Ariel. "We should go. We have a long way to travel yet before nightfall."

They resumed their trek. Sawyer walked behind Ariel, trying to start a conversation, while Geoff walked with Jane a few paces behind.

After a while Geoff looked at Jane. She saw from his expression he was concerned about something.

"Jane," he said quietly, "that giant wolf track was headed in the same direction we're going now."

Jane nodded. She had noticed that, too. Sawyer appeared to be too interested in Ariel to notice.

"Geoff," whispered Jane, "what do you make of her? Do you really think we can trust her?"

Geoff thought for a moment. "I don't know now. I think maybe yes, but I'm not sure. Why not?"

"I'm starting to get a little worried. I know she saved us from those…those…what did she call them? Orcs?"

Geoff nodded.

"And she fed us last night, but I don't think she is being completely honest with us. She keeps to herself mostly."

"Jane, what if no one can help us get home? What if we're stuck here?"

Jane's heart sank. It never occurred to her they might be in this beautiful yet dangerous world for the rest of their lives.

"Oh, Geoff," she said. "Don't even think that. We're going to get home. Soon."

They marched on for a few miles before entering another forest. Ariel found some blackberry bushes along the way and they all ate their fill while they sat and rested.

"We will need to quicken our pace if we hope to arrive at Silverthorne by nightfall," said Ariel.

"I thought we were moving at a pretty good clip," said Sawyer. "You mean we may be walking in the dark again?"

"Are we still being hunted?" asked Geoff.

Ariel stood and surveyed the forest ahead of them. "No."

Jane studied at Ariel. She had ignored Sawyer's attempts to start a conversation, and now when she did speak she said very little. Jane was a little apprehensive by her short answer; she expected more of an explanation. What is she not telling us, she thought. Maybe Ariel didn't want to upset them. Or was it something else?

Soon they were trotting, trying to keep up with Ariel, who looked about more and paid closer attention to their surroundings as they moved through the forest. Their rate of movement increased as the sun began to set. Ariel stopped long enough to wait for them to catch up to her and to cast another spell to mask their trail.

Jane's feet and ankles were aching. She also noticed she was winded. She held up a hand. "Wait. I need to rest. I can't go on."

She sat on a moss-covered boulder, breathing heavily. Geoff plopped down beside her. Because he was smaller, he had a particularly difficult time trying to keep up. Even Sawyer was needed a rest, and he was accustomed to physical activity.

As they sat and gathered their breath, Ariel joined them.

"At this pace, we will not make it to Silverthorne before sunset. Rest awhile and we will continue."

"I'm thirsty," said Geoff between breaths.

Ariel handed him a leather flask filled with water.

"Take a drink and pass it to the others," she said.

"What's the hurry?" asked Sawyer, who was lying at the foot of a large oak tree.

Ariel glanced at Sawyer and walked away, ignoring his question.

At that moment something snapped in Jane. Her nostrils flared and she felt her cheeks getting warm as she stood up.

"Hey," she said louder than she intended, "you've been ignoring Sawyer all day and you keep pushing us to run I don't know how far through the forest with no rest to speak of. Why are you pushing us so hard?"

"Hey, Jane, chill out," said Sawyer. "It was a question. That's all."

Jane, offended by his remark, faced Sawyer and put her hands on her hips.

"No, it was a good question. Geoff and I've been wondering about that all day, among other things."

"What other things?" asked Sawyer.

"Well, what's going to happen when we get to Silverthorne, for one. Why are we rushing to get there? Are they going to be able to help us? Will they help us? And why do we need to get there before nightfall? I mean, if something isn't chasing us, then why are we killing ourselves to get to Silverthorne before it gets dark? What happens after sunset?"

"Are you not in a hurry to return home?" asked Ariel with her back to Jane, scanning the forest.

"Yes," said Jane, "but do they have a key and an archway thing in Silverthorne?"

"No," said Ariel.

"Then why the heck are we going there?"

Ariel did not answer, which infuriated Jane.

"Well? Are you going to answer me or not? Why don't you call us by our names? And what do you have against humans anyway? You say that word with such distaste."

Ariel whirled on Jane, her eyes flashed, "Take care how you speak to me, *Jane*." Jane stepped backward, matching each step forward Ariel took toward her. "You humans are little better than orcs! You have no respect for each other or each other's property. You seek to rob, cheat, betray, and steal from anyone for whatever you covet. You eagerly lie and twist the meanings of words to suit your own selfish needs. You care nothing for the elderly and downtrodden, always seeking an abundance of riches to fill your own coffers.

You have no regard for nature. You hunt and kill for sport, seeking to adorn your homes with bits of animals as trophies. You cut down entire forests to build your towns and castles, never caring a moment for the wildlife you disturb. You war with anyone, especially yourselves. Throughout the ages, whenever there was a war, a human was behind it and why? For nothing but power and glory or riches.

This realm is on the verge of war because a human lord seeks more power and more lands. Many will die because of the greed of one man. So, to answer your questions, I push you *humans* to move faster so we can reach the nearest human village before dark because you will be safer there than in the forest. I do not know if they can or will help you, nor do I care. What was it you said? Oh yes. 'It's not my fight.'

And yes, you are being stalked. You are being stalked by a monster. A werewolf. That is what made the tracks you found and that is what stalks you. That is what killed the orcs. I did not speak of this because you are only children and I sought not to alarm you. However, I am a druid and rank among the leaders of my order and I will not be spoken to in such a disrespectful manner. As I said, humans — little better than orcs. Now have I answered your questions, *Jane?*"

Jane stood perfectly still. She was speechless. She had never received such a tongue lashing. She swallowed and in a softer tone asked, "Then why are you helping us?"

Ariel took a deep breath before answering. "Because you saved the unicorn. I assure you that had you not done so I would have left you to whatever fate awaited you. I have decided to give you safe escort to people who may help you. Perhaps the local lord will help you find your key and an 'archway thing' as you call it. For now, this is the best I can do. There are other more pressing matters that demand my attention. Perhaps one day I will come for a brief visit."

"Why…why would a werewolf hunt us? What did we do?" asked Geoff.

Ariel turned away from Jane, looked at Geoff, and shook her head.

"Other than being an excellent source of food? I do not know. It is said that the beast hunts those who are good and innocent."

Jane, Sawyer, and Geoff were silent. Ariel's harsh words had caught Jane off guard. She didn't expect Ariel's reaction; all she wanted were answers to her questions. She stood there not knowing how to respond.

"Hey, Ariel," said Sawyer, "people…are like that where we come from, too. But I don't think any of us are greedy or selfish."

Ariel said nothing. She walked a few yards away then turned around.

"Come. We have an hour or two left before it gets dark. We will not make it to Silverthorne tonight. We should look for shelter."

Jane looked at Sawyer, who met her gaze and then looked at Geoff. Then he followed Ariel. Geoff got up, gave Jane a quick smile, and joined Sawyer. Jane took a deep breath and tried to steady her trembling hands. She looked over her shoulder at the darkening forest behind her and then she fell in line behind Geoff.

Later, Ariel found a good spot to camp for the night as the sun was setting. It was a covered rocky outcropping behind a small grove of weeping willows.

"This will do," she said. "It is concealed yet defensible. If we are careful and have a small fire no one will know we are here."

Ariel leaned close and whispered something to a weeping willow tree and it moved. The willow stretched its branches and intermingled them with the other weeping willows, which, in turn, formed a semicircular, lattice-like structure around the small outcropping. Kind of like an igloo, Jane thought.

Next, Sawyer and Geoff gathered stones and placed them in a circle while Ariel and Jane gathered wood for a fire. Ariel lit the kindling by bending close and uttering a single word, "*Ignara*."

"Cool! I gotta learn how to do that," said Geoff.

Later, after they had eaten, Ariel said, "Take care to stay here and do not wander off."

"Are you going somewhere?" asked Jane.

"I am going to scout the nearby forest. If the werewolf or any other danger draws near then perhaps I can distract it or lead it away."

"Shouldn't we all stay together?" asked Geoff as he looked at Jane and Sawyer for support.

"Yes, humans should always stay together when lost in a forest," said Ariel, "but I am not human and I am not lost."

Sawyer, Jane, and Geoff looked at each other uneasily, but no one said a word.

"Sawyer," said Ariel as she was about to leave their tree-covered haven, "I will need you to stand watch." She pulled a slender, slightly curved dagger from her belt and handed it to him. "This is an elven blade. It is far superior to the goblin spear you carry."

Sawyer nodded. "Okay. Hurry back."

Ariel looked about the small hidden camp as if she were inspecting it. Then, without another word, she turned and walked to the wall of weeping willows, which parted for her, let her pass, and then closed again.

"Will it do that for us if we have to make a quick exit?" asked Jane.

"Let's hope we don't have to find out," said Geoff.

They sat around the fire, staring at the flames as they danced among the wood and embers.

"What do we do if she doesn't come back?" asked Jane.

The thick mist covering the ground brought it all back. The silence of the forest offered undeniable proof that he was not welcome. Understandable, he thought. An outcast of man and nature. Accepted only by the moon. The cold, harsh moon. He shook his head, trying to clear the images that haunted him. But it was no use; the memories flooded in. The hooded figure draped in tattered animal skins looked into the flickering flames of the small campfire. The only thing missing was the torrential rain. He remembered his friends. That night long ago when Shaun and Lionel rode beside him, followed by Zorn and Maelord.

They had been hunting a monster. The beast had been terrorizing the countryside, killing livestock and farmers. He had tracked it into the Eldritch Forest, which was looking especially sinister that night. The Eldritch Forest had been a pleasant woodland, much like the Spirewood

Forest to the south. But now it was changing. It was a forbidding woodland with twisted, blackened trees and uneven terrain.

All manner of slithering, stinging, biting, crawling death lurked behind every tree and under every stone, waiting for the chance to strike at unsuspecting prey.

At the heart of the forest was a great festering swamp said to be impassable and home to dark woodland denizens. Five riders carrying torches raced through the trees of the Eldritch Forest in a heavy downpour.

Their torches flickered in the wind and rain, threatening to die as they rode. They were on the trail of their quarry and they were close. The trees swayed and seemed to move and swipe at them as they ventured deeper into the darkness.

"Time has changed so much..." he said as he threw a stick onto the campfire, sending red glowing ash fluttering upward. "I was an excellent tracker," he growled.

He remembered how he had come to a stop and swept the ground with his torch, looking for the tracks of their prey.

"Alex! This is madness!" shouted a dark-haired rider with a large war hammer slung over his shoulder.

"We must turn back! We'll never follow its tracks in this weather!"

"Shaun is right," said the rider in the rear. "We should go back!"

Shaun and Maelord's advice should have been heeded. It wasn't, he thought. Maelord had a slight build and a thin, dark beard and moustache. He carried a narrow staff made of dark brown wood and topped with a large white glowing gem. Normally, it would be impossible to try to track at night in such a downpour. This quarry left heavy, clawed tracks deep in the mud, however, and knocked small saplings aside as it passed.

"There!" said Alex as he pointed to signs on the ground. "It's close! It's headed for the ravine! There's a chance we can corner it!"

Without a glance backward he spurred his horse forward into the darkness with the others in close pursuit. Lionel was directly behind Alex. He had clear blue eyes and dirty blond hair that was now thoroughly soaked. Behind Lionel came Shaun, then Maelord followed by Zorn, who carried a hunting bow and a sword slung over his back.

"We were heroes," he said as he broke off another stick and tossed it into the campfire. "And we were best friends. Together we were unbeatable." Those were grand days. Days of adventure. The best of days.

They pressed on through the storm, horse and rider dodging branches and weaving in and out of twisted, gnarled trees that swiped at them. Alex halted his horse when they arrived at a small clearing. The others pulled their horses close and huddled together.

"We can't be far behind the beast now. I see fresh breaks in the undergrowth and broken saplings. Be on your guard," said Alex. He saw the concerned looks on their faces and nodded. "Yes, this is madness to chase such a monster into its lair on a night like this or any other night. But we may not have another chance to slay this beast. We can't turn back now. It's close."

The other riders said nothing. Their gazes fixed on him as they sat silently in the cold rain, their breaths rising from their mouths.

"Alex, even if we find the beast," said Shaun as he leaned forward in his saddle, "do we have the means to kill it?"

"Aye," said Alex. "We can kill it."

He looked at the rain-soaked faces of the others. They were frowning and looking at each other. Their uneasiness had been understandable, thought Alex now as he sat by the fire. But what other choice did he have? He did his best to rally his friends.

"If we turn back now, what happens to the townspeople of Somerdale? What of them? Do we let them continue to suffer?" He shook his head. "No, we've been charged with this task and we must see it through."

Maelord had been the first of the riders to speak. "So be it. We'll destroy the beast or die." He grabbed Alex by the shoulder. "But I sense something else working its will here tonight. Dark magic is all around us. Be careful!"

"I sense it, too," said Zorn. He readied his bow and peered into the darkness around them.

"What do you think it is, Maelord?" asked Lionel.

The wizard shook his head, "I don't know. I've never felt anything like it before. I'm not sure what kind of magic we're facing, but it permeates everything here."

"What? Are you saying the trees are cursed?" asked Lionel. Maelord nodded. "Perhaps." Lionel winced as he turned again to look into the darkness. Alex wondered if they had ever faced anything so dreadful. He couldn't remember the last time they were in such a fix, and more important, wondered if they would survive the night.

Shaun sighed as he pulled the war hammer from his back and wiped the rain from his face. "Stormy night, marauding beasts, haunted forest…it's not so bad. Could be fun."

Alex smiled at Shaun's words. They weren't cowards, not even remotely. He looked at his friends. Each had proven himself time and time again in battle. However, he had long ago learned that if Maelord urged caution it would be wise to heed his warning.

At that moment the horses gave a start. Lionel's horse nearly lost its footing in the mud.

"Easy. There now. Easy, boy," he said in a reassuring voice as he scanned the tree line around them.

"We shouldn't linger. It's too dangerous! We should move on," said Zorn.

Alex nodded and spurred his horse forward. Zorn looked at a thoroughly drenched Shaun and laughed.

"Having fun yet?" said Zorn as he raised his eyebrows and urged his horse to follow Alex.

"Ha!" laughed Shaun, sputtering and spewing water. They followed Alex into the darkness.

Not one of them noticed a pair of yellow eyes hidden in the trees following their movements as they rode. Only after the riders disappeared into the darkness did it move. Its brownish- gray matted fur was a perfect disguise as it followed the riders. The beast slowly began to quicken its pace, for it sensed the kill.

Up ahead, the riders continued their determined passage through the forest. Alex noticed the ground had begun to change. It was rockier. The ravine was close.

He was sure the beast's lair was in that ravine, but what had begun to worry Alex was the fact that it had been some time since he had seen any tracks. He glanced left and right, holding the torch close to the ground in an effort to discern any trace of the beast.

Water poured from his brow and the tip of his nose as he bent forward. The others scanned the trees in every direction.

Alex turned in his saddle and called, "I've lost it, and I've lost the trail. I don't see any sign of it now. It must have doubled back on us. Be on your guard! It could be anywhere!"

"What?" said Shaun, "Alex, if you've lost the trail—"

The thunder overhead was interrupted by the horrific, tormented howl of a wild beast.

"It's close! Where the hell is it?" shouted Lionel.

"Gods and demons!" shouted Shaun, turning his head and looking about.

Lionel and Alex drew their swords, the hair on the back of their drenched necks standing up. Maelord's horse reared in fright, causing the wizard to desperately cling to his reins to avoid being thrown to the ground. Alex dismounted and started to search the edge of the ravine for a safe way down. The other riders remained mounted and kept scanning the woods, all the while trying to calm their mounts. Alex moved along the edge of the ravine, scrutinizing the terrain. There could be no mistakes, not if they were going to survive.

The footing along the edge of the ravine was treacherous, but Alex managed to keep his balance.

"I can't find a safe way down and there are no tracks!" he said.

Lionel dismounted and walked along the ravine in the opposite direction. Alex remembered Lionel had wandered away from the group, however. He moved toward Lionel and as he did so, he called over his shoulder, "Maelord, we need more light!

The wizard stood in his saddle while he raised his jeweled staff high overhead. "*Iluminara!*" shouted Maelord, and the large jewel in the tip of his staff began to grow brighter and brighter. The white light continued to expand and cover more area. The shadows among the trees retreated against the growing intensity of the magic illumination.

Behind his companions, the bright light revealed a large, furry form already in full charge toward Lionel. It was huge, roughly manlike, yet it seemed to alternate between running on all fours and leaping with its hind legs. The beast was covered with thick brownish fur that failed to conceal the large corded muscles that rippled beneath. Its enormous head housed two glowing yellow orbs that were fixed on Lionel.

Its snarling jaws were lined with large fangs. Its massive, fur-covered claws tore at the ground as it propelled itself toward Lionel at incredible speed.

Maelord's horse reared and neighed, as did the other horses. The beast charged past the riders as they were trying to regain their balance on their steeds and bring their weapons to bear. Its lips were now peeled back, further revealing its fangs, which now resembled jagged daggers.

Alex turned and saw the monster was closing in on Lionel, and moved as fast as he could to aid his friend. Lionel had heard the beast's approach and turned to meet it. As he did so he lost his footing and dropped to one knee. He couldn't take his eyes off the monster, and he cursed as he struggled to regain his balance as the werewolf drew near.

"Look out!" yelled Shaun as he leapt from his horse to aid Lionel. Alex was closer and already running. Lionel regained his balance and braced himself for the impending attack. He was pushed aside at the last moment by Alex, however, who readied his sword to meet the charging beast.

It lowered itself to the ground and gathered speed. It launched itself at Alex, slamming into him with frightening force, knocking the warrior backward as it tore and ripped at him with claws and teeth.

As Alex and the monster hit the ground, the werewolf closed its jaws on Alex's left shoulder, its fangs piercing Alex's armor. Alex screamed in pain and plunged his sword deep into the beast's left side. Then he pulled out his dagger and stabbed at his attacker again. He could barely feel his left arm and noticed it was no longer responding as it should.

"Alex!" shouted Lionel as he pulled himself to his feet and ran to Alex's aid. The werewolf swung around and turned its malevolent gaze on the others as Shaun and Lionel together struck it with their weapons. Shaun ducked under a vicious biting lunge and swung his war hammer at the beast, striking it on its left side. Lionel plunged his blade deep into its belly. The beast lashed out at Shaun with a massive claw that struck him squarely on his chest and sent him sprawling several feet away.

As Shaun sailed through the air, Lionel spun and slashed at the beast, slicing into its right shoulder. The werewolf snarled and rose on its hind legs. It was about to pounce on Lionel when it was suddenly blinded by a sharp light that was focused on its eyes. Maelord had altered the magically generated light at the end of his staff and sent a beam directly at the beast.

It held up its massive, blood-covered paw to shield its eyes. This hesitation was all Lionel needed. He leapt forward and stabbed at the beast with his weapon, then followed that attack with a slash to its midsection.

Shaun climbed to his feet and was charging to help as fast as he could, his war hammer high overhead ready to strike. The beast lashed out with renewed ferocity and struck Lionel on the left shoulder. The force of the blow sent his left pauldron flying in one direction and Lionel in the other.

Shaun brought his hammer down on the monster's back. It whirled, its head colliding with Shaun as it snapped savagely at him. The collision knocked Shaun off balance and sent him tumbling into the mud. The monster then leapt onto Lionel. As the beast's jaws were about to close on Lionel's throat, Alex buried his blade deep in its back and then collapsed.

A short yelp escaped from the beast as it turned on the prone Alex. Something glinted and sparkled and caught its attention. It raised its head and looked at the rider with the silver-tipped arrow and snarled. In another instant Zorn's silver tipped arrow had found its mark.

Five riders had entered the Eldritch Forest. Only four emerged. The man in the tattered skins flung another stick on the fire and shook his head.

"I was careless," he said. "Now I'm an exile. It must be this way. For the sake of all, it must be this way."

"Ah, here she comes," he said, looking into the dark forest. "Here comes my old friend."

Chapter Nine
Meeting by Night

AN EVENING MIST HAD FORMED, which made it difficult for Ariel to see any tracks. She quickened her pace as she walked deeper into the darkness. She detected the faint smell of smoke from another campfire. As she moved toward the distant fire, thick, dark hair grew all over her body and her posture changed to that of a four-legged animal. Long whiskers grew from her cheeks and her teeth grew into fangs.

Ariel's senses were heightened and she detected the scent of a human. It wasn't the first time Ariel had smelled this particular scent, but she had hoped to never encounter it again. She shivered in her cat form. She wasn't sure what would happen or what she would do if things went badly when she met him again. She admitted to herself that she was afraid—for herself and for the others. She growled deeply with irritation as she raced toward the unwelcomed scent.

The mist covering the ground had become thicker, permeating the entire forest floor. Soon her senses told her that she was close to him. Very close. Ariel slowed and navigated her way through the trees. She heard the bubbling sounds of a brook nearby and moved in that direction. The smell of the campfire was much stronger now. She made no sound as she stalked toward the human scent. She saw the glow of a small campfire through the trees in front of her.

She crouched lower to the ground and began to circle. Each time she circled she moved a little closer until she could clearly see a lone figure crouched by the fire. It was a cloaked man, and his hood was pulled up, making it impossible to see his face. He was dressed in torn animal skins. Ariel hid roughly fifty feet away, facing him.

She lay down and watched the figure by the campfire. She knew him. He moved very little; only once in a while he would throw another piece of wood on the fire. Ariel could see that his large animal skins and cloak were soiled and ripped like the rest of his clothing. The only sounds were the crackling and popping of the campfire and the rushing water of the creek, which was between him and Ariel. He was still large and muscular. That much was easy to see, even if he wore raggedy skins.

There they were, two predators facing each other and all alone in the dark, misty forest. The fur on Ariel's back stood up and her muscles tightened. Her entire body was tense, ready to flee or attack. The man's breathing had become heavier and more ragged. Ariel heard his raspy breaths and could see his shoulders heave up and down in the firelight. The man shook and coughed, which almost caused Ariel to leap up from her position.

Slowly she stood, all the while keeping her eyes on the lone figure sitting by the fire. Every fiber in her being told her that she was in extreme danger being this close to him.

She knew the best thing for her to do was flee from him as fast as she could, but she didn't. She was curious as to why he was here and she hoped to find him in a sane state of mind. She couldn't be sure of his sanity, however—or his intentions.

With all the concentration and resolve she could muster, Ariel returned to her elven form. To make such a rapid change of form caused her to feel weak for a short period of time. Only the most powerful druids were able to change shape quickly and not suffer any ill effects. The man sitting by the fire made no move, nor did he indicate he was aware of Ariel's presence. She stayed motionless in the dark, not daring to make a single sound. Her hands were shaking and her palms were moist with sweat. Ariel didn't frighten easily, nor did she panic at the first hint of danger. She had seen her share of battle.

Now, however, Ariel was in danger, and it took nearly every bit of willpower to keep from fleeing. The man raised a gnarled hand and pointed at her. A sense of dread came over her, but before she could turn and run away he beckoned her to come closer.

Ariel knew that the further away she was from the man the better her chances of surviving this encounter. She took a deep breath, steadied her nerves, and then stepped from the trees onto the moist bank by the brook. The man beckoned Ariel to come closer, but she hesitated and her hands moved nearer to her weapons.

"Why do you fear me, old friend? Are we not both woodland beings?" asked the sitting figure with a deep, raspy voice.

Ariel didn't answer. She was trying to decide if she

should trust him. He was once an honorable and noble man, but that was a long time ago. Again he motioned for her to come closer and he offered her a seat by his fire. Ariel looked around. If she had to flee she could not escape through the forest. She would have to find another way to safety.

She placed her hands on the hilts of her blades and stepped into the cool, shallow waters. The water bubbled and splashed about her ankles, refreshing her and helping her to focus. She walked to the other side and stepped onto the bank. She was careful to position herself by the fire opposite her host. She still couldn't see his face under his hood.

She stood for a moment, then knelt down in front of him, keeping the fire between them.

She licked her lips and swallowed. "What are you doing? Why are you following us?"

He sat silently for a moment, and then replied, "Have you not sensed it? Do you…not know?" Ariel tightened her lips and shook her head. This was a lie and he would certainly know, but she didn't dare answer him truthfully.

"I'm sure you know by now there is something about them. They are…special," he said.

"They are three human children. That is all," Ariel said flatly.

He pointed at her. "No, they are much more…at night I sense their power. I believe they can—"

"Can what?" interrupted Ariel. "Help you? They cannot help you. They have no powers and seek only to return home."

"No, Ariel. They are much more…they're powerful."

She was taken off guard for a moment hearing him speak her name after so many years.

"They are children. They are here only by chance."

"No. I believe fate brought them to us. They shine, Ariel. They shine so brightly. Surely you can see this. They are here for a reason and that reason must be to—"

"No!" shouted Ariel. "Do not involve them in your dark affairs. They are only children. Leave them be."

They sat in silence for a few moments, staring at each other. Then Ariel spoke. "I cannot protect them from you. This you know. Go away and leave them be."

The man lowered his head and thought for a moment, then answered. "You know they are so much more. I have seen their auras just as you have. They may be mere children, but I believe they can help. I sense they have true power, especially—"

"Stop. Please stop," said Ariel. "You do not know what you ask. Just leave them be."

"Even if I did as you ask, do you think *he* would listen to you? Do you think the Shadowlord would leave them be?"

Ariel shook her head. "I...don't understand."

"He hunts them. He has gathered his armies and has begun to wage war against the free kingdoms. No one is safe. Not from him. He commands the darkness and he will not stop until he conquers all."

Ariel's eyes widened. She was not aware of these dire tidings.

"Why would the Shadowlord hunt them? And how does he know of their presence?"

"I don't know," said the man. "His powers have grown.

Perhaps he senses their potential, too. We will soon be at war. It would be a mistake for you to take them to Chalon. Lionel can't protect you. He can't defeat the Shadowlord's legions."

Ariel thought for a moment. She wasn't planning to travel to the capital city of Chalon. Perhaps they could elude him. Buy some time, she thought. Perhaps all the talk of war would be a good distraction.

"The elves and dwarves will aid in this war…there are other human kingdoms…if we band togeth—" she said.

"The dwarves and elves struggle for their very existence," he said.

"The dwarves fight cave to cave in their subterranean strongholds against unknown dark minions. It is rumored the remote mountain fortress of Bhregendain has already fallen. For the moment, the elven fortress of Selra'thel stands. If it should fall, then the rest of the elven kingdoms would follow. The outlying human villages and forts are being destroyed. Millhaven—"

"Has fallen…I know," said Ariel. She dropped her eyes and looked into the smoky fire. "I lost many friends there."

"Then you know I'm not lying," he said with a hint of disgust. "You druids keep to your forests while not giving a second thought to the world beyond your trees, preferring to maintain the balance and protect nature." The man's voice lowered. "Heed my words, Ariel. There is nowhere to run; our world is burning. Your precious balance is in peril. Once you leave the relative safety of this forest, you will be risking their lives."

Ariel sighed. Her heart was heavy with the news he had shared with her.

"Then what would you have me do? I have given them my word to safely guide them out of the forest. If our world burns as you say then there is no sanctuary anywhere."

There was no answer from him.

"You were destined to be a great ruler!" cried Ariel. "If you know of a safer haven than Chalon tell me. I trust the counsel of the wizard Maelord. Perhaps he will know how to return them…" Ariel's voice trailed off.

"Return them?" he asked. "Where are they from?"

Ariel took a deep breath, "They came here through a wizard's portal. They say the smallest had a wizard's key."

"A wizard's key, eh? Where did he find such a treasure?"

Ariel shook her head. "I do not know."

The man leaned back and seemed to consider what Ariel had just revealed. "Then perhaps I'm mistaken," he said. "Lionel and Maelord are good men. They will help you. I'm sure of it. But beware. The Shadowlord has spies everywhere. Anyone you meet may be his pawn—anyone."

"Lionel is a fool," said Ariel. "He should never have been chosen to sit on the throne. The people of Chalon need their rightful king. Now more than ever."

The man in tattered skins shook his head.

"He's dead. Forget him. He can't help."

Ariel knew he was right. But how did the Shadowlord become so powerful? How did he come to have the military might to challenge elves, dwarves, and men? This didn't make sense. Perhaps she did spend too much time in the forests and not enough time staying current with the affairs of men. No, she thought. Her place was here, in the forests.

"Does Lionel know the elves and dwarves are fighting for their lives?" asked Ariel.

"I don't know," the man said. "Even if he did, I don't think he can help them. His troops are spread too thin already trying to protect the outlying villages. He's calling up reserves, but time is not on his side. It's a brilliant strategy, what the Shadowlord has done. Wouldn't you agree?"

"Of course," she said. "He was always a brilliant tactician." The Shadowlord is not the only foe we need to avoid, she thought as she glanced at the figure seated in front of her.

"I believe the safest place for us will be in the city of Chalon," she said. "If the battles are still being waged in the outer villages and towns, then the children will be safe there."

The man coughed and shuddered a little.

"Aye. Perhaps you are right," he said. "If you can reach Chalon, then maybe you will find safety—at least for a while. Remember what I said about spies."

"And what of Caladar? Do they know of our peril? Will their knights aid us?"

"I don't know."

"You must stop following us," she said. "It is too dangerous! If you find us on a night when the moon is full—"

Suddenly, he coughed and began to shudder.

"Go," he croaked. "Run." He shuddered again, more violently than before. Ariel leapt to her feet, her eyes focused on the man. His body convulsed in the firelight and he rolled over on the mist-covered ground.

"Run! Get away," he growled as he swung his hand in a shooing motion. His hand was almost fully covered with coarse black hair, and long, razor-sharp claws grew from his fingers right before her eyes.

Her old friend had been so unintimidating that she had spent too much time talking to him. Ariel took a step backward. She was trembling and her mind raced. She was in danger. The mist was heavy enough to partially cover the man writhing on the ground. First he sounded like he was in pain. Then the sounds became low growls.

Ariel was horrified, but she had to summon her senses or she would die. She leapt into the air and her body quickly assumed the shape of an owl. As she took flight, a massive dark figure exploded from the mist, scattering ashes from the fire everywhere. All she could see were two glowing yellow orbs set above a large, fang-encrusted maw. An expression of rage covered the monster's snout as it closed in on Ariel, who was flapping as hard as she could to gain more height.

Her head was spinning from such a rapid shape change, however, so her reflexes were slowed. Fear overtook her as she frantically flapped her wings and moved higher. She could feel the hot breath of the monster and she heard the violent snapping of its jaws closing in on her.

A massive clawed hand tore at her, causing her to swerve and dip slightly in order to avoid being shredded. Ariel summoned every ounce of her strength and with a final flap of her wings she propelled herself away from her attacker, but not before the monster's other claw raked one of her wings. The glancing blow dislodged a few feathers and sent Ariel careening sideways.

The close call actually helped Ariel, as the blow knocked her further away from the monster and gave her room to maneuver. She changed direction and shot straight up, spiraling upward as fast as she could fly. Down below, she could hear the werewolf snarl with rage.

Once she had reached a safe height, Ariel looked down at the mist-covered landscape and clearly saw the shape of a large black beast disappear into the trees. She saw it was below, following her. Every now and then she caught a glimpse of those yellow, hate-filled eyes.

She changed her route and flew in the opposite direction, away from Geoff, Jane, and Sawyer. The werewolf howled. To Ariel it sounded like a scream of rage in the darkness. It was a sound she had heard before, but every time she heard that howl she was chilled to her core. If it was somehow able to follow her then she must lead it away from the others. Ariel flew as fast as she could; hopefully she would somehow be able to lose the werewolf.

She flew with the wind for several minutes until she reached a small clearing, then circled and peered into the misty darkness below. She watched for disturbances in the mist, but her first pass revealed nothing. Even as an owl, Ariel could feel herself tremble. She had just escaped being ripped to pieces and she was upset with herself for walking into such a dangerous situation. But she had to try to reason with her friend.

She had learned much, however. War was at hand and everything was going to change. No longer would she be able to live in her forests and let the outside world take care of itself. Ariel dropped lower and made another circle around the small clearing. Her keen owl's sight enabled her to catch a glimpse of an irregular swirl of mist along the tree line. She swooped lower for a better look. Ariel found an old oak tree and quietly landed on a branch.

Her perch was over twenty feet from the ground, which gave her plenty of time to take flight and escape danger. Her talons gripped the branch tightly and she peered into the mist below. All she could see was the thick gray mist rolling over the ground. Then she noticed the eerie silence that had fallen on the forest. The only sound was a slight breeze that blew through the trees and rolled the thick mist along

Ariel swiveled her head around and searched the mist behind her as well. She wondered if she had flown high enough and far enough to lose the werewolf. Certainly it couldn't track an owl in flight. Even a supernatural beast like a werewolf would have realized the futility of pursuing prey that could escape so easily. She swiveled her head around again, looking for any additional movement. The sensation of being watched overtook her, and a feeling of danger washed over her. She shifted nervously. A single bit of bark had become dislodged by her claws and fell to the ground.

The small piece of bark fell, tumbling through the branches and leaves. Ariel wasn't aware of the pair of yellow eyes in the mist that watched it fall to the ground and disappear into the mist. The yellow orbs slowly moved their gaze upward to the owl sitting on a limb close to the oak tree's trunk.

Without a sound, the werewolf moved closer until it was directly below the owl that sat on a branch above. Ariel swiveled her head left and right, looking all about for the creature. Suddenly the mist below her erupted and the monstrous shape of the werewolf leapt upward. The beast roared and grasped the trunk of the oak tree. It quickly scrambled up the trunk toward Ariel, ripping huge gashes in the side of the tree and sending chunks of bark and pulp flying.

Ariel was taken off guard by the sudden attack. She only caught a glimpse of those glowing eyes as the dark shape of the beast lurched its way higher up the tree toward her. Her avian instincts took over, and she instantly took flight, propelling herself into the night air again. This time, she thought, she would lead it many leagues away before returning to the others. She swooped lower, staying away from the beast's reach but close enough to maintain its attention.

The werewolf had dropped to the ground and continued to follow her, attempting to conceal itself in the mist and the darkness. Ariel's keen night vision allowed her to keep a close watch on the beast. She flew even lower, below the tree line. She knew this was risky, but she flew faster as well, as fast as she could fly. She hooted a few times, taunting the large black shape that followed her. She darted in and out of the trees as she kept circling deeper into the forest. The werewolf followed her for a mile or two, but then suddenly broke off its pursuit and changed direction. It was headed straight toward Sawyer, Jane, and Geoff.

Ariel flew as fast as her owl form could fly. She passed the werewolf and flew a mile further before landing on the forest floor and returning to her elven form. Ariel's hands trembled as she drew her scimitars. She closed her eyes and took a deep breath to steady herself.

"Alex," she said, "go away. Please go away. You are right.

There is something special about them. I do not know if they can save you—or us. But they do shine so bright, so very bright in a world full of darkness."

Ariel scanned the forest, waiting for the beast to burst through the mist-shrouded undergrowth at any moment. She looked at the trees and shrubs nearby.

"*Bar'athel envora*," chanted Ariel over and over.

Then she saw the werewolf. It was running. Sometimes it crouched on all fours, yet it also ran on two legs like a man. As she watched, it stood and raised its snout and sniffed. She continued to watch the werewolf as she chanted. It moved slowly and methodically, like the predator it was. Ariel's heart sank and she swallowed. She knew she had no hope of defeating such a creature, but she had to try to slow it down.

She saw the furry hulk moving in her direction with its eyes gleaming in the moonlight. She smelled a strong musky odor as it came closer. Her heart raced.

Perhaps the trees would be able to hold the beast long enough for me to escape, Ariel thought. She could clearly see the hair rise up on its back as it crouched very low to the ground. She watched as the beast crept closer. It stayed in the underbrush and moved silently, never taking its eyes off Ariel.

Suddenly the werewolf charged. Ariel finished her spell and she turned and dashed away as fast as she could, her graceful legs carrying her over fallen trees and rocks and through the brush. Behind her, the werewolf had become ensnared by tree limbs and vines. It roared and gnashed its teeth as it ripped and tore through its leafy attackers. Ariel dared not look behind her.

Her only concern was returning to the others and getting them as far away from these woods as possible. Soon she saw the small glade ahead of her. As she entered the weeping willow barrier, a blood-curdling howl pierced the silence of the night.

"Up!" shouted Ariel. "Now!" Sawyer, Jane, and Geoff leapt to their feet.

"Do you think we can make a stand here?" asked Sawyer, clutching the elven dagger Ariel had given him.

"No! We do not stand a chance against such a beast," said Ariel as she motioned for them to follow her. "We dare not stay a moment longer!"

Sawyer, Jane, and Geoff dashed from their sanctuary, close behind Ariel. "We will try to lose it at the Restless Serpent River!" said Ariel.

CHAPTER TEN
STORMBLADE

Sawyer heard the sounds of rushing, churning water getting closer as they followed Ariel through the forest. Jane and Geoff ran close behind Ariel, while he brought up the rear. He carried the elven dagger Ariel had given him, holding it tightly. Behind them, he thought he heard faint snarling sounds drawing nearer.

"Quickly!" shouted Ariel, motioning to the others. "Run faster!"

"How close is it?" asked Geoff as he ran, nearly tripping over a tree root as he spoke.

"Very close! Run!" said Ariel.

"I think it's coming!" cried Sawyer as he looked over his shoulder.

Up ahead, Ariel had stopped at a ledge. When the rest of them caught up, Sawyer realized what he had heard. The rushing water was a huge waterfall crashing nearly a hundred feet below. Further downstream were dangerous looking rapids. His heart sank and his stomach churned as a wave of dizziness fell over him.

"We have to jump," said Ariel. "Hurry."

"Jump down there?" asked Jane. "In the dark? Are you crazy? We could be crushed on rocks or something."

Ariel looked at Jane and pointed back toward the weeping willow glade they had just fled.

"Or you could stay here and be ripped to shreds."

Jane and Geoff stepped closer to the edge and looked down. Sawyer maintained his distance several feet away from the edge. "There has to be another way," said Jane. "Can't we just climb down?"

"I don't think so," said Geoff. "It's too dark to see where to climb."

Sawyer swallowed. Geoff's remark was not what he wanted to hear. His palms were moist. He wiped them on his jeans and looked for another route to escape the werewolf.

"Be sure to jump outward as far as you can," said Ariel as she pointed to a dark pool of water at the base of the waterfall, "and keep your arms close to your body."

Jane stepped onto the ledge and looked down again.

"This is the only way?" she asked.

"Yes," said Ariel, who was growing more anxious. "You will be fine. Jump."

A beastly howl rose from behind them. The werewolf was close. And by the sound of it; moving fast.

"Go!" said Ariel.

Jane jumped off the ledge and screamed as she fell, landing in the middle of the pool below.

"Geoff, go!" said Ariel.

Geoff stepped onto the ledge and jumped.

A deep, ferocious snarl erupted behind Sawyer. He spun around and saw the black shape of the werewolf charging.

"Sawyer! Go!" said Ariel, who had also seen the werewolf.

Sawyer swallowed again.

"You go! I'll be right behind you!" he said.

"Sawyer, you must jump now!" yelled Ariel.

"I know! Go! I'll jump after you!"

Ariel turned back to the ledge and jumped, leaving Sawyer alone.

Sawyer shivered as he grasped the cold, wet metal of the dagger's hilt. He watched as the werewolf continued to rush him, its yellow eyes flashing as it bared its sharp fangs.

Down below he could hear the others calling his name. He saw the werewolf rear up on its hind legs and lunge for him. It was so close Sawyer could detect its musty, earthy smell. He started to scream, and without even thinking, he turned and jumped off the ledge. The werewolf's large clawed hand just missing him by inches

Sawyer continued to scream as he fell. He thought he saw the others swimming to the other side of the river. He hit the water with a loud *smack*, the force of the impact causing him to lose his grip on the dagger. Since he had rushed his jump at the last moment, he had not jumped as far out from the ledge as the others. He landed much closer to the edge of the pool and was immediately swept toward the rapids by the current.

The cold rushing water turned Sawyer over and over until he was able to regain his orientation and right himself. The only sound he heard now was the roaring of the water all around him. The current tossed him about as he struggled to remain afloat. He was heading straight for a mass of tangled tree roots protruding from an overgrown bank.

Seeing his chance, Sawyer grabbed a handful of roots, slowing his momentum. He caught his breath as he came to a stop in the cold water. He looked upstream, but didn't see the others. He heard a loud sucking sound in the bank behind him. It reminded him of the sound water makes as it drains from the bathtub. Suddenly the current pulled him to the darkest part of the bank.

Sawyer noticed a large half-submerged hole in the bank. Water was flowing into the hole so fast that he was swept into it before he could react. Water sprayed him as he fell twenty feet into another pool. He struck the bottom, scraping his back on a rock. Sawyer grimaced. The water was waist-deep and frigid. He found his footing and stood up. He took a few deep breaths and immediately regretted doing so.

"Ugh! What is that smell?" Sawyer held his nose. "Smells like rotting leaves and dead fish."

Above him he could see the hole he had just fallen through. The moonlight shone down into the cavern, allowing Sawyer to see most of his surroundings when his eyes adjusted.

"Yeah," said Sawyer. "This is kinda spooky."

A large moss-covered boulder sat half-submerged in the water, partially obscuring Sawyer's view of the rest of the natural oblong-shaped cavern. Overhead was a tangle of tree roots and earth. The walls were stone and earth with moist vines settled in among the rocks.

Sawyer noticed his breath as he exhaled; the temperature was much cooler here. He waded in the waist-deep water, staying close to the walls for support. He walked to the boulder, which was almost beneath the hole he fell through. It was wet, with sickly, scrubby, half-rotten vegetation covering it.

The fetid, decaying smell was much stronger near the boulder. Sawyer coughed and covered his nose and mouth with his shirt collar.

"Oh man! What stinks? Maybe this big rock landed on something and killed it."

Sawyer walked around the boulder, looking for a way to climb on top of it.

"Here we go," said Sawyer as he brushed away a bit of moss and found some handholds. He climbed the boulder, which was ten feet high above the water. He stood and cupped his hands around his mouth.

"Ariel!"

He waited, but heard no answer.

"Ariel! Jane! Geoff!"

He frowned and lowered his arms.

"They probably can't hear me over the sound of the water. I hope they got away from the werewolf."

Sawyer shivered. He wasn't sure if it was because of the cold cavern or the beast from which he had just escaped.

"Jane!" he called again. Still no answer. Sawyer sighed and turned around, nearly slipping off the boulder.

In the far corner of the cavern something glinted in the moonlight. Something beneath the surface of the water.

"What's that?" he said aloud.

Sawyer climbed down from the boulder and stepped back into the chilly dark water. He waded his way to the other side of the cavern. C'mon, where are you? Flash again, he thought. Sawyer realized he was blocking the moonlight with his body, so he stepped to one side, placing his back against the rocky wall.

Then he saw the something glint again.

"That's something metal down there," said Sawyer.

He was startled by a low gurgling sound followed by what sounded like something growling underwater. He whirled and looked around, but the only object nearby was the smelly boulder.

"Okay, enough of this," he said out loud. "I'm scaring myself. Don't be a wuss, Sawyer."

There was another glimmer and sparkle in the water, then another. The dark, swirling water made it difficult to see, but Sawyer was able to glimpse a silvery metallic surface partially buried in the mud and rock.

"What are you?" Sawyer muttered as he made his way to the object. "Another key like Geoff's? Are you our ticket home?"

The object glittered, almost like an arc of electricity. Sawyer took a deep breath and plunged into the cold water. He saw the glimmer again and he swam closer. It was right in front of him. It wasn't a key. It looked like a metal handle or grip protruding from the muddy bottom of the pool. He reached out and grasped it. A tingling sensation pulsed through his body, but he didn't feel any pain. He pulled at the object and tried to wriggle it back and forth, but it didn't budge.

Sawyer grasped the handle with his other hand and pulled, but the object barely moved. He gathered his strength and pulled again, but his hand slipped and sank into the soft deposit, disturbing the sediment and further obscuring his view. A few seconds later, the murky water cleared. Sawyer's slip of the hand had unearthed a human skull. Startled, the last of his breath escaped his lungs and mouth. He rose up out of the water and stepped backward, gasping for air and coughing.

As Sawyer caught his breath, he looked down at the grinning face of the skull in the object's flickering light. He shivered again. Holy crap! Someone died here! Then he saw what the object was—the grip and pommel of a sword.

"Whoa...," he said. "Look at you."

He stepped closer and positioned his feet so he could use his legs to help pull the sword free.

In the darkness behind Sawyer, the boulder he had just climbed upon shuddered and rolled slightly to one side. A huge, slime-covered clawed hand rose up out of the water and grasped a stone on the edge of the stream. A massive misshapen head with a twisted nose slowly rose from the dark water and turned toward Sawyer.

Its dull, sunken black eyes opened as the creature focused on Sawyer. It stood up, rising to a height of over twelve feet. It had abnormally long slime-covered arms the size of tree trunks ending in long, slender fingers. It also had a grotesquely hunched back. It raised its head and sniffed the air to catch Sawyer's scent. Sawyer was so busy trying to pull the sword out of the mud and rock that he didn't hear it approaching.

The creature started to salivate uncontrollably. It opened its quivering mouth, revealing an uneven set of jagged gray teeth. Long, putrid strands of saliva dripped from the corners of its mouth and knobby chin. It reached out with its clawed hands and moved toward Sawyer.

The sword was slowly rising from its watery prison. It tingled in Sawyer's hands as he exerted himself one last time and pulled the blade free from the debris in the bottom of the stream. Then an electrical arc ran along its length, briefly lighting the cavern.

"Oh wow," said Sawyer, mesmerized.

The sword reminded him of the ancient ceremonial swords that adorned the walls in Geoff's house. The blade was over four feet in length and showed no signs of rust or pitting. In the pommel was a dark blue oval sapphire the size of a plum. The sword hardly weighed anything, yet its blade was straight and sharp. Another electrical discharge escaped from the sapphire, running the entire length of the blade and illuminating the room again.

The creature snarled and shielded its eyes from the sudden burst of light. Sawyer heard the snarl and whirled around in time to see the hideous creature closing in on him.

He screamed and tried to back away, but he slipped and stumbled in the muck. He held the sword up with both hands to fend off the creature. As he did so, the blade began to flash and sparkle with energy discharges.

The creature lunged at him, but missed as Sawyer ducked under its outstretched arms and dove into the water. Two powerful kicks later and Sawyer found himself behind it. He rose out of the water with a sputtering gasp and quickly turned to face the creature as it swung around and lashed out with a clawed hand. Sawyer felt a searing pain in his left shoulder as the claw ripped through his shirt and scratched him. The force of the blow sent Sawyer sprawling backward.

The back of Sawyer's head struck a submerged stone and almost knocked him unconscious. He grimaced as he struggled to regain his footing on the slippery bottom of the stream, his vision blurry and his head spinning. The creature's cold black eyes glared first at Sawyer, then the sparkling sword. It growled and moved toward Sawyer.

Sawyer screamed and ducked his head and closed his eyes, bracing for the impact of the oncoming attack. As he lifted his arms to protect himself, he raised the sword up toward the creature. It lunged at Sawyer, the blade piercing its eye as it pounced. Sawyer felt the creature shudder as it howled in pain and then stood twitching and quivering as small arcs of electricity rolled over its body for several seconds. Then it fell backward in the pool and died.

Sawyer opened his eyes and looked at the body of the creature lying half-submerged in the water. Its clawed hands rose from the water and still looked as if they were grasping for something. Sawyer wiped his face. His hand shook so much he could barely control it. He blinked several times, not sure what had just happened.

Sawyer crept over to the body. Its clawed hand was larger than Sawyer's head. The pommel and crossguard of the sword remained above the dark water. The sword remained stuck in its eye. Sawyer nudged the creature with his foot to be sure it was dead. Satisfied, he removed the sword. It no longer sparked with energy.

"All out of juice, huh?"

Sawyer glanced about again. There was no way to climb out. He found a relatively dry niche in the wall and curled up in it. He thought for several hours, but still had no idea how he was going to escape.

He sighed and wrapped his arms around himself to keep the chill away. As he did so he noticed he could see better. The cavern was starting to become brighter. He looked at the hole from which he fell. The sun's first rays were shining through the opening. The added light also brightened his spirits a little. He walked to the sunlit area beneath the hole and tilted his head back, letting the sun warm him.

"Help! Ariel! Jane! Geoff! Help!"

He listened, but didn't hear anything but the water flowing into the cavern. He cupped his hands around his mouth again and called to the others. He continued calling for help for over an hour before he heard a response. It was Geoff.

"Sawyer! Where are you?"

"Geoff! I'm down here in this hole! Are Jane and Ariel with you?!"

"No, but they're close! Hang on, I'll get them!"

Several minutes later, Geoff returned with Jane and Ariel.

"Sawyer," called Jane. "Are you okay?"

"Yeah! I'm okay," he said as he gripped the sword.

"Stay where you are," said Ariel. "We will come to you."

Sawyer heard two loud splashes in the river above, and a minute later Ariel appeared at the opening with Jane.

"There you are," said Ariel. "We feared the worst."

"Hey, guys," said Sawyer. "I found a sword and got attacked by a monster."

He pointed at the creature's carcass with the sword.

"Oh my god!" exclaimed Jane as she finally noticed the large claws protruding from the water.

"What is that thing?" she asked.

"Dunno," said Sawyer. "But it's dead now."

Ariel looked at the body. At first she didn't seem to recognize it, but a moment later she did and raised her eyebrows.

"You killed that creature?" she asked.

"Yeah. It attacked me and I stabbed it with this sword," said Sawyer.

"Come. Take hold of this tree root," said Ariel.

No sooner had she finished her sentence than a long, thick root snaked its way down into the hole and wrapped around Sawyer's waist.

"Oh no, Sawyer!" cried Jane as Sawyer emerged. "You're hurt!"

Sawyer looked at Jane and saw she was pointing at his injured left shoulder. He was still bleeding. The cold water had numbed him so much he barely felt any pain.

"Oh," said Sawyer. "Yeah, it scratched me. I'll be fine. It's not bad."

The current buffeted Jane and threatened to sweep her away. She held onto the tree root with one hand and lifted Sawyer's shirt collar to look at his wound with the other.

"No, Sawyer. This is serious. You're bleeding a lot."

"Nah. It looks worse than it really is," he said.

He was lifted out of the water, along with Ariel and Jane. The tree roots gently deposited them on the ground before returning to their normal sedentary state.

"Thanks. That was cool," said Sawyer, looking at Ariel.

"We were afraid the werewolf got you," said Geoff. "We've been looking for you for a long time."

"I'm glad you're okay," said Jane, "and didn't get eaten or anything."

"Me too," said Sawyer. "So what happened to the werewolf? It almost had me."

"We don't know," said Jane. "After you jumped it disappeared back into the forest and we didn't see it again."

Ariel walked over to Sawyer and examined his shoulder. She performed the same healing spell she used on the unicorn and immediately the pain left him. He felt warm and refreshed.

"You are lucky," she said. "Not many can singlehandedly kill a river troll."

"Well, I had this," said Sawyer, holding the sword up for all to see.

Ariel took the sword from Sawyer and looked at it. She looked as if she recognized an old friend.

"Sawyer," she said quietly, "you found this and killed the troll with it?"

"Yeah," said Sawyer. "It lunged at me and I stabbed it."

He motioned with a finger to his eye, indicating where the fatal blow landed.

"Wow!" Geoff looked at the shiny sword as it reflected the sunlight. "That is awesome! I've never seen anything like it. Ever."

"Yeah," said Sawyer. "It's really sharp. It lights up too, just like your key. Hey, you guys think there may be a connection between them?"

Geoff and Jane looked at Ariel, who was still examining the sword. Sawyer was about to repeat the question when Ariel looked at him. Why is she staring? She looks like she is surprised or sizing me up, thought Sawyer.

"Stormblade," she said quietly. "The lost sword of heroes."

Chapter Eleven
Silverthorne Manor

"Sword of heroes?" asked Jane. "What do you mean?"

Ariel held the sword high and studied it, looking over every detail of the weapon. She studied the large sapphire embedded in the hilt and the intricate etchings along the blade.

"This...is the sword of legend." Ariel stared at Sawyer. "The Stormblade had been lost for over a hundred years. How did you find it?"

"Like I said," said Sawyer, swallowing, "I was swept into that hole and found the sword in the mud. When I pulled it out that's when the monster—"

"River troll," interrupted Ariel.

Sawyer blinked and looked at her.

"Yeah, okay. The river troll attacked me and I killed it. The sword electrocuted it or something when I stabbed it in the eye."

"Just as easy as that?" asked Ariel.

Sawyer looked at the sword in her hands and nodded. "Yeah. I wouldn't call it easy, but that's what happened."

"It's beautiful! Look at the workmanship. I wonder who made it," Geoff said.

"No one knows for sure," said Ariel. "It is said the Stormblade was forged when Alluria was young. Long before men. Long before elves and dwarves."

Ariel handed the sword back to Sawyer. As he grasped the hilt she said, "By right of combat, the sword is yours. But know this: the Stormblade is an arcane weapon, carried by the greatest heroes of the realm."

Then she leaned forward and whispered, "Are you heroic?"

Before Sawyer could reply, Ariel released the sword and turned away. Sawyer held up the enchanted blade. It tingled in his hand.

"Are you mad at Sawyer?" asked Jane.

"No," said Ariel, shaking her head. "I know not how arcane weapons choose who wields them."

"Wait a minute," said Sawyer. "Are you saying this is a *magical* sword? And it *chose* me?"

Ariel nodded. "Yes. Now come. We must be at Silverthorne Manor before nightfall."

"But why? I mean…why me?" asked Sawyer.

"An excellent question," said Ariel. "I, too, am puzzled by the sword's choice."

"Sawyer," said Geoff, "can I hold it?"

"Yeah, sure. Here ya go."

Sawyer handed the sword to Geoff and fell in line behind Ariel and Jane, who had already started walking away. Geoff stumbled along behind Sawyer, studying the sword.

"Sawyer, it's so light! Look! The balance is perfect!"

Geoff stopped and balanced the sword on his index finger. "This is what they call a long sword. It's more of a chopping and thrusting weapon, but with this balance and how sharp it is, you could do anything with it."

Geoff stopped and examined the blade.

"Hey," said Geoff, "if this sword is so old and it was buried in the mud for a hundred years why is there no pitting? No damage whatsoever?"

"The enchantments on that sword protect it from damage," said Ariel, looking over her shoulder.

"Oh yeah," said Geoff. "I forgot. Magic. Cool!"

He carefully handed the sword back to Sawyer, who saw that there was a sort of reverence in the way Geoff held it, not unlike the way Ariel had handled it. Sawyer swung the sword a few times. It felt like he was simply waving his arm. The blade whistled as it sliced through the air. He held the sword up again. Wow, the sword of heroes, he thought. He noticed Ariel was watching every move, every swing he made. Sawyer lowered the sword and smiled. He felt his cheeks warm.

He noticed Ariel said nothing, but the look of disapproval on her face revealed her feelings about his possessing the sword. He quickened his pace so he was directly behind Ariel and Jane, who had started a conversation.

"So if Sawyer's sword is magic, what does it do?"

"The wielder of the Stormblade is said to control the elements themselves—if the sword allows," Ariel said.

"What does that mean?" asked Jane. "Is the sword alive or something?"

"Oh, yes," said Ariel. "It is a sentient being in its own right. However, only a handful of arcane items have been known to form a bond with their masters. It is an extremely rare thing."

"If it is alive," said Jane, "then is it dangerous?"

"Not to the Stormlord," said Ariel. "Once Sawyer proves himself and fully masters his blade, he will become the Stormlord, master of the elements."

"Whoa, whoa, whoa," said Sawyer as Jane began to giggle. "Stormlord? Sword of heroes? Master of the elements? What the heck is all that? It's just a sword I picked up. I mean…I don't want all that. I just want to get home."

Ariel stopped and turned around. She regarded Sawyer for a moment.

"Then rid yourself of it," she said. "Cast it away. It matters not to me."

Ariel turned and continued walking with Jane beside her.

"But it's really valuable," said Geoff.

"Priceless," said Ariel. "The Stormblade has been found after a hundred years and chosen its master. No one has ever declined such an honor. Until now."

Sawyer frowned. He felt trapped. It reminded him of the feeling he had when his dad forced him to play Little League sports when he was younger. He simply had no choice. The first sport he ever played was soccer. He loved the game, but he was embarrassed when he missed a penalty kick that would have won the game, which ended in a tie.

The missed attempt wasn't what actually embarrassed him; his dad did. He could still hear his dad's shouting and cursing from the sidelines, almost to the point of having to be restrained by other spectators. "If you lose, then you're a loser." That was his dad's favorite saying, and he never wasted an opportunity to berate Sawyer and point out his mistakes.

"Geoff, you think your dad would wanna buy it?" asked Sawyer, holding it out to Geoff.

"Oh heck yeah!" said Geoff, his eyes opened wide as he smiled and took the sword.

Ariel turned and looked at Sawyer.

"You would sell such a treasure?"

Sawyer stopped and looked at Ariel, whose acidic gaze cut right through him.

"Yeah, I guess so," he said. "You just said 'cast it away' I might as well get something for it. Geoff would take care of it and he knows all about swords and armor. Besides, I could use the money."

Sawyer noticed Ariel's cold, emotionless expression had returned.

"What?" he asked. "I don't want it. I'm not a hero."

"Agreed," said Ariel as she turned and resumed walking.

Sawyer shook his head and fell back in line behind Ariel and Jane. Geoff followed close behind.

They walked in awkward silence for over an hour in the morning sun before Sawyer heard Ariel say to Jane, "Tell me why you saved the unicorn from the goblins."

Sawyer was about to say something, but Jane answered, "It was the right thing to do."

Sawyer noticed Ariel quickly glanced at Jane, but she didn't say anything. They continued in silence for the rest of the morning before they heard the distant rumble of thunder. Sawyer looked up and saw the dark clouds gathering.

"Great; werewolves, trolls, and now thunderstorms," said Sawyer. "Will we ever catch a break?"

"Silverthorne Manor is not far," said Ariel. "We will be welcome there."

"Thank goodness. How much further to this Silverthorne Manor?" asked Jane.

Ariel pointed to the northwest. "Just past the next valley. The manor sits on a small hill in the village."

By midafternoon the first cool drops of rain began to fall. They didn't mind the rain, however. It refreshed them as they walked. Lightning flashed sporadically overhead and the wind began to pick up. Ariel changed direction and turned north. The others followed, matching her pace. After another half hour, the rain began to fall heavily, striking the leaves of the trees and bushes with a loud *tap tap tap*.

"How much further?" asked Jane. "We're going to get soaked!"

"Yeah," said Geoff. "Sawyer, can't you make the rain stop with this sword?"

"Just a little further," said Ariel. "Silverthorne Manor is close."

In the distance they could see the large, dark shape of a walled manor house nestled in a small village. Trails of smoke rose from small chimneys, and the warm glow of firelight peeked through the shuttered windows. The manor reminded Sawyer of a small castle, with its two turrets and a large wooden gate. With their destination in sight they sprinted toward it in the pouring rain. They found a well-traveled muddy path that led through Silverthorne Village and then sloped upward to the manor house. Streaks of muddy water ran down its length and formed small pools. Jane slipped and would have fallen face first in the mud had it not been for Sawyer's quick reaction; he reached out and caught her arm as she started to fall.

As usual, Geoff was bringing up the rear, struggling to maintain his balance, too. Being smaller, he had to take two steps for every one of theirs as they made their way.

"Geoff, are you okay?" asked Jane.

Geoff kept his eyes on the ground and nodded as he trudged through the mud. Ariel quickly reached the top of the hill and patiently waited for the others. The front gate was a formidable looking ironbound set of wooden doors twenty feet wide and just as tall. Another flash of lightning revealed a pair of large iron knockers that were mounted on the doors with heavy rings. Ariel grasped a ring and knocked five times. Sawyer was surprised by how loud each booming knock was; he had no trouble hearing them over the thunder and falling rain.

"Who lives here?" asked Jane, who was thoroughly soaked and looked miserable in the rain.

"Eben Silverthorne," said Ariel. "An old friend."

Sawyer, Jane, and Geoff shivered as they huddled together next to the front gate. Ariel looked back to the forest, her eyes searching the trees for movement. A minute after their knock they heard a scraping, grinding sound from the other side of the large, thick doors. A small rectangular opening appeared in the door as an eye slit opened and torchlight filtered through the opening.

Through the slit, Sawyer could see two beady blue eyes surrounded by a multitude of wrinkles and a gray, scraggly head of hair.

"Who is it? What do ya want?" asked an elderly voice on the other side.

"Old Thomas," said Ariel. "Greetings. It is I, Ariel. These human children are Sawyer, Jane, and Geoff. We seek shelter for the night."

At the sound of Ariel's voice the old man's blue eyes brightened.

"Ah, Ariel! It's been too long, dear. Where have you been hiding? No doubt singing and dancing in your forest, eh? And now here you are with three children. They look too young to be traveling in such weather if ya ask me."

Ariel smiled. "Then perhaps Eben will be kind enough to feed them and give them a warm bed tonight." The old, wrinkled face in the narrow opening nodded. "Aye, I believe he would," the old man said with a chuckle.

They heard the jingle of keys and the scraping of metal on metal as he unlocked the door and let them in.

"Come along. The master'll wanna see ya right away!" Thomas was a tall, scruffy, doddering old man with a wide, welcoming grin. He had a bit of a slouch to his posture, and he walked with a slight limp. His face was leathery with age and stubby whiskers protruded from his chin. He carried a crooked walking stick, which he leaned on as he limped along. His worn black cloak opened as he walked, revealing a dark blue tunic over a white shirt. His breeches were black and well kept, and he wore a pair of short black boots.

They followed the old servant into a large, rectangular courtyard. Standing in the middle was a marble fountain with a large statue of a dragon at its center. The dragon reared on its hind legs with its wings outstretched and its head facing upward to the sky. Several thin streams of water spewed upward from its opened maw. A flash of lightning revealed small, silvery specks on the dragon's scales that sparkled brilliantly against the reflections in the fountain's water.

"It's beautiful," said Jane as she passed the fountain.

"S'ppose so. Yep," said Thomas with a shrug.

When they reached the manor house, Sawyer noticed the walls were almost completely covered in ivy. It reminded him of the old ruined keep they had found by the stream.

The interior of the manor was well lit and the smell of freshly baked bread and roasting meat wafted over them as they entered. Sawyer leaned close to Jane and whispered, "That smells good. I hope they feed us 'cause I'm tired of nuts and berries." Jane smiled and nodded, and then Sawyer's stomach rumbled. He held his hand over it and made a face of mock embarrassment.

Overhead in the entry, there was a large wooden chandelier, which held what seemed like hundreds of candles that illuminated the entire room. Multiple torches burning in sconces along the walls shed light on the thick, elaborate tapestries that decorated the entry.

"Wow!" said Geoff as he walked over and looked more closely at one gaudy black tapestry with golden embroidery.

"This is awesome! Look at the artwork! It looks like a history of the kingdom or a noble family's history! It must have taken years to make."

"Geoff, don't wander off," said Jane.

Geoff turned and hurried back to join the others as they walked down the corridor toward a great hall.

When they reached the two large wooden doors that

led into the hall, Thomas grasped the handles and pushed for all he was worth. The massive doors slowly swung open, revealing a large, inviting room. More ornate tapestries hung on nearly every wall. At the far end of the great hall was a raised dais with two large wooden chairs sitting on it. In the larger of the chairs sat another old man. He appeared to be in his sixties, and he regarded them with warm gray eyes. He stood and motioned quickly with one hand for Thomas to enter with their guests.

They followed Thomas across the room to the man sitting in the large chair. Large dining tables lined the way. Sawyer thought they looked like extra-long picnic tables and benches. They appeared to be dark brown and were worn smooth from use in several spots. The tables looked wet, or even greasy. Suits of armor and weapons adorned the various alcoves of the great hall.

"My dear Ariel!" said the old man. "How long has it been? Five years, I'll wager." With those words he held his arms open wide and beckoned to her.

"My Lord Silverthorne," said Ariel as she smiled and hugged the old man.

"Too long, my old friend. It has been far too long," she said as she embraced him. The old man looked at her and smiled. "And what brings you here on a night like tonight?"

"We seek shelter for the night," said Ariel. "Is your hospitality as warm as it ever was?"

The old man threw his head back and laughed while he nodded. "Aye," he said. "The daughter of Lorne and Llywella Windsong is always welcome at Silverthorne Manor."

Sawyer glanced at Jane and smirked, then turned his

attention back to their host. He seemed over accommodating. In fact, he seemed infatuated with Ariel. He looks kinda buff, thought Sawyer. He looks like he works out. He must be strong for an old guy.

Ariel turned and motioned to them. "I happened upon these human children in Spirewood Forest. They are outlanders and have become lost. This is Sawyer, this is Jane, and the little one is called Geoff."

The old man turned to them and said with a smile, "Welcome to Silverthorne Manor. I am Eben Silverthorne."

"Thank you," said Jane, who tried to smile.

"My Lord Silverthorne," said Ariel "There are other matters that I would discuss with you. May I speak with you alone for a moment?"

The old man raised his eyebrows. "Of course, of course. Thomas, would you see to our three guests?"

Thomas nodded. "Aye, my lord. Come along, younglings. We'll find you something to eat and...maybe something dry to wear...never seen clothes like that before. Where could you be from, I wonder?"

Sawyer and Jane looked at each other and then looked at Ariel, who gave them a reassuring nod. They followed the slouchy old servant out of the great hall and up a flight of stairs.

Ariel watched them until they had left the great hall then she turned to Eben Silverthorne. "You should know we are being hunted by a werewolf. It has followed us for two days now." The smile left Eben's face as he listened to Ariel.

"A werewolf? I've never heard of a werewolf stalking

prey for so long. Do you have any idea why the beast has taken such an interest in you?"

"I cannot say for sure," said Ariel. "But this is no ordinary werewolf. This one is covered with fur as black as the night."

Eben turned and walked to his chair.

"Is it *him*?"

"Yes."

"Why would he stalk you? Surely there must be easier prey than a druid…" Eben's words trailed off. "The children you travel with…," he continued as he turned to Ariel. "He's stalking the children, isn't he? But why?"

Ariel took a deep breath and thought for a moment before answering. "He knows there is something about them, as do I. They are strangers here. Yet within each of them is a reservoir of power…and good. To elves and those with the ability to see auras, there is something special about them. They shine so bright. Their auras are as the sun."

Eben blinked and shook his head.

"I don't understand. They are children—like any other child in the village here."

"So they appear, yes," agreed Ariel. "But they have the potential to be so much more. Did you notice the sword the taller boy carried? It is the Stormblade."

"Stormblade?" Eben raised his eyebrows. "How in the name of the gods did he find it? That sword has been lost—"

"For a long time," interrupted Ariel. "Yes. He killed a river troll for the sword. How many children can accomplish such a feat?"

Eben walked to a small table upon which rested several

filled decanters. He poured wine into two pewter goblets and offered Ariel one.

"So if the Stormblade has been found," said Eben, "then Sawyer, the tall boy, is the Stormlord. And according to prophecy, we will need him."

Ariel looked up from her goblet.

"There's more. Lord Zorn has gathered a great army and marches against the free peoples of the realm," said Eben.

"I have heard," said Ariel. "One by one, our old friends return."

"What happened to Zorn? He was courageous and good," said Eben. "He was a great warrior. Only Alex matched his skill in battle. How could they have fallen so?"

"I do not know," said Ariel. "I suspect they are not the only ones to have been afflicted by evil. I believe a dark druid follows us as well, keeping just out of sight. I hope I am wrong. But if I am not, then another friend has fallen and I dread the task that lies before me."

Silence descended as they pondered the unpleasant tidings they shared.

"Bhael? Is it Bhael?"

Ariel nodded. "I cannot be sure, but that is what I suspect."

"This cannot be a coincidence," said Eben. "Not with finding the Stormblade too."

Sawyer noticed a couple of chambermaids scurrying about with buckets and brooms as they followed Thomas to their rooms. The maids smiled and curtsied as they walked past.

Jane, Sawyer, and Geoff were surprised at their room's furnishings, which consisted of large canopy beds, washing basins filled with fresh water, and finely crafted solid oak tables and chairs. Bowls of fruit sat in the middle of each table. A hot bath had been readied for them and a change of clothes was neatly laid on their beds.

"It looks like they were expecting us," said Geoff.

"Yep, looks like," said Sawyer as he flopped on a bed. "I could sleep for a week."

"Me too," said Geoff. He and Sawyer shared a room while Jane had the room next door to herself.

Sawyer and Geoff each had tunics and breeches waiting for them as well as leather boots. Geoff's boots were too big for him, however, and his feet made a slight flopping noise as he walked, so he put his soggy tennis shoes back on. His dark blue tunic and breeches were also too big for him and hung loosely from his frame.

The thunderstorm outside continued, with the pounding rain echoing throughout the manor house. Sawyer finished tucking his tunic into his breeches when out of the corner of his eye he noticed a tiny flicker of light. He glanced in that direction, but saw nothing except his sword lying on his bed. He looked at the Stormblade for a moment, trying to decide if he imagined the light.

"Sawyer? You ready to eat? What're you looking at?" asked Geoff. Sawyer looked at Geoff, "Hmmm? Oh... nothing." He gave his new attire one last inspection and then followed Geoff out of the room. Just before he closed the door behind him he looked at his sword one last time, but didn't notice anything unusual. Must have been a reflection from a candle or something, he thought. Sawyer closed the door. The smell of fresh bread and meat made his stomach growl again.

"Let's eat!" he said as he grabbed the back of Geoff's tunic. He pulled Geoff back and stepped in front of him.

"Hey!" said Geoff in protest, but by then Sawyer had opened a considerable lead to the food. As he and Geoff raced each other down the hall and around the corner, neither noticed the faint blue-white glow that was now visible from under the door to their room.

CHAPTER TWELVE
THE COMING THREAT

SAWYER AND GEOFF RACED DOWN the long hallway toward the winding staircase that led to the first floor and the great hall. Sawyer leapt onto the stairs and nearly crashed into Jane, who was trying to navigate the steps and breathe in her dress and corset. Jane had found a beautiful dark green dress on her bed, along with slippers and corset. With the help of a servant she was able to squeeze into the corset—and still manage to breathe somewhat.

"Oops! Sorry!" Sawyer said, patting Jane on the head as he dashed by. "You look great!"

"Yeah. Sorry, Jane!" said Geoff, who bounded down the stairs after Sawyer.

"Hey! Stop running, you two!" said Jane.

By the time she had finished speaking, however, both Sawyer and Geoff had already reached the bottom of the stairs and turned the corner toward the great hall. All Jane could do was take a deep breath, pull her skirt up enough so she could run, and try to catch up with them.

They reached the entrance of the great hall with Sawyer

in the lead and Geoff several paces behind. Jane brought up the rear, with her dress making swishing sounds as she ran.

"Guys! Wait!" said Jane. "I can barely breathe! This is horrible!"

"Then why are you wearing that dress?" asked Sawyer, smiling.

"Well, what else am I going to wear? They took my clothes," said Jane.

"Same here, but these tunics they gave us are comfortable," said Geoff.

Jane eyed Sawyer and Geoff for a moment. "Now why can't I have something like that to wear?"

"Because young ladies wear dresses."

The answer came from Eben Silverthorne, who was sitting at the end of a long table. Ariel was seated to his right, looking at the three of them from over the lip of her goblet as she drank. Two servant girls stood behind them with large pitchers in their hands. Jane noticed their eyes remained on Sawyer as they entered the hall. On the table sat a large turkey as well as plates of potatoes, cheese, and rough, round loaves of bread. The combined aroma of such a feast made Jane's stomach growl.

Eben motioned for them to take a seat, which they did, opposite Ariel with Jane sitting between Sawyer and Geoff.

"Help yourselves. Eat! You must be famished."

"Oh, we are! Thanks!" said Geoff as he reached for the potatoes.

Across the table, Ariel sat quietly and watched them as they launched themselves at their tasty dinner.

"Ariel tells me you wield the Stormblade," Eben said as he looked at Sawyer.

Sawyer tried to speak, but his mouth was full of turkey and bread so he simply nodded.

"He found it in a cave," said Jane. "He killed a large monster. What was it? A river troll?"

"Indeed?" said Eben, raising his eyebrows. "A river troll is a formidable enemy. I admire such bravery. Well done, young man! Or should I say Stormlord?"

He raised his goblet to Sawyer. The others did the same. Jane noticed Sawyer's cheeks were a little pink. He was never embarrassed before, she thought. He likes all the attention he always receives at school. She took a bite of turkey. It was greasy and had little flavor, but she didn't care; she was hungry enough to eat whatever was placed in front of her. She shoveled a chunk of potato into her mouth and nearly swallowed it whole.

"Perhaps tomorrow, when you are rested," Ariel said to Sawyer, "we can spar? I would like to see your skills with the blade."

Sawyer stopped chewing and the blood seemed to rush from his features. He had a mouthful of turkey and had to swallow twice before answering.

"Um, yeah. Sure."

"I too would like to see the Stormlord in action," said Eben, lightly beating the table with his fist. "But I'm afraid I have duties elsewhere. Try not to harm her, okay? But beware, she is quick as lightning with her blades! Ha!"

"We've seen her fight. Yes, she is fast," said Jane, expecting to see Sawyer squirm more.

"Yeah, she's awesome!" said Geoff.

The meal disappeared in short order, with Sawyer, Jane, and Geoff each eating seconds and Sawyer inhaling a third serving of turkey. Jane felt a low rumble in her stomach. Uh-oh, she thought. She hoped she wouldn't get sick from eating so much. The young serving girls made sure no cup was empty. One girl had a dark red wine for Eben and Ariel, and the other filled the rest of the cups with cold water.

"Thank you again for this meal and letting us stay here," said Jane.

Eben looked at her and smiled. "You're quite welcome. I haven't had many visitors in recent years. It's good to have guests again." Eben turned to Sawyer. "Tell me, have you conjured the power of the tempest yet?"

Sawyer looked confused for a moment. "No, I'm afraid not."

"Sawyer has only possessed the Stormblade for a short time. Perhaps such powers will eventually come to him," said Ariel.

"Indeed," said Eben as he regarded Sawyer. After they had finished their meal Ariel and Eben remained in the great hall while Sawyer, Jane, and Geoff went to their rooms.

"I'm stuffed," said Sawyer as they made their way up the stairs.

"Me too," said Jane. "I ate way too much. I'm just glad to eat something other than berries and fruit."

"Get some rest, Sawyer," said Jane with a smirk. "You have a big day tomorrow."

"Yeah," said Sawyer. "I gotta get my butt kicked by Ariel."

Geoff snickered.

"She just wants to embarrass me," said Sawyer.

"Maybe she will show you some of her elven ninja tricks with the sword," said Geoff.

"Yeah, right. Whatever," grumbled Sawyer.

"A little humility may be just what you need, *Stormlord*," Jane said with a smile. "Good night, guys."

She opened the door to her room and immediately began to remove her corset. As she readied herself for bed, Jane realized it was good to breathe deeply again and she was exhausted. She crawled under the blanket and was soon fast asleep. Outside, somewhere in the distance, a wolf howled in the night.

The next morning after breakfast, Ariel led Sawyer, Jane, and Geoff to a small, flat clearing in the woods just outside the village.

"Before we begin…," said Ariel. "Have you ever held a sword in your hand?"

"Yeah, sure I have," said Sawyer, glancing at Geoff for support.

"And until the day when you slew the troll, had you ever used a sword in combat?"

Sawyer felt warm. Ariel circled him like a shark about to attack. A small bead of sweat ran down his temple.

"Well?" said Ariel.

Sawyer shook his head.

"I see," said Ariel as she pursed her lips and looked at the ground.

"It isn't his fault," said Jane. "We don't have sword fights and trolls and unicorns and—"

"And elves and orcs," finished Ariel. "Oh, you do not have those where you come from, either. You had already mentioned that. But you are not home, are you?"

As Sawyer watched, Ariel walked to an old oak tree on the other side of the clearing and produced two wooden practice swords that had been hidden behind it. She gave one to Sawyer.

"Now," she said, "show me how you killed the river troll."

Sawyer swallowed.

"Well, first it was behind me and then it came at me and clawed me and then I just swung at it, like this."

He held his makeshift weapon up and swung it much like he would swing a baseball bat. But before his swing ended, Ariel had made a single flip of her wrist and disarmed Sawyer, sending his practice weapon flying. Then she pointed her wooden sword at Sawyer's chest.

"I do not think so," she said. "A river troll may be large and stupid, but it is deceptively fast and very strong. Such an attack would have been futile."

Sawyer's hands were moist and his heart beat fast. He knew she was going to humiliate him. He wished Jane and Geoff were not there.

"How did you manage to thrust your blade through the troll's eye? An attack that precise is difficult for even the most accomplished warrior," Ariel said.

Sawyer retrieved his wooden sword and sighed.

"Okay, okay," he said. "I don't know how I did it. It just lunged at me and I held the sword up. It was luck. That's all."

Ariel took a step closer, and Sawyer looked into her green eyes. Her stern, emotionless expression had returned.

"Now," she said, "we can begin your training. We will start with how to properly hold a sword."

"Hey, wait a minute," said Jane. "Training? For what? I thought we were going home. We are going home, aren't we?"

"The Stormblade is known throughout the realm," said Ariel. "Sawyer should at least learn how to use it. Others will seek it for themselves, even kill for it."

"Whoa, wait a minute," said Sawyer. "Kill for it? Kill *me*? Now I really don't want the sword. Take it and go find another Stormlord guy. I'm not the one."

"Yes," said Ariel. "You are."

"Why don't you take it, Ariel?" asked Geoff.

Ariel shook her head. "The sword did not choose me."

"Well, it can choose again," said Sawyer, throwing his practice sword down. "I'm not doing this."

"Sawyer, pick up your sword," said Ariel as she positioned herself so her face was inches away from his. "What I have to teach you may save your life."

He looked into her green eyes. Finally he understood what she was trying to do. She had no intention of embarrassing him. Instead, she was going to teach him how to defend himself with a sword. She's serious. This could be a good thing, he thought.

"Why are you helping me?" said Sawyer.

"Hey. Hello. When do we get to go home?" asked Jane. "You said when we got to Silverthorne Manor we could go home."

"No," said Ariel. "I said I would escort you here. What happens to you now is up to Eben Silverthorne." Ariel looked at Sawyer and raised her chin. "I am helping you because if I do not, you will never survive."

Silence fell over the clearing as they contemplated Ariel's words.

"But if we go home," said Geoff, "we're safe, right? I mean, we won't be here, so we won't get eaten by a troll or a werewolf, right?"

Ariel turned away from Sawyer and walked toward Geoff and Jane.

"In order for us to return you to your home," she said, "we need a wizard's key and an arcane portal. We have neither, so while you are here you may as well learn to defend yourselves."

"Doesn't Eben have a key or an archway?" asked Jane.

"No," said Ariel.

Another moment of silence followed.

"Okay," said Sawyer as he raised the wooden sword he had just picked up. "I'm ready. Let's do this."

"You need to know that learning how to cast spells or how to use a sword requires discipline and study. You may have talent, but that is not enough. If I am to instruct you, then I expect complete dedication from you."

Ariel spent the rest of the morning and most of the afternoon teaching Sawyer the correct way to hold a sword as well as how to swing it and thrust with it. Sawyer listened to every word Ariel said, as if she were his football coach.

She introduced him to the guards and stances all warriors must master, along with the basic footwork. But Sawyer struggled to remember them. He remembered only one, the "ox" stance. When they sparred, Sawyer always received a crack on a knuckle or a swift strike to the stomach or back.

Ariel moved effortlessly as they sparred. She leapt

over and around Sawyer and dodged his strikes with ease. Sawyer thought she was a gymnast at times, because she was so graceful.

"How do you do that? That's awesome! Will you teach me how to move and fight like that?" he asked.

"Perhaps. After you have learned the basics of human swordsmanship," Ariel said as she disarmed him again and gave him a whack on the rear with her wooden sword.

Jane and Geoff snickered. Ariel walked over to Jane and leaned on her wooden sword.

"And now," she said, "perhaps you would like to learn a spell?"

Jane leapt up from her spot in the tall grass.

"Yes, yes," she said. "Can I? I'd love to! But *can* I cast spells?" A grin spread across her face.

"We shall see. You will need to learn the magical qualities of each plant, each tree of the forest," said Ariel. "Certain spells require specific materials."

Jane nodded. "I understand."

"Excellent. Gather some basic components. A few oak leaves, a handful of green grass, and a few cherry blossoms."

"Okay, I will! Thank you!" said Jane. She turned and was about to dash off, but Ariel stopped her.

"Wait. Geoff, you accompany her. Do not leave each other's sight."

"All right!" said Geoff. "I'm on it! C'mon Jane! Woo- hoo!"

Jane and Geoff ran into the forest as fast as they could. Geoff scanned the ground for lush clumps of green grass while Jane searched for oak leaves and cherry trees.

"Oh, this is gonna be so cool!" shouted Geoff. "Hey, Jane, what spells do you want to learn?"

Jane stopped and thought for a minute before answering.

"I don't think I have a choice. Whatever she wants to teach me I'll learn. I guess I'll just have to trust her."

"Yeah," said Geoff. "So we trust her now, right? We've kinda been through a lot together, haven't we?"

Jane looked at Geoff. My goodness he's right, she thought. They had some close escapes with Ariel. Without Ariel, they would not have survived this long in this world.

"Yes, we have," she said quietly. "Didn't you say we had no choice but to trust Ariel?"

"Yeah, I guess," said Geoff.

Suddenly a dreadful feeling came over Jane and her newfound enthusiasm faded, as did her smile.

"Geoff," she said as she picked up a handful of oak leaves, "what if we can't get back home? We could be stuck here forever."

"Jane you can't think like that," he said. "We're gonna get home."

"Back at school," said Jane, "a lot of people thought you were just a little nerd. But now I see that you're actually really cool. I never understood why everyone picked on you. Sawyer and his jock buddies picked on you a lot, didn't they?"

Geoff nodded and then lowered his head a little.

"Yeah, I'm used to it by now...I guess. I don't expect an apology or anything. He's Sawyer. It's what he does."

"Well, he should apologize," said Jane. "And those bullies should leave you alone."

"Yeah," said Geoff. "But we gotta work on getting home first."

"You know," said Jane with a frown, "I just realized we aren't any closer to going home. What if we don't find the key? And even if we did find it, Ariel says we need to find an archway, too."

"We're gonna be okay," said Geoff. "We have Ariel. You've seen what she can do. She can handle anything."

Jane laughed. "Where did that come from?"

"Well," said Geoff, "she's a druid. A badass."

Jane laughed.

"Badass," she repeated. "She is, isn't she?"

"Oh yeah," said Geoff. "Don't worry, Jane. We're gonna be all right. We'll get home soon."

Jane sighed.

"I hope so. I really do."

She felt better about their situation after listening to Geoff.

"Okay, I think I have enough grass," said Geoff. "Have you found your leaves and stuff yet?"

"No," said Jane. "We better hurry before Ariel changes her mind."

"Yeah. Good idea," said Geoff.

After another ten minutes of searching, Jane and Geoff returned carrying the items Ariel had instructed them to locate. "Okay," said Geoff. "We got the stuff you told us to get. What's next?"

Jane held her hands out and displayed a mix of cherry blossoms, grass, and oak leaves.

"Yes," said Ariel as she examined the contents of Jane's hands. "These will do nicely."

"Jane, use your pouch to hold your components," said Ariel. "I will teach you about their properties soon. I must continue with Sawyer because he is in dire need of training."

"Huh?" said Sawyer. "What? I—"

"Cannot even hold onto your weapon," said Ariel. "How many times have I disarmed you? Jane is a natural healer. You are not a warrior, not yet. But you could be if you work at it."

Jane smiled and looked at Sawyer. His eyebrows were raised and his mouth had dropped open.

"Again, your grip is all wrong. You swing your sword like a club and your balance is nonexistent. Do you remember what happened when we began your training?"

"Oh! I do!" said Jane with a giggle. "He dropped his sword."

Jane looked at Sawyer. He had narrowed his eyes and was glaring at her. Jane smiled as broadly as she could.

"Yes," said Ariel. "Such a mistake should never happen to a warrior."

"Well…like you said…," said Sawyer, "I'm not a warrior. Besides, we don't need swords back home."

Ariel walked up to Sawyer and looked him in the eyes.

"Again, you are not home."

Jane watched as Sawyer stood at attention and swallowed, he hung on every word she said.

"You must ask yourself this," said Ariel. "In a sword fight, can I kill someone?"

Sawyer winced and shook his head. "I don't know."

"Because, I assure you, they will try to kill you. Expect no quarter from your foe. You appear to have some athletic ability, but that will not keep you alive."

Sawyer stood in silence. To Jane he looked like he had been called into the principal's office at school. She felt a little sorry for him.

"You somehow managed to slay a river troll and win the Stormblade," said Ariel. "Whether that was luck or fate I do not know. However, if you are to be the Stormlord you will have to grow up."

Sawyer nodded.

"I will give you time to consider what I have said."

Ariel turned and walked to the campfire.

"I don't need any time," said Sawyer. "I'm ready. I am. I don't know how to fight with a sword, and at the moment I can't tell you that I can kill someone. The truth is I hope I don't ever have to, but your world is dangerous. I know this sword is a weapon and not a toy. I want to learn how to use it so I can help you protect us, and maybe protect others."

Jane wasn't sure how Ariel would react to his answer, but she was sure Sawyer meant it. He had never spoken so passionately about anything.

Ariel turned back to Sawyer.

"I did not think I would hear such an answer from a young human. Perhaps it was fate that dropped you in that dark hole with the Stormblade," she said.

Jane watched as Ariel took out one of her scimitars and showed Sawyer the differences between her weapon and his long sword.

Jane watched Sawyer and Ariel. He was totally focused on learning swordplay. He looks very serious, she thought.

Ariel provided a small lunch that consisted of berries, bread, and water. She sat beside Jane and ate while Sawyer, after wolfing down his portions, continued practicing the techniques Ariel showed him.

"Balance," called Ariel. "Maintain your balance at all times."

"Oh, yeah. Okay," said Sawyer.

Jane and Ariel watched Sawyer for a minute before Jane spoke.

"How is he doing for a beginner?"

"Not bad," said Ariel with a nod. "I admire his tenacity. It will serve him well in battle."

"Battle?" said Jane. "Are we going into battle?"

"I hope not," said Ariel. "But these are dangerous times."

"In that case," said Jane, "you got any more swords?"

Ariel smiled.

"I think we will choose a different weapon for you," she said. "After all, you are a natural healer."

"What sort of weapon?"

"I am not sure yet."

"Okay," said Jane. "How about I concentrate on healing and leave the killing to you and Sawyer?"

"I think that is an excellent suggestion," said Ariel.

She lay down on her stomach in the grass beside Jane and motioned for her to do the same.

"What? What are we doing?" asked Jane.

"I will teach you how to mend small plants. Look here."

Ariel pointed to a wild tulip with a bent stalk. It was crumpled and was missing a few of its deep red petals.

"Watch," said Ariel as she placed an index finger on the broken stalk.

"*Ehlia talo.*"

The broken stalk straightened and the tulip grew a few more inches. What was once a dying flower had become healthy and robust, displaying vibrant colors.

"Wow! It even grew!" said Jane.

She looked at Ariel. The elven druid was smiling at her reaction to the wondrous event.

"Yes. That spell will also help a plant grow and invigorate it," said Ariel. "Look, there is another. Now you try."

Jane looked where Ariel indicated. There rested another trampled tulip, this one sporting deep lavender petals.

"Place your finger on the stalk," said Ariel.

Jane did so.

"Now concentrate on the flower and speak the minor charm of healing, *Ehlia talo*."

Jane took a deep breath and studied the tulip. She hoped her spell would work.

"*Ehlia talo*."

As soon as she finished the last syllable the lavender tulip straightened and flourished just like its deep red cousin had done.

Jane laughed aloud. A warmth flowed over her, lifting her spirits.

"I did it! Did you see that?"

"Yes," said Ariel. "Well done."

"Did what?" asked Sawyer, who had stopped his sword practice and walked over to Jane and Ariel. He was breathing hard and sweating.

"Look, Sawyer," said Jane. "I made that flower grow."

"Yeah? That's pretty cool! Can you use those spells back home? If so, you could open your own florist shop."

"Smart aleck," said Jane.

She turned to Ariel. "That's a good question. Will these spells work when we go home?"

"I do not know," said Ariel. "But I do not see why not. Remember, the power of spells comes from within you."

"Oh, I hope so," said Jane. "I could heal sick pets and make plants grow all over."

"I'd say you got that spell down," said Sawyer.

An exciting thought suddenly occurred to Jane. She looked at Ariel, her eyes wide.

"Hey, can I heal people too? I mean, with different spells? Can you teach me how to cure diseases?"

"Yes," said Ariel. "You would make a wonderful healer, I think."

"Can I save someone from dying? You know, bring them back?"

Jane spoke so fast in her excitement that she wasn't sure if Ariel understood her rapid questions.

"No," said Ariel. "The ability to return someone to life lies with a greater power. You cannot return the dead to life, but so long as breath remains in their body, you can save them."

Jane nodded and looked at her lavender tulip again. "Yeah, I guess you're right. I want to learn every healing spell there is. Will you teach them to me? All of them?"

"I will," answered Ariel. "But you should know some spells you will learn may exact a price from you. Weaken you."

"Can casting spells kill me?"

"Only if you use the last remaining energy within you. Then your spirit will depart from your body."

"How many spells will I be able to cast before I get weak?"

"That," said Ariel, "only you will know. There are limits to magic. Each druid has their own limitations according to their inner strength."

"You better not go crazy, then, Jane," said Sawyer. "You don't want to kill yourself over a flower garden or something."

"But I don't feel weak," observed Jane. "I feel like I just did something good."

She smiled at Sawyer and Ariel. "Actually, I feel great."

Ariel leaned forward and smiled. "As did I when I cast my first spell."

"Hey, Jane," said Sawyer. "The next time I get hurt playing football, could you throw a healing whammy on me?"

Jane laughed. "I don't know. You heard Ariel. It may take too much out of me.

"Come," said Ariel. "That is enough for one day."

"Hallelujah," said Geoff as he jumped up from a comfortable spot under the oak tree. "I'm hungry. Ariel, will you show me how to fight with a sword too?"

"No," said Ariel. "Not with a sword. But perhaps you and Jane would like to learn about this."

Ariel unsheathed a dagger from her belt and held it up.

"Aww, man," said Geoff. "I want to fight with a sword."

"I think you are better suited for something smaller," said Ariel. "At least for the moment."

"But I like swords," said Geoff.

"Perhaps one day I will teach you," said Ariel. "But for now, use this. It is my last dagger."

"Oh, all right," said Geoff as he took the dagger from Ariel.

They returned to Silverthorne Manor as the evening sun was setting.

Sawyer noticed worried servants whispering among themselves and hustling about. He looked at Ariel, who also spotted their strange actions.

"Go and prepare for dinner," said Ariel. With that, she walked toward the great hall.

"What's happening?" asked Jane.

"Dunno," said Sawyer.

"I'm going to wash up," said Jane.

Jane turned and went upstairs while Sawyer and Geoff stayed in the hall.

"Geoff," said Sawyer in a quiet voice, "I think something's going on."

"What?" asked Geoff.

"I'm not sure," said Sawyer. "Look around. People seem worried, even scared."

Geoff looked about, watching the other residents of the manor.

"Yeah," he said. "I think you're right."

"Well, I guess we'll find out soon enough. C'mon, we better get cleaned up too," said Sawyer.

They went upstairs to their room. Two water basins and jugs rested on a table. Sawyer tossed the Stormblade on his bed and went straight for the basins.

"Wow, it gets dark fast here," said Geoff, looking out the window.

"Yeah," said Sawyer as he dunked his face into the cool water in the basin.

"Sawyer, what's that?" asked Geoff.

Sawyer looked at Geoff, who was pointing to his bed. A strange blue-white glow was coming from the Stormblade. Sawyer didn't say anything. He motioned for Geoff to stay put while he slowly walked to the bed. Something is wrong, he thought. He grasped the sword and felt an abrupt jolt. He slowly unsheathed it. It pulsed with a small arc of electricity that traveled the length of the blade.

Sawyer examined the sword for a moment, and then he touched the large sapphire.

A sense of doom overwhelmed him. Danger was near. In his mind he could see the dark forest surrounding Silverthorne Manor, but he was running. Running through the forest. He ran fast. Faster than a man could run. He felt the cool evening air rushing through his thick black fur. He was drawing closer. Closer.

Geoff watched Sawyer grip the sword and fall into a trancelike gaze.

"Sawyer...," he said. "Sawyer...what is it? Are you okay?"

Sawyer didn't answer. His brown eyes had rolled up in his head. Geoff inched closer to Sawyer and poked Sawyer's arm. "Sawyer?"

Sawyer still didn't respond. Geoff had never seen Sawyer like this. He mustered all of his courage and pushed Sawyer's shoulder. "Sawyer!"

Sawyer snapped out of his trance. "Geoff, we're in danger! It's coming for us!"

Geoff jumped back, startled by Sawyer's actions. "What? What's coming, Sawyer?" Sawyer looked at his sword again and then back at Geoff.

"I saw it again, Geoff. It was huge...and it wants *us*." Geoff stepped back, barely managing to keep his balance by grasping the arm of a nearby chair.

"What wants us? Is it the...werewolf?"

Sawyer nodded. "We have to warn the others!"

CHAPTER THIRTEEN
BATTLE AT SILVERTHORNE MANOR

JANE HAD ALREADY REMOVED HER sandals and started the lengthy process of removing her corset, which she wore on the outside of her dress like one from the Middle Ages. She was fumbling with the laces when Sawyer and Geoff burst into her room.

"Oh!" she gasped. "You guys! What are you doing? Are you crazy?"

She glared at them. She wasn't amused by their intrusion, nor was she in the mood for their practical jokes or horseplay.

"Jane! We're in trouble," said Sawyer. "We need to warn Ariel. We're no longer safe here!"

The look in Sawyer's eyes and the slight quaver in his voice confused her. Geoff grabbed her hand. "Jane! The werewolf is coming! It's close! We gotta tell the others! We gotta hide!"

Jane looked at Geoff then back at Sawyer.

"How do you know…," her words trailed off as she saw the look of urgency in their eyes. Geoff's hand trembled in hers. They were genuinely frightened.

"Please, Jane! Let's go!" begged Geoff as he pulled her toward the door.

"Jane, it's true. The werewolf is coming closer every second," insisted Sawyer.

"I don't understand. How do you know?" she said with a quick shake of her head.

"The sword," said Sawyer, holding it up. The blue-white glow and electrical arcs had stopped. "It warned me. I don't know how to explain it, Jane. It just sorta...showed me that we were in danger. For a moment I was a huge, ferocious werewolf running through the forest. I knew our scents. It's coming, Jane. It's coming for us. I felt it."

Jane studied Sawyer for another moment then said, "This better not be a joke, because it's not funny."

"It's no joke! The werewolf is close!" Sawyer's eyes never wavered.

"Please, Jane!" said Geoff again. This time he was almost in tears.

"Okay," she said. "Let's go tell Ariel and Eben!" With that, they dashed out the door.

Eben and Ariel were just leaving the great hall when Sawyer, Jane, and Geoff came charging around the corner running as fast as they could.

"Ariel! It's coming! The werewolf is coming!" shouted Geoff.

They stopped in front of Ariel and Eben and started to speak at once. Ariel held up her hand for silence and they quieted down.

"Now, what is it?" she asked. Geoff, who was a bit winded from trying to keep up with Sawyer, was the first to speak. "The werewolf is coming. It's coming...to get us!"

Ariel raised her eyebrow slightly. "Yes. We knew it was following us, but we are safe here. Why are you so alarmed?"

"Sawyer saw it!" said Geoff as he pointed at Sawyer.

Ariel turned her attention to Sawyer. "Is this true? Where did you see it?"

Sawyer took a deep breath. "I didn't actually *see* the werewolf. It was like I was looking through its eyes as it ran…the sword showed me."

Ariel looked at Eben.

"The Stormblade showed you the werewolf was coming?" asked Eben in a slow, deliberate tone.

Sawyer nodded. "Yes. I think the sword was telling me we're all in danger. The sword was glowing when Geoff and I returned to our room after dinner. And when I touched it, I saw the werewolf running through the forest. It was huge and had black fur. It's the same one…"

The look on Eben's face became grim. He looked at Ariel and then turned and shouted, "Thomas! Rouse the guards! Secure the gates and walls! Nothing and no one gets in tonight! I need my armor!" The old caretaker, who had come to see what the noise in the corridor was all about, nodded and hurried away.

Eben looked at Ariel, "As much as your magic and weapons would be sorely needed, I think it would be best if you and your companions leave while you can. Use the secret route through the catacombs."

"No, Eben. I will fight at your side."

"And if we cannot stop the beast? What of them?" asked Eben as he motioned toward the three teenagers.

Jane was confused. "Wait," she said. "Aren't we all in danger?" She looked at Ariel and then Eben. "Aren't we?"

"We are," agreed Eben. "But for reasons I do not know the beast stalks you. Heed my words. If what Sawyer Stormlord says is true, death hunts you this night."

Eben turned to Ariel. "You must get these three safely away. We will stop the beast...or die trying."

Jane shivered. She thought she saw Ariel's eyes well up slightly as she met Eben's gaze. Eben shook his head. "Whatever happens here will happen whether you are with us or not. Now go. Quickly."

Ariel nodded and raised her chin. "Then allow me to leave you with a druid's blessing, old friend."

Eben frowned and shook his head. "Oh, very well. But be quick about it. I know how you druids love long, drawn-out spells and charms. I have a werewolf to do battle with. Now hurry up."

Ariel managed a slight smile as she placed her right hand on Eben's chest and closed her eyes. "*Eth'nara ban'ethel lo'gara nee'salar.*"

Eben tilted his head to one side and raised an eyebrow. "Happy now?" Ariel looked at him and forced a quick smile as she nodded.

"Good. Now if you will excuse me, I need to prepare to defend my home." Then he turned to the others. "You three go and pack your things and take whatever supplies you wish. Go!"

Sawyer, Jane, and Geoff ran back to their rooms to gather their things. When they rounded the corner Sawyer and Geoff disappeared up the stairs while Jane had to stop and untangle her dress, which had become wrapped around an iron gothic- looking door handle. As she freed herself she overheard Eben and Ariel speaking.

"In all the years I have known you, you have never been so dedicated to a human, let alone three human children. You're taking a tremendous chance, Ariel. Are they worth it? What makes them special?"

"I am not sure. I cannot explain it, but there is something about them. I sense it. I can see their auras. I think they possess power. Perhaps they can help us, but they have no idea of their potential."

"And if they do have power," said Eben, "what can they do? How can they possibly help us stand against the Shadowlord? After all, they're only children."

"They are more than children. Perhaps these three outlanders may well deliver us from darkness."

Eben took a deep breath. "I have never heard you speak so well of anyone." They looked at each other for a moment, saying nothing.

"Very well. Go. The beast will not harm you or your friends. Not here. Not this night."

Jane peeked around the corner just in time to see Ariel embrace Eben and whisper, "Thank you."

Upstairs, Sawyer and Geoff wasted no time in changing and throwing their tunics along with an extra blanket or two in their newly furnished knapsacks. Geoff watched Sawyer's hands. They were shaking. "Sawyer…," he said. Sawyer stopped, closed his eyes, and hung his head. Then he pinched the bridge of his nose and sighed.

"Sawyer," Geoff said again, "are you…"

"Yeah, I'm fine," said Sawyer without looking up. "At the waterfall. I saw it up close. I thought I was gonna die."

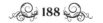

"Why didn't you jump with the rest of us? What took you so long to jump, Sawyer?"

"Heights," said Sawyer. "I'm afraid of heights."

Geoff looked at Sawyer for a minute longer. "Okay. I'll go and check on Jane and make sure she's ready to leave," he said. "I wish I had a gun with silver bullets."

"Geoff, you don't understand. The thing's really big. It isn't like any of the werewolves you've seen on TV or at the movies." Sawyer raised his head and looked at Geoff. "It's a monster, Geoff. A real monster. And it's coming. Coming for us."

Geoff's smirk faded away and a feeling of anxiety rushed over him. He saw that Sawyer was frightened by what the sword had shown him.

"Sawyer," said Geoff, "why is it after us? What did we do to it?"

"I don't know, Geoff. I just don't know. C'mon, let's get outta here."

They picked up their full packs and hurried out the door. Jane was just leaving her room when Sawyer and Geoff nearly ran into her. Jane was dressed in her jeans, tennis shoes, and blouse.

"Got everything, Jane?" asked Sawyer.

Jane nodded. "Here. A maid brought us some food," she said as she handed a sack to Sawyer.

"Let's go. Hurry," said Sawyer.

Shouts of men preparing for battle resonated throughout the keep. Armor clattered and weapons clanged as guards equipped themselves and hustled to their posts. Their heavy footsteps echoed like drumbeats. Servants were scurrying from room to room closing shutters and locking doors.

They could also hear shouts from the guards outside as they worked to secure the main gate and walls. Ariel and Eben were waiting at the bottom of the stairs.

"Got everything?" Eben asked. He looked at all three of them as they nodded. "Good. Listen carefully; this is important." He placed a hand on Sawyer's shoulder and leaned forward.

"Beneath this manor is an escape route through the catacombs. Ariel knows the way, so you stay close to her and do not wander."

He paused and looked into their eyes and continued. "Don't worry. Heed Ariel's words and you'll be fine." He gave them a quick nod and pointed back down the hall to the great room, "Go. I need to speak with Ariel." Without a word, they obeyed and ran to the great room.

Eben turned to Ariel. "Take care. Alas, I haven't been in the catacombs for several years. I don't know what—if any— strange creatures now call it home."

Ariel unsheathed her twin scimitars and held them out to Eben. "This werewolf can only be harmed by enchanted weapons and spells. Take these. Protect yourself and your men."

He shook his head. "Keep your elven blades. I'm no damn good with them anyway. Get to Chalon and tell Lionel what you have seen and heard. Tell him to prepare for war before it's too late. Keep safe."

Ariel held out a hand. "Your sword. Give it to me."

He drew his sword and handed it to Ariel. She knelt on both knees and held the sword in front of her. She slowly ran her slender hand along the length of the blade and chanted, "*La'olonara telna seda ith ruln del nuvale ith ruln anath*" over and over until the blade of the sword began to glow with a faint green hue. Ariel stood and handed the sword back to Eben. "This is the best I can do. I will not flee and leave you defenseless. The enchantment will last until dawn."

He looked at his newly enchanted sword and then at Ariel and smiled. "Harrumph! Well, at least that wasn't as long as your usual spells. Thank you. Now go. I have preparations to make. The beast will not get past us this night. That much I promise you."

Ariel kissed him on the cheek and smiled. Eben didn't say a word; he simply nodded and turned away. Ariel hurried to the great room, where Sawyer, Jane, and Geoff were waiting. The windows were shuttered and locked. Along the walls torches were being lit by servants. Ariel walked to them and took a deep breath. "Remember, stay close to me. Do not stray, and be alert. I do not know what dangers we may find in the darkness of the catacombs."

Sawyer and Jane looked at each other for a moment then back at Ariel. Jane swallowed and said, "Okay. We're ready."

"Let's go," said Sawyer. The corners of Ariel's mouth slowly turned upward, revealing her attractive dimples. "To the catacombs then."

Ariel walked to the far wall and ran her fingers along a specific section of the stonework. As she did so, a loud click echoed in the great room. A stone door in the wall slowly swung open and a horrible stench overcame them.

"Oh! Oh my! What is that? I'm going to be sick!" cried

Jane, as she covered her mouth and nose with one of her hands and stepped back.

"It stinks!" said Geoff as he stepped backward too. Sawyer held the collar of his tunic over his nose. While he looked into the dark opening, Ariel reached into a pouch and removed a gem the size of a plum. She held it overhead and said, "*Iluminara.*" The gem began to glow a bright green. She ducked inside and surveyed the passage, then motioned for the others to follow. Sawyer was next to enter, then Jane, still covering her mouth and nose, with Geoff close behind. The passage itself was a rough-hewn, dank gap through solid stone that led into darkness.

Outside the manor, the torrential rain ceased to fall. The moon peeked through the clouds, shedding a pale glow over Silverthorne Manor. At the rear gate, two guards had just finished placing a large, iron-shod bound beam across the heavy wooden doors. "There. That'll do 'er," said the elder of the two guards. "Yer wife and children'll be happy to know yer safe now." The younger guard grunted. "Any idea what this is about?"

The older guard just shook his head and answered, "Nah. Just do as yer told and keep yer eyes open."

"Keep my eyes open for what? No damn thing's gonna get through these gates 'cept a full army with a battering ram. A large battering ram."

"Aye, but we have our orders, so we stay up all night patrolling the grounds and—"

The older guard saw movement out of the corner of his eye, something behind his younger comrade. The large gate slowly moved inward, as if someone was trying to gauge its strength.

"What? What is it? Have ye gone daft, old man?" The young guard rubbed his black scraggly whiskers and turned away from the gate.

The older guard held up his hand for quiet, and then slowly stepped toward the gate they had just barred. He thought he heard heavy breathing and a growl, but he wasn't sure. Maybe his eyes and ears were playing tricks on him. After all, he was the eldest of the guards and his eyesight wasn't what it used to be. He stepped close to the gate and peered through a crack between the large wooden doors.

Just as he did, the gate suddenly and violently lurched inward. The beam that secured the gate cracked and groaned from the pressure, nearly splitting from the force marshalled against it. The old guard was struck by the gate and fell over backward, his head striking the ground. A deep, vicious growl came from the darkness beyond the gate.

"What the hell?" said the younger guard as he drew his sword.

Holding his head, the old guard struggled to his feet and drew his weapon.

"Alarm!" yelled the older guard. "Something's tryin' to break down the rear gate! We need help! Hurry!"

The younger guard stepped toward the gate and examined the damaged beam that barred it.

"By the gods! It's nearly broken in two! What could've done this? What did you see, old man? What's out there?" he demanded.

"I…I…dunno…something was out there. Something big…and then…" The old man's voice trailed off.

"Speak up! What was it?" The younger guard held up the lantern they had carried with them.

"Answer, you old foo—" He had glanced over his shoulder and saw the elder guard was standing still with his mouth agape. His gaze was fixed upward, somewhere overhead.

Something warm and syrupy splattered on the young guard's shoulder. He spun toward the gate. As he did so a deep, guttural growl from above pierced him to the core. He turned his gaze upward and was instantly overcome with the same fear that had stricken the older guard.

Crouched on top of the wall was a large, sinister shape that was darker than the surrounding night. Two malicious yellow orbs peered down on him. Below the two burning eyes was a massive twitching snout. The creature opened its maw, revealing long, jagged fangs. Streams of drool rained down around the guard.

Without warning, the black beast leapt upon the young guard, crushing him beneath its weight while it savaged him. The young guard didn't even have time to scream; it was over too quickly. The elder guard backed away and again called for help. The monster turned its gaze to the old guard, who trembled as he stumbled backward. He could barely breathe. Instead he only gasped as a large, fur-covered claw reached out and snatched him off the ground like a rag doll. He managed to scream as he was lifted toward the gaping razor-lined jaws.

In the distance, more armed men were hurrying toward the commotion at the back gate.

"There!" shouted one of the guards in front. "A beast from the pits of hell! There it is! Hurry!"

A large black silhouette shone against the wall, then two glowing yellow eyes flashed and the monster quickly bounded away toward the keep. The guard who had glimpsed the beast turned to the subordinate guards behind him and ordered, "Sound the alarm! We are under attack! Warn Lord Eben that a beast has entered the grounds! The rest of you come with me!" Two guards in the rear obeyed without a word while the other four guards in the group followed him as they ran to their fallen comrades.

When they arrived, they saw the carnage left behind in the light from an overturned lantern.

"May the gods help us," said the leader. "What manner of beast could do this to a man?" He looked away and steeled his nerves.

"Come! The beast went this way! Stay alert, men! It cannot be allowed inside the manor." They turned and rushed toward the keep, following the path of the beast they had seen only moments earlier. They failed to notice the shape of a black, winged creature slip from the shadows and crawl onto the top of the wall. There it sat and observed them as they ran.

Inside the manor, Eben Silverthorne was finishing his preparations for the defense of the manor when the alarm sounded.

"Hurry! Get in here! Bar the doors and check the windows!" he shouted. "Bring more torches!" He turned back to the great room. He had ordered his men to move the long tables and benches to the sides of the room, creating an open space in the middle. Several barrels of oil were brought in and positioned around the edges of the room.

"I don't know of any sort of wolf that likes fire," he said as he walked about inspecting the room.

"Any wolf'll burn," he added. "If he makes it this far we'll give him a warm greeting indeed."

Eben also had numerous brown, pint-sized clay jars of oil placed about the room so that they could be easily reached and hurled at a target. If hurled hard enough they would break on impact, splashing the target with a thick, flammable liquid. Eben had planned to use these should his keep ever come under siege.

Additionally, he had placed a dozen or so lit torches in the sconces around the room and positioned a guard near each one. The guards also carried torches, which caused an eerie, murky haze throughout the great hall. The smell of burning wood permeated the air.

Satisfied with his defenses, Eben turned to his men. "Very well, when I give the order I want you men to throw the clay jars and douse the beast with oil then throw your torches at it. Men, let's hope it doesn't come to that, but our unwelcomed guest is a spawn from the infernal regions and that's exactly where we're going to send it!"

Cheers rose from the men, and they thrust their swords, spears, and torches into the air.

"We will defend this manor with our lives!"

Eben held his sword high into the air for all to see the greenish glow.

"And in doing so we slay an old friend," he said to

himself. "I wish this night had not come, Alex. I would have liked to see you again. Just not like this."

He paused and looked at his men to be sure he had their complete attention. "If I fall, then one of you must take up this sword and finish the task. It's an enchanted weapon. It's enchanted by the druids to slay all manner of evil."

In truth, he knew Ariel's minor enchantment was not nearly so powerful, but his men needed to hear something else. They gave a rousing cheer as Eben thrust his sword higher into the air.

Then they heard it, a bloodcurdling howl from somewhere in the courtyard. The cheers faded. There were shouts from outside as well. Inside the great room not a noise could be heard except the crackling of the torches.

"Steady, men," said Eben. "Steady." The silence that had descended on the great hall covered everyone with a blanket of fear.

"Be ready, men. Together we'll slay the mons-"

The farthest shuttered window exploded, sending glass and bits of wood flying throughout the room.

A large dark shape landed on one of the long tables. Eben thought it was a bear, a large, misshapen black bear. Its fur was matted and wet and it was heaving. Its large head hung low, as if it was out of breath. It had a strong musky smell and its heavy breathing slowly turned into a low growl as it raised its head. It had a large, blood-soaked snout that twitched as its lips pulled back to reveal an array of bloody fangs. Its eyes glowed with hatred as it scanned the room. It was hunched over on all fours and its arms were the size of small trees. They were covered with thick black fur and ended with large curved claws over three inches in length that left deep gouges in the wooden table.

No one moved. Everyone stood transfixed on the terrifying creature that had suddenly intruded upon their world. Pools of blood and drool formed on the table and floor beneath the creature as it continued looking about, sniffing the air.

Then it settled its hateful gaze on Eben. It slowly crawled off the table and stood on its hind legs. It was well over seven feet tall and its furry canine ears twitched as it rose.

Eben steeled himself and pointed his sword at the beast. He stepped toward the werewolf, but just as he did, one overzealous guard rushed it from behind with his spear raised. "No!" shouted Eben. But it was too late. The guard struck the beast with a clear thrust to the back, but the shaft of his spear shattered against its hide. The monster whirled around and lashed out with one of its great claws, striking the guard across the chest. The force of the blow dented the guard's breastplate and sent him flying backward into the wall.

Eben seized the opportunity and slashed at the beast's lower leg. The blade sliced through fur and flesh, causing the werewolf to roar in pain and shock as it swung back to face him. Its horrible growl resonated loudly throughout the room.

"Wait for my word!" yelled Eben. He knew he had merely succeeded in angering the beast with such a minor wound. But now he knew he had a chance, and he could kill it.

The beast's large snout tilted downward and its face

wrinkled with rage as it focused its attention on the warrior with the green sword. Suddenly it leapt forward, its massive claws stretched out, ready to rend and shred him. The speed and ferocity of its attack surprised Eben, who only managed to step aside as the beast struck. Its jaws snapped shut and barely missed Eben's face. Its hot, putrid breath smelled of iron and death. The werewolf's left claw struck Eben's side and sent him flying backward. Eben grimaced with pain. He felt at least one rib break from the impact of the blow.

He landed hard on his back, pain erupting from the back of his head. The room started to spin.

He tasted his own blood as he struggled to clear his head. The werewolf wasted no time as it leapt on top of him. The beast's crushing weight nearly caused him to lose consciousness. Several of the guards rushed forward, yelling and striking at the beast with their weapons, attempting to draw the werewolf's attention.

It swung around, slashing with its claws and viciously snapping side to side. One guard struck the werewolf from behind with a sword, but the blow merely glanced off the beast's hide. The guard stood looking first at his sword and then at the werewolf, which had turned around and now faced him. It sprang forward, locking its jaws around the guard's neck and bore him to the floor. The other guards rushed to the aid of their comrade, but it was too late.

Eben staggered to his feet with his head still throbbing with pain. He removed his helmet in order to breathe better. He felt the back of his head and looked down at his hand. It was red with blood. The pain in his side and chest made it difficult to breathe. Gasping for air, he spat the blood from his mouth and shouted, "Ready the jars!"

He lunged forward and stabbed the werewolf from behind. The werewolf howled in pain and spun around, ripping and slashing with its massive claws. This time a claw landed flush on Eben's breastplate, sending him crashing into the tables and chairs that were stacked along the wall.

He lay against the wall gasping for air. He watched as the beast wrenched his sword from its body. The glowing blade was covered with blood. Taking a deep, painful breath, Eben summoned enough strength to rise on one knee and shout, "Now! Throw the jars! Burn it! Burn the beast!"

Then he slumped back against the wall in a sitting position. The guards by the sconces immediately threw their oil-filled clay decanters at the werewolf. Some of them shattered on the wall behind it, splashing its hide with the flammable liquid. A few jars, however, struck the creature square in the chest and arms, further dousing it.

Next numerous torches came flying through the air toward the werewolf. The oil pools beneath it and the soaked furniture ignited. Then the werewolf's fur caught fire. The beast let out a howl and dropped to all fours, locking gazes with Eben. The werewolf snarled and glared at him.

Eben coughed up more blood and smiled.

"It was…a great…battle, Alex," he said. "And it is…a good death. A warrior's death."

Fur ablaze, the beast leapt over the flames and out the window it had crashed through moments earlier. The room was filled with smoke and the smell of burnt hair, oil, and scorched wood. Eben continued to smile as he watched the werewolf flee, its fur still on fire as it disappeared into the night.

"Good-bye, old friend." They're safe, he thought. He had kept his promise. Lord Eben took one final breath as darkness closed in around him.

CHAPTER FOURTEEN
CATACOMBS

"Oh wow," said Jane. "I can't believe we're doing this. We're creeping around in a dark, scary tunnel running from a werewolf."

Ariel held a finger to her lips for quiet. "Come. We should not make any noise," she whispered. "Stay close." She held her glowing gem before her and stepped forward into the dark passage. As Geoff watched, she opened her hand and the gem floated above her head.

"That's a cool trick," said Sawyer. "How long'll it glow like that?"

"Shh!" said Ariel. She lowered her voice. "As long as I wish. Mage stones obey the will of the one using them."

"Can I try?" asked Geoff.

"Only those who possess arcane talent can control a mage stone," said Ariel. Geoff frowned and looked over his shoulder. He was last in line as they traveled single file down the dark, dank passage.

"On second thought...," Ariel stopped, reached into her pouch again, and produced three more gems. She held them in her open hand.

"Take one," she said as they gathered around her. Sawyer was the first to take a gem, then Jane and Geoff. Jane gasped as her gem immediately began to glow green like Ariel's. Geoff's gem shone with a soft white radiance.

"That's awesome!" said Geoff, hardly containing his enthusiasm. His hands trembled as he watched his gem rise above his head and emit a soft white glow.

"So why is Geoff's gem glowing white while ours is green?" asked Jane.

"I think mine is burned out," said Sawyer as he gave his gem a vigorous shake. "Do you have another one?"

"Interesting," said Ariel. "How rare it is to see a mage stone glow white. You have the inner makings of a wizard, Geoff."

Hearing Ariel speak his name for the first time startled Geoff. After all, he didn't think Ariel cared much for him—or the others, for that matter. His thoughts went from the mage stone to Ariel, which caused the gem floating above him to extinguish and fall, striking the top of his head with a *thud*.

"Ow!" said Geoff as he rubbed his head and picked up the gem that lay at his feet.

"However, you will need to train if you want to be a competent wizard," said Ariel.

"So mine is green," said Jane. "What does that mean?"

"It means you have an affinity for woodland magic, the magic of the druids," said Ariel. "And that too is interesting."

"Yeah, okay," said Sawyer. "But mine won't do anything. I think it's broken."

"No. It is as I suspected," said Ariel. "You have begun

to train as a warrior and that is your path. Jane and Geoff have to rely on their minds, while you must rely on the strength of your arm."

"So I can't make my gem glow? Why not?" Sawyer held up his sword. "Isn't this sword magical?"

"It is. But a warrior relies on his balance and the use of his wits differently."

"Yeah. All right," said Sawyer. "Guess I'm in the dark." He handed the mage stone back to Ariel who placed it in her pouch and led them deeper into the dark passage.

As they slowly made their way, Geoff noticed that only he, Sawyer, and Jane were making noise as they walked. Ariel was silent. She never makes any noise, he thought. He heard each footstep and every breath they took. Geoff couldn't help it; he was so nervous his hands trembled and a shiver ran up his spine. He looked behind them, but couldn't see anything stirring except their shadows against the rough-hewn walls in the green and white light. He exhaled a sigh of relief and saw his breath. Geoff wrapped his arms around himself and rubbed his upper arms. He could feel goose bumps on his skin.

"Hey," whispered Geoff. He cringed when he heard how loud his whisper resonated around them.

The others turned and looked at him.

"Why is it so cold down here?"

"It's always colder underground," said Jane. "No sun gets down here to heat things up. You know that."

"Quiet," said Ariel, and she motioned for them to follow. The passage had a slight downward slope, and at various places jagged, cobweb-covered rocks poked out from the walls. In another hundred yards, the passage leveled out and opened into a carved stone room.

Ariel stopped, grabbed her mage stone, and held it in front of her. The green light shone forward and illuminated the room. It was rectangular, and contained three semicircular alcoves in each of the walls. The alcoves contained various dusty clay urns and brass vases. There were etched plaques in the stonework above the alcoves, but time had rendered them worn and unreadable. Some alcoves also had rolled bits of parchment. Geoff detected a dirty, musty smell in addition to the stale scent of decay.

Ariel crouched near the floor and slowly panned her glowing mage stone left and right.

"What are you doing?" whispered Jane.

"Looking for disturbances in the dust," said Ariel. "Extinguish your mage stones and stay here."

An arched doorway on the opposite wall opened into more darkness. The stonework in the room was hand carved and fit neatly together. Geoff watched Ariel scan the floor. His heart raced and the goose bumps on his arms tingled. He tried not to breathe so loudly, but when he attempted to do so his lungs ached for air. He peered behind them, imagining they were going too slowly and the werewolf would lunge at them from out of the darkness at any moment. His mind conjured up images of a fanged maw and yellow, malicious eyes coming closer. A shiver ran down his back and his breathing became shallow.

When he turned back around, Ariel had unsheathed one of her scimitars and was already in the middle of the room. As Geoff watched, she moved without a sound, her gaze fixed on the opening ahead. He took some satisfaction in seeing Ariel use the same toe-heel method he utilized from time to time. She extinguished her mage stone and stepped into the arched doorway. She stood there for a minute, listened, and looked down the dark passage.

Geoff and the others found themselves enveloped in a sea of pitch-black. He could hear Sawyer and Jane breathing faster, and he felt someone brush against his arm and grab his wrist. Another moment later the room was illuminated in green light as Ariel once again activated her mage stone. Geoff saw that it was Jane who had latched onto his wrist, but he didn't mind the support, either. Ariel motioned for them to enter. Jane released Geoff and stepped into the room, with Geoff and Sawyer behind her.

"Stay alert," whispered Ariel. The ceiling of the room was nearly fifteen feet high. Two bats, disturbed by Ariel's light, circled overhead. The beating of their small wings echoed in the chamber. Their darting shadows against the green illumination sent another shiver down Geoff's back.

"This has to be the creepiest place I've ever seen," said Sawyer.

"Yeah," was all Geoff could say. He was looking all about the chamber while trying to keep constant vigil on the bats.

"What kind of dangers are down here?" asked Jane. "What did Lord Eben mean?"

"I do not know," said Ariel. "That is why I want you to be quiet and stay close."

Geoff noticed a rather ornate urn in one of the alcoves and went to have a closer look.

"Do not touch anything," warned Ariel.

Geoff looked over his shoulder and saw Ariel had

directed her comment at him. Dad would love to see this place, he thought. Too bad he's not here. He stepped away from the alcove and joined the others.

"We will use only my mage stone," said Ariel. "Three will cast too much light and alert enemies to our presence."

Ariel turned and walked into the corridor, her green gem glowing above her head.

Geoff could see no end to the corridor; it continued into the darkness beyond Ariel's light. Cobwebs dangled from the ceiling and fluttered slightly as they walked past. Soon they arrived at a four-way intersection that was shrouded with cobwebs. Small black silhouettes of spiders raced away as the light from Ariel's mage stone shone on them. Ariel signaled the others to stay where they were and not to move. She unsheathed another scimitar and advanced into the intersection as she cut away the cobwebs.

Geoff imagined Ariel's cobweb cutting would enrage a giant black spider that would attack them at any moment. Once Ariel entered the intersection she looked left then to the right. She motioned for them to stay put. Geoff could barely see her as she went down the right corridor. She crouched and examined a large, dark lump lying on the floor.

"Ariel, is everything okay?" whispered Jane.

"Stay where you are," said Ariel.

Geoff exchanged a worried glance with Jane. What was she looking at? If everything was fine why should we have to stay where we are?

Geoff edged closer until he was barely in the intersection. He couldn't help it, he was curious. Something had given Ariel reason to be concerned. She returned to the others.

"Ariel, what—" Jane started to ask but was interrupted by Ariel placing a slender finger over her own lips for quiet.

"Grave robber," she whispered. "And that is not all. He was killed most likely by a carrion mite. We are in danger and must be very quiet now."

"Carrion mite? What's a carrion mite?" asked Sawyer.

"They are predators. They make their homes in dark, moist places," answered Ariel. "They tend to feed on dead things, but have been known to attack the living."

"But mites are just tiny little things," said Sawyer, holding up a hand with his thumb and forefinger pinched together. A moment of silence passed as Sawyer looked at the others.

"Aren't they? They're real small, right?" he asked.

"And you said *mites*," said Jane, stressing the plural. "How many mites are there?"

"Carrion mites live in colonies. I do not know how many are here, but if we encounter even one we will be in danger."

Ariel looked at Sawyer.

"I assure you that you will be able to see them. Our best strategy is to move quickly and quietly while we are here."

"So…that was a body? What you just looked at? Who was he?" asked Geoff.

"Someone who was neither quick nor quiet. Come. Stay close together," said Ariel as she moved back into the intersection. She walked straight ahead this time. Geoff glanced down the right corridor as he passed. He saw a dark, crumpled shape next to the wall. It reminded him of a pile of clothes, but the rotting stench made it difficult for Geoff to breathe.

They continued straight, passing through three intersections. Geoff counted his steps as he walked, figuring it was about fifty yards or so. Along the way he noticed strange, jagged gouges and scrapes in the stonework on the floor and walls. They looked to him like someone was wildly swinging a pickax in the corridor.

As they walked, the gouges became more numerous and they had to step over debris that had been torn from the walls and ceiling. Geoff felt many gashes in the stones beneath his feet, and the treacherous footing caused Jane to stumble twice, although she managed to stay on her feet.

Every sound they made echoed throughout the subterranean passages, causing Geoff to cringe. He tried to imagine what sort of monstrosity could cause such damage to solid stone, but only succeeded in sending another shiver down his back.

Suddenly Ariel stopped and remained very still. Just ahead, faintly visible in the green glow, were several large, rough holes in the walls on both sides of the passage. Each hole was roughly three or four feet in diameter and dripped with moisture.

Ariel turned back to the others and held a finger up to her lips. Here the passage was nearly filled with debris. The stench of decay coming from the holes made Geoff's stomach churn. He placed a hand on the wall to steady himself. Ariel, weapons in hands and her mage stone hovering above her head, crouched and hurried past the gauntlet of fissures.

Once on the other side she turned and motioned for Jane to follow. Jane scurried past the openings in the wall, nearly falling over a loose bit of debris. The sound echoed in the corridor and continued for several long seconds. Geoff held his breath and they waited in silence for any sound in response. Beside him, Sawyer let out a long sigh of relief and shook his head. Ariel signaled for Geoff to come across next. He let out a deep breath and swallowed. He took slow, deliberate steps, trying to be as quiet as possible. The foul odor emanating from the openings in the walls caused him to cough and gag and nearly throw up.

He tried to suppress his coughing as he rushed past the gaping holes and joined Ariel and Jane. He couldn't help but take a peek as he passed, but he couldn't see anything in the darkness. Sawyer followed close behind Geoff.

Click-clack.

The sound rang out from the last opening in the wall. Geoff and Sawyer looked at each other, then Geoff glanced behind him. Something moved in the darkness. He reached into his pocket to withdraw the mage stone Ariel had given him. But a firm hand on his collar yanked him backward and he found himself sitting on his backside next to Sawyer, who had received the same treatment.

"We must go," whispered Ariel. "Now!"

As Ariel spoke a large, bloated insect-like creature emerged from a hole in front of them. It had large, sharp mandibles that resembled a giant pair of scissors, and these were making the distinct *click-clack* sound. A pair of large, wiry antennae waved about on its head. It had no eyes, at least none that Geoff could see. Its grayish body was covered with moist, smooth plates that resembled scales. Its powerful hooked claws stabbed the stonework, leaving large gashes. Geoff thought it looked like a giant tick. It was four times his size and moving quickly toward him.

 210

"That's a mite? How can they be so big?" Geoff said.

Geoff looked up and saw Ariel slash at the carrion mite.

"Run!" shouted Ariel.

The creature opened its mandibles, revealing a beaklike mouth lined with several rows of triangular teeth. The next instant, two moist, sinewy tentacles shot from its maw at Ariel, but her quick elven reflexes allowed her to move out of their way. Before Geoff and Sawyer could get to their feet, another carrion mite emerged from an opening on the other side of the corridor.

Jane screamed so loud it caused Geoff to wince and cover his ears. He saw that Ariel was dodging two sets of tentacles while Sawyer had drawn his sword. Ariel reached up, plucked her mage stone from above her head and held it forth.

"*Iluminara!*" she shouted, and the green glow from the gem exploded in a brilliant green burst of light. The carrion mites let out a shrill screech and retreated as the bright light engulfed them. Geoff watched as they shuddered and sizzled in the light.

"Run!" shouted Ariel again as she looked over her shoulder at them. "Run now!"

"Oh, no! Look!" said Sawyer as he pointed past the two carrion mites Ariel battled. Geoff could see the bloated forms of at least three more mites in the corridor. Their clicking had become almost deafening as the sound reverberated throughout the catacombs.

Geoff, Sawyer, and Jane turned and ran down the corridor. Jane managed to pull her mage stone out while she ran. She repeated the command word Ariel had taught them and her gem began to glow. As they ran, Geoff looked behind him and saw Ariel was running in their direction. Behind her the corridor writhed with swarming, clicking carrion mites.

"Guys!" shouted Jane. "I don't know where I'm going!"

"Just keep running straight," answered Sawyer.

Geoff barely heard Jane and Sawyer over the increasingly louder clicking noises behind them. Jane held her glowing gem out in front of her as she ran. The green light bounced and bobbed about, which further added to their eerie surroundings. As they ran, Geoff noticed some of the floor stones ahead were heaving upward.

"Jane!" called Geoff.

"I know! I see it!" said Jane.

Jane leapt over the upheaval of stones first, then Sawyer. Geoff barely made the jump as a pair of large, hooked claws emerged from the floor accompanied with the *click-clack* noise.

They ran down the corridor and stopped at an intersection. Jane bent over and gasped for air. Geoff looked back and saw Ariel slash at the burrowing carrion mite as she leapt over it. The wounded creature screeched and retreated back down the hole from which it had emerged.

"We should keep going," urged Geoff. "Those things are everywhere."

"Hell, yeah," said Sawyer. "C'mon! Let's go!"

Sawyer pointed straight ahead as Ariel caught up with them. She was followed by a dozen carrion mites, which seemed to be appearing from everywhere in the corridor.

"Run!" she said, using a scimitar to point in the direction Sawyer had just indicated.

With the added light from Ariel's mage stone, Geoff

saw another intersection a few feet ahead of them. With Jane leading the way, they dashed down the corridor as Ariel turned to face the pursuing carrion mites.

Geoff glanced over his shoulder and saw Ariel use her mage stone to blind them and then slash and slice the ones closest to her. Their screeches echoed throughout the corridor, even drowning the clicking noises they made with their mandibles.

As Jane, Sawyer, and Geoff reached the next intersection the walls collapsed on both sides of the corridor. Geoff looked around. Through the dust and debris, he saw that he was cut off from Sawyer and Jane. He was trapped. He had fallen behind when he had looked over his shoulder at Ariel battling the carrion mites.

Geoff heard Jane call his name. He saw the light from her mage stone had drawn the attention of the carrion mites. They lumbered toward her and Sawyer.

Geoff looked back at Ariel for help. She was about twenty feet away battling a new group of carrion mites that was dropping into the corridor from the ceiling.

"Ariel!" shouted Geoff, but the noise of combat and the screeching accompanied by the deafening clicking noise made it impossible for her to hear him.

Then he noticed something moving nearby. A carrion mite had emerged from the fissure in the corridor and was rushing at him. He screamed and ran down the nearest corridor.

As he ran, he kept one hand touching the wall and the other stretched out in front groping. He heard the clicking mandibles of the carrion mite coming closer. Oh, no! Please! No, he thought over and over again as he ran down the corridor. His fingers were scraped raw from feeling his way along the wall.

He fumbled in his pocket for his mage stone, but was unable to grasp it as he ran. His chest ached and he could barely breathe. He thought his lungs were going to explode. He reached into his pocket one more time and found his mage stone. He pulled it out, and as he turned to face the oncoming carrion mite he tripped.

Geoff landed on the cold, hard surface with a *thud*. He opened his mouth and said "*Iluminara*." Descending on him from the darkness was the beaklike mouth with rows of jagged teeth surrounded by a pair of gnashing, clicking mandibles. Geoff screamed and held out his arms to ward off the attack. The light from his mage stone exploded into a bright flare until all he could see was white. He heard a horrible screeching and smelled burnt meat. Geoff's head spun wildly and he gasped for air. He could barely keep his eyes open, and before he faded into unconsciousness, he thought he heard voices.

"Ye see that?"

"Aye," answered a deeper, rough voice. "Thought no more wizards existed 'round these parts."

"I hear others coming," said the first voice.

"Get our loot. Better bring 'im too. A young wizard's gotta be worth somethin'."

CHAPTER FIFTEEN
MAGE FIRE

JANE MANAGED TO RAISE HER mage stone above her head and illuminated the area around herself and Sawyer, who had drawn his sword. They were positioned behind Ariel in the center of a rough-hewn intersection. Jane saw more carrion mites pour into the corridor from everywhere around them. Ariel slashed and sliced at them with her scimitars, holding them back.

Jane looked around, but she didn't see Geoff anywhere.

"Geoff!" called Jane, but she could barely hear herself over the maddening clicking noises of the carrion mites.

"Sawyer, where's Geoff?" shouted Jane.

She grabbed Sawyer's arm, causing him to start and almost drop his sword. He shrugged her off and quickly regained his grasp.

"What?" he said as he glanced at Jane.

Jane grabbed his shoulders and shouted in his ear. "Where's Geoff?"

"Dunno," said Sawyer with a quick shake of his head. "Isn't he here?"

"No! I don't see him," said Jane.

The carrion mites' numbers continued to grow. Ariel whirled and attacked with such grace that she looked like she was dancing, but the mites were pushing her back into the intersection.

Jane looked all about for an escape route. Her palms were sweaty and her forehead was moist. This has to be a bad dream or something, she thought. It can't be real.

She watched Ariel swirl about in circles, killing one mite after another with her dance of death. She killed them in such a way that their corpses formed a bottleneck. The remaining mites were forced to attack her one or two at a time, but Ariel's two scimitars made quick work of them.

"Holy crap! I've never seen anyone move like that," said Sawyer. "Have you?"

Jane shook her head. Watching Ariel fight reminded her of a ballet. She opened her mouth to tell Sawyer she agreed with him when out of the corner of her eye she saw movement to her left. Down the corridor and saw a wave of carrion mites surging toward them from a new direction. She screamed, grabbed Sawyer's arm, and turned him around so that he saw the oncoming mites.

"Get back!" he shouted and raised his sword. Jane took a few steps back.

"Sawyer!" she cried. "We have to get out of here!"

"I got this!" called Sawyer.

In the green glow of her floating mage stone, Jane saw his hands trembling, and he rapidly shifted his weight from foot to foot. The leading mite charged at Sawyer and raised up on its hind legs as it prepared to lunge. Sawyer jabbed at the underside of the creature with his sword, but he lost his balance and missed. He fell forward and landed directly in front of the mite.

"Sawyer!" screamed Jane.

A bright green light flashed from behind Sawyer and Jane, blinding the mite above him. Jane covered her face with her hands, shielding her eyes from the intense green light.

"Move back!" shouted Ariel.

The flash had lasted only a moment, but that was enough to scare the mites away.

"Get up, Sawyer!" said Jane.

She saw that Sawyer was struggling to get to his feet. He had dropped his sword and reached down to pick it up when a mite burst through the wall beside him. Ariel stepped in front of Sawyer and thrust a blade through it.

Jane sprang forward and grabbed Sawyer by the hand. She pulled him to his feet and looked at Ariel. The elven druid was slicing and slashing at the blinded mites, driving them backward.

"Ariel!" shouted Jane, "What do we-" She stopped. There was a white glow behind her. She turned and saw a rolling wall of white flames approaching. The writhing, violent flames tumbled toward them. The light hurt Jane's eyes, and she looked away and tried to step back. The heat increased. Jane screamed. The pain from the searing heat was such that the air she breathed burned her nose and lungs. She felt the skin on her arms begin to burn.

Oh no, no. Too hot. Too hot, she thought over and over. She closed her eyes tightly and held her arms up to brace for impact. Then she heard Sawyer's voice.

"Aarrgghh! Where'd that fire come from?"

The next instant she felt a strong hand grasp her arm and jerk her out of the corridor. She was thrown into the hole in the wall just made by the mite, and landed beside its body. Suddenly she felt Sawyer land on top of her with a painful "Oof!"

Ariel laid down beside her while covering them with her arm and cloak. The carcass of the mite provided additional cover as the small cavern where they lay exploded with light and heat. Jane and Sawyer both screamed. From under Ariel's cloak, Jane could see bits of bone and broken stones and debris all about the cavern. She squinted. The heat hurt her eyes, but she saw the stones scorch and the bone fragments char, some even turning to ash. The mite in the opening fell apart as it was incinerated. It seemed to Jane that the whole world was shaking, like a giant train had just rumbled by. Several stones fell from the ceiling of the cavern.

A few seconds later Jane heard the high-pitched screeching of the carrion mites as they were engulfed by the rolling white inferno. She closed her eyes as pulsing waves of sweltering heat rolled over her. When the heat from the fireball faded and didn't feel as intense, Jane opened her eyes. The cavern was too dark to see. She still heard the stones sizzling and the smell of burnt flesh clung to her nostrils. Jane lay still and coughed a few times.

"*Iluminara*."

Ariel's mage stone lit the cavern with a familiar green tint. A thick layer of smoke lingered overhead. Jane looked around at the black earth and black stone. Everything the white flames had swept over was charred.

"What *was* that?" cried Jane.

"Yeah," said Sawyer as he brushed himself off. "That was close!"

Jane watched as Ariel carefully walked to the opening and peered out into the smoky corridor. Suddenly a horrible thought occurred to Jane.

"Ariel! Geoff! Is he—"

"I do not know," said Ariel. "Only a great wizard can cast such a destructive spell."

"He couldn't survive that," said Sawyer. "No one could."

"He may have hidden," said Jane. "Got out of the way, like us. He may be okay, right?"

Jane looked at Ariel for support, but the druid said nothing. Jane looked back at Sawyer. His eyes were wide with dread. Jane guessed what he was thinking, because she was thinking the same thing. Geoff may not have survived.

"Well, we have to find Geoff! He may be hurt or—"

Ariel held up a slender hand. She silently stepped into the blackened corridor, looked to the left and then to the right.

"I heard him cry out during the battle with the mites," said Ariel. "Perhaps he did survive. Come. It is clear."

Ariel moved down the corridor, disappearing from view.

"Oh no!" said Sawyer. "My sword!" he called. "I dropped it!"

"Sawyer, forget your sword," said Jane. "Geoff could be dead. And if you dropped it in the corridor it must be melted by now anyway."

"Perhaps not."

The voice was Ariel's. She had reappeared at the opening and tossed the Stormblade to Sawyer, hilt first. He caught the sword and examined it.

"Wow, no damage. It's just a little warm," he said. "Why isn't it melted?"

"Some magical items are imbued with great power, making them difficult to destroy. That sword is such an item."

Ariel disappeared from the opening again. Jane noticed she went right this time.

"Come on, Sawyer," she said as she stepped through the opening. "We have to find Geoff."

Jane still felt the heat from the flames that had scorched the entire corridor as far as she could see. The stench from the charred mites was stronger in the corridor and the smoke was thicker. She coughed and covered her nose and mouth with her hand. The heavy smoke clung to her as she walked.

"I can't breathe," she said as her stomach churned. "This smell is making me sick."

"Crouch lower, Jane," said Sawyer from behind. "Like this."

Jane glanced back at him. He also had his hand over his nose and mouth, but he was bent over as he walked.

"The smoke is what gets ya."

"I know," said Jane as she crouched. "It's all those burned monsters."

The air was less smoky closer to the ground, which allowed Jane to tolerate the stench somewhat. The smoke mostly lingered overhead, barely moving except to swirl when they passed by. They made their way toward a carved opening at the end of the corridor.

"Sawyer," whispered Jane.

"Yeah?"

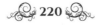

"What if Geoff is the only one who can get us back home and what if he is…you know. Gone."

There was no answer.

"What would we do?"

"I dunno."

Jane turned to speak to Sawyer, but as she did she stepped on a loose stone and fell. She put her hand out to break her fall. A jagged piece of stone pierced her palm. She cried out in pain and quickly sat up. She was covered with soot. Jane was relieved to find she could sit on the stone floor without burning herself.

"Jane," whispered Sawyer, "are you okay?"

He reached down to help her up, but Jane waved him off, irritated with her clumsiness.

Jane looked at the blackened piece of stone sticking out from her palm. Her blood looked black in the green light as it ran past her wrist and down her arm. Ariel knelt beside her and quickly plucked the sharp stone from her palm. Next she withdrew two leaves from her belt pouch and placed them firmly over the wound.

"Here," she said. "Press this over the wound. It will ease the pain for now and stop the bleeding."

Jane did as she was told. Ariel wrapped a leather strap around Jane's hand to keep the leaves in place.

"Better?" she asked.

Jane blinked for a moment and looked at her injured hand. The pain was already subsiding. She nodded.

"Thank you."

Jane struggled to her feet and looked down. She was filthy, like she had just finished cleaning a few chimneys.

Without a word Ariel went forward into the room at the end of the corridor.

"Jane, are you okay?" asked Sawyer.

"Yeah. I feel better," she said.

They followed Ariel into the room, but soon realized it was a dead end. In the middle of the room lay part of a charred mite.

"That's strange," said Sawyer. "Looks like only half of the room is all burned up, starting with that mite there."

Jane looked at the walls and crypts. Sawyer was right. Only half of the tomb was scorched. The white hot flames had started at the carrion mite and flowed out of the room and down the hall toward them.

"So where's Geoff?" asked Jane. "What happened here?"

Jane looked to Ariel for answers. The druid was examining the base of the far wall, which had not been scorched.

"Ariel?" said Jane. "Where's Geoff?"

"You don't think that he was caught in the flames and got cremated, do you?" asked Sawyer.

"No," said Ariel. "I do not think Geoff perished in the flames. I think perhaps he accidentally conjured the ball of fire to defend himself."

Jane stood still and thought for a moment, not sure if she heard Ariel clearly.

"Um, what?" she asked.

Ariel glanced over her shoulder at Jane and Sawyer.

"Earlier Geoff had shown an affinity for wizard magic. Do you remember his mage stone glowed white? I think he ran into this room and the mite followed him. However…"

Ariel's voice trailed off as she knelt and began studying the floor.

"Hold on," said Sawyer. "You mean to tell us that Geoff sent that ball of fire down the hall? No way. That's just crazy."

"Geoff's just a kid. What does he know about magic?" asked Jane.

"He was not alone," said Ariel. "There are two more sets of footprints here."

"Huh? Who else would be down here?" said Sawyer.

"More grave robbers," said Ariel.

"Then where are they? And where is Geoff?" asked Jane again.

"Yeah," said Sawyer nodding and looking about.

"It appears they took Geoff," said Ariel. "If Geoff did conjure that fireball, the strain must have been too much for him to bear."

Jane shook her head and snickered.

"You're kidding, right?"

"Jane's right," said Sawyer. "Geoff can't cast spells. He doesn't know any magic. We don't have spells and that kind of stuff back home."

"I cannot say what happened to Geoff with certainty," said Ariel. She turned around and began running her fingers over the stones in the wall.

"However," she said, "since there is no sign of Geoff or his blackened bones, it is safe to assume he either escaped or was taken."

"Jane," said Sawyer, "maybe Geoff can do magic. I mean, when he first touched that key it lit up. It didn't do that for me. And his mage stone glowed white."

Jane thought for a moment. It was true that Geoff was the one who was responsible for them being here in the first place. After all, they had tried to save him and they were all pulled through the portal. She looked at Sawyer.

"Do you know how insane that sounds?"

Sawyer nodded, "Yeah. But here we are."

Click.

"There it is," said Ariel. "Secret door."

"What secret door?" asked Jane.

They watched as Ariel pushed against the stone wall and a concealed door opened. Ariel stepped through and looked down.

"Two sets of human-sized footprints," said Ariel. "I do not see Geoff's footprints."

Jane and Sawyer walked through the newly discovered door and found themselves in a natural cave. The ground was moist and tree roots hung from the ceiling. There was a damp, earthy smell, but Jane felt a fresh breeze and took a deep breath. She was relieved to find the air was cooler and not filled with stifling smoke.

"So if a couple of guys got Geoff," said Sawyer, "how bad are they? These grave robbers."

"They are the worst sort," said Ariel. "One who robs the dead is capable of the basest acts. They would not hesitate to kill anyone for their valuables."

"They won't hurt him, will they?" asked Jane.

Ariel looked at Jane. "I do not know. But we must hurry if we are to save him."

With that, Ariel, Jane, and Sawyer followed the passage to the mouth of the cave. The opening was covered by a thick layer of tree branches, concealing the entrance. They pushed their way through the branches and emerged into the cool night air. They found themselves back in the forest. Moonlight infiltrated the trees, seeping through their branches and casting a soft radiance on them.

"This way," said Ariel.

She grabbed the glowing mage stone floating above her head, extinguished it, and returned it to her pouch.

"Oh," said Jane.

She searched her pockets and realized her mage stone was missing.

"I think my glow gem was destroyed in the fire."

"At least you had one and could use it," said Sawyer. "Hey, look at how bright the moon is. I can see."

Ariel stopped at a small copse of trees.

"Horses," she said and pointed down. "Their horses were tied here. Their tracks will be easy to follow."

"Yeah, but they're gone," said Sawyer. "We can't outrun horses."

"We must hurry," said Ariel. "For Geoff's sake and to distance ourselves from the werewolf."

"Maybe Eben killed it," suggested Jane hopefully.

With all that had happened, she had forgotten they were being stalked by a werewolf.

Jane looked behind them. There was the silhouette of Silverthorne Manor on a hill. An orange glow emanated from the center of the walled compound.

"Hey, look," said Jane, pointing back toward the keep. "Is the keep on fire?"

Ariel turned and walked past Jane.

"Yes," she said. "It burns."

As they watched the burning keep Jane thought she

heard Ariel quietly sigh and whisper "Eben" under her breath. Then her heart sank as she realized their situation had drastically deteriorated.

"Ariel," said Jane, "We don't have Geoff with us anymore and we still don't have the key or an archway. What do we do now?"

Chapter Sixteen
The Brigands

"C'MON! FASTER, HORSE! HAH!"

"Rolf, whaddaya think a small hedge wizard'll fetch?"

"Dunno," said the first, deeper voice. "Ole Aiden'll decide."

"Wonder what that was we heard in the bushes rolling around outside Silverthorne Village?"

"Bah! Musta been a bear."

"Bear? That was one big bear! Well, whatever it was, I'm glad we left it alone. I heard tell of strange creatures roaming about in the forests at night."

Geoff awakened to the sound of rough voices. He strained to hear more. He found himself bound, gagged, and draped over a horse's saddle. He lifted his head so he could see where he was, but a hand grabbed the back of his neck and forced him back down. The hand was callused and large—large enough to wrap itself nearly all the way around his neck.

"'ey there! Get yer 'ead down an' stay still!" growled the deep, rough voice.

In the darkness all Geoff could see was the ground as it flew by in a blurred motion. Who are these men? Geoff wondered. Why was he tied up?

"Trouble there, Rolf?" asked the first voice.

"Nah. The boy woke up is all."

Geoff felt a tingling sensation deep in his chest and a sharp pain in his head. It reminded him of how he felt when he gulped down too much cold soda at one time, a brain freeze. He moaned and closed his eyes. He let his body go limp, surrendering to whatever situation he found himself in. The cool night air rushed by while he bounced on the saddle. Before he went unconscious again, he heard the large man above him speak.

"Almost there. Better lemme do the talkin'. Aiden'll be mad we didn't come back with nothin' shiny, but at least we got this lil wizard."

The next thing Geoff knew, cool water trickled from his scalp past his temples and into his ears. It caused Geoff to shudder and turn his head. A wet cloth fell from his forehead. He was lying on a hard wooden surface and he smelled the smoke from a nearby fire. He heard voices and every now and then someone laughed.

The pain in Geoff's head had subsided, and with the exception of a bruised neck, he was fine. He opened his eyes. It was dark. He raised his head and surveyed his surroundings. His hands and feet were still bound, but his gag had been removed. He noticed bars all around and realized he was in some kind of cage. The cage was sitting on the back of a wagon, and bits of straw were scattered about the floor.

"You should be still," said a girl's voice from behind him.

Geoff looked over his shoulder and saw a girl in the dark corner of the cage. He was unable to see her face because it was covered by her dark blond hair. She was small, about his size.

"Who are you?" Geoff croaked. His throat was dry.

The girl didn't answer. Geoff squirmed and twisted himself around so he was facing her.

"Where are we?" he asked.

"Trouble," said the girl. "We are in trouble."

"What kind of trouble?"

"The worst kind," she said. "Are you really a wizard?"

"Me?" asked Geoff. "A wizard? No way."

The girl leaned forward, and Geoff could see she was a young elven girl. Her face was smudged, but not enough to conceal her attractive features. The angular contours of her jaw and cheeks reminded Geoff of Ariel. Her hands were bound too.

"They think you are," she said, nodding toward a group of men gathered around a campfire.

"Huh?" said Geoff.

"They think you are some kind of wizard. Are you an apprentice, perhaps?"

"No." Geoff shook his head.

She leaned back into the darkness and sighed.

"Then we are doomed," she said.

"What do you mean?" asked Geoff. "I don't understand."

He scooched his way to the bars at the side of the cage opposite the elf girl. It was a small cage, but large enough for their two slight figures.

"Who are these people?" he asked.

"Thieves," said the elf girl. "Robbers and slavers. In other words, typical humans."

"What do they want with us?" asked Geoff, ignoring the slight.

"Simple," she said. "They wish to sell me to the highest bidder, and you…well, if you are not a wizard then I suspect they will try to make a slave of you and then perhaps kill you…eventually."

Geoff frowned. He licked his lips, then wriggled his hands and wrists in an effort to free himself. Almost got it, he thought. Just a little more. He had nearly worked one hand free when he heard a familiar voice.

"There he is. That lil hedge wizard there'll fetch us a pretty sum of coins."

It was the booming voice of the big man who had Geoff draped over his saddle.

Geoff stopped what he was doing and looked in the direction of the campfire. A giant of a man was standing beside the cage pointing at him. He had a thick, bushy mustache that rested under a crooked, scarred nose. His bald head glistened in the firelight. He was dressed in a mismatched bit of leather armor that was clearly too tight for his large belly. A shorter man with a medium build emerged from behind the giant and held a lantern up to the cage.

The first thing Geoff noticed were his eyes. They were black. He sneered at Geoff with an expression that was devoid of any compassion. His thin beard and mustache were as black as his eyes, and his olive skin looked rough and leathery. He wore a leather jerkin over a long white shirt that was unbuttoned enough to reveal a gold chain around his neck.

"So, boy," said the man. "Rolf here says you're a wizard. Tell me, can you cast spells?"

Geoff shuddered and swallowed, but said nothing. He knew a bully when he saw one.

"I asked you a question, boy," snarled the man with the lantern.

Geoff stared at him.

"Aiden, I tell ya he was in them catacombs of that there Silverthone Castle an' he casted a spell that not only fried a buncha them fat, dead-eatin' mites, but his friends, too. Cedric 'ere saw it too."

A small, chubby man appeared on the other side of the man called Aiden, nodding his head.

"True enough," said Cedric. "This here boy lit everything up. White flames everywhere! Rolf and me barely got out with our lives. We thought ye might like 'aving a wizard around. We heard they was good luck and all."

"'ere," said Rolf, presenting the dagger Ariel had given Geoff. "He had this 'ere elven knife, too. Figured 'e was doin' a bit o' grave robbin' 'imself."

"Him? Hah!" said Aiden as he took the elven dagger and without a word he reached into the cage and jabbed Geoff in the arm.

"Ow! Aarrgghh!" Geoff jerked away, grabbing his arm. The pain shot right through him. Geoff looked at Aiden. He didn't have to do that, he thought. What does he want?

"So he can speak," growled Aiden. "But I'll be damned if he's a wizard. Come the morning he better be castin' spells or it'll be yer hides."

Aiden leaned forward so his long, thin nose protruded through the bars.

"And if you don't cast any spells that'll make me rich, then I'll cut you into lil bits and use you as bait next time we go fishing."

Aiden halfheartedly lunged at Geoff through the bars with the knife. Geoff scooted away. Tears welled up in his eyes. Aiden laughed, and Rolf and Cedric joined in.

"At least we'll have some sport with him," said Aiden. "Make him squirm and squeal before we're done."

The three men walked back to the campfire. Geoff lay against the far side of the cage looking at his arm as tears rolled down his cheeks. He felt the warmth of his blood as it ran down the length of his arm to his wrist. Sawyer and Jane are dead? That can't be, he thought.

"Is it true? Did you kill your friends?" asked the elven girl.

Geoff looked at her and shook his head.

"No. Well…I don't think so. I couldn't have," he said as he winced in pain.

"That is a strange answer," she said.

"What I mean is I don't remember," said Geoff. "I was running in the dark. A big carrion mite was chasing me. It got closer and closer until it was on me. Then…"

Geoff paused.

"I thought I was going to die. I felt a pain deep in my chest and my head began to ache. I think I screamed, but I'm not sure. The next thing I remember I was a prisoner. It seems like a dream now."

The elven girl sat silently in her corner of the cage.

"I don't know what they're talking about," said Geoff. "I wouldn't hurt anyone."

He heard fabric ripping and before he knew it the elf was next to him binding his arm. Geoff watched her. Now that she was closer, he could see that she looked to be his age. Her smooth, slender hands moved quickly to stop the bleeding. He was amazed at how she was able to bind his wound with her hands tied.

"Thanks," he said. "I'm Geoff."

She glanced at him for a second as she finished tying the bandage.

"Ishara," she replied.

Geoff smiled. "That's a nice name."

She returned to her corner without a word. Geoff opened his mouth to continue the conversation, but he couldn't think of anything to say. He was tired and his arm hurt. He leaned back against the cage and continued to wriggle his hands. Was it true? His memory is fuzzy. Cast a spell? Him? Sawyer and Jane can't be dead, and especially not Ariel. She's such a powerful druid. But what if they were dead? There wouldn't be any way to get home now.

His heart sank. If he did kill them, then that made him a murderer. What was he going to do?

As he sat in his corner, he overheard Aiden and his band of brigands talking by the campfire.

"Are ye sayin' we gotta leave an' go south?" said an unknown voice.

"Aye. That's exactly what I'm saying," said Aiden. "When the barbarian hordes of the Shadowlord sweep through these lands I for one don't want to be here."

"So it be true, then?" The deep voice was Rolf's.

"True enough," said Aiden. "Two days ago Bertram there and I were returning from trading our loot at Geegan's Hold. We planned to stop at Millhaven for a night's rest and entertainment."

Geoff heard a few grunts and snickers.

"Aye," agreed someone by the fire. "But we saw smoke rising before we got to Millhaven. We heard the sounds of battle and screams."

"Then," continued Aiden, "we crept closer. Till we found a hill overlooking Millhaven."

There was a moment of silence and then Rolf spoke. "An' what did ya see?"

"We saw him," said Aiden. The others became quiet.

"We saw Lord Zorn. We saw that evil bastard."

"He just appeared. Dressed in armor as black as the night," said the one called Bertram. "Swinging a wicked blade, cutting down everyone like they was grass. He was strong and fast. Too fast for any man. No one could stand against him. The whole town was overrun by his barbarian horde."

"From what we could see," said Aiden, "they killed everyone and burned Millhaven to the ground."

Another moment of silence passed and then Rolf spoke. "What're we gonna do, then?"

"Run," answered Aiden. "We run as fast and as far south as we can. I tell you no one can stop him, the Shadowlord. His black hordes are covering the lands like a plague of locusts. War is here."

"I 'member hearin' tales 'bout him," said Rolf. "I 'eard he was a 'ero, though."

"Ha! He was. Not anymore," said Aiden.

"But what about the kingdom of Chalon?" someone asked. "Surely they can stand against the Shadowlord? They have a powerful army, don't they?"

"Aye," grunted Rolf. "And what 'bout them Knights of Caladar? They ne'er lost a battle."

"Chalon and Caladar were nowhere to be found," said Aiden. "And if they had been, they wouldn't have made any difference. Millhaven would still be gone. Every man, woman, and child. Gone."

"I still hear the screams," said Bertram. "It was a slaughter, I tell ya. Aiden and I got outta there as fast as we could."

As Geoff listened, he noticed the mood of his captors had become anxious. Whoever Lord Zorn was, he frightened them. He wished Jane and Sawyer were there. Ariel too. He wanted to go home now more than ever. Geoff looked at Ishara. Her green eyes were open, and she was also listening to the conversation.

"Too bad you are not a wizard," she said softly. "You could make these bars disappear and we could escape."

Geoff thought about what she had said for a moment.

"If I were a wizard," said Geoff, wriggling and turning his hands. "I'd be home."

"And where is your home?"

Geoff thought for a moment, then said, "It's a long way from here. It's a different—"

To his surprise, Geoff worked his hands free before he had finished.

A second later Geoff heard footsteps as someone approached the cage.

"Ha!" said a voice Geoff didn't recognize. "You? A

wizard? Don't think so. Rolf and Cedric musta been drunk in the catacombs again. You're just a lil runt."

Geoff turned his head and saw the backside of another brigand as he bent over and began gathering up his sleeping blankets. A large, rusty key ring dangled loosely from his belt. Without thinking, Geoff reached through the bars and grabbed it. The key ring easily detached itself from the brigand's belt and Geoff quickly tucked it under his shirt.

He looked at Ishara. She was leaning forward, watching him intently. The brigand, none the wiser, collected his blankets and returned to his spot by the campfire.

"You may not be a wizard," whispered Ishara, "but you are an excellent sneak thief."

Geoff tried to smile, but the best he could manage was a quick nod. He thought of Jane, Sawyer, and Ariel. Did the bandits see him kill his friends? He shook his head. No way, he thought. He didn't kill them. He just couldn't do that.

"We will make our escape when they are asleep," said Ishara. "My weapons are there."

She pointed at a large brown tent facing the campfire. As Geoff watched, most of the brigands started to settle down for the night near the tent.

"How're we going to get in there?" he asked. "They're all around the tent."

"We sneak," said Ishara, smiling for the first time, "little sneak thief."

"Just like that?" he said. "What if we get caught?"

"Then you will not have long to await your fate," said Ishara. "As for me, I would rather die than live as a slave to a human master."

Geoff sighed and turned his attention back to the brigands, who were still talking among themselves.

"Seems ta me, Aiden," said Rolf, "that'll be better for us if we ride 'round Zorn's armies. We can pass through Eldritch Forest an' he'll ne'er know."

"It's no forest anymore," said Aiden. "'Tis a marsh, I tell ya. The Eldritch Marsh. It's changed. Something evil resides there. There is talk of a great beast roaming the marsh. A beast that cannot die. Even the trees and flowers and bugs will kill ya. No, it's too dangerous. The evil in that bog is seeping out, oozing into the surrounding countryside. Nearby crops have withered and the water is polluted. The townsfolk of Somerdale have abandoned their homes. That is no place for us. We go south. Keep to the trees."

"I heard druids protected that forest," said Cedric. "What happened to them?"

"Who knows?" said Aiden.

"Who cares?" said another brigand, prompting a raucous chorus of laughter from the others.

"Guess the druids left, too," said Aiden. "Or they were killed. It's not our concern. Let's turn in. We've an early start tomorrow."

Geoff looked on as Aiden disappeared into the large tent that held Ishara's weapons. The other outlaws merely bedded down for the night by the fire.

Geoff quietly slid over to Ishara.

"We should just run for it when we open the cage. If we try to go into that tent we'll get caught."

"No," said Ishara. "We will need weapons."

"But we're going to get caught," said Geoff.

"It is worth the risk," she said. "However, if you think

you can conjure another fireball and turn our captors to ash…"

Geoff shook his head. He sat beside Ishara and leaned his head back against the bars.

"I don't think any of that happened," said Geoff. "I just can't remember how I got out of the catacombs. I'm not a wizard."

"The two brigands who brought you here are convinced you are a wizard," said Ishara, "and if they are right, you killed your friends."

Geoff turned his head away. "I don't think I did that. I *couldn't* do that."

Several minutes passed before Ishara put her hand on Geoff's wrist.

"We wait until they are asleep," she whispered. "Then we escape."

"Here," whispered Geoff as he handed her the keys. "You take them."

A few hours later they heard snoring coming from around the dwindling campfire. Geoff watched as Ishara silently moved to the front of the cage to gain a better view of the slumbering bandits. A moment later, he followed her and observed them for himself. As far as he could tell, they were all asleep. He looked at the large tent. It was dark.

"Now?" he asked.

Ishara gave him a quick nod and crept to the cage door. She reminds me of Ariel, Geoff thought again. She never makes a sound, either. I wonder if they know each other. He made a mental note to ask Ishara when they were away and safe.

Geoff watched Ishara try a couple of keys on the lock

before she discovered the correct one. She slowly turned it in the lock until Geoff heard a faint *click*. He glanced over his shoulder at the group of sleeping men. He felt a rush of adrenaline run through him. Oh crap, he thought. Are we really going to try this? What if we get caught?

No one appeared to have heard Ishara unlock the cage. She looked at Geoff, raised her eyebrows, and smiled as she quietly opened the cage door.

Ishara hopped down off the wagon. She motioned for Geoff to follow. Geoff, still holding his injured arm, walked as quietly as he could to the cage door. When he reached it, he grasped the bars to steady himself, but the door swung open further, squeaking as it did so. Geoff winced and looked at Ishara, who was glaring at him.

They listened for sounds of movement from around the campfire, but heard nothing other than an occasional pop or crackle from the fire. Ishara took Geoff by the arm, lifted him off the wagon, and quietly set him down. Wow, she's strong, he thought. They stepped away from the wagon and made their way to the tent. Geoff was using his usual toe-heel method to sneak. He saw that Ishara, like Ariel, also employed that technique.

When they got closer to the tent, Geoff noticed the large shape of Rolf slumbered in front of the opening. His chest rose and fell as he slept. Geoff concluded that he couldn't safely step over the large man. He squeezed Ishara's hand to get her attention. She turned and looked at him. Geoff shook his head frantically while pointing at Rolf.

Ishara tugged on Geoff's hand and nodded, signaling that he should follow her and step over the large outlaw. Geoff scanned the campsite. The other men were still asleep.

Ishara let go of his hand and easily, gracefully stepped over Rolf. She turned around and motioned for him to follow. Geoff lifted his foot, but he was so frightened, he couldn't stop his leg from shaking. He put his foot down and took a deep breath. He just had to get over this big guy. C'mon Geoff. You can do it, he told himself.

He steadied himself again. Ishara held her hand out to assist him. He took her hand and stepped over Rolf. He was about to bring his back foot over when Rolf shifted. The large man rolled over onto his side, scratching his exposed belly. Geoff's back foot was caught under his heavy leg.

A small bead of sweat rolled down Geoff's forehead and cheek, and his whole body started to shake. He looked at Ishara, pleading with his eyes for help. Ishara bent down and gently slid Geoff's foot from under Rolf. Geoff wasted no time. He quickly stepped over the big man. Ishara still held his hand, which comforted Geoff.

They quickly opened the flap at the front of the tent and stepped inside.

CHAPTER SEVENTEEN
LESSONS

"COME," SAID ARIEL. "WE DO not know if Eben killed the beast. Hurry."

She turned and continued following the deep horse tracks that lay before them. Jane and Sawyer looked at each other for a moment and then hurried after Ariel. They jogged behind the elven druid, whose graceful, brisk walk outpaced them. At times Jane and Sawyer stumbled over unseen tree roots or rocks. Ariel hopped over and stepped around obstacles with ease. From time to time she stopped and waited for Jane and Sawyer to catch up.

After a few hours of trotting through the forest, Jane gasped for air and her lungs began to ache. She took a deep breath and blurted out, "Can we stop and rest?"

"Yes," said Sawyer. "Please."

Ariel stopped and watched Jane and Sawyer make their way to her.

Jane sat on a mossy rock and Sawyer sat with his back against a tree.

"I thought I was in better shape than that," he said. "That was rough."

Jane noticed a throbbing pain from her injured hand. She untied the leather strap and peeled the leaves away.

"Ouch," she said with a grimace. "I hope it doesn't get infected."

Ariel walked over to Jane and knelt on one knee. She took Jane's hand and examined it. Jane felt the softness and warmth of Ariel's touch, which surprised her. She had expected Ariel's hands to be rough and coarse. To Jane, Ariel was an Amazon warrior or martial artist. She had muscles and moved and fought like an action hero.

"You said you lost your mage stone. Take this one."

Jane looked at the round, faceted gem in Ariel's palm. It was bigger than the one she had lost. She took the gem and deposited it in her pocket.

"Thank you."

"You are in need of healing," said Ariel.

Jane nodded. "It's really starting to hurt now." She held her hand out to Ariel expectantly.

"You can do it," said Ariel.

Jane looked at her for a second and rubbed the dryness from her eyes. She was tired from their nighttime trek through the forest and she wasn't sure she had heard Ariel correctly.

"I…I don't understand," said Jane. "What do you mean? You aren't going to help me?"

"I do not need to help you," said Ariel as she knelt in front of Jane. "You can heal yourself. Would you like me to show you?"

Jane glanced at Sawyer. He was sitting with his back against a tree. In the moonlight, she could see he was looking on intently.

"Jane," said Ariel, "just as I believe Geoff has the makings of a wizard, I believe you have the potential to be a druid. Do you remember the wounded unicorn? How your first instinct was to try and stop the bleeding and help it?"

"Yes," said Jane. "I remember, but you healed its wounds, not me."

"Yes, but it is your *instinct* to which I am referring at the moment. You tried to help it, did you not?"

Jane nodded. The goblins had inflicted grave wounds on the poor beast. It had broken her heart to see such a beautiful creature suffer.

"Okay," said Jane. "What do I do?"

Ariel took Jane's hand in hers and removed the leaves from Jane's palm. They were warm and moist and soaked with blood. The cool night air flowed over Jane's wounded palm. It felt refreshing, even a little invigorating.

"Do you remember the incantation?" asked Ariel.

Jane shook her head. "No."

The druid once again removed a few small dried leaves from her pouch and crushed them with her fingers. Then she took Jane's uninjured hand and dropped the leaf bits in it.

"Now," said Ariel, "sprinkle and press these leaves over your wound and repeat the charm of healing, *Ilinara tae ullnara taethos.*"

Jane did as Ariel instructed. The throbbing pain in her hand subsided the instant the leaves touched her skin. She looked at Ariel. It was amazing. She had never felt such a peaceful sensation.

"*Ilinara tae ullnara taethos,*" said Ariel.

"*Ilinara…,*" said Jane, still looking at Ariel.

"*Tae ullnara*," said Ariel slowly.

"*Tae ullnara…*"

"*Taethos.*"

"*Taethos*," repeated Jane.

As soon as she completed speaking the spell, she saw a tiny green glow and the wound in her palm closed. It's tingling, she thought. It feels like a thousand little needles, but it doesn't hurt. It feels good.

"Well done," said Ariel. "You have more power within you than you realize."

"Wow, Jane," said Sawyer, who was now standing. "That was awesome!"

Jane smiled and looked at her palm again. The leaf bits had turned to dust. When she tilted her hand and poured the dust out she didn't see the nasty cut anymore. She looked closer and wasn't even able to see *where* she had injured herself.

"I don't feel any pain," she said with a laugh. "It feels great."

"Yeah," said Sawyer, "Wouldn't it be cool if you could do that when we get home?"

Jane looked at Ariel, who had stood up and was smiling at her.

"Can I do it when I go home?" she asked. "I mean, will I be able to heal?"

Ariel shrugged. "Why not?"

Jane looked at Sawyer. He also shrugged.

"Yeah, why not?" he said. "You just gotta hope no one burns you at the stake for being a witch."

Ariel turned to Sawyer. "They burn spell casters in your world?"

"Well, no," he said. "Not anymore. People were burned for being witches, but that's different. Isn't it?"

He looked at Jane for help.

"It was a long time ago," said Jane, "but you aren't a witch. A druid isn't a witch, right?"

"No," said Ariel. "Druids are not witches."

"So will I be able to heal people with spells?"

"Yes," said Ariel.

"Suppose magic won't work where we come from?" asked Sawyer. "What then?"

"Then you will live your lives as you desire. You have lost nothing."

"Can I use that spell to heal animals too?" asked Jane with newfound enthusiasm. "Will it work on other injuries? Broken bones? Diseases? What about age? Will it extend an animal's life?"

"The spell you just learned will mend bones and wounds," said Ariel, "but it will not cure diseases, nor will it extend life. There are, however, other spells that can accomplish such things."

Jane shot to her feet.

"Will you teach me? I could do so much for others if I knew which spell to cast!

Ariel regarded Jane for a moment. Jane's mind was racing with possibilities.

"Perhaps," said Ariel. "We shall see. It takes time to learn those spells. Humans do not usually have the compassion or desire to help others unless circumstances are dire."

Jane felt the air leave her lungs. She couldn't believe what she had just heard.

"But didn't Jane just prove she has what it takes to cast healing spells?" asked Sawyer.

"Yes," said Ariel. "One healing spell does not prove anything. As I said, we shall see. The sun will rise soon. We must resume our journey if we are to find Geoff. Come."

Jane watched Ariel turn away and continue tracking the same hoof prints they had been following since they emerged from the catacombs. Jane was irked. How could Ariel be so untrusting? What's the harm in healing people or animals? Jane lowered her head as she thought.

"It's okay, Jane," said Sawyer.

She felt him wrap an arm around her shoulders and gently pull her along with him as they followed Ariel.

"That's why we have doctors, right?" asked Sawyer. "I bet that mumbo jumbo spell stuff won't work when we get home anyway."

"Why doesn't she trust me? Does she hate all humans?" said Jane.

"Not sure about that," said Sawyer. "But she did show you that spell and she got us through the catacombs. And I think she is trying to help us get home."

Jane frowned. Ariel had done much for them already, but her manner and refusal to teach more healing spells confused her.

"Yeah," she said. "But why won't she teach me more healing spells? I know I can do it. I showed her I can cast spells. She should trust *me*, at least. Otherwise, why even bother?"

Jane walked along with Sawyer, his comforting arm still around her shoulders. In the distance she saw Ariel waiting for them again at the top of a hill. Jane imagined she was annoyed with their slow pace and slowed down even more.

Too bad, she thought. We'll get there when we get there. You just wait.

As she walked, Jane saw the sky begin to lighten and she realized they had been traveling all night. A wave of exhaustion rolled over her. She blinked to stay alert and awake.

"Dunno," said Sawyer. "But I guess she has her reasons."

Jane just shook her head.

"Well, as I see it, we need to get back home, and we need Geoff in order to do that," said Sawyer. "So let's tough it out 'til we get home. This whole place is so weird."

As Jane heard Sawyer's words she grasped what he said. He's right, she thought. We do need Geoff so we can go home.

"Okay," she said. "Let's find him and go home."

Jane and Sawyer quickened their pace. When they reached Ariel she said nothing. She simply turned and continued on. They marched in silence for a couple of more hours with Ariel in the distance, bobbing in and out of their sight as they hurried. They rounded a bend and saw Ariel had made camp beside a small grove of trees.

A small fire burned, giving off wisps of white smoke as Ariel laid out a small breakfast of bread, cheese, and raspberries.

"You should rest," she said without looking at them. "We will resume our search for Geoff before midday."

"All right," said Sawyer. "How much further? Do we have any idea where the bad guys are taking Geoff?"

"The tracks head northeast," said Ariel. "I suspect the brigands' camp is not far."

"What if they don't have a camp?" asked Jane. "What if they already packed up and left?"

"Brigands are outlaws," replied Ariel. "They must move from place to place in order to escape justice. If they have moved on then we will follow them."

Jane frowned at her answer.

"You know," said Sawyer, "I was really looking forward to sleeping in a warm bed. Too bad that werewolf tracked us down. Now I have to find a nice comfy rock to rest my head on. Hey, Ariel, why didn't my sword warn me about those carrion mites like it did with the werewolf?"

Ariel shook her head. "I do not know. Your sword will reveal what it wishes. Perhaps in time it will warn you of other dangers."

"I know brigands are outlaws," snapped Jane. "How do you know they have a camp? Do you know who they are?"

"Hey Jane…," said Sawyer.

"Just a minute," said Jane with a flushed face. "I'm getting tired of you putting us *humans* down. If you don't trust us by now then you never will. Why are you helping us? That's what you're doing, right? Helping us poor *humans*?"

Ariel stood up and glared at her. Jane could see her nostrils flare, and the elf's green eyes drilled into her. Jane swallowed and continued. "You show me how to cast one small healing spell and a spell to make flowers grow. But when I ask you to teach me more spells you say 'Perhaps'. Why won't you trust me?"

"Have we not covered this before?" Ariel asked as she approached Jane. "Your manner is ungrateful, which is characteristic of your kind. Humans are greedy, disrespectful, selfish, and have no honor. You think that

because you have an aptitude for casting druidic spells you are entitled to learn more. But you have no idea of the power that resides within you. None of you do. I choose what I teach and to whom. I did not refuse you earlier, but given your temperament perhaps I should. Your selfish nature betrays you. Our order has never had a human within our ranks. Why? Because humans cannot be trusted with power. Invariably they want more and that lust for power always dooms them."

Jane opened her mouth but closed it. She took a deep breath. Her knees were shaking as she spoke.

"I didn't start any wars here! Neither did Sawyer or Geoff! You unfairly lump all humans into a big pile and label us. We aren't all bad. All we want to do is go home, so if you're looking for a thank you then I'll say it. Thank you. Believe me, no one wants to see us go home more than we do. If you don't want to teach me more spells so I can help others then don't."

Jane glanced at Sawyer. His eyes were opened so wide they looked like they were going to pop out of his head. Suddenly Ariel was in her face, looking down at her.

"Do not," she said through clenched teeth, "ever speak to me like that again. You need to learn to channel your anger into something useful. Take heed; I will not tolerate another one of your tantrums."

Jane was trembling, but she tried to conceal it. Ariel maintained eye contact as she stepped around her and disappeared into the forest.

Jane could only watch as Ariel walked away.

"Holy crap, Jane!" said Sawyer. "Are you crazy? She could cut us into little bits and feed us to the rabbits. What's gotten into you? She's trying to help us. Okay, so maybe she won't show you how to cast more spells, so what? We don't plan on being here much longer anyway. Just tough it out till we get home."

"Oh shut up, Sawyer."

Jane sat down by the small fire Ariel had made and crossed her legs.

"I know," she said, her eyes welling up. "I know she is trying to help. But look at us. Things aren't getting better. We aren't any closer to going home and Geoff has been kidnapped. So you tell me, where is the silver lining in all this?"

Sawyer looked away from Jane and put a handful of dried twigs on the fire.

"Yeah," he said. "Things aren't good. We've been through a lot. Werewolves, elves, orcs, killer mites. Seems like everything wants to either kill us or eat us."

Jane put her head between her knees and let her tears fall to the ground. She wished she hadn't blown up at Ariel like that. It was stupid.

"Hey, do you think she's coming back?" asked Sawyer.

Jane couldn't help but chuckle at Sawyer's question. She realized he had a knack for saying just the right thing to cheer her up. She lifted her head and brushed her hair back, then looked at Sawyer, smiled, and wiped her eyes.

"No idea," she said.

"So what do we do if she doesn't come back?" he asked.

"No idea," she repeated.

Sawyer laughed. Jane looked up at the sky.

"Looks like a sunny day," she said. "We should try to get some rest before our commander returns—if she returns."

"Yeah," said Sawyer. "After what you said to her that's a big if."

"You know me," she said as she laid her blanket beside Sawyer and settled down on it. "Greedy, selfish, and ungrateful."

Sawyer laughed and put his sword aside. He kicked off his shoes and lay on his side facing Jane.

"You know," he whispered, "she may be wrong about the three of us, but on the whole she *is* right about the human race, isn't she?"

Jane closed her eyes and nodded. "Mmhmm."

She drifted off into a deep sleep and awakened a few hours later to the sound of birds chirping. She opened her eyes to find that she had snuggled herself into Sawyer's arms. She felt warm and safe. She closed her eyes again and took a deep breath. Suddenly, her eyes flew open. Huh? What the heck? She quickly slid away from Sawyer and looked around. The sun was shining overhead and there was the slightest hint of a breeze.

She was relieved to find Ariel had returned while they slept. She had even prepared a meal consisting of dried meats, cheese, bread, and berries for them. A cup of water was sitting beside her, and there was a small stack of firewood by their blanket.

"I am not your enemy, Jane," said Ariel from an overhead tree branch.

Jane sat up and rubbed her eyes. She opened her mouth to say something, but a belated yawn prevented her reply.

"I have no love for humans," Ariel said as she dropped silently to the ground beside her, "and perhaps I never will.

Your race is a scourge on these lands. But I will honor my promise to help the three of you return home."

Jane put her hands on the ground to push herself up, but Ariel knelt and presented her with a small brown leather pouch.

"In this pouch are more components needed to cast stronger healing spells," she said, her eyes fixed on Jane's. "I do not know when I will be able to get you home, but you should learn to use the gifts I believe you have. If you wish, I will teach you how to understand the ways of nature and how to communicate with both plant and animal."

Jane took the pouch and stared at it. Ariel stood and walked to the campfire.

"Thank you," said Jane quietly.

She looked at Ariel.

"I'm sorry I got angry. I have a bit of a temper. And I was tired. I was wrong to argue with you."

Ariel knelt by the fire. "Apology accepted. I did not expect that from you," she said. "Perhaps I should not speak ill of your kind so often."

"No," said Jane. "You have your reasons. To tell the truth, you're pretty much right about us…in general. I suppose our race has a lot of growing up to do."

"Perhaps," said Ariel. "But maybe not the three of you, I think."

She pointed at Sawyer with a smoldering twig she had taken from the campfire. "I will also continue to teach him how to fight with a sword. After all, we cannot have the Stormlord always dropping his weapon during a fight."

Jane looked at Sawyer and giggled. He was still fast

asleep. A thin line of drool seeped from the corner of his mouth.

"With Geoff having been taken," said Ariel, "I realized that you need to learn to use your talents."

"Will you also teach Geoff how to cast spells?"

"No," said Ariel. "I cannot. If my suspicions are correct about Geoff then he will need to learn his craft from a wizard."

"You mean there are wizards here too?" asked Jane.

"Most assuredly," said Ariel. "And witches, sorcerers, necromancers, warlocks, and—"

"And druids?" interrupted Jane.

Ariel smiled. "And druids, of course."

She has a beautiful smile, thought Jane, smiling back at her. Maybe everything will be okay after all.

"Okay, so wizards are different from druids and all those other spell casters you mentioned," said Jane. "So if you can't teach Geoff how to be a wizard, who can?"

Ariel stoked the fire.

"There is a wizard," she said. "His name is Maelord. He does not live far. He is not likely to take on a new apprentice, but if he chooses to teach Geoff the ways of a wizard it will be a difficult path for your friend. Do you think Geoff is strong enough for such a rigorous undertaking?"

Jane thought for a moment before answering. "I don't know."

Ariel nodded.

"But I think if Geoff did cast that fireball in the catacombs, he almost killed us. So he needs to be taught and he should be given a chance to learn."

"I agree," said Ariel.

"Me too," said Sawyer.

He had awakened but chose to lie still and listen to Jane and Ariel.

"Otherwise," he said as he sat up, "he might be more dangerous to us than that werewolf or any carrion mite. He could fry us. We'd be crispy critters, ya know?"

"That's true," said Jane.

Sawyer hopped to his feet, dusted himself off, and wiped his moist chin. Then he looked at Ariel.

"Okay," he said. "Let's eat and go get Geoff."

After their meal, the three of them set off again, Ariel again outdistancing Sawyer and Jane as they journeyed through the forest. Every now and then she would stop and examine the ground for tracks. After another couple of leagues, Jane became winded and fell behind. She stopped and held up her hand for the others to stop.

"We'll make a long distance runner out of you yet," said Sawyer.

Jane sat on a fallen tree and took a long drink of water from her water pouch.

"How much further, do you think?" she asked between gasps for air.

There was no answer.

Jane looked at Ariel. She had dropped to one knee and was closely examining something on the ground.

"What is it?" asked Sawyer. "What do you see?"

Ariel stood and placed her hands on the pommels of her scimitars. She looked at the clearing ahead and then turned to Sawyer and Jane.

"We are not the only ones tracking Geoff."

CHAPTER EIGHTEEN
ESCAPE

THE ONLY LIGHT IN THE tent came from a dying candle on a rusty holder hanging in the center. Geoff saw several closed chests stacked on top of each other along the left wall. To the right, an assortment of weapons and a few pieces of fine silk rested on three wooden tables. Geoff watched Ishara walk to one of the tables without hesitation and pick up a bow and a quiver full of arrows. She quickly and quietly slung the bow and quiver over her back, then strapped a curved sword and knife around her waist.

Ishara glanced over at Geoff and smiled. She motioned for him to follow her, and they crept to the back of the tent. Geoff heard slight snoring coming from a low cot. The source of the snoring was buried beneath a blanket. Geoff stopped. Even before Ishara pulled the blanket back he knew who was sleeping there. Geoff shook his head but he was unable to move. He watched as Ishara stood over the slumbering Aiden, leader of the brigands.

Then, to Geoff's horror, Ishara pulled the dagger Ariel had given him from Aiden's belt and held it to his throat in one fluid motion. Aiden started and woke, looking up at

Ishara. Geoff saw fear in his dark, evil eyes. Aiden raised up on his elbows and opened his mouth to speak.

"Shh," said Ishara, holding a finger to her lips.

Aiden closed his mouth and remained quiet. Ishara removed the knife from his throat, turned to Geoff and smiled. Then she whirled back around and punched Aiden in the face, knocking him unconscious. She handed the dagger to Geoff and smiled. "Here," she whispered. "This belongs to you."

Geoff took it and looked at Ishara. The look on his face must have amused her because she grinned.

"I could not help myself," she said. "That felt good."

"I thought you were going to kill him," whispered Geoff.

"Me too," answered Ishara. "He deserves to die."

She walked to a back corner of the tent and took out her knife. Geoff watched as she cut an opening along the seams and stepped out into the night. He glanced over his shoulder to the front of the tent. He didn't see or hear any movement from the rest of the brigands. He swallowed and walked to the opening and peered through. A slender hand emerged from outside and grabbed his shirt collar. Before he realized what happened he was pulled through.

Outside Geoff found himself face to face with Ishara, who was smiling from ear to ear. She seems different now that we're out of that cage, he thought. She is kind of friendly. Happy, maybe? Before he was able to further consider the elven girl's change in demeanor he found himself dragged along behind her as she dashed into the forest. Geoff crunched and crashed through the underbrush and trees, unable to keep silent as they ran. He looked back at the brigands' camp to be sure they hadn't awakened any of them. When he didn't see any movement he let out a sigh of relief.

They ran until they came to a small meadow. Ishara released Geoff and sped ahead of him. Geoff stopped, put his hands on his knees, and tried to catch his breath. Ishara twirled about and leapt into the air with exemplary grace. She was elated to be free of her captors. She's like a ballerina, Geoff thought. She's so graceful, so fluid when she moves, just like Ariel.

"Um, excuse me," said Geoff, "but do you know Ariel?"

Ishara whirled, her eyes opened wide.

"Ariel Windsong? How do you know her?" she asked.

Geoff paused, wondering if he had made a mistake.

"I...I don't think she ever mentioned her last name," he said, "but she's a druid and fights with two scimitars like the one you carry."

Ishara ran up to Geoff and grabbed his shoulders. Geoff tried to step back, but she was too fast.

"You have met her! Where is she?"

Geoff swallowed hard.

"Well?" said Ishara, shaking him. "Tell me!"

"Oh...uh...yes. I met her but..."

"But what?"

Ishara grasped his head with her hands. Uh-oh, he thought. He hoped she wouldn't kill him if he had killed Ariel.

"You must tell me," she insisted. The smile had faded from her face.

"I...well, I'm not sure. Like I said in the cage, I don't

remember. The last time I saw her was in the catacombs of Silverthorne Manor. So, if those brigands were right…"

"Then you killed her too," said Ishara.

She released him, then turned and walked away. Geoff moved back a few steps. He wasn't sure what his new companion would do next.

Ishara stopped and shook her head.

"No."

She turned and again ran at Geoff. He braced for impact. But instead of attacking him, she wrapped her arms around him. Geoff tried to say something, but only managed a shocked mumble. He felt his cheeks run warm. Ishara pulled away and laughed.

"Sneak thief or wizard," said Ishara. "I do not believe you could kill Ariel. Not even by accident. She is a friend of the forest, a powerful druid. So you see, I think her destiny lies elsewhere."

"Yeah," agreed Geoff. "But the two brigands said they saw me kill her and my friends."

Ishara tilted her head and looked at Geoff.

"And you believe them? Brigands?"

Geoff considered Ishara's point for a moment.

"No. I guess not."

"They found you below Silverthorne Keep, in the catacombs?"

Geoff nodded.

"What possible reason would a human boy like yourself have to be in such a place?"

"We were…uh…running from a werewolf," said Geoff. "It's been following us for a while now."

"A werewolf?" said Ishara incredulously. "Why would a werewolf be hunting you?"

"I don't know," said Geoff. "But we can't lose it."

"I have never heard of such behavior from a werewolf," said Ishara. "Can Ariel's magic not protect you?"

"No. I don't think so. No matter where we go it's always right behind us."

Ishara walked past Geoff, looking at the ground in deep thought.

"I do not understand," she said.

"Neither do we," said Geoff. "But we wish it would go away and leave us alone."

As Geoff watched, Ishara walked in a circle around him while she considered what he had said. He looked around for a familiar landmark or terrain feature but found none.

"Hey, um, Ishara. I'm lost," he said. "Can you help me get back to Silverthorne Manor? Please? I have to try and find my friends."

Again the elven girl turned and walked to Geoff. Her movements were quick and deliberate. Geoff stepped backward. He wasn't sure what her answer would be, much less her physical reaction.

"Yes," she said with a smile. "I will help you, little sneak thief. Your quick thinking and quicker fingers freed us. It is the least I can do."

Geoff smiled. That was easy, he thought. She's pretty cool.

"Thanks."

"Follow me," she said and she took him by the hand and led him into the forest. Geoff stumbled and tripped once in a while, but he kept up with Ishara for the most part.

"We have to go back the way we just came," she said, "so we must give the brigand camp a wide berth."

"Okay," said Geoff. He had no desire to meet them again, especially Aiden.

They traveled until daybreak and then found a cool, shady spot to rest. She doesn't get tired, either, Geoff realized. She's just like Ariel. He wondered if all elves were as fit.

"Ishara," said Geoff as he bit his lower lip, "how did they capture you?"

Ishara raised an eyebrow.

"Sorry," said Geoff. "I just meant it seems like it would be really hard for anyone to catch you, let alone those brigands."

"On any given day you would be right," Ishara said. "But I was foolish and careless. Their leader, the one who stabbed you, is as cunning as he is cruel. He set a trap by the roadside. I was scouting for orc raiding parties when I came upon an injured man lying in the grass—or so I thought. I went to see if I could aid him and before I could react, I was surrounded by a dozen outlaws."

Geoff nodded and yawned unexpectedly. He quickly covered his mouth so as to not be rude, but Ishara noticed anyway.

"Try and get a little sleep," she said. "I will stand watch."

"Okay. Thanks."

He found a comfy spot on the grass and lay down. He watched his new companion walk about and survey their surroundings. She looks so different from when we met in the cage, he thought. She seems happy. Maybe being free agrees with her. Geoff shook his head. Of course it does, stupid.

He closed his eyes and drifted off to sleep. The next thing he knew Ishara was shaking him.

"Wake up," she said. "We should go."

"Ugh. How long was I asleep?"

"At least three hours," said Ishara. "We have remained here long enough. Come. We must go."

Geoff grunted as he lifted himself off the ground and rubbed his face.

"Do elves ever sleep?" he blurted out.

Ishara giggled.

"Of course. But we do not require as much sleep as humans. We can go for days before taking rest."

"Must be nice," said Geoff.

He wiped the sleep from his eyes and fell in line behind Ishara.

"Hey, that Zorn guy," said Geoff, "the one those brigands were talking about. He's the bad guy invading and conquering everything, right?"

"Mmhmm."

"Why?"

Ishara replied, "Why do humans always seem to start wars?"

Geoff grinned to himself. Yep. Just like Ariel.

"More power, more land, more riches. How much of each does a man need to be content? Greed will be the downfall of men. And they will drag us all to our deaths."

"Okay," said Geoff as he scratched his head. "Sooo from what you and Ariel say about us—humans, I mean—we're the bad guys?"

"Elves learned a long time ago not to trust men. Those brigands were a small sampling of what humanity has to offer the world."

"But," said Geoff, "there are some good humans, right?"

"Indeed," said Ishara. "They are rare, but they do exist."

"Hmmm. So back to Zorn," said Geoff. He felt at ease with Ishara; he felt he could talk to her. "What did they mean when they said he *was* a hero? He was a good guy?"

"Yes," replied Ishara. "Once he was a noble and just knight. Now he is an evil, twisted tyrant."

"So what happened?" asked Geoff.

"What do you mean?"

"Well, if he was a noble knight and all that, what changed him? Something must have happened."

They walked a few minutes, the sun warming them. The forest was not as thick with trees as the Spirewood Forest. The sounds of squirrels chattering and birds chirping filled the air.

"I do not know. Perhaps the same greed that infects all men finally found him."

Geoff shook his head. "I'm not sure about that. If he was a noble lord wasn't he rich?"

"Perhaps," said Ishara. "Then maybe he craved more power. He was always a great swordsman and a formidable opponent. You should ask Ariel; that is, if you didn't kill her and your friends in the catacombs."

Geoff stopped.

"Wait a minute," he said. "Ariel knows that Zorn guy?"

Ishara turned and looked at Geoff.

"Yes. She didn't tell you?"

Geoff shook his head.

"She *knew* him. They were once good friends, but that was a long time ago."

"Oh wow," said Geoff. "Is that why Ariel doesn't like us? Humans, I mean?"

"Perhaps, but I do not think so," said Ishara. "Men have shown their true colors longer than Zorn has been alive. Ariel knows this well."

"She doesn't seem to like us much," said Geoff. "But she is trying to help us get home…I think."

"*I* think if she is trying to help you find your way home," said Ishara, "then she likes you."

Geoff considered Ishara's words and smiled.

"Yeah, I guess you're right. We better get a move on, huh? Find the others."

Ishara and Geoff continued on their way through the forest. By the position of the sun in the sky, Geoff guessed it was midmorning. He couldn't help but notice that Ishara had a bounce in her step; she really did seem to be happy to be free and in the forest. They didn't speak as they walked, but after a few miles, she became solemn and turned to him.

"If we do find your friends," she said, "and if they are dead, what will you do?"

Geoff frowned. This is something he hadn't considered until now.

"I don't know," he said. "Try to find my own way home, I guess."

"Where is your home?"

Geoff thought for a moment, not sure how to best answer the question.

"Well," he began, "it isn't anywhere near here. My friends and I come from very far away."

"Where?" asked Ishara again.

Geoff laughed a little and smiled.

"We come from a place called Earth."

"Earth? Is that the name of your village? I have not heard of it."

"No. It's a planet," said Geoff. "Like I said, we aren't from around here. I don't know where we are—another planet or dimension or whatever."

Ishara stared at Geoff for a minute before speaking.

"This is the world of Alluria," she said. "How did you come to be here?"

"That's a long story," said Geoff. "In a nutshell, I found a white alabaster key and a stone archway in my father's study. When I touched the key it sort of activated the archway and we were sucked in. When we woke up, we were here."

"A key?" asked Ishara.

"Yeah, Ariel called it a wizard's key, I think. I've never seen one before."

Geoff continued for several more steps before he realized he was alone. He turned and looked for Ishara. She had stopped several feet back and had the most inquisitive look on her face.

"A wizard's key is a rare thing," she said. "There are few who can use such an item. Only the most powerful wizards can safely wield its power."

"Well, that leaves me out," said Geoff with a loud laugh. "Otherwise, we would still be home. Not being chased by werewolves and such."

"Yet you did use the key and you found yourselves here. I wonder, little sneak thief," she said, "if you possess wizardly abilities but you are unaware of them."

"Dunno," said Geoff. "Ariel let me hold this gem. She called it a mage stone. It was really cool. It floated and glowed with a white light. Jane's was green, like Ariel's, but I lost mine in the catacombs."

Ishara threw her head back and laughed. Wow, even her laugh is cute, Geoff thought. She's really cool. He watched her and couldn't help but smile.

"Then you *do* have the makings of a wizard," she said. "The mage stone proves it! You really have no idea, do you?"

"What? Me?" Geoff shook his head. "No way."

Ishara walked to Geoff and put her arm around him, turning him around so they could continue on to Silverthorne Keep. She had such a warm smile that Geoff couldn't take his eyes off her.

"So, what is to be done with you? A wizard combined with a sneak thief can be very useful. I wager those brigands would have gotten rich from your talents."

"But we don't have spells and magic where I come from," protested Geoff. "I can't cast any spells. I'm just a little guy. Not like Sawyer. Other kids pick on me and stuff."

Geoff hung his head. He hadn't meant to reveal that much to Ishara.

Geoff felt her arm tighten around him as they walked.

"I do not know this Sawyer, but I believe," she said with a confident tone, "those days are behind you. I am glad to have a wizard to travel with. I feel much safer now."

Geoff smiled. He felt like he was floating on air. Ishara

was nice and beautiful and she noticed him. She smelled like a sweet summer breeze. No girl had ever noticed him before. Hey, if she wanted him to be a wizard, he thought, then he'd be a wizard. No problem!

"However," she said in her serious tone, "if you *are* part wizard, you will need to become an apprentice and study. That will take time."

"Ha!" said Geoff. "Who's going to teach me? How many wizards do you have running around? How much is tuition? How do I—"

Ishara had stopped and crouched, pulling Geoff to his knees as she did so.

"What's the matter?" asked Geoff.

Ishara held up her finger for silence.

Geoff's heart began to beat faster. He looked around but saw nothing out of the ordinary.

"Shh," said Ishara as she unslung her bow and nocked an arrow in one move. "We are no longer alone."

She nodded and indicated that something or someone was straight ahead.

Geoff licked his lips and crouched lower.

"What do we do? Should we run?" whispered Geoff.

"Follow me," said Ishara.

Still crouching, she moved forward with slow, deliberate steps.

Geoff crouched and followed her. He made sure to stay close as they advanced. They crept silently for another thirty yards.

Ishara stopped and pointed at a small, overgrown brook in front of them. Geoff squinted. He saw movement past the shrubbery. On the opposite bank a hooded, solitary

figure in ragged furs was bent over trying to snatch a fish out of the water with its bare hands.

"What is that? Is that a man?" he whispered.

Ishara clenched her jaw and raised her bow.

Chapter Nineteen
Ol' Bleet

"WHAT? WHO ELSE IS AFTER Geoff? Oh, I don't believe this." Jane pushed herself up from her resting spot and walked over to Ariel. Sawyer got there first and stared at the ground by Ariel's foot.

"Oh, no," he said. "I don't believe it. No way."

Jane looked down to where Ariel had pointed to a blemish in the soft black dirt. She gasped and her hand shot up to her mouth as she shook her head in disbelief. A large pawprint of a wolf was clearly visible.

"That's…that's not real," she said. "Is it the same-"

"It is," said Ariel. "It is a fresh track from last night. The werewolf survived Silverthorne Manor and is now in front of us."

"Aww, man," said Sawyer. He stepped away, then took out his sword and swung it angrily in the air.

"So what are we going to do?" Jane asked, feeling a tear in her eye and staunching it with a trembling hand. "If we find Geoff, then the werewolf can't be far away."

Ariel stood and surveyed the path ahead of them.

"We continue on," she said. "We find Geoff and rescue him. We cannot stop. Not now. Hurry."

Jane and Sawyer fell in line behind Ariel, who had picked up her pace. At least she's staying within sight, thought Jane. That's good.

"Sawyer," she said between gasps for air, "how're we going to get out of this?"

"Dunno," said Sawyer. "Let's keep looking for Geoff… figure the rest out after."

"Okay," said Jane.

Soon Sawyer and Jane arrived at the clearing the brigands had used for a campsite. Ariel had arrived a few minutes earlier and was in the process of searching the abandoned camp. Only a wagon with an empty cage remained, along with a several rough sacks of flour and grain and a few miscellaneous items.

"Where's Geoff?" Sawyer asked. "And the kidnappers?"

Ariel studied the tracks in the ground by the wagon for a bit and pointed northeast.

"He and another prisoner escaped. They were pursued by the brigands," she said. "This is a good opportunity. We may be able to find Geoff first."

"But they left their wagon and food," said Jane. "Why would they do that?"

"The wagon and supplies would have slowed them. They intend to return," said Ariel. She looked at Jane. "Can you continue or do you need to rest?"

Jane shook her head and leaned against the wagon. "I need to rest for a little while."

"I could use a breather, too," said Sawyer. "Just a few minutes."

Ariel nodded. "Very well. Take a brief break. I will scout further ahead and return."

Jane watched Ariel sprint away, again disappearing into the forest.

"We're slowing her down," she said. "Maybe we should let her go after Geoff by herself."

Sawyer looked in the direction in which Ariel had run and shook his head. "We shouldn't split up," he said. "Didn't Geoff say something like that when we first arrived here?"

"I guess. I don't remember," said Jane. "But Ariel keeps taking off on her own and scouting or whatever. Let's just let her go get Geoff."

"Yeah. Maybe," said Sawyer. "But she keeps coming back. I think she's doing all she can. I say we do as she tells us."

"All right," she said. "It's just a suggestion anyway. Ariel knows what she's doing."

"You know, it's funny," said Sawyer. "At football practice I run circles around everyone. No problem. We come here and I can't even keep up with an elf girl. Hey, aren't elves supposed to be good at baking cookies and stuff? Mom used to buy that brand in the store."

Jane laughed.

"Jane, do you think they put Geoff in that cage?" said Sawyer, gesturing toward the wagon.

She looked at the crude cast iron cage sitting in the back of the old wagon. "Probably," she said. "I hope he's okay."

"Yeah," said Sawyer. "Me too. If he isn't, I have no idea what we're gonna say to his dad and stepmom."

The mention of Geoff's stepmother made Jane cringe. Geoff's stepmother was such a mean, rude woman. How could Mr. Vincent marry her? He's always nice and compassionate.

"She would probably have us arrested," said Jane. "His dad is really cool. He would understand, I think."

"When Ariel gets back we'll—" Jane was interrupted by a loud *snap* of a twig in the bushes behind her.

She whirled about and Sawyer jumped to his feet, drawing his sword. Neither made a sound for at least a minute. They listened and watched the bushes for movement. They heard another *snap*. This one was closer, but quieter than the first.

"Is that Ariel?" asked Jane in a hushed voice.

"No way," said Sawyer. "She never makes that much noise."

As Jane listened she became more aware of something approaching them, and that something was making an attempt to be as noiseless as possible.

"Who's there?" shouted Sawyer.

Jane was breathing fast. She backed away from the bushes until she was standing beside Sawyer. Jane noticed his front leg quivered a little. She looked about for a weapon. Finding none, she picked up a rock and readied herself.

"Who's there, I said!"

There was a cough from the bushes and then a figure appeared. It was an older man, middle-aged by Jane's best guess. He was pudgy, had a slight limp, and was slouched over. He wore no armor and his clothes were dirty and patched. His black and silvery hair was unkempt and matted, his face was round and his nose was a scarred, bulbous mass. His chin bristled with gray whiskers of various lengths. He breathed heavily through his mouth, which was missing some teeth. Those that remained were yellow and gray, turning black near the gums. He was in dire need of a bath, too.

The foul, smelly man took a step forward. Sawyer responded by raising his sword so it pointed at his chest while Jane cocked her arm and prepared to throw the stone. The man stopped and looked at them with his beady, mole-like eyes.

"Ye be in my camp," he said between wheezes. "Think ye can rob ol' Bleet an' get 'way with it?" He drew a rusted sword from his belt.

"Ye'll be sorry fer that. Oh yes, ye will."

"Stay away, old man," said Sawyer. "We aren't here to rob you and I don't want to hurt you."

The old man smiled, revealing several gaps in his yellow teeth. "Aye, maybe so. Maybe so. But I wanna hurt you. I like that sword ye be pointin' at me. Yes, I like it very much."

"We aren't trying to rob you," said Jane. "We're looking for our friend."

"Ah, ye be needin' a friend, eh? Well jest set right there an' ol' Bleet'll be with ya in a minute." The smelly old man grinned at Jane and licked his cracked lips.

"Ewwww. Gross," said Jane.

"Hey," said Sawyer. "Look at me. Where's our friend?"

The old man feinted a lunge at Sawyer, who stepped back.

"Dunno what ye mean," said Bleet. "Jest gimme that sword an' leave the girl then ol' Bleet'll let ya live, eh?"

"Get behind me, Jane," said Sawyer. "Get way back."

Jane stepped back another ten feet, keeping her arm raised and ready to throw the stone she had picked up.

"Ye think that'll save 'er, boy?" Bleet feinted again, this time to Sawyer's right.

"Sawyer! Be careful!" said Jane.

Sawyer appeared to remember Ariel's lessons. He maintained his balance, which he rarely did with Ariel, and kept the point of his sword pointed at his foe.

"I got this," he said.

"What ye got, boy?" said Bleet. "Ye think ye'll get the better of ol' Bleet?"

"I think ol' Bleet is about to have a bad day," said Sawyer. "From the looks of it, he's had a lot."

Jane looked at Bleet and then at Sawyer. The uncouth old man continued to feint, observing Sawyer's reaction each time. He's crafty; he's testing Sawyer, thought Jane. She threw her stone at Bleet, but he simply ducked his head and let it fly by.

"Now, now," said Bleet. "That's cheatin', it is. Ye shouldn't be throwin' nothin' at ol' Bleet."

Jane quickly found another stone. "Sawyer, he's dangerous!"

"Yeah," said Sawyer. "I know, I know."

Jane noticed Sawyer never took his eyes off the old man, another one of Ariel's lessons. Suddenly, Bleet thrust at Sawyer's midsection with his sword. Sawyer sidestepped the attack and parried Bleet's spinning backswing, which was the real attack.

"Ahhh, so ya know a lil somethin' 'bout swords, do ye?" said Bleet. "Been a long time since I 'ad this much fun."

Sawyer slashed with his sword, then followed with a thrust of his own. Bleet easily dodged both attacks and laughed. Jane noted the old man was no longer limping as he and Sawyer circled each other in the center of the camp.

Jane cocked her arm and readied another stone. This time the old man noticed from the corner of his eye and pointed at her. "Oh no ye don't," he growled. "This's a fight between two gentlemen, eh boy? That's what we are, two gentlemen. Right?"

Jane threw her stone as hard as she could. It struck Bleet just above his left eye.

"Ow, girl! I done told ya…," said Bleet as he staggered and collapsed.

Sawyer lowered his sword and looked at Jane. "What're you doing?" he said. "Thanks, but I had him."

Sawyer walked over to the prone figure and bent over to pick up his sword.

"Sawyer! No!" called Jane, but she was too late. Bleet suddenly swept Sawyer's legs out from under him with a hard kick. Sawyer landed with a heavy thud, but he kept his grip on his sword. In an instant Bleet was on top of him, smiling and drooling through the gaps in his yellow teeth.

"So ye think ye had ol' Bleet, eh?"

Jane watched as Sawyer tried to raise his sword, but the old man pinned his arm to the ground and forced Sawyer to release it. Sawyer struggled to get up, but the old man was much stronger than he looked.

"Now it's all o'er for ye. Oh yes, tha'll be truth, boy."

Bleet pulled a knife from his belt. He licked the blade. "I'ma stick ye real good, yes I am, and watch—"

Whack.

Jane had found a stout branch and hit Bleet on the back of his head as hard as she could. Bleet's eyes widened and then rolled up in his head. He slumped forward. Sawyer extended his arms to prevent Bleet from landing on him.

"Sawyer, are you okay?" said Jane. "Is he…is he…"

"Oh man, this guy is heavy," said Sawyer. Jane dropped the old branch she had used to club Bleet and helped Sawyer free himself.

As she helped Sawyer to his feet she noticed his face was red and he didn't make eye contact with her.

"Thanks," he said. "Like I said, I had him. Easy. We need something to tie this ugly perv up with."

"I just saw some rope in the wagon," said Jane.

"Perfect," said Sawyer. He put the point of his sword on Bleet's grungy neck. Jane got the rope and returned.

"Sawyer," she said, observing where he held his sword, "you aren't going to kill him, are you?"

"Nah," said Sawyer. "We need to make this grubby dude talk. Tell us what happened to Geoff. Let me have that rope, Jane."

Jane was relieved that Sawyer had no intention of murdering the old man. She looked at Bleet as Sawyer bound his hands and feet. She pinched her nose and took a couple of steps back. "Ugh! He really stinks, Sawyer."

"Yeah," said Sawyer. "He probably hasn't had a bath in weeks."

"More like years!" Jane said. "Ugh! I bet he has lice and fleas too."

Sawyer finished tying Bleet and sat him against a wagon wheel.

"Don't forget to wash your hands," said Jane. She was still holding her nose. Sawyer snickered and sat on the nearest rock, keeping his sword ready. Jane studied Bleet from a distance. He's horrible! Just horrible, she thought. Then an alarming thought occurred to her.

"Oh wait!" said Jane, looking around. "There might be more like him!"

Sawyer stood and looked around. "Yeah. You're right," he said. "Let's hope Ariel gets back before they do."

Jane picked up her makeshift club and stood guard on the other side of the camp while Sawyer kept an eye on Bleet. She hoped Ariel would return soon. Bleet was a handful for them, but Ariel would've made short work of him.

Another ten minutes passed and Jane started to worry. She expected Ariel to have returned much sooner. She set her club down and wrung her hands as she turned completely around, looking for Ariel.

"'Ey boy. Gimme some water, 'kay?" said Bleet. He licked his lips. "Ye bashed my noggin good, girl. Ye didn' 'ave to hit me so hard."

"I'm not getting you water," said Sawyer.

"The only water you need is for a bath," said Jane.

"Aww, ye wouldn't let an old man be thirsty, would ye? Now be a nice girl an' fetch ol' Bleet some water."

"Hell no," said Jane. "I'm not getting near you."

"That's jest downright cruel, that is," said Bleet. "Ye captured me fair. I be your prisoner now an' I need a bit o' cool water for my parched throat."

"All right, all right," said Sawyer. "Just shut up. I'll get you some water. Keep an eye on him, Jane."

"Aye," said Bleet, grinning at Jane. "I like ye lookin' at ol' Bleet, girl. Makes me feel wanted."

Jane winced. "Eww! You're just a dirty old toad. Stop talking before we do something bad to you."

"Somethin' bad? To poor ol' Bleet? Now, now. That's not very nice, is it?"

Sawyer had poured some of his water into a broken clay cup he found by the wagon. He walked over to their prisoner and bent over to let him drink. As he did so, the old man produced a knife he had hidden beneath his jerkin and put it against Sawyer's throat.

"Sawyer!" shouted Jane, picking up her club.

"Easy there, girl. Ye don' want me to filet yer boyfriend, do ya?"

"Let him go!" said Jane. She gripped her club with both hands and prepared to swing.

"Jest as soon as he unties ol' Bleet. Then I'll—"

A scimitar appeared from nowhere and brushed firmly against Bleet's throat. Bleet's eyes opened wide at the sudden occurrence.

"She said let him go," said Ariel. She placed a point under Bleet's chin and raised it, forcing him to look up at her.

"Aagh! Okay, okay!" Bleet dropped his knife and released Sawyer, who immediately stepped back and raised his sword.

"'Ey! Ye be an elf!" said Bleet.

"So?" said Ariel.

"We 'ad one an…an…" Bleet realized what he was saying.

"And?" asked Ariel, applying more pressure with her scimitar.

"Ow! An' she run off, she did. She run off with that lil hedge wizard Rolf and Cedric brought back."

"You mean the boy?" asked Ariel.

"Aye, aye. The skinny lil yellow haired runt. Oh, but I didn' do nothin' to 'im, ye see. Ol' Bleet liked 'im, that's true. Ol' Bleet didn' harm the boy. Was Aiden who…" Bleet let his words trail off.

"What happened to the boy?" said Ariel.

"No, no. Nothin' happened. He's right as rain, he is. Aiden jest stuck 'im a lil with his knife is all."

"What?" said Jane. "Geoff's been stabbed?"

"Who's Aiden?" asked Sawyer, taking a step toward Bleet.

"Aarrgghh! Easy with that point, will ya? Aiden'll be our leader, he is. Makes lots o' gold for us, he does."

"Yeah, you look like it," said Sawyer.

Jane lowered her club. Ariel had returned and the danger from Bleet was over and done. She watched as Ariel searched the old outlaw for further weapons. She found another knife in one of his boots.

"If you decide to take prisoners," she said, "always remember to search them thoroughly for weapons." Ariel threw the knives into the woods and stood up.

"Now, now. They'll be jest for carvin' dinner an' such. I forgot I—"

Without a single word Ariel punched Bleet in the face. Jane heard a *crunch* and Bleet was unconscious. His nose looked even worse now, she thought. It was red and swollen and had a nasty bend to it.

"You broke his nose," said Jane.

"Good. Maybe he looks better," said Sawyer. His face was still a little red, and he still seemed a bit embarrassed.

"I followed Geoff's trail," said Ariel. "He travels with someone and he is being pursued by the rest of the brigands. We should hurry."

"Did Geoff get captured by someone else? And what are we going to do with him?" said Jane, pointing at Bleet.

"Leave him," said Ariel. "He will survive and find a way to escape. Worms like him always do. Geoff is no longer a prisoner, but that may change if we do not find him in time."

"Are you sure? I mean, what if he gets loose and warns the other brigands? Isn't there a police or sheriff's office or something? We're just going to let him go?" said Jane.

"Do you wish for me to kill him?" asked Ariel.

"No," said Jane. "But shouldn't he be punished for kidnapping Geoff?"

"Who cares?" said Sawyer. "The rank old fart is on his own. I hope some animals eat him."

"We do not have time," said Ariel. "Geoff may need our aid even now."

"Yeah," said Sawyer, putting his sword back in its scabbard. "Let's roll."

Jane didn't want to waste any more time with Bleet, either. They needed to find Geoff, and from the tone in Ariel's voice, he must be close and in trouble.

They dashed into the forest, following Geoff's tracks. Jane and Sawyer no longer tried to keep quiet. They ran as fast as they could, crunching and crashing through the woods in an attempt to keep up with Ariel.

"Sawyer," said Jane, "do we have any idea who's with Geoff?"

"No," he said. "Bleet mentioned an elf girl. But maybe one of those brigands helped him escape? Dunno."

Jane frowned. Sawyer's guess didn't make any sense to her. Why would one of the brigands betray their own? And if Bleet was any indication, the brigands were crafty, merciless, and hateful. She remembered how dangerous this world was; brigands might be the least of their worries. The werewolf was still hunting them.

Jane searched for Ariel as she ran. But as usual, she was too far ahead, she thought. Sawyer was running twenty feet ahead of her and he made a lot of noise, so Jane easily followed him along a small woodsy ravine and over a few mossy boulders. They passed through more trees and found Ariel standing in a small clearing holding her hand up while she covered her heart with the other.

Two figures emerged from the far side of the clearing and approached Ariel.

CHAPTER TWENTY

BRIGAND BATTLE

"So what do we do?" asked Geoff, staring at the large, ragged figure by the water.

Ishara didn't answer. She remained tense, ready to let her arrow fly. Geoff's heart began to race and he could feel goose bumps on his arms again.

"Ishara," said Geoff urgently, "what do we do?"

"Quiet. We should avoid that stranger," she whispered. "I do not have a good feeling about him."

"Yeah," said Geoff. "Me either."

Geoff stepped back. He glanced back over his shoulder at the route they had taken.

"Geoff!" said Ishara. He spun back around at the urgency in her voice. She stood and it looked to Geoff like she was going to fire her arrow.

The tattered figure stood up and looked at them.

"He sees us! What are we going to do?"

Geoff turned to Ishara. She had a clear shot at the stranger.

"Are you going to shoot him?"

The solitary figure motioned for them to come closer.

He didn't appear to be afraid of Ishara aiming an arrow at him. He made no threatening moves, nor did he appear to be armed.

"Do we run for it?" asked Geoff.

Ishara lowered her bow and took a deep breath. Geoff looked at her and raised his hands, not sure what was going to happen next.

"Keep your knife handy, little sneak thief," said Ishara. "Be ready to run."

"What?"

Geoff couldn't believe what he had just heard.

"You're not going over there, are you? Who knows what that wild man will do to you!"

"No," said Ishara, "I am not going over there. We are."

"Huh? Look at him! We don't know what he's capable of doing. We can't trust him," said Geoff.

Ishara raised an eyebrow.

"You have great power indeed if you can but glance at someone and determine if they are trustworthy."

"But…sorry," said Geoff. "It's just that since we arrived we've been running for our lives."

"Mmmhmm," said Ishara with a slight smile. "Remember, remain vigilant. I do not believe this meeting is by chance."

As they made their way into the small glade, Geoff detected a strong musty smell, like an animal's scent.

He stayed behind Ishara as they approached the stranger and kept his hand on the knife she'd reclaimed from the brigand leader. He also noticed that even though she had lowered her bow, she kept an arrow nocked and ready to fire.

They stopped almost ten feet away from the water's edge. Geoff couldn't see much of the stranger's face under the frayed hood, only a dark, whiskered chin. The man was over six feet tall and had broad shoulders. He—or the animal skin he wore—was the source of the musty smell. He must be some sort of mountain man or something, thought Geoff. He's big, and he looks wild and dangerous.

"I am Ishara. My companion is—"

"Geoff," said the man in animal skins.

Geoff's jaw dropped. Ishara looked at Geoff. He blinked a few times.

"How…how did you know my name?" asked Geoff.

"I know who you are," said the man. "And I know of Sawyer and Jane. I've been watching you."

"How do you know of Geoff and his friends? Have you been following him?" demanded Ishara.

"Do you not see him with your elven sight?" said the stranger. "See how his aura shines. So beautiful."

Geoff was speechless.

"I see *your* aura," retorted Ishara. "It is both light and dark. Dark as night."

The man in animal furs slowly nodded, but said nothing.

"What do you want?" asked Ishara. From the corner of his eye he saw her tighten her grip on the bow. The stranger pointed at Geoff. His hand was burnt and raw.

"You have lost something, haven't you? Something important? A key, perhaps?"

"Oh yes, yes!" said Geoff, leaning forward. "It was taken from me! Have you seen it? Do you know where it is? My friends and I need it."

"Aye, I've seen it," said the stranger. "It's in a dark, tainted place. Far too dangerous for you."

"Tell me…please," said Geoff.

"If you journey there, you will not return," said the tattered man. "Perhaps I'm not doing you a kindness if I tell you."

"You have been touched by the darkest of evils," said Ishara. "Why should we trust you? Perhaps you are trying to trap us."

"Aye, that is true enough," said the stranger. "Know this—I profit nothing by helping you. Besides, it may already be too late."

"What? What do you mean?" said Geoff.

The stranger looked at Ishara. "I've seen the armies and great war machines of the Shadowlord. The realm of Alluria is about to tear itself apart with war. An age of chaos is upon us."

Geoff looked at Ishara. Her somber expression confirmed what the strange, wild man said.

"What do you mean that it may already be too late?" asked Geoff. "We've got to find that key. I need to know where it is. We've got to get home."

The tattered man sat in silence for a moment.

"Very well," he said. "North of here is a dead forest. It was once the Eldritch Forest, a green and beautiful place. But now it is a festering swamp."

"Yeah," said Geoff, looking at Ishara. "That's what the brigands said, too."

"Your key resides in the center of that swamp. But I warn you not to go there."

"Why not?" said Geoff.

"Something sinister dwells there. You and your friends will perish if you enter."

"Wait, you've seen them?" asked Geoff excitedly. "Are they alive? Where are they?"

"I don't know."

Geoff looked at Ishara. "We have to find them!"

Suddenly the stranger shot to his feet, and Ishara to hers, her bow ready with arrow fully drawn and aimed at his heart. Geoff thought she was going to shoot him.

"Riders," he said, looking in the direction behind Geoff and Ishara. "From the south. You've been followed."

Geoff listened. He didn't hear anything except the rushing water of the brook.

"I hear them too," said Ishara. "Geoff, we need to hide."

"It's gotta be the brigands," said Geoff with a frown. Without a word, Ishara grabbed his hand and pulled him along as she ran into the woods. Geoff glanced back at the lone raggedy figure. He wondered what they would do to him if they captured him.

"Run!" said Geoff while he waved at the stranger to flee. "Shh!" said Ishara sharply while she jerked his hand so hard Geoff thought he might lose it.

"Quiet," she said tersely. "You will betray our whereabouts!"

As they ran through the trees Geoff looked over his shoulder one last time. The stranger had not moved. Instead, he was watching them run away. Ishara led Geoff down a slight slope and then across a small meadow. Geoff heard the sounds of hoofbeats now. Their pursuers were coming closer. Once they reached the other side of the meadow, Ishara grabbed Geoff firmly by the shoulders and planted him behind a large oak tree.

"Do not move. Understand?" she said. "No matter what happens, you must not move from this spot."

Geoff swallowed and nodded. His breathing was fast and shallow. The thought of being captured again by Aiden and his gang of cutthroats terrified him. Ishara peeked from around the trunk of the oak tree.

"What are you going to do?" asked Geoff.

"What I must to save us," she said. "Stay here."

Geoff watched Ishara raise her bow. Her eyes narrowed. Then he heard a low *pffft* followed by a sickening thud and a scream. Ishara had another arrow nocked in an instant. She loosed the arrow and again Geoff heard a scream. This time Geoff heard something heavy hit the ground nearby.

Ishara nocked another arrow and dashed to the next tree, firing sideways from her hip. Another thud and scream. Geoff trembled so much that his knees felt weak. Then he heard something fly by, grazing the tree that concealed him. There was a loud *thwack* ten feet away. Geoff saw an arrow protruding from the tree just beyond his hiding spot.

"They're in the trees! Get after 'em!" It was the unmistakable sound of Aiden's voice commanding his men to attack.

Ishara raced to the next tree, spun, aimed, and *pffft*.

Geoff heard her arrow strike her target. Then he heard another scream followed by a loud gurgling sound. He watched Ishara spin and move between the trees and fire arrow after arrow. Every one she let fly was followed by a thud and then a scream. A few arrows whizzed by her and

hit a neighboring tree. She was lightning fast and used her surroundings for cover with perfection.

Wow! thought Geoff. She's amazing! She doesn't miss!

He heard a few alarmed voices coming from the meadow. Shaking, he peeked from behind the tree and saw two more brigands coming in his direction. Two more were running in the opposite direction. A hand touched Geoff's shoulder and he jumped. It was Ishara.

"Shh," she said, putting her finger to her lips. "I have no more arrows."

Geoff's heart sank. He heard the two oncoming brigands. They were close. Ishara leapt from behind the tree and ran deeper into the forest, away from Geoff. The brigands followed her. They ran past Geoff, failing to notice him standing flush against the tree. Geoff peeked from behind the tree again. He was relieved not to see any more brigands attacking. Suddenly he felt a vicelike grip on his shoulder. He was spun around and pushed against the tree. His head hit the tree trunk and he grunted with pain as he saw a white flash. Something cold and sharp pressed against his throat.

"So you and your little girlfriend think you're smart, eh?" It was Aiden.

Geoff opened his mouth to scream, but Aiden covered his mouth with his hand.

"Oh, I don't think so," said Aiden with a sneer. "Your sweetheart wiped out my men. I should kill you right now."

Geoff looked at those cruel dark eyes hovering over him. He felt his knees wobble and his eyes welled up.

"But I'm going to take great pleasure in hearing you scream and—"

Geoff saw a large, blistered hand grab the hair on top of Aiden's head and yank him backward. Geoff no longer felt the sharp edge of the sword against his neck. His knees buckled and he sank to the ground. Geoff looked up and saw the strange man in tattered animal skins slam Aiden's head into the tree with a *whack*. Aiden's body immediately went limp and fell to the ground.

"Are you okay?" the man asked.

Geoff nodded. The tattered man picked him up off the ground. Wow, he's so strong, thought Geoff.

"Go," he said, pointing into the woods. "Find Ishara. Find your friends."

Geoff took a few steps then turned around.

"Th…thank you."

The tattered man nodded. Geoff ran into the forest. His legs were a little wobbly, so he stumbled a bit. Nearly fifty yards further he found Ishara. She was holding her bow like a club and standing over the two prone figures of the brigands.

"Ishara!" said Geoff. "That was awesome!"

She winked at him and smiled.

"How did you do that?" said Geoff. "They didn't stand a chance!"

"They should not have followed us," she said. "How are you?"

"I'm fine," said Geoff. "That wild man saved me. Aiden was about to kill me, but then this big, hairy figure appeared out of nowhere and slammed Aiden's head against the tree."

"Truly?" asked Ishara, raising her eyebrows at this news.

"Oh yes," said Geoff. "I think maybe he's a good guy."

Ishara said nothing. They walked back to the meadow

where the brigands had attacked them. Geoff scanned the area. The tattered man was gone.

"Pity," said Ishara, also looking about. "I would like to have spoken with him again."

"Me too."

Geoff looked at the bodies that littered the meadow. Ishara's arrows had found their mark with unerring accuracy.

"You never miss, do you?" asked Geoff.

Ishara smiled at him.

"No, really," Geoff continued eagerly. "How did you do that?"

"Many years of practice," said Ishara. "I am an archer, but in times of war I am also a skirmisher."

"Skirmisher?" Geoff asked, shaking his head.

"I seek out and attack enemies from a distance. I harass them."

"Yeah," said Geoff, licking his lips. "I think you got that down."

He stopped and regarded Ishara.

"You could've killed them anytime, couldn't you?"

"Yes," she said. "But not until I was free, and I have you to thank for that. Stay here. I want to be certain we are no longer being followed."

Geoff nodded and lowered himself to the ground, leaning against a small tree. He saw Ishara walk into the meadow, but she quickly disappeared in the foliage. He put his head in his hands and rubbed his sweaty forehead.

Geoff leaned his head back and closed his eyes. A bead of sweat trickled down the back of his neck, relaxing him a bit. He took a deep, weary breath. So tired, he thought. He could go to sleep right there.

Ishara returned a few minutes later, wiping blood from several of her arrows.

"You got your arrows back," he said, noticing she had a full quiver again.

"Yes," she said. "I looked for the man wearing the animal skins, but I could not find him."

"Oh," said Geoff. He was disappointed their conversation with the tattered man had come to an abrupt end.

"I did, however, find the two brigands who fled," said Ishara. "They were dead."

"See? He helped us," said Geoff. "He didn't seem so bad."

"I would not count him as an ally," cautioned Ishara. "As I said, he has a darkness about him. He is dangerous. Remember that should you encounter him again."

Geoff thought for a moment, then said, "How can you see if someone is good or bad? What's all that 'aura' stuff?"

"Elves," said Ishara, "and a few other races in Alluria are able to see or sense whether one's spirit or inner self is moral or corrupt."

"So, it's like seeing if someone is lying?" asked Geoff.

"No," said Ishara shaking her head. "But it is wise to be suspicious when dealing with someone like that stranger. There is a duality about him."

"Duality? What does that mean?"

"Two halves," said Ishara. "There is a struggle inside him, I think. But I cannot say how or why."

"But all humans have good and bad in them," said Geoff.

"No," said Ishara. "Not like him. He is…cursed somehow."

"Cursed," repeated Geoff. What could that mean? The man in animal skins was odd and smelly. But he had helped them.

"It must be lonely living wild like that," mused Geoff. "He looked hurt, too. Did you see his hands?"

"Yes, but I think his true pain comes from within," said Ishara. "Are you ready? We should find Ariel and your friends."

"Yeah. You're right. I guess we better get going," said Geoff as he got to his feet.

As they left the meadow, Geoff glanced over his shoulder at the bodies in the meadow.

"Geoff," called Ishara. She had stopped about twenty feet away to wait for him.

"Oh," said Geoff. "Sorry."

He hurried to catch up with Ishara. They walked in silence for almost a league before Ishara spoke.

"You have not seen death, have you?"

Geoff shook his head. "Not like that."

"In your realm, Earth, you do not have death?"

"Yes," said Geoff. "It's just…I don't know. My mom died a couple years ago, so we do have death."

"I am sorry for your loss, but no matter what realm we are from," said Ishara, "we are all on a journey to somewhere else. We elves may live forever, but there is something eternal in all living things, even humans."

Geoff nodded.

"We each have our own destiny. When we have completed our destiny then our time here is done."

"I wonder," said Geoff as they walked. "What was their destiny? The brigands, I mean."

Geoff looked at Ishara, who pursed her lips while she thought about an answer. After a minute she said, "If not for the brigands then we would have never met. And who knows? Perhaps when they pulled you from the catacombs they saved your life."

"Yeah," said Geoff. "I like the first answer. We wouldn't have met if not for them, would we?"

Ishara smiled and nudged him with her shoulder, nearly knocking him down.

"Hey!" said Geoff, laughing, "You're pretty strong…for a girl." He returned the nudge.

Geoff was surprised and even a bit elated when Ishara responded with a playful giggle. He didn't expect that sort of reaction. She seemed to enjoy his company. This is new, he thought. Normally girls didn't talk to or even notice him. Ishara, however, was different.

"So," said Geoff, working his mind for something to say, "elves live forever? You're immortal? Do you ever get… you know…bored?"

"No," said Ishara, "Why would we? Such a silly question."

"Well, I never met an immortal before you and Ariel," said Geoff. "I just wondered what elves do since they live forever."

"We do what all the other races do, except we do it for a longer time."

Geoff looked at Ishara. She was grinning at him. He grinned back at her. "Good answer."

They continued their trek back to Silverthorne Manor

for another hour. Geoff and Ishara chatted about the differences between elves and humans. Geoff was pleased to discover Ishara had more tolerance for humans than Ariel. As they walked, his spirits rose. He enjoyed being with Ishara. He enjoyed the leisurely pace of their stride, too.

More than once he looked about and took in the beauty of nature. The trees grow so tall here, he thought. There's so much wildlife and the smell of the forest is relaxing.

"Geoff," said Ishara in a serious tone, "we should arrive at Silverthorne tomorrow morning."

"Okay."

"You need to prepare yourself for the possibility those brigands were right," said Ishara. "If your friends are dead…"

Geoff looked down. "Yeah," he said. "I hope they're still alive. I don't know what I'd do if they were gone. How would I get home?"

"I do not know," said Ishara. "Ariel knows more about such matters. However, if you used a wizard's key to travel from your Earth to this realm, then you must continue your quest for the key. Exactly how did you lose it?"

"It was taken by a giant," said Geoff. "I left it at our campsite and when I returned, the giant took it, changed into a black winged thing, and flew away."

"Oh," said Ishara, "Some creatures are drawn to items of magic. Do you know where this key-stealing giant is now?"

"No," said Geoff, shaking his head. "It just flew away. But I think Ariel knew something about it. She seemed to, anyway."

"True, she would know of such creatures," said Ishara.

"Is she like a tribal leader or something? She knows a lot about a lot." Geoff winced at his last sentence, not sure if it had made sense.

"She is a druid," she said. "A very powerful one, too. In her order she holds the rank of archdruid."

"So she is the leader of the druids?"

"No," said Ishara, "The high druid is the leader of all the druids. Ariel is among those who are next in rank."

"How many druids are there?"

"I do not know," said Ishara. "Those born with druidic talents and abilities are a rarity. Only elves have the capacity to become druids."

"Wait. Only elves? Not humans?" said Geoff.

Ishara nodded.

"But I said earlier that my friend Jane could make one of those floating gems glow green," said Geoff. "Ariel said she had druidic abilities."

"Who is this Jane?"

"She's one of my friends. She came here with me."

"She is human?" asked Ishara.

"Yep."

"There has never been a human druid. Humans simply do not have the empathy, compassion, and fortitude for such a calling. It is a gift, even among us elves."

"Okay," said Geoff. "But I saw her gem glow green, just like Ariel's."

From the corner of his eye, Geoff saw Ishara look at him with a puzzled expression. He smiled to himself. He wasn't sure if she believed him, but that didn't matter to Geoff. He took a small amount of comfort in knowing something she didn't.

Another hour passed. They walked in relative silence before Geoff asked, "Where are we?"

"The Feral Thicket," said Ishara. "A place full of wild magic and creatures. It is—"

Geoff felt Ishara grab his shoulder and pull him down. She placed a finger over her lips and unslung her bow with her other hand. In another second she had an arrow nocked and was aiming at something in front of them.

"What is it? Is it that wild man again?" said Geoff quietly.

"Shh," said Ishara. "Something or someone is coming."

Geoff looked where Ishara had pointed her arrow. He didn't see anything except trees and undergrowth. A few seconds later, he heard the sounds of something running through the undergrowth, coming their way.

CHAPTER TWENTY ONE
THE ELDRITCH SWAMP

"ARIEL!" CALLED GEOFF, HIS FACE beaming. "You found us!"

He ran to Ariel and flung his arms around her. She smiled and returned his embrace. Jane and Sawyer arrived several seconds later. Jane hugged Geoff and Ariel while Sawyer gave Geoff a pat on the back.

"Oh, Geoff!" said Jane. "We were worried about you! We didn't know what happened."

"Yeah, we thought you were a goner," said Sawyer. "It's good to see ya! Are you okay?"

"Yeah, I'm fine," said Geoff. "But I was worried you guys were dead. I was kidnapped by brigands and they said I killed all of you."

Jane and Sawyer looked at each other.

"Well, there was a giant ball of fire that rolled down the hall and almost fried us," said Sawyer. "You did that?"

"I don't know. I can't remember," said Geoff. "All I remember is being trapped in a dark room by one of those mite-monster things. I thought it was going to eat me. I must've blacked out. When I woke up, I'd been kidnapped."

"So where are the brigands and who is she?" said Sawyer, motioning to Ishara.

"Oh, that's Ishara," said Geoff. "She took the brigands out all by herself."

Jane turned her head and saw Ariel speaking with a small elf girl armed with a bow.

"Hal'inari," said Ishara, placing her hand over her heart.

"It is good to see you again, little one," said Ariel with a smile.

"Forgive me, but I bring ill tidings. The Shadowlord has attacked Selra'thel. Our homeland stands alone against his hordes."

Jane saw the smile leave Ariel's face.

"I have other grave news," continued Ishara. "Evil has consumed the Eldritch Forest. An evil that is growing, expanding beyond its borders. The forest is now twisted and warped, Ariel. Creatures that should not exist, hideous things, are spat out from that once green woodland."

Ariel looked to the north, the direction of the Eldritch Forest.

"I know," she said quietly. "I must go to there and confront my friend."

Everyone fell silent and looked at Ariel. A few moments later Jane walked to where Ariel and Ishara were standing.

"What are you talking about?" she said. "Who are you going to confront? Are you going to fight someone?"

Jane studied Ariel and looked at Ishara for an answer. Ishara merely cast her eyes downward.

"Ariel," said Jane, "I don't understand. Who are you going to fight and why?"

She looks worried and sad, thought Jane. Something awful has happened.

"Ariel?" repeated Jane.

"I do not wish to speak of it," said Ariel. "It would be better if all of you went to the capital city of Chalon while I see to the task before me. Ishara can take you there."

"What?" said Sawyer. "No way. We're going with you."

"Yeah," said Geoff. "Safety in numbers, right?"

Ariel shook her head. "Not this time."

"We're going with you," insisted Jane. "We can help. And Geoff is right; there is safety in numbers."

"I am sorry," said Ariel. "But it is too dangerous."

"Perhaps," said Ishara, "you will allow us to accompany you as far as the village of Somerdale? We can wait there for your return."

"Even that is dangerous," said Ariel. "Somerdale has been abandoned. Whatever evil dwells within the Eldritch Forest reigns there."

"But if something happened to you," said Geoff, "we'd never know."

"I will stay with them and keep them safe," said Ishara.

Ariel took a deep breath and nodded. "Very well," she said. "We travel to Somerdale Village. But you must listen and do as I say. Your lives may well depend on it."

"Okay," said Jane. "We only want to help, so don't send us away."

"The village is a day's travel northeast of here," said Ariel solemnly. "We should leave now."

"We stick together," said Jane. "It's what we do."

"It's what…we do," repeated Ariel. She looked at Jane and raised an eyebrow as she tilted her head. Jane met

Ariel's confused gaze. Did she say something wrong? She must have struck a nerve, she thought. Ariel turned and walked away. Ishara motioned for them to follow as she joined Ariel.

Sawyer and Geoff joined Jane as they fell in line behind Ariel and Ishara.

"What's up with her? Never seen her like this," said Sawyer. "Why would she fight a friend? Is she going to kill him?"

Jane shook her head, "I don't know. Something's wrong. She obviously doesn't want to do this."

"Yeah," said Sawyer. "I couldn't kill my best friend."

"By the way," said Jane. "Who *is* your best friend?"

"Dunno," said Sawyer. "You, maybe?"

He looked at her and smiled. Jane returned his smile and gave him a nudge with her elbow.

The day's journey to Somerdale Village was uneventful. They arrived late in the afternoon and stopped at the outskirts of the small farming village. Ariel and Ishara scanned the area for movement. The entire town was overgrown and the buildings were starting to show signs of disrepair.

A light mist rose from the ground and surrounded doors that hung ajar and shutters that dangled from their windows. The fields of the once thriving hamlet were nearly barren. The crops had withered away until nothing more than scraggly shrubs remained.

Ishara pointed to three bodies lying near the doors to a large brown barn. They were armed and wore chainmail armor.

"I see them," said Ariel. "They look like soldiers from Chalon."

"Their weapons are strewn about. It looks like they died in battle," said Ishara. "Typical patrols from Chalon number twelve soldiers. I do not see the others."

"Agreed," said Ariel. "Lionel would be foolish enough to send a smaller patrol here. He has not changed."

"What happened here?" said Jane. "It looks like a ghost town. And who is Lionel?"

"Lionel," said Ishara, "is the lord magistrate of the great capital city of Chalon."

"Ugh! I can already smell the swamp," said Sawyer, holding his nose.

"Guys," said Geoff. I don't think we should be here."

"Me too, Geoff," said Jane. "We're in danger."

Ariel looked at Jane. "I have the same feeling."

She too senses danger, thought Ariel. She knows so little about the druidic ways. Yet she surprises me. Her skills grow.

"Hey! My sword is pulsing! Ariel, the last time it did that we were at—"

"Silverthorne Manor." Ariel scanned the forest behind them.

"Is the werewolf near? Is it coming after us again?" asked Geoff, following Ariel's gaze.

"How…how did you come by that sword?" asked a wide eyed Ishara. She had recognized the blade Sawyer carried.

"He found it in a troll hole," said Jane. "Is it the werewolf, Sawyer?"

"No. It's something different," said Sawyer. "It's

like we're surrounded and something knows we're here. Something bad. Really bad."

"It is too early in the day for a werewolf," said Ishara.

Ariel felt her stomach churn. The Stormblade's warning was undeniable. They were being watched.

"Stay here while I have a closer look," said Ariel. "Ishara, watch them."

The young elf girl nocked an arrow. Ariel crouched and moved toward the barn while Ishara drew her bow and prepared to fire.

"What's she looking for?" asked Geoff.

"Enemies," whispered Ishara. "And a safe place for us."

Ariel crept to the barn and peered inside. With the exception of several mounds of rotting hay in a corner, the barn was empty. She turned her attention to the three bodies that lay just outside and examined them. From their condition, she guessed they had been dead for a couple of days. They must have tried to make their way to the barn, she thought. They had hoped it would be a more defensible position.

Ariel turned and crept around the barn toward the center of town. Every building and cottage was dark and empty. The townsfolk had left Somerdale Village a long time ago. She found the village barracks and armory near the center of town. The one room building was a mess inside. Bedding and utensils were strewn about, but there were no weapons in the wall racks. A useable cooking pit lay in the center of the barracks.

Ariel ran her fingers along the stout wooden construction of the walls. It's well built, she thought, nodding. This will do.

She went outside and signaled for the others. They hurried to her through the center of the village.

"Wow, what happened here?" said Jane. "This place looks like a hurricane blew through it."

"At least it's strong," said Ishara, knocking on a wall. "We should be safe here. The shutters on the windows appear to be intact."

"Okay, so what exactly is going on?" asked Sawyer. "You're going into the swamp while we wait here. I figured that much out. Are you sure you don't want us to come with you?"

"The swamp is dangerous," said Ariel. "You are to stay the night here. If I have not returned by morning, Ishara will take you to Chalon. Once there, seek the wizard Maelord. Tell him what happened. He will be your best chance to get home."

"Don't go, Ariel," said Jane. "You don't have to go. We can all go to Chalon together."

Ariel smiled at Jane. "I am learning much from the three of you. And I have more to learn about humans. When I return, perhaps you can teach me."

"Perhaps. I'd like that very much," said Jane with a grin. "But only if you teach me more spells."

"Agreed," said Ariel.

"Yeah," said Sawyer. "And you gotta show me more sword fighting moves and stuff."

"We'll see you in the morning," said Geoff with a smile.

Ariel gave Ishara a quick nod and turned for the door. The sun was starting to set; the shadows from the cottages and buildings of Somerdale had grown since their arrival. Ariel stopped in the doorway and looked at them. She never thought these three human children would be her friends. She smiled, turned, and exited into the coming twilight.

She ran to the edge of the village. The swampy terrain was starting to encroach on Somerdale. The mist was thicker and clung to her as she moved. Ariel stopped and looked into the dim, misty swamp. The once thriving trees had been twisted into dark, grotesque shapes. She took a deep breath. The stench of decay assailed her senses.

She let her mind wander back hundreds of years when she and her elven friends ran and played with all manner of fairies in the Eldritch Forest. She first learned the ways of the druid here, studying the trees and animals. Those were magical, happier times.

This was once the most beautiful forest in the realm, thought Ariel. She knew what she had to do, but she had hoped the rumors were false—that she would not be the one to face her beloved mentor. Bhael, the dark druid. Yes, she knew him. If her sight failed her she would still know him.

Deep inside Ariel felt a yearning, a calling. Something was beckoning to her from deep inside the swamp. It was like a voice in her head and a painful, sinking feeling in her heart. She was being drawn into darkness.

Her hands trembled slightly and she clenched and released her fists several times to steady her nerves. Suddenly the feeling of being watched again descended on her. Something knew she was there and she had no choice but to continue. So be it, she thought.

Ariel entered the mists and the stinking, malignant marsh. Pools of bubbling muck littered the ground and her vision was hindered by the ever thickening mist.

Something to her left moved and hissed. She spun to face the unknown enemy, but saw nothing. Satisfied no attack was forthcoming, she returned to her original course.

She had walked twenty feet when something black flew up from the ground in front of her. A whirlwind of wings and claws struck at her. Ariel drew one of her scimitars and slashed at her attacker. Her blow missed, but managed to chase away a large raven. It flew up and landed on a moss-covered branch in a nearby tree, its cawing echoing throughout the swamp.

Several other ravens landed in the same tree, their black eyes watching her. Ariel ignored the chorus of caws and resumed her trek deeper into the swamp. Sounds of crickets chirping and frogs croaking filled the air. Every now and then she heard a loud splash as something disturbed the dark waters around her.

Eventually she came upon a ring of large carved stones that were overgrown and covered with moss. The stones were carved from granite and set three feet apart. They surrounded a small basin that rested on a raised dais which was also carved from granite.

Ariel knew this place. This was a sacred site. Many years ago she had been anointed here and became a druid. It was here that she performed her first druidic rite, the ceremony marking the first day of spring. Once flowers bloomed all about and the ground was carpeted by lush green grass. This had been a second home. She used to lie in the grass and watch the clouds roll by. It saddened her to see it now.

The basin that rested at the center of the dais appeared to be in decent condition, with the exception of a large chip in the lip of the bowl. Ariel walked up the cracked steps

of the dais to the basin. It had once been filled with clear rainwater, but now it was full of murky water and rotting leaves. She ran her finger along the worn rim.

Something shot out of the dark water and narrowly missed Ariel's hand. She stepped back as a diamond-shaped snake's head reared back and flicked a black forked tongue at her. The snake's body was olive-colored with a dark yellow underbelly. Before it could lunge at her, Ariel turned sideways, and with a single backhand slash she severed the snake's head.

Ariel hopped off the dais and moved along the edge of the dark swirling water of the bog.

"Summoned," said Ariel. "I am summoned. You must follow the old druidic ways. Even a dark druid is still a druid."

She heard a deep melancholy voice in her head bidding her to continue. Strange dark shapes darted among the haunted, gnarled trees. They were ghostly shapes that flitted about in the mist. Ariel remembered hearing tales of ghostly spirits that led unfortunate villagers to their end.

"Ariel."

She whirled about. Someone whispered her name again. Then she heard several voices whispering to her from the trees.

"Are you worthy?"

The whispers taunted her. It is the swamp, she thought. The swamp spoke to her as the water swirled a few feet away. She looked down and saw a small stream of bubbles in the water near the edge of the muddy bank. She stood perfectly still for a moment and then slowly backed away from the water's edge.

 **305**

An explosion of dingy water and muck blinded her as a great head with large, tooth-lined jaws arose from the swamp. The jaws of the alligator snapped shut with an abrupt crunch, missing her by inches.

Ariel stumbled backward and fell onto the wet ground as the alligator again snapped at her and missed. She scooted backward on the ground as quickly as she could as the alligator raised its tremendous form onto the bank. It was a dull gray-green color and its broad head ended with a rounded snout. Its armored body was twenty feet long and covered with thick leathery scales.

It charged Ariel, its powerful jaws snapping at her with bone-crunching ferocity. As Ariel continued to scoot backward, her hand fell across a rotten tree branch. She picked it up and hurled it into the alligator's gaping maw. Its massive jaws clamped down on the soft wood. It shook its reptilian head, shredding the branch to bits.

Ariel jumped to her feet and ran. Perhaps she could lose it in the mist. She heard the alligator pursuing her. Just ahead, she saw the dark, twisted shapes of several downed trees.

They had fallen close together in such a way that they formed a loose pyramid. There was enough room for Ariel to crawl under the trees, but the alligator's bulk would not fit. She dove for the opening under the downed trees and slid through as the alligator crashed into the trunks. It wedged its snout under the opening, but it was much too large to follow her. Ariel slashed the reptile's snout and left a deep gash across its nose. The alligator hissed and pulled its head back while it clambered onto the fallen trees, their trunks straining and cracking under its weight. Bits of bark,

mud, and rotten wood fell on Ariel as she looked about for an escape route. The tree trunk above her cracked loudly. It wouldn't support the alligator's weight much longer.

Ariel slid herself backward until she reached the trunk that supported the others. She drew her other scimitar and positioned herself so she had enough room to defend herself. There was another loud crack, and the tree that had shielded Ariel from the alligator split apart. Half of the trunk and the alligator fell on the ground in front of her.

As the alligator lunged, Ariel looked into its yellow-green eyes and drove her scimitars home. The alligator hissed again and fell to the ground.

Ariel caught her breath while she cleaned her weapons, then she resumed her journey to the heart of the swamp. It was not far now. She would be there by midnight.

Ariel heard more strange whispers. Their haunting voices mocked her as she made her way to the sacred grove. She still saw the dark, wispy shapes among the trees. Spirits of the damned, she thought. They would accompany her the rest of the way.

Ariel walked for another half hour. She stumbled onto a nest of huge black widow spiders that were nearly a foot in diameter. They descended from the trees and tried to land on her. She slashed through several spiders and avoided the large mass of webs that was their nest.

When Ariel reached the grove at the center of the swamp, the moon was high in the night sky, drenching everything in a bluish-white glow. She came to a clearing in the morass of twisted, tortured trees. It was over sixty feet wide and twice as long. Dense brushwood and wild tangled grass filled the grove. At the center was a round, overgrown pool about twelve feet in diameter. Carved stones ringed the pool. In each stone was carved a druidic symbol of power.

The pool was filled with filthy dark water and reeked of decay. This was once a druid's gathering place. Long ago she had come here to refresh herself in the clear waters of the sacred pool. She wiped a tear from her cheek. She remembered the many classes she attended here. Her mentor was kind and wise.

Suddenly, she became aware of the eerie silence that surrounded her. The mist began to recede and the shadowy figures that had haunted Ariel faded into darkness. A slight breeze blew through the trees, causing their branches to scrape against each other.

Ariel shuddered. She wasn't alone any longer. She felt sinister eyes upon her. Something close yet unseen watched her, measured her.

Ariel held her arms out to her sides. "I am here. Show yourself."

A few moments later something large moved beyond the far side of the clearing. The soggy ground beneath her feet shook. Several trees snapped and fell as some giant unknown thing approached. Ariel's heart pounded in her chest. Her breathing became shallow and fast as she gripped her scimitars.

Chapter Twenty-Two
Druid's Duel

THE MASSIVE SHAPE PUSHED ITS way toward her, snapping and splintering trees as it moved. Ariel heard its deep, raspy breathing as it drew closer. She took a step back and tensed.

It lumbered into the clearing opposite Ariel and stood there watching her. It was an abomination, a thing born from nightmares. Its humanoid shape stood over ten feet tall. It walked upright on cloven hoofs and it was covered with greenish-brown fur. The head was crowned with an enormous set of antlers, each the size of a small sapling.

Below the antlers was a thick green mane like that of a lion. The tips of pointed ears protruded from the mane. The creature's face was twisted into a scowl and twitched with rage. It regarded Ariel with large black eyes.

Its muscular arms ended with long clawed hands, one wielding a gnarled tree trunk for a club. It wore a torn leather loincloth.

The creature let out a low growl and lowered its head as it studied her.

"I know you," it said with a deep, booming voice.

Ariel raised her chin and returned its stare. She said nothing.

"You have come to...challenge me?"

Ariel noticed it tightened its grip on its club.

"I was told you would come," it growled. "How dare you enter my grove, little elf."

"I do not wish to challenge you," said Ariel. "But I am called and must obey. And I know you."

The beast-man blinked. "You...know me?"

Ariel took a step forward, "You are Bhael Treemender."

The giant narrowed its eyes and gave another low, throaty growl.

"What has happened to you, Bhael? Look at what you have become," said Ariel. "Let me try to help you."

Bhael's face twisted as he snarled, revealing a set of fangs.

"Why would I want your help?" roared Bhael. "*I* am the stronger! *I* am the high druid!"

Ariel's leg muscles became taut as she readied herself for an attack.

"No," she said. "A dark druid can never be the high druid. You have lost what you once were."

Bhael's dark eyes drifted toward the ground. "Whoever controls magic controls destiny. But there is...a price to pay for such power."

"Oh, Bhael, what have you done?"

"Done?" The giant raised a bushy green-gray eyebrow. "I have become more," he roared. "I am more powerful than ever! My power is absolute. My thoughts become reality."

Ariel shook her head and looked into Bhael's black eyes.

"You have betrayed us. Betrayed our order. Look

around. You have destroyed and perverted that which you swore to protect. You have become a thing of evil, nothing more."

Bhael lowered his head at Ariel. "You should not have come here. You cannot defeat me."

"I am drawn here by a power greater than either of us," said Ariel.

"Then you came to challenge me," he said. "You were drawn to your death."

A shiver ran down Ariel's back. Such challenges, or duels, as they were known in the druidic world, were how one gained rank. The combatants always fought to the death.

Ariel exhaled. "You have left me no choice. Yes, I challenge you. For the sake of all, I challenge you."

As she finished, Ariel drew her weapons. Bhael roared, lowered his head, and then charged. His powerful legs propelled his large form forward with astonishing speed. He was on Ariel in seconds. Ariel saw the sharp antlers as they bore down on her.

She turned sideways and stepped back, easily dodging his attack. As Bhael thundered past, Ariel whirled in a circle and slashed his back with both scimitars. He roared and spun around, swinging his massive club. Ariel leapt backward as the club crashed to the ground. The impact sent dingy water flying, along with chunks of dark, soggy soil.

Ariel backed into something cold and hard. It was one the ceremonial stones that ringed the pool. Bhael bellowed and swung at Ariel again. She dove away, hit the ground, and rolled to her feet as he shattered the stone. The attack also splintered his club. Bhael hurled the sizeable chunk that was left at Ariel.

Ariel gasped as the heavy stump sailed at her. She tried to spin out of its path, but the wooden missile grazed her left side and knocked her to the ground. She winced as a sharp pain shot through the left side of her body. She scrambled to her feet and faced the giant.

Bhael growled as he raised one enormous clawed hand palm up and pointed at Ariel with the other.

Ariel felt the ground tremble beneath her feet. All around her she heard loud crunching and snapping sounds. She glanced about and saw the dead, rotting trees and foliage began to writhe.

The gnarled trees and plants were uprooted. In a few seconds, the mass of dead vegetation churned and thrashed and shaped itself into a giant serpent. It was over fifty feet long and its body continued to writhe as it reared back and opened its round, cavernous maw.

Ariel turned and ran. The serpent of churning trees and vegetation slammed into the ground where she had just stood. The impact of the tree serpent's attack shook the ground, knocking Ariel off her feet. She rolled over and sprang to her feet. The writhing, twisting serpent raised its head from the soggy ground and turned toward her.

That last attack was too close, thought Ariel. How does one defeat such an enemy? Her mind raced as she grabbed her side in pain. She had never faced a foe like this. She didn't dare fight it. The earlier injury impaired her movement, and her weapons were useless. She couldn't even think of any helpful spells.

From the corner of her eye, Ariel saw Bhael. He stood in

place and continued to point at her, his eyes never leaving her. An idea popped into Ariel's mind and she changed directions, running straight toward Bhael. This might be her only chance, she thought, looking over her shoulder as she ran. The writhing serpent was gaining on her.

Ariel sheathed her weapons and stretched out her arms. Feathers sprouted from her body while her nose and mouth formed a beak. She assumed the shape of a large hawk, flapping her wings and shooting skyward as the tree serpent lunged and missed.

Once she had gained sufficient altitude, Ariel turned and plummeted straight at Bhael. She extended her talons and crashed into the giant, ripping and tearing at his face and eyes. He swiped at her, causing him to lose his concentration. As soon as he did, the tree serpent fell apart, crumbling into a large decaying pile of debris and muck.

Bhael snarled and tried to crush Ariel between his hands as he clapped them together. Ariel disengaged and flew upward, leaving him with several cuts on his face. Ariel looked back and saw Bhael watching her fly away. His lips peeled back over his teeth, forming a sneer. The giant closed his black eyes. His skin grew black-purple scales and his arms became leathery wings. He grew a long snout embedded with several rows of razor-sharp teeth. He sprouted a long thrashing tail that ended with a large stinger. Bhael's new wyvern shape was easily three times the size of Ariel's hawk form.

Bhael leapt into the air, and with two flaps of his leathery wings he was in pursuit of Ariel. She flew as fast as she could. She zigzagged back and forth, dodging Bhael's toothy maw as he snapped at her. He can match my speed, she thought, but she can outmaneuver him. She plunged down into the trees, Bhael was close behind her.

Ariel wove her way in and out of the mossy, gnarled trees. Their branches moved and swayed, as if attempting to catch her or slow her flight. She was relieved to see Bhael collide with the branches, which hampered him and caused him to fall behind. Ariel heard his wyvern's screech. He was frustrated and angry, and she realized she could use that to her advantage.

She looked behind her. There was no sign of Bhael. Where was he? Perhaps he had assumed a different shape. Even with her hawk's keen eyesight, Ariel found it difficult to see well in the mist. She stayed below the tree line and doubled back to the grove. One of the carved stones provided excellent cover as she landed and resumed her elven shape.

Ariel crouched and peered out from behind her hiding spot. She saw nothing. Bhael could be anywhere. He could assume the shape of nearly anything. His wyvern form was proof he also possessed the ability to assume the shapes of magical and unnatural creatures. She didn't possess such a high level of shape-shifting ability; Ariel could only change into typical animals.

She changed shape again, this time into a panther. The moonlight glistened on her sleek black fur as she glided through the trees and undergrowth, stopping every now and then to listen. She stayed low to the ground and circled the grove.

Something large moved in the mist to her left. Ariel stopped and crouched. The scent of another predator filled her nostrils, and the fur on the back of her neck stood up. The other predator was close. She scanned the mist-shrouded grove. This time she saw a pair of large yellow eyes watching her.

Suddenly, a large greenish-brown cat with long saber-shaped canine teeth burst from the mists and charged Ariel. She leapt up and hurtled herself at the oncoming attacker. The two great cats collided in midair and landed as a rolling mass of fur and claws in shallow water. Bhael's saber-toothed cat form was heavier and stronger than Ariel's panther form, but again she was faster. They tore at each other with sharp claws and teeth.

Bhael swatted Ariel's neck with a powerful strike. The force of the blow knocked her on her side, and before she could recover, he pounced on her. His heavy frame pinned Ariel and partially submerged her. Bhael lunged for her exposed neck but Ariel raked his face with a quick strike. It was enough for her to wriggle free. Now the two cats circled each other in the shallow water.

Ariel saw an opening and sprang. She sank her teeth into Bhael's thick shoulder. He roared and swatted Ariel, sending her flying twenty feet away. Landing hard on a muddy bank, she sprang to her feet and faced Bhael. The saber toothed cat was already charging her. Ariel leapt at him. With claws extended, she sailed through the air. Bhael rose on his hind legs and struck Ariel's midriff with a heavy paw.

His claw slashed across Ariel's abdomen, and the force of the blow sent her flying toward deeper water. She struck the water with a loud splash. She paddled to the surface and gasped for air. Her midsection and left side were on fire and throbbed with pain, making breathing painful.

Bhael charged again. This time he changed shape as he ran. The fur of the saber-toothed cat melted into hard scales and his face elongated and formed a toothy snout. Her injury prevented her from swimming fast. If she tried to climb onto the bank Bhael would be on her almost immediately.

Ariel gulped in as much air as her sore ribs would allow and slipped beneath the surface of the water. She changed shape again, her arms and legs fusing with her body. The panther form elongated and she became a brown and green striped snake. She swam downward, her body forming an *S* shape as she turned left then right. She felt the thunderous splash as Bhael dove into the water above her.

She hid in the weeds and bramble on the bottom of the swamp. She raised her head a little so she could see the surface. Bhael's alligator form had entered the water exactly where she had shape changed into a snake. He glided through the water near the surface, swinging his head from side to side as he searched for her.

Ariel swam to the bank and hid in an area thick with slimy reeds, lying half submerged in the dark water. No matter what form she chose, he would always be stronger. He knew this too. He was overconfident because of his great strength and the varied forms he could choose to assume.

A moment later something large swam past, creating a swell of water that rolled over her. Ariel dared not move while he was close. She waited. An hour later she heard a splash. Almost thirty feet in front of her Bhael emerged from the water. He stopped and transformed back into the large beast-man form. She watched him survey his surroundings.

Having lost his prey, he shape-shifted into the saber-toothed cat. The cat form was a better hunter, a formidable combination of strength and speed. The great cat raised its head and sniffed the air. Ariel froze. She didn't even breathe. Bhael sniffed a few more times and then walked toward the grove.

Ariel slithered out of the water and watched him from a distance. If his physical strength was too much to overcome, another tactic must be used. An idea came to her. Ariel shifted into the form of blackish-gray snake. It was smaller, but faster and much more lethal. She slithered through the grass and approached Bhael from behind. Slowly and carefully, she maneuvered to within striking distance.

She lay still and flicked her tongue. The cat's musty odor excited her senses. If he discovered her while she was in snake form she would be ripped to shreds. She had one chance to end the duel. Everything depended on her being able to surprise him with a timed strike at his vulnerable neck. Some of the poisons she would inject into him would paralyze him in seconds. Those seconds were what worried her; she had to avoid Bhael's teeth and claws.

Ariel slid beside him and coiled her body. She raised her head. Bhael sniffed and began to growl. He had picked up her scent and would discover her at any second. Ariel uncoiled her body and struck. Her fangs pierced his hide. She injected her venom and fell away, immediately slithering into taller grass. Bhael roared and jumped into the air. He swung his head about, searching for Ariel.

A moment later she felt Bhael bearing down on her. She shape-shifted into a brown hare and bounded away. All she needed was time. Bhael chased her, but the form she had selected was much quicker. She ran around the grove, randomly changing direction when he swiped at her. She jumped over a fallen tree and skittered across the grove.

When she reached the far side of the grove she realized she no longer heard Bhael chasing her. She stopped and looked back. He was standing near the circular pool, gasping for air. Ariel watched as the large cat shuddered and fell on its side.

She returned to her elven form. A tear rolled down her cheek. She held her left side; the pain in her ribs was excruciating. She staggered to Bhael and knelt beside him.

"Forgive me," she said as she gently stroked the great cat's head. She let her fingers drift through his coarse fur.

The cat's form slowly changed and became that of an older, handsome elven male. This was how Ariel remembered him. He was her beloved friend and mentor. Bhael.

Ariel helped him roll over and she looked into his eyes. They were no longer black, empty orbs. Instead, they were a familiar dark green. Ariel bit her lip while she held back more tears.

"Ariel," said Bhael. "I am glad it was you. My nightmare is finally…over. Thank you."

"Lie still. I can try to remove the poison."

"No. It is…too late for that. The poison has already reached…my heart. I…do not…have long. You must listen."

Ariel nodded and forced a smile.

"The three children you…travel with…they are the key. They can…save our world."

Ariel frowned. "I do not understand."

"I was…the one who created the…werewolf…that

attacked Alex. It was necessary...to remove him from... power. Chalon is...a weaker kingdom without him."

He arched his back in pain. Ariel placed his head in her lap.

"A dark age comes. If the children cannot—" Bhael coughed and a trickle of blood ran from the corner of his mouth. Ariel wiped it away with her hand.

"What happened to you?" she asked softly.

"I was...attacked in the night. Red...bright red wings. Such evil...I have never felt before."

He coughed up more blood. Ariel again wiped it away.

"I fought...tried to resist...but I was not strong enough..."

Ariel caressed his cheek as he spoke.

He took her hand in his. "You will need...to be stronger than I...was. Ariel...Ariel...You must...protect the balance...of life."

His breathing became labored and raspy.

"We were to...cause fear and panic...draw... attention..."

"Who else, Bhael? Who was helping you?"

"Zorn."

Ariel gasped. How could her beloved mentor be in league with the Shadowlord? Ariel shook her head. This made no sense to her.

Bhael fumbled at a small pouch around his neck but was unable to grasp it. Ariel steadied his hand and helped.

"She...fears...the children...you travel with...they are not...safe...here."

"She?" asked Ariel.

Ariel saw the light fading from Bhael's eyes, yet he

struggled to hold on. He gave the pouch to Ariel. His lips moved, but no sound came from him. Ariel leaned closer. She heard him whisper under his breath, "Zorn...is...not the...true enemy..."

Bhael convulsed and a gurgling sound came from his throat as he exhaled and died. Ariel stared at him and squeezed his hand.

"No," she said. "Don't go...please don't go."

Ariel threw her head back and let out a loud wail. For a long while, she couldn't stifle the screams that came out of her. Her heart ached and her body shook as she sobbed. A wave of guilt and grief washed over her.

"Forgive me," she whispered.

She wrapped her arms around Bhael and held him for another hour. She kissed his forehead and remembered the lessons he had taught her. How he shared the wonderment of nature's secrets with her. Each day was a new discovery.

Afterward, Ariel built a traditional funeral pyre for Bhael in the grove. She lit the pyre with a torch, and as the flames burned into the night, she felt a surge or a tingling deep inside. Though she was sad, Ariel somehow felt reinvigorated. Something of Bhael's spirit had remained with her and strengthened her.

Dawn was approaching by the time the pyre had burned out. Ariel walked to the center of the grove and reached into a small pocket in her tunic. She opened the pouch and withdrew a single white seed. She sang an ancient druidic song of joy and rebirth as she planted the seed in the soil. When she finished, she cast the spell she had taught Jane, *Ehlia talo.*

She stood and as she did a small sprout pushed itself up from the dark soil. A sweet, light rain began to fall.

"I give you back your life. You shall once again be a beautiful forest. No longer shall you be filled with hate. You will know goodness again, and love. Grow strong and flourish, for you are blessed."

Ariel opened the leather pouch Bhael had given her. It was a key made from white alabaster. A wizard's key. She smiled.

"Geoff's missing key," she said.

Ariel walked to an area tangled with dense undergrowth. It obeyed and fell away when she waved her hand. Standing before her was a large, ornately carved archway.

Chapter Twenty-Three
The Werewolf

"You three should try to get some sleep," said Ishara. "I will stand watch."

"Well," said Jane, "I suppose there's nothing else we can do."

"Wanna take turns with the watch?" asked Sawyer.

"No," said Ishara. "I will be fine."

Jane, Sawyer, and Geoff each located a cot and settled in for the night. Jane looked at the small, stone-ringed cooking pit in the center of the barracks.

"Should we start a fire? It's already dark," she said.

"Not tonight," said Ishara. "Even with the windows shuttered the firelight will likely attract enemies. This is not a good place to be noticed."

Jane glanced at the secured windows and barred door. This is a safe place for one night at least, she thought. She yawned, laid her head down, and closed her eyes. In her dreams she was lying on a comfortable bed. There was a warm, blue-white light in the room and someone was shaking her, trying to wake her up.

"Jane!" said Geoff. "Wake up! Something's wrong!"

Jane's eyes shot open. Her vision was blurred, but she knew she wasn't dreaming anymore. She blinked and rubbed her eyes. How long had she slept? Who was shining that light in her face? The brightness of the light hurt her eyes so much she raised a hand to shield them.

"Wha...what's happening?" she asked.

"It's Sawyer," cried Geoff. "The sword lit up again and he's in some kind of trance!"

Still shielding her eyes, Jane looked in the direction of the bright light. Sawyer was sitting up in his cot, trembling. In his hands was the Stormblade, its blade glowing with the blue-white radiance. Sawyer's eyes were open, but they were rolled up in his head. Jane gasped. The sight of Sawyer's white eyes terrified her.

"We gotta do something! The last time the sword did this was at Silverthorne Manor," yelled Geoff. "Just before the...oh my god...!"

"Just before what?" asked Ishara, who had stepped away from the window and nocked an arrow.

Jane stood up and looked around. She shuddered. Oh no. This isn't good, she thought. We're trapped in close quarters.

"Just before the werewolf attacked," she said.

Ishara spun around and visually inspected the windows and door.

"If the werewolf attacks," she said, shaking her head, "we have nowhere to run."

At that moment the sword in Sawyer's hands ceased glowing. He looked around with glazed eyes, not seeming to recognize where he was.

"Sawyer," said Jane as she approached him with her hand out in a reassuring manner. "Are you okay?"

 323

Sawyer's eyes returned to normal as he awakened from his trance and leapt out of his cot.

"It's coming again! The werewolf really is close!" he shouted. "It knows we're here. It can smell us."

"What're we gonna do?" asked Geoff, wringing his hands. "We barely escaped it last time because we jumped off that cliff at the waterfall."

"Sawyer!" snapped Ishara. "Where is it? From which direction does it approach?"

"It followed our route," said Sawyer, pointing in the direction from which they had come. "It's here. I saw this building through its eyes!"

Jane's skin tingled with goose bumps. Her heart raced.

"What are we going to do? Ariel isn't here," she said, her voice rising. "How are we-"

"Quiet!" demanded Ishara, holding her hand up.

The room fell silent. Jane looked at Sawyer and Geoff. Sawyer's forehead was moist with sweat, and Geoff's eyes were wide open and he was shaking. Ishara aimed her arrow at the door. As Jane watched, Ishara slowly moved her aim from the door to the first shuttered window, as though she was tracking something.

Jane heard movement outside. Something sniffed the air, then there was a low, guttural growl by the shuttered window.

"Ishara," whispered Geoff in a near panic. "It's at the wi-"

Pieces of wood exploded into the room as a large clawed hand burst through. It was covered with black fur.

Jane screamed as Ishara fired her arrow. It struck the hand and shattered. A vicious snarl came from the werewolf as it retracted its hand. Two more arrows hissed through the opening in the window, but with little affect. The werewolf ripped the remains of the shutter from the window and stuck its large head through.

Jane screamed again, but this time she was joined by Geoff, who had retreated to the far wall and shielded his face with his arms. Ishara fired another arrow. This one struck the werewolf between the eyes and shattered, as the previous ones had.

"Only magical weapons can kill it!" yelled Geoff. "That's what Ariel said."

"I have no such weapon! What I wouldn't give for a silver-tipped arrow," replied Ishara, firing another arrow. This one merely bounced off the werewolf's throat.

The beast's maw was glistening in the moonlight. Drool ran down the length of its fangs and puddled on the floor beneath the window.

Jane saw movement to her left. She was horrified at the sight of Sawyer running toward the werewolf.

"Sawyer! No! What are you doing?" she screamed, "Stay back!"

The werewolf was in the process of tearing much of the wall away so it could enter.

"It'll rip you to bits!" Jane covered her mouth with both hands.

"Stormlord!" Ishara had no choice but to cease firing. "You are in my way!" She stepped further to the right, trying to find a clear shot.

Sawyer swung the Stormblade with both hands, striking the werewolf's arm. It yelped and snarled, then turned its blazing yellow eyes on Sawyer. It snapped at him with bone-crunching ferocity, but bit only air. Sawyer had stepped back just in time, holding his sword up in the defensive stance that Ariel had shown him.

"It can't fit through the window!" shouted Jane. "It's going to tear through the wall!"

"Look! it's bleeding!" yelled Geoff. "Sawyer hurt it!"

Jane looked at the black mass of fangs and claws that was trying to enter the room. Sawyer had wounded the beast. Its blood ran down the wall and mixed with the puddles of drool. Jane was overcome by the irony-smell of blood mixed with the musty odor of the werewolf. She coughed, reached into her pocket and retrieved her mage stone.

She held it overhead and said "*Iluminara.*" The entire barracks was engulfed in green light. The werewolf looked at her with hate-filled yellow orbs, causing her to scream and step back.

With the werewolf's attention on Jane, Sawyer thrust the Stormblade at it, this time, stabbing it in the shoulder. The beast snarled and snapped at the sword, but Sawyer had again retreated to safety. The werewolf disappeared from the window. Jane was breathing heavy and she was still shaking.

"Is anyone harmed?" asked Ishara as she maneuvered to the center of the room. She looked at Sawyer.

"Be alert," she said. "It's still out there. Somewhere near."

Jane was about to extinguish her mage stone when Geoff stopped her.

"No, don't," he said. "It distracted the werewolf. Can you make it glow really bright? Maybe try to blind it?"

"If you can, maybe we can escape," said Ishara. "With

the beast blinded, the Stormlord may have a chance to kill it."

Jane looked at Sawyer. He was trembling and his eyes darted from the window to Ishara.

"Jane?" said Geoff. "Do you think you can do it?"

"What? I…I don't know," said Jane between breaths. "I don't think so."

"I'm pretty sure I can," said Geoff. "Give it to me."

He held out his hand and Jane dropped the mage stone into it. As soon as it touched his skin, the green radiance became white.

"Unbelievable…," said Ishara as she watched the transaction.

There was a loud thump at the door. Ishara whirled and aimed another arrow in that direction.

"Listen carefully," she whispered. "It must come through the door because of its size. When it does, the Stormlord will keep it at bay while the rest of us escape through the hole in the wall."

"Wait," said Jane. "We can't leave Sawyer to fight the werewolf all alone."

"Yeah," said Sawyer. "I'm not that good with a sword. I've only just-"

The heavy wooden door, bar and all, smashed and shattered. Again a hail of wood and debris showered them as the werewolf loomed in the doorway.

Its hulking form completely blocked the doorway. It was still drooling and it flexed its clawed hands.

Ishara fired two arrows, each bouncing off the beast's chest and breaking. It turned its head and swung at her.

"Now, Geoff!" Ishara called as she dove to the floor, avoiding a slash that would have surely killed her.

"*Iluminara*!" yelled Geoff and suddenly the room became brightly lit. The werewolf turned to Geoff when it heard him, catching the full effect of the light from the mage stone. It held up a clawed hand to cover its eyes and stepped backward.

"Strike him, Stormlord!" yelled Ishara. "Kill it!"

Sawyer hesitated, then stepped toward the doorway. Jane felt Ishara grab her arm and all but throw her through the opening in the wall that was once a window. She hit the hard ground and rolled to her feet.

"Wait!" Jane cried. "We can't leave Sawyer and Geoff in there!"

"Come on!" said Ishara as she nocked two more arrows and ran toward the front of the barracks. Jane heard the werewolf snarling and growling. Oh no! she thought. Sawyer and Geoff are going to die! She followed Ishara around the corner and there was the werewolf. It was still blinded by Geoff's light, but it was swinging its claws wildly. Each swing made a violent *whoosh* as it missed.

Sawyer advanced, but maintained his distance while he kept his sword raised. Geoff followed Sawyer out of the barracks, keeping the light from the mage stone focused on the werewolf's eyes. Jane saw the wounds on its arm and shoulder. The fur on its right arm was moist with blood. Ishara fired her arrows. Each struck the beast in the chest and broke.

"Keep the light on him, Geoff!" called Sawyer.

Ishara nocked another arrow and fired. This one struck the werewolf on the side of the head, causing it to snarl at her. Ishara kept firing arrows and Geoff did his best to keep the beast blinded. Sawyer maintained his defensive stance and stayed out of arm's reach.

"What do we do now?" asked Sawyer, looking over his shoulder at Ishara.

"Strike! Attack the beast," she said. "Time your attack and strike!"

"The hell with that!" said Sawyer, shaking his head. There was no way to approach the werewolf without being shredded by its claws.

Jane looked around for something to throw and noticed how overgrown the area was. Thick, thorny vines wrapped themselves around trees and climbed the walls of every building. The grass had not been maintained, and had grown almost two feet high. If the werewolf can be held in place, we might have a chance, she realized. What were the words to that spell? Bar-something envora.

Suddenly the beast lunged at Sawyer. It swung and missed, but Sawyer lost his balance and fell, dropping his sword again.

"Sawyer!" screamed Geoff as he tried to blind the werewolf.

Ishara moved to the beast's right flank and fired arrow after arrow, each bounced off its hide or broke. The werewolf ignored Ishara's arrows and leapt at Sawyer.

"*Bar'athel envora!*"

A mass of vines caught the werewolf in midair, suspending it just above Sawyer. It snapped at Sawyer, its massive snout mere inches away from his face.

Jane kept chanting *Bar'athel envora* over and over. She felt the willingness of the vines and plants to do her bidding.

She realized as she chanted she had control over all nearby plants. She pictured the grass and trees also restraining the werewolf. Immediately the roots and limbs from the nearest trees wrapped and coiled around the beast. The thick grass entangled its legs, drastically slowing it.

"Now, Stormlord! Strike!" said Ishara, who had just fired her last arrow at the werewolf.

"Hurry, Sawyer! It's breaking free!" shouted Geoff.

Jane could only watch and chant as the werewolf ripped its way through its woodsy prison. She felt the strength of the beast as the vines and limbs that had held it captive gave way. The werewolf was just too strong.

Sawyer grasped his sword and scrambled to his feet. The snapping and crunching of vines and limbs echoed throughout the deserted village. Sawyer ducked another swing from the werewolf, and as he did, he thrust his sword up into its midsection. It howled in pain and chomped at the last of the tree limbs that restrained it. Sawyer stepped to the side and slashed its leg. This time, the werewolf flinched and yelped.

Sawyer raised his sword overhead and was about to strike when the werewolf broke free. Instead of attacking Sawyer, however, it stumbled backward. It snarled and glared at them with a malevolent look in its eyes.

"Kill it!" shouted Ishara. "Kill it now!"

Sawyer didn't move. The werewolf growled and limped into the night.

Jane dropped to her knees. She felt drained, she was tired. So tired. Ariel said this could happen, she thought. Everything's spinning, turning black. Then she lost consciousness.

Chapter Twenty-Four
A New Day

"Wake up, Geoff."

Geoff felt a hand on his shoulder shaking him.

He had tried to remain awake all night but failed.

"Wake up." It was Ishara.

He opened his eyes and saw her kneeling beside him. Her dark blond locks were tussled and dangled over her shoulders. She smiled at Geoff.

"Hmmm? What is it? Jane. Is she okay?" he asked as he squinted and rubbed his eyes.

"She is fine. She needed rest. It's morning," said Ishara. "A new day for us."

Geoff sat up. "What about Ariel? Is she back?"

He looked over at Sawyer and Jane, who were also waking up.

"What's all the commotion?" groaned Sawyer. He lay on his cot, stretched his arms, and arched his back.

"Ariel's here?" asked Jane.

"Yeah," said Sawyer, standing up and stretching. "Where is she?"

A burst of light entered the barracks as a lone figure stepped into the doorway. Geoff shielded his eyes. The morning sunlight sparkled about the new arrival, creating a nebulous radiance. Geoff squinted and looked at the glittering familiar figure in the doorway.

"Ariel!" Geoff said as he scrambled to his feet.

"Hello," said Ariel.

A warm smile spread across her face. Jane ran to Ariel and wrapped her arms around her.

"We were so worried about you!" said Jane. "Thank goodness you came back!"

"Careful," said Ariel with a slight grimace. "That side is still a bit tender."

"Can I help?" asked Jane. "I know a spell…"

Ariel laughed. "Thank you, but I have already healed myself."

She looks more beautiful than ever, thought Geoff. Maybe it was the way the sun played off her hair, but Ariel was simply luminous. He felt his spirits rise. Sawyer was also grinning as he hugged Ariel.

"Your friend. Did you…do it? Did you fight him?" asked Geoff.

The smile faded from her face and she lowered her head. "Yes," she said. "The dark druid has been defeated."

"I'm so sorry, Ariel," said Jane. "I really am. Are you okay?"

Ariel nodded. "I did what had to be done."

"Hal'inari," said Ishara, bowing slightly to Ariel. "We are honored."

Ariel smiled. "Hal'inari, little one."

Geoff watched the interaction between Ishara and Ariel.

They were obviously fond of each other, but he noticed that Ishara now spoke to her with a more reverent tone. Something was different now.

Ariel looked at the damaged wall that once contained a window and the splintered door that was strewn about.

"What has happened here?" she said.

Before Geoff could answer, Ishara spoke.

"We were attacked by the werewolf."

Ariel looked at them. "Truly? Is anyone injured?"

"No," said Geoff. "We chased it off."

"You...chased it off?" said an astonished Ariel. She looked at Ishara.

"No. Not me," said Ishara. She motioned toward Sawyer, Jane, and Geoff.

"They did."

Ariel raised her eyebrows, "How did you manage such a feat? That werewolf is a most fearsome foe."

"Together," said Ishara. "They fought as one and chased away the beast. My arrows were of no consequence. Geoff blinded it with the light from a mage stone while Sawyer kept it at bay. However, it was Jane who cast the spell which ensnared it and gave Sawyer the chance to drive the werewolf away."

A smile beamed across Ariel's face.

"Magnificent," she said. "Simply magnificent."

"We thought it was going to kill us," said Jane. "We were so scared."

"Yeah," said Sawyer. "It tore this place apart to get us."

"They were brave," said Ishara. "As brave as any warrior."

"Indeed," said Ariel. She glanced at Sawyer, Jane, and

then Geoff. "I suspected as much. I am glad none of you were hurt. Come. I have something to show you."

They gathered their belongings and followed her outside. Geoff looked around. The morning sunlight fell on the green leaves of the surrounding shrubbery and the freshly sprouted grass. Trees that had been black and twisted resumed their natural colors while small white daisies had sprung up, revealing their yellow centers.

"Hey, what happened here?" said Geoff. "This place isn't so scary now."

"Yeah. It looks…kinda normal," said Sawyer. "There's no more mist or creepy stuff here anymore. And it doesn't stink."

"Looks like a nice, quaint village," said Jane, scanning their surroundings. "Do you think the townsfolk will return to Somerdale now?"

"Yes. I believe so." said Ariel.

"Cool," said Sawyer. "I like it here now."

"Me too," said Geoff. "Looks like a nice place to live."

The sun shone on them as they continued past the edge of the village. The bright rays warmed them and lifted their spirits. Geoff found himself smiling. He had a bounce to his step and he felt energized. He looked at Sawyer and Jane and saw they were also smiling.

"Oh, wow," said Jane. "The swamp is…is it changing back into a forest? I don't understand. How could it change so much overnight?"

"Because," answered Ishara, "the high druid desires it."

They looked at Ishara, who was looking at Ariel.

"Oh, yeah," said Sawyer. "So you're the commander, right? The highest rank?"

"High druid," said Ishara. "Now she is the greatest druid."

"Well, I think Ariel was always the greatest druid," Jane said.

"I agree. Amen to that," said Sawyer.

"Thank you," Ariel said with a slight bow of her head. "Though I wish the circumstances of my ascension had been different."

"Hey...do you hear that? I think I hear birds singing," said Geoff. "Don't you?"

They paused and listened.

"I hear 'em too." Sawyer said.

They looked overhead. At least three large flocks of birds were flying by on their way to the recovering forest. Then a flash of yellow and green fluttered by and caught Geoff's attention. He watched as two butterflies flitted and danced about Jane before they landed on her shoulder. Jane was unaware of her visitors. That's the second time butterflies did that, thought Geoff. Maybe they just like her for some reason.

"Come," said Ariel. "Follow me."

She stepped forward and held her hands out to her sides, palms extended upward. The nearest trees that were twisted and deformed moved. Their trunks straightened and unraveled while the branches spun out of Ariel's way. As she walked by them, their black, oozy bark changed and became various shades of brown and green.

Thick grass grew in Ariel's wake and flowers bloomed beside her as she walked. Geoff's mouth fell open as he watched the forest flourish around her. Ishara nudged him. She winked and hurried after Ariel. He looked at Sawyer and Jane, who were beside him. They also stood transfixed and astonished.

"Oh," mumbled Jane. "Have you ever seen anything like that?"

"No way," said Sawyer. "Maybe in the movies…"

"Is this what she wanted to show us?" asked Geoff.

"I guess. I've no idea what could top this." Sawyer was still gaping at the wondrous sight.

Ishara turned around and beckoned them to come along.

"Yo, Geoff," said Sawyer. "I think she likes you."

"Huh? No way!" Geoff felt his cheeks grow warm.

"Sawyer may be right, Geoff," said Jane. "She isn't shy about you; that's for sure."

"That's true," said Sawyer. "What exactly did you two do while you were kidnapped by the brigands?"

Geoff looked at them. Jane's eyes were wide open. Sawyer was rubbing his chin and feigning suspicion.

"Mmhmm," said Sawyer in a low tone.

"Aww, c'mon, guys!" Geoff laughed, but felt awkward. The idea of a beautiful elven girl being interested in him was just not possible. She couldn't be, he thought. But it would be awesome! Geoff swallowed and fidgeted where he stood.

"Okay, okay. We better get going, loverboy," said Jane.

Geoff exhaled. He was thankful for the change of subject. Following Sawyer, Jane, he ran after Ariel and Ishara.

Soon they walked into a picturesque grove. Birds zipped about and chirped at each other while bees meandered among a rainbow of colorful wildflowers. At the center of the grove was a circular pool of clear water. Large carved stones displaying odd symbols and runes littered the grassy knolls here and there.

"Oh, wow! This is awesome," said Jane. "I think it's paradise. It's like the Garden of Eden."

Ariel waited for them by the pool, with Ishara standing a couple of steps behind her. Near the center of the grove grew a small tree. It shone with a light green luminescence that sparkled in the sunlight. Jane went over to the tree for a closer look. Sawyer and Geoff followed.

"It's beautiful," said Jane. "Just beautiful."

"It's an oak," said Geoff, circling the tree, "but it's, like, perfect. Why is it glowing?"

"Magic. I think it's a blessing," said Jane.

"How do you know that?" asked Geoff.

"She knows," said Ariel. "This tree will nourish and strengthen not only this grove but the entire forest."

"Very cool," said Sawyer. "So is it changing the swamp back into a forest?"

Ariel smiled and nodded.

"It's so peaceful here," said Jane, running her fingers over the growing trunk. "I wish we had a place like this back home."

"Come here," said Ariel. She beckoned to them and they walked over to her.

She looked at Geoff. "I believe this belongs to you," she said as she held out her hand. Resting in her palm was the familiar white alabaster key they had found in his father's study. It glimmered as the sun's rays caressed it.

"Wow!" Geoff's heart leapt. "You found it!" His mouth

dropped open. He never thought he would see it again, but there it was, mere inches away. "I can't believe it!"

"Oh my god!" said Jane, putting her hands over her mouth.

"Believe it," said Ariel with a big smile.

Geoff's fingers trembled as he took the key from Ariel. He felt the same strange tingling sensation he had experienced in his father's study. Little arcs of electricity, like tiny lightning bolts, zoomed up and down the key. He couldn't take his eyes off it.

"I thought it was gone," said Geoff. "This can't be. It's impossible."

"Impossible? How can it be impossible when it has happened?" said Ariel.

Jane removed her hands from her mouth. "Will we… can we…go home now?"

"But…we need an archway," said Geoff. He looked at Ariel. "Don't we?"

Ariel stepped aside, Ishara did the same. Thirty feet behind them stood an archway similar to the one in Geoff's house. It was made of white marble with a dramatic array of green and gold veins of varying sizes. Instead of gargoyles and dragon heads, this archway was exquisitely adorned with a collage of vines, leaves, and flowers.

"Yes! Jane, we're going home!" said Sawyer, grabbing Jane and giving her a bear-hug.

Ariel placed a slender hand on the back of Geoff's neck and ran her fingers through his blond hair.

"Before you go, Geoff," she said, "we must discuss your key."

"I know," he said. "Something like I should put it back and forget it? That's exactly what I plan to do!"

"I am not so sure about that," said Ariel. "A wizard's key is an extremely rare thing. One does not simply happen upon them. I do not know how a portal and key came to be in your home, but it must have taken great effort to place them there."

Geoff frowned. "So what do I do with the key? If I lose it my dad will be angry."

"That choice is yours. Perhaps you can hide it," said Ariel. "I am only saying someone of great power placed it in your house. And their intentions may not be good. Be careful."

"I never thought about that. You're right," he said, scratching his head. "There's no way the portal could even fit through the door. How could it have gotten there?"

"Magic," said Ariel. "It could only be placed there with powerful magic."

"Okay, but why Geoff's house?" Sawyer asked. "Why Geoff? I was with him when he found the key. Why not Jane's house? Or mine?"

"I do not know," said Ariel. "Perhaps you will discover that for yourselves when you return home. Take care. I fear evil may try to seek you in your world."

The five of them walked to the archway at the far side of the grove. It's exquisite, thought Geoff. Look at the detail in the carvings. Each leaf and vine intertwines with the others. It's so lifelike and there isn't a mark on it.

"Hey, Geoff, this one's in a lot better shape than the one in your dad's study," said Sawyer.

"That one has been damaged," said Jane to Ariel. "Like it was in a fire or explosion."

Geoff watched Ariel's reaction. She frowned, pursed her lips, and looked at the archway.

"There are but a small number of these portals known to exist. No one knows the true number or their locations."

"Ariel…" Ishara began. Ariel gave her a quick nod and gestured with her hand. "One moment."

"Remember, when you go home," said Ariel, "look after one another."

"Okay," said Jane. "Hey, will I still be able to make plants grow and heal injuries?"

Ariel smiled. "Why not?"

Jane's face beamed as she gave Ariel another hug. "Thank you!"

"You are welcome," said Ariel. "I am honored and grateful to have met each of you."

Jane turned away from Ariel and wiped a tear from her eye. Sawyer stood before Ariel and smiled. He held up his sword.

"Here, you better take this," he said. "It belongs here. Use it on the Shadowlord. Besides, if my dad found it he would probably pawn it."

"The Stormblade has chosen you," said Ariel. "It is yours."

"Yeah, but somehow I'd lose it. I know I would. You better keep it. Give it to the next guy."

"There is no 'next guy,'" said Ariel. "However, if you wish, I will keep it safe for you should you return."

Sawyer laughed. "Ha! Return? No offense, but no way! Once we're back home I'm putting this place behind me.

Who needs werewolves and orcs and trolls? You can have 'em!"

Ariel accepted the sword with a slight nod. Geoff saw Ishara's jaw drop. She appeared astonished that someone would give up such a weapon.

"Thank you for everything," said Geoff. "I hope you win the war. Beat that Shadowlord guy, okay?"

"Hell yeah!" agreed Sawyer.

Ariel bowed slightly to Geoff, but didn't say anything as he walked to the portal. The tiny arcs of electricity on the key increased in frequency and his hair once again stood up.

"Geoff," said Ishara.

She went to him and ran her fingers through his hair, mimicking Ariel. Her eyes met his then she kissed him on the cheek. Geoff immediately turned a bright red.

"Good-bye, little sneak thief. I will miss you."

Geoff blinked. He had never been kissed by a girl before. What was he supposed to do now? His heart began to beat faster. He smiled at her and put his hand on his warm cheek. "I'll miss you, too. I wish we had met sooner."

"Mmhmm," said Sawyer.

Ariel walked to the portal and put her arm around Geoff.

"You must concentrate on your destination," she said. "Think only of your home when you step through."

"Geoff," said Sawyer, holding up a fist, "you better not mess up and send us somewhere else."

"Concentrate, Geoff," said Jane. "Get us home."

Geoff closed his eyes and pictured his house and his father's study. When the image was clear, he opened his eyes, placed the key in the slot, and turned it. White and gray swirling mists appeared in the portal.

"The mists," said Jane. "They were green before."

"Each place has its own color," said Ariel. "Do not worry."

She looked at Jane, Sawyer, and then Geoff. "When you are home," she said. "From time to time, if you have a free moment, think of us. Will you?"

"Are you kidding?" said Jane, wiping another tear away. "How could we ever forget you? Or this world, Alluria?"

She hugged Ariel again.

"Is it safe to go through?" asked Sawyer. "Can we go home?"

Ariel nodded.

"All right. Watch out. I got this," said Sawyer. He positioned himself in front of the archway. He took a few deep breaths, then shook his arms out and let them dangle at his side. Next he rolled his head on his shoulders and crouched. Geoff noticed Ishara's mouth had fallen open again as she watched Sawyer's preparations. Sawyer waved at Ariel and Ishara. "Thanks for teaching me how to fight with a sword! Good luck! See ya!"

He lowered his head and charged into the swirling mists of the portal, yelling "Yaaaaaaaaaaaaa!"

"Does he always behave like that?" asked Ishara with a shocked look on her face.

"Yes," said Jane and Geoff in unison.

They laughed and then Jane walked to the archway. She looked back at Ariel.

"I won't forget," she said. "I'll remember. I promise."

She took a deep breath and stepped through the portal. Geoff smiled at Ariel and Ishara.

"Now that we're going home," he said. "I want to stay." He felt a slight ache in his heart. He also took a deep breath and waved good-bye. He followed Sawyer and Jane into the mists but as he did he heard Ishara and Ariel speaking.

"You're letting them go? Surely they must be—"

"Yes," said Ariel, "they are the three travelers. Their arrival was foretold many years ago."

The rushing sound of wind filled Geoff's ears and he felt the familiar spinning sensation. He closed his eyes as he spun faster and faster. When the spinning stopped, he opened his eyes. He was standing in his father's study. The usual musty smells of old books and rusty artifacts welcomed him home. Jane and Sawyer were jumping for joy and hugging each other.

"Yes! We're back! We're back!" shouted Jane. "I thought we'd never make it home."

She ran to Geoff and hugged him tightly. "Geoff, you're awesome!"

Sawyer gave Geoff a high five and put his hand on Geoff's shoulder. "Wow! Some adventure, huh? Was that crazy or what? No one's gonna believe that!"

Geoff looked down at the key in his hand. It still crackled with energy.

"You better put that key back where you found it," said Jane. "Let's get out of here. I'll bet everyone is looking for us. We're in so much trouble."

"But guys," he said, "Ariel said maybe we should hide the key, right?"

"Yes, but it's your key, Geoff," said Jane. "You decide."

"I don't care what you do with it," said Sawyer. "We made it! No more monsters! Life is good again!"

"I better put it back for now," said Geoff. "In case dad misses it."

Geoff placed the white alabaster key back in the small plastic bag and then in the box on his father's desk. It's good to finally be back, he thought. They had survived an extraordinary adventure and returned home. Now he realized life was going to return to normal. Back to the bullying. Back to dealing with his icy stepmother. Back to lonely nights doing homework. Geoff frowned. He was going to miss Ishara's smiling face. Then he recalled the conversation between Ariel and Ishara before he stepped into the archway.

"I heard them talking before I left," he said. "Ishara and Ariel. They said something about us being travelers and our arrival was foretold."

"Foretold? What're you talking about? We're home!" said Sawyer thrusting his arms in the air. "Let's get the hell outta here. C'mon."

"He's right. Let's go, Geoff," said Jane as she placed a hand on his cheek. "I'm going to miss them too. They saved our lives."

Geoff nodded and looked down at his feet. The adventure they had just been on was incredible. He hoped to return to Alluria and see Ishara again.

"What do you think they meant about our arriving being foretold, Geoff?" asked Jane.

"I'm not sure," he said. "But it sounded like Ariel knew more than she told us...and maybe it isn't over. Does that mean we'll return to Alluria someday?"

"I don't know, Geoff," Jane said with a smile. "I just don't know. Maybe…someday."

They left the study and went downstairs. Geoff looked about, searching for any detail that may be out of place. Everything looks exactly the same, he thought. How long have we been gone?

"Hey, what day is it?" he asked.

"Good question," said Jane. "How long were we in Never-never Land?"

"Dunno," said Sawyer. "But how're we gonna explain this? We better get our stories straight."

"I have no idea," said Jane. "We need to come up with something."

They walked through the living room. Geoff saw a newspaper on the coffee-table. He picked it up and looked at the date.

"This can't be right," he said.

"What?" asked Sawyer.

"This paper. It's the same date we…you know…left."

"Yeah. Whatever. Look, I say we took a trip and had car trouble," said Sawyer. "If we tell people we got sucked into a fantasy land they're gonna think we're nuts."

Geoff set the paper down and turned to Sawyer and Jane.

"But who's going to believe the three of us went on a trip together?" Jane asked.

Sawyer looked at Geoff. "Yeah. I guess you're right. So what're we gonna say?"

Something in Sawyer's voice made Geoff stop, "So… what happens now?"

"Whaddaya mean?" said Sawyer. "We're back! We made it! Hell yeah!"

"No," said Geoff. "I mean what about us? Are we, like, you know, friends now?"

Sawyer and Jane fell quiet and looked at each other. A few seconds later Jane answered, "Yes. We are."

Geoff smiled. "Good."

Sawyer gave Geoff a fist bump and said, "We're cool."

They went into the kitchen. Jane's purse was on the kitchen table.

"There's my purse! It's still here, right where I left it."

"Guys, I don't think anything has changed since we left," said Geoff. "Jane, do you still have that check from my dad?"

Jane looked in her purse. "Yes. Here it is." She held the envelope up.

"And here is the book you gave back, Sawyer." Geoff held up his copy of *The Once and Future King*.

"So…nothing's changed? Were we in some kind of time warp or alternate reality or something?" said Sawyer.

The phone rang and all three of them jumped. Geoff looked at Sawyer and Jane, then the phone, which continued to ring. He wasn't sure if he should answer it.

"Go ahead," said Jane.

He gulped and picked up the receiver.

"Hell..hello?"

He recognized the voice on the other end, "Oh, hi, dad. No, everything's fine. Jane is here. She dropped by to get your check." Sawyer and Jane exchanged grins.

"Where are you? Oh, the dinner? How is it? Yes, of

course. Okay. When will you be home? Great. I'll see you then. Bye."

He hung up the phone and looked at a clock on the wall. "Hey, guys," he said, pointing at the clock, "either dad and mom have been at their banquet for almost a week, or we're back at exactly the same time we left."

"Oh, wow. This is so weird," said Jane. She walked over to a candy dish on the kitchen counter and fished around. "I need chocolate."

"Ya know," said Sawyer, "I kind of liked it in Alluria – when we weren't running for our lives."

"Me too," said Jane. "But I'm so glad to be home."

Geoff sat down at the table and put his head in his hands.

"Aww, man," he groaned. "I still have an algebra test tomorrow. I haven't even studied for it."

They looked at each other for a moment and then all three of them laughed. Their adventure was over and they were home...for now.

THE END

Coming soon by Mitch Reinhardt

The Iron Citadel
Book Two of the Darkwolf Saga

The Scarlet Queen
Book Three of the Darkwolf Saga

Bloodmoon
Book Four of the Darkwolf Saga

About the Author

Mitch Reinhardt grew up in the central Piedmont region of North Carolina and is currently a business analyst for an international software firm. An avid animal lover, he enjoys hiking, tennis, classic movies, and, of course, reading and writing. He lives with his faithful dog, Murphy, who doubles as a proofreader – when he isn't sleeping or digging in the backyard. *Wizard's Key* is the first book of The Darkwolf Saga, a four book series.

Visit his web site at
www.mitchreinhardt.com

Made in the USA
Middletown, DE
08 January 2020